Ministry of Defence in 1983. He _____
at the Cabinet Office and on _____
now lives in Gloucestershire wit_____
is the author of *The Cup of The World*, *The Widow and the King*,
and *The Fatal Child*. *The Lightstep* is his first adult novel.

The Lightstep

John Dickinson

BLACK SWAN

TRANSWORLD PUBLISHERS
61–63 Uxbridge Road, London W5 5SA
A Random House Group Company
www.rbooks.co.uk

THE LIGHTSTEP
A BLACK SWAN BOOK: 9780552774468

First published in Great Britain
in 2008 by David Fickling Books
a division of The Random House Group Ltd
Black Swan edition published 2009

Addresses for Random House Group Ltd companies outside the UK
can be found at: www.randomhouse.co.uk
The Random House Group Ltd Reg. No. 954009

The Random House Group Limited supports The Forest Stewardship Council
(FSC), the leading international forest certification organisation. All our titles that
are printed on Greenpeace approved FSC certified paper carry the FSC logo.
Our paper procurement policy can be found at www.rbooks.co.uk/environment

Typeset in Bembo by Falcon Oast Graphic Art Ltd.
Printed in the UK by CPI Cox & Wyman, Reading, RG1 8EX.

2 4 6 8 10 9 7 5 3 1

To Pippa

Contents

Note

Three years after the outbreak of the French Revolution, the new republic of France declared war on the old regimes of Europe. Chief among these was the Holy Roman Empire, a loose confederation of mainly German princedoms and bishoprics under the leadership of the Austrian Hapsburgs.

The French revolutionaries hoped that the peoples of Europe would rise against their rulers. However, only a few small uprisings occurred, in Belgium and in Germany. The men who led these efforts may have been inspired by the revolutionary ideals of liberty and equality, but fate was cruel to them. Their causes did not prosper.

In the summer of 1793 a French army was occupying the German city of Mainz, with the support of some of its citizens. Austrian, Prussian and other German forces had arrived to retake the city. The siege lasted for months.

Cast List

Michel Wéry *A petty gentleman from Brabant*

THE ADELSHEIMS

The Knight August von Adelsheim

Lady Constanze von Adelsheim

Franz *Their elder son*

Albrecht *Their younger son*

Maria *Their daughter*

Anna Poppenstahl *Governess and companion*

Tieschen *A servant at Adelsheim*

Dietrich

Johann } *Servants at the house in Erzberg*

Pirenne

Ehrlich *A coachman*

IN ERZBERG

The Prince-Bishop of Erzberg

The Countess
Wilhelmina Pancak-Schönberg *His aunt, and mistress*

Bergesrode } *His secretaries*

Adhelmar Fernhausen-Loos

Gianovi *First Minister of Erzberg*

Count Balcke-Horneswerden *Field Marshal of Erzberg*

The Knight von Uhnen	
Karl von Uhnen	*His son, an Erzberg hussar*
Baron Altmantz	*Hussar colonel*
Colonel Knuds	*Commander of the citadel*
Major Skatt-Hesse	*Infantry officer*
Captain Heiss	*Aide to Balcke-Horneswerden*
Lieutenant Bottrop	*Militia officer*
Asmus	*A clerk*
Canon Rother-Konisrat	*A leader of the peace party*
Baron von und zu Löhm	
The Knight and Lady Jenz-Hohenwitz	*Associates of Canon Rother*
The Knight and Lady Machting-Altstein-Borckstein	
Doctor Sorge	*An Illuminatus*
Canon Steinau-Zoll	*A leader of the conservative clergy*
The Comte d'Erles	*A French émigré*
Captain Jean-Marie Lanard	*An officer of the French Republic*

IN MAINZ TERRITORY

Ludwig Jürich	*A judge, and cousin of Anna Poppenstahl*
Emilia Jürich	*His wife*
Maximilian Jürich	*His nephew*
Kaus and Madame Kaus Hofmeister and Madame Hofmeister	*Friends and relations of the Jürichs*
Father Septe	
Hartmann Heinrich	*Servants*

PART I:
CROSSING

July 1793

I
Crossing

A young man saw his dreams broken. He saw that he had helped to betray them. That was why he came to hate.

That was why Michel Wéry, once a petty gentleman of Brabant, was in Mainz in the spring and summer of 1793. It was why, on a dimming July evening, he followed a guide from his cellar shelter on the first stage of a long journey.

He was a tall man. His brow was high, rounding backwards into the soft browns of his hair. Hunger had hollowed his face and pinched his neck. His skin had lost its natural tan. It was blotched and bad after the months spent penned in the city. His whiskers straggled over his cheeks and throat. His eyes were sunk, and the skin in the pits was brown, as if it had been stained. The downward jut of his nose lent him a hawkish look, as he glanced to left and right for signs of danger.

Beneath his greatcoat he was naked to the waist.

He had emerged in the shadow of a ruined church. The church had once been beautiful, with tall windows and a steep-pitched roof reaching up three-quarters of the height of its octagonal tower. On the tower there had been a clock-face with gilded hands, and an onion-dome like the cap of a priest. But the roof was fallen, the clock stopped, the dome gone altogether. The stones were streaked with great tongues of soot and the timbers were charred by fire. Wéry did not look up.

A sound swelled in the air, passing overhead – the liquid hum of a cannon-ball, followed by the crash. (And where did that one fall? The cathedral again? The house of some citizen?) Here came another. Wéry did not duck. Ducking did no good.

The street was empty and scattered with rubble. It was scattered too, with a thick layer of earth and dung, laid by once-proud citizens to damp the impact of mortars and solid shot firing into the town. The dung was everywhere, moist and dark after the recent wet weather. It coloured the cobbles and the lowest few inches of the house walls with its foul brown stains.

Everything must stink. Wéry knew that he too must stink, but he had lost the sense of it long ago.

The guide caught his arm. The two men hurried down the street and across the Square of Our Lady. To their left rose the huge, six-towered, red-stone cathedral. Part of the great roof had collapsed. The east towers stood like broken teeth, wrecked by fire. In the porches were carved the figures of fiends, blank-eyed and grinning. Wéry did not see them as he passed. The fiends went on grinning after he had gone.

The houses were half-timbered, with elaborate diagonal patterns of black and white. They were tall, under steep roofs, and their upper storeys leaned out over the streets. But the doors were fast and the windows shuttered. Few if any people were inside them. The inhabitants were crammed into cellars and crypts across the town, sheltering from the bombardment. The streets were empty. Even the population of stray cats had vanished, because the people were hungry now, and in the lulls they would come out to hunt anything they could eat. They would hunt for food, and for firewood, and the ragged republican militiamen would beat up and down the streets and scream at them to observe the curfew. But they would come out all the same. They were weak and desperate. When the sickness came, it would kill them in hundreds.

At the end of the street a row of houses had been gutted by fire. The house fronts leaned dangerously outwards. The roofs were gone and the windows were as empty as the eyes of skeletons. And another ball smashed uselessly into tiles somewhere close by.

Not long ago the defenders had sneered at the shot, when they saw how few killed anyone. They had been brave, and laughed. But bravery starved. Courage was wearing away. They did not sneer now. And in the darkness, sometimes they wept. Rumour said that the French garrison was negotiating its surrender. The French would abandon their allies, the Mainz republicans. The republicans could not hold the city alone. They would have no escape from the revenge of the besiegers, and of their own townspeople.

Order was breaking down. Commands were not obeyed any more. Tasks that should have been done were not done. Down by the waterfront, under the walls of the baroque palace, a corpse lay unburied. It was a republican militiaman, shot by firing squad. The dead man's arms lay flung wide, like a victim of crucifixion. Someone had taken his musket and coat and boots, but then they had left him here, in a pool of his own blood.

Beside the body Wéry and his guide crouched and waited. The guide was scanning the waterfront fortifications. There were not many defenders here, because the Rhine protected this side of the city from assault, and because the fortifications themselves were dreadfully exposed to enemy cannon fire from across the river. All the same, the two men did not want to be seen, or stopped or questioned.

As his guide peered around the corner of the palace building, Wéry gathered his breath. His eyes rested on the corpse beside him.

The face, twisted with shock and pain, was familiar, but he could not remember the man's name. The cheeks were hollow, the eyes rolled their whites at the sky. The mouth was open in a silent howl. The teeth were bad and bloody, and many of them were missing. The shirt was lifted halfway up his chest, showing how tightly the skin had drawn over the ribs, and how it swelled over the pot-belly. Hunger did that. It had done the same to Wéry. But this man would not be hungry any more.

Something was moving around the dead man − something crawling or trembling on the dung-scattered cobbles at his shoulder. Yes, lice: a small tide of lice, creeping out from the filthy collar, leaving the body as it cooled, looking for some other way to live now that their host was dead. Wéry had seen that before. The man must have died in the last hour. He must have been shot by the very men to whom he was going. Did anyone remember why?

Lice were everywhere, like the dung. Wéry had them too.

'Come on!'

The two men scuttled into the open space between the palace and the low river wall. The wall was littered with rubble and wrecked guns. The few serviceable cannon were silent and unattended for want of powder. Here the two men were most at risk from enemy shot. But now, after the close, hellish world of the city streets, they could see.

It was sunset. The air moved, cool and steady on the skin. To their left the palace was a shadow – a mass of black shapes of roofs and gables, battlements and the cupola of the corner tower, all outlined in living gold. To their right, across the grey flow of the Rhine, the thick light yellowed on the hills. Smoke gathered around the complex of earthworks at the bridgehead on the east bank, which was still held by the French garrison. Beyond, out on the slopes, more smoke-plumes trailed across the land. Peeping among them were the brown lines of the nearest trenches and batteries aiming inwards at the city. As they hurried along the waterfront Wéry saw the low bank of smoke grow suddenly, in a thick, silent puff. He heard the ball drone by, and the distant thump of the gun. That was the Prussians firing. The Prussians always seemed to have ammunition.

Ahead of them, beyond the corner of the palace and the bastion at its feet, the Rhine bent westward. It curled through three long river-islands that lay like dead whales in the flow. On the far bank the attacker's lines curled to follow it: first the Saxons, Wéry knew, then the Franconian contingent, and then the Prussians again, camped at both ends of the bridge of boats that linked their positions on the far bank with the main besieging force, dug in around the town on this side of the river.

Breathless, the two men reached the bastion at the foot of the squat little corner tower of the palace. They threw themselves down in the shelter of the low wall.

There were men in the bastion. They were a handful of the Mainz republican militia, posted here because it was not one of the immediate points of danger which the French felt they must guard for themselves. They were a ragged and filthy crew, ill-armed, with a mix of cross-belts and military-style coats over the remains of civilian clothes. There were patches on their elbows, long whiskers on their cheeks, and their feet were bare or tied with rags.

Their commander was another young man, once a student at the Mainz university. He was short, hatless, with wild dark hair and heavy brows. He crouched at the parapet, looking sombrely over the rubbled lip of the wall at the batteries on the far bank. It was he who had ordered the killing of the man by the palace, half an hour before. If that weighed upon him yet, no one could tell.

'Jürich,' called one of his followers hoarsely. 'Hey, Jürich!'

The bastion commander looked around.

'The Belgian's here.'

Another ball moaned inwards. Somewhere nearby a fire must have started, because there was smoke in the air.

The commander beckoned. Wéry crawled over to him.

'Look downstream,' said the commander.

Wéry lifted his head above the battlement.

'The islands are held by the French, still,' muttered the bastion commander. 'They will be watching out. They'll watch harder as the dusk falls. The main flow of the river is this side of them. You must stay this side, too. Stay with the current until you pass the last of them. Then you must strike for the far shore. Save your strength for that. If you leave it too late you'll be swept down to the bridge, and the Prussians will shoot you in the water. Understand?'

Wéry peered down at the islands, now fading into the dusk. There seemed to be very little space between the tail of the last French-held island and the Prussian bridge. Very little, for a half-starved man who must swim that great current at night.

'I understand,' he said simply.

'Now. Follow the line of the bridge inland on the far side. There. That encampment. Look – you can see the fires, now. That's what you are making for. They're troops of the Franconian Circle – mostly from the Erzberg bishopric. See it?'

'Yes.'

'You must surrender as soon as you have a chance – to the Franconians if at all possible. Ask for the Erzberg contingent, and then for an officer called Adelsheim. If you find him, you use my name. Understand?'

Wéry was still trying to measure the distance he would have to swim, and weighing the chances of reaching the far bank before he was swept down to the bridge.

'This officer,' he said at last. 'This Adelsheim. How do you know him?'

The bastion commander grimaced. 'My cousin was his governess. She taught him French. She still lives in their house.'

Wéry shrugged at the human ties that had been ruptured by war. 'Will he get me to the Imperial Headquarters?'

'No. His superiors will have to do that. But you must ask for him first, for your own safety.'

Wéry's eyes brooded on the river – the great, grey river, cold and heavy, that drowned men every year. Darkness cloaked the far bank, where soldiers patrolled with muskets and would shoot at any sight or sound. As he watched, one of the batteries on the far bank loosed all its guns together, and a pale light flickered in the clouds of smoke.

Drone, drone, drone and *thump-thump*. And crash.

Crash, thought Wéry absently. The sound of another dream breaking.

The two men shared so many things. Both were radicals, who

23

had taken arms to overturn the old, privileged order in their homelands. Both had looked to the new republic of France for help. They had heard and believed the calls of a common freedom sounding from Paris. But Wéry had seen his new state of Belgium betrayed and abandoned. And now France was about to betray the republic of Mainz, too. In the struggle of the great powers there was no room for the little causes any more. There was only a lethal, dwindling game to be played and played until it was lost. No power was truly a friend.

'I've been saying goodbye to your uncle,' Wéry murmured.

The man Jürich glanced sharply at him. His uncle was no sympathizer with the city republic. He had come to Mainz to extract his nephew before war closed the city gates, and had been trapped there by the siege. 'And?'

'Small comfort. He understands that you are trying to open negotiations with the Empire. But he thinks it is too late. He says the Imperial commanders won't listen to you. He says they don't have to. They'll deal with the French. The French will leave, and the Empire will come in and pick up the pieces. Why promise anything to men who rebelled against their own prince?'

The bastion commander looked at him sombrely. 'And what do you think?'

Wéry grinned. 'I agree, of course. But I'll still go for you.' He added softly, 'My rule now is to decide first what Paris would want me to do. Then I do the opposite. And those fellows over there are less likely to shoot me than they are you. My crime against them was a while ago.'

The bastion commander nodded. He gestured to his followers. 'The rope.'

The rope was fastened to the carriage of a wrecked gun. Over the parapet it went, long and dark and snaking in the dusk. There was a faint splash as it touched the water. Wéry took it just below the knot and tugged hard, flinging his weight backwards. The dead gun did not move.

'Good, then.'

A whisper, hoarse and urgent, from the upstream side of the bastion.

'The boat! Look out, lads! The boat!'

A sudden flurry broke out on the bastion top. Down in the river, the boat patrol was approaching. Now that it was dark, it was safe for the French to put armed men on the river, rowing up and down outside the walls to guard against any attempt by the besiegers to cross over the river by stealth – and to catch anyone who tried to leave the city without permission. Men hurried to the downstream side of the bastion and began to haul up the rope.

'Leave it!' hissed the bastion commander. 'Leave it, and get your heads down!'

As they ducked, he stood, and showed himself calmly at the wall.

Crouching at his feet, Wéry looked up at him. He saw the man's face turn slowly, following the swift progress of the boat down-river. He saw the reflection of distant muzzle-flare wink in the man's eye. Silence had fallen on the platform. Wéry bent his head, listening.

(Drone, drone, drone and Thump. And crash. *Goodnight, Mainz!* said the guns.)

And another noise, much closer: something on the river. An oar, washing through the water. Wéry crouched lower. In the dimness he could see his own hand in front of him. There were white marks on the skin. He knew them well. They seemed to float now, in the grisly light. They floated like dreams before his eyes.

The creak of oars. Muttered voices from the boat. Would they see the rope? The rope must be a dark line, still and quiet in the downstream crook of the bastion. It would be far less easy to see than a bustle of men and something disappearing furtively up the wall. But the current would carry the boat to the downstream side. They would come in close, because the flow was slower under the bastions. They would want to row upstream right against the wall. Where were they?

It was cold. His heart was beating. It would be colder still in the water.

God! That one was close! It must have hit less than fifty paces away. He had not heard it coming. He had felt it, though. He had felt the city tremble as it hit. Was that why he was going? This was a hopeless mission. Hope? Meaningless. Everything had been betrayed. Brussels was betrayed, and Liège was fallen, and Paris was sick and vengeful – a tyranny worse than the one it had destroyed. And here in Mainz there was tyranny too, where there should have been liberty and justice. There were dead on the cobbles and dung in the streets and people who had been driven out like animals to starve beyond the walls. Dreams were nightmares now. The white marks on his hands were the scars of his rage.

But it was not meaningless. Not yet. There was still a way to go, into the river and beyond. There were still things to do, against the men who had stolen the dream.

What else was there to live by?

Wash, wash, wash, went the oars on the river, diminishing. The boat had begun its long labour upstream. The crew had not seen the rope. The river beckoned to him.

'Maximilian,' he whispered. 'Thank you.' And he gripped his friend's arm. 'Good luck.'

'Good luck.'

Then Wéry was standing, kicking off his battered shoes, shaking off his greatcoat and feeling the cold touch of the air on his skin. Maximilian Jürich held the rope out for him. He gripped it, passed it around his back, and scrambled to the lip of the parapet. There he teetered, facing in, leaning backward until the rope bit into his back and wrists and his feet were braced against the stone.

'Quickly!' someone hissed. He did not know who. They were all dark shadows now – the shapes of head and shoulders, flat against the night sky. He could not look for footholds. His bare feet felt their way down the stone. White light flickered along the wall. (God! What an irony if a cannon ball struck him now!) But nothing happened. He did not even hear the passage of the shot. He was nearing the water. Here it was – leaping up to lick at his heel like a ghostly hound, wet and cold. He felt for a foothold and did not find one. Deeper, maybe. Carry on down. His feet slipped on weeds and suddenly he was up to his armpits in wet, cold river, and bruising his shoulder at the same time against the wall. Ugh! His feet found the muddy bed. He stood there, chest deep, holding himself up with the aid of the rope. He was already shaking. The Rhine sucked at his body.

Goodnight, Mainz! bellowed the guns. That was the Empire, firing. That was everything he had first taken up arms to fight: privilege and aristocracy and the smothering hold of church and

27

feudal dues; the power that had once been his enemy. That was where he was going now.

Over there the gunners must see little of their target – perhaps just the crown of spires, sprawling under the afterglow of sunset, the burst of an incendiary shell like a sudden star, and the occasional white flare as the garrison fired back on its tormentors. They would hear nothing but their own batteries: not the crash of shot landing; the weary jokes or cries; the sobbing of those who had already passed so many nights like this and could not bear one more. From over there, Mainz would endure its hell in silence. And they would work calmly, by lamp-light and muzzle-flash, taking their bearings from the stakes and markers, bringing more ammunition, handling the matches care-fully in the dark. There would be no hurry. A city is hard to miss, and it cannot run away.

Goodnight, Mainz!

The flashes plagued his vision. He could not see the line of the islands that Maximilian had pointed out to him. He could not see the watchfires. He could only guess the direction to the Erzberg camp. *Ask for an officer called Adelsheim. If you find him . . .*

'Adelsheim.' That was all he had.

Maximilian might be looking down on him from the battle-ment. Probably he was, waiting for the moment when the tell-tale rope could be hauled back to safety. But Maximilian could not help him any more. He could give no more directions. He might as well be on the moon. Down here there was nothing but darkness and gunfire, the coldness of the water, and the name.

The name might mean anything: any future at all.

Or none at all.

Now, the river.

PART II:
THE SISTER

MAY 1797

II
A State of Germany

Peace came after four years, and a string of disasters for the Empire at the hands of a General Bonaparte far away in Italy. And the early days of peace found Michel Wéry once again at a river bank, with only the word 'Adelsheim' to guide him. But this river was just a muddy stream running in the bottom of a wooded valley. And the word was not a man any more.

Nor had anyone directed him, this time. Only his own conscience had nagged and prodded him to make his way here along the forest tracks of Germany. At each turning and mud-hole and rain-shower, it had grumbled at him: *Well, if you don't do it, who will? And when?*

He rode a handsome, dark-brown horse. On his head was a tall military cap of green and black, with a white plume and a trailing wing of green cloth. Under his greatcoat his uniform was green and white. His moustache was trimmed to the fierce curl of a light cavalryman, and a long, curved sabre hung from his saddle.

Only his eyes were unchanged: sunk, and rimmed with brown skin. They brooded on the water.

There was a ford here, and in the black mud at the water's edge there was a stone, covered in a shroud of moss. He dismounted to pull the moss away. Beneath it he found, as he had expected, the letter A, cut in deep lines that were packed with dirt.

A for *Adelsheim*.

It was an estate marker. But here, in the heart of the Empire, it was also a frontier marker. On this unimpressive bank the territory of the Prince-Bishop of Erzberg ended. On the other, a different ruler held sway: a man who owned no lord but God and the distant Emperor.

Adelsheim! declared the revealed dirt importantly, and touched the emptiness in his heart.

Wéry straightened. The estate from which the Adelsheim family took its name appeared to be just one village and one house, sitting glumly together in a mile-long cleft between two great wooded hills. He could see all the way across it from where he stood. The brown fragments of a small castle stood abandoned on a shoulder of rock above the valley. And his horse, with the callous disregard of an invading army, was already crossing the border. It was standing in mid-stream, head turned back towards him, as if wondering what he was waiting for.

He waded after it, scolding. The horse allowed him to remount, lifting its head as he took the reins. He took a moment to pat its neck and speak to it, not because it was misbehaving, but because he did not want to go up to the house to say what he had to say.

At length he nudged it to the far bank, and presumed to invade another soil.

He passed fallow and barns, small herds and a trough that leaned so drunkenly it could hardly serve its purpose any more. He passed a gang of peasant men carrying axes and wearing broad hats. Some were in clogs and some in bare feet, he saw. There was a woman drawing water from the stream, and a ragged and bare-footed child watching over a flock of ducks. They stopped and stared at him as he rode by.

The cottages had a mean and dilapidated look. None could have had more than two rooms. Several roofs were in poor repair. There was no sign of new work here, not a water channel or a granary, just as there was no sign of clover crop or any other modern farming method in the fields. The place smelled of dung and damp and wood smoke.

The schoolhouse was empty. The children would be off at their chores. The schoolmaster would be out working his furrows, or doing whatever else he did to supplement his living. And there was no one to tell pupils or schoolmaster or parents what good there was to be had from education, which they would never gain by drudgery in their fields.

The watermill was a sad thing: broken paddles and an ill-fitting sluice-gate, the roof sunk and ragged, and no doubt teeming with rats. What did the landlord charge his peasants for using that?

There was no sign of life at the church.

Disappointment grew on him as he passed across the estate, like the chilly wind that warned him of rain. Neglect met his eyes wherever he looked. The Imperial Knights were famous for lacking interest in their subjects. And it seemed that the Knight of Adelsheim was one with his kind, whatever the views of his second son had been.

So, my friend, he thought. *Is this the home you spoke of fondly? Is this where you were raised, in your little cot of privilege?*

Now the house was coming into view again, as the road curved by a grove of broad-leafed trees. It was a square block, three stories high, perched on a low rise with a steep, wooded slope at its back. The porch was supported by classic columns. On each side of the door three tall windows stared solemnly down across the bottom of the valley. The windows were stripped of their paintwork by the weather. There were dark streaks on the wall below a bad gutter. The roof, missing tiles and lead, sagged like the back of a horse. Here was more neglect, and some shortage of means too, no doubt. But in Wéry's eyes the neglect of the house did not excuse what he had seen on the estate. Here, sullen in its dignity, was Privilege again. He met it wherever he went. The Knight of Adelsheim was lord of his tiny land, in this land of little lords. And Wéry did not doubt that he wrung his tired peasantry for every crust they had; the emptier a knight's pockets, the stiffer his neck with pride.

'The guillotine loved stiff necks when I was in Paris, sir,' he murmured. 'And I do not love aristocrats myself.'

He spoke aloud to steady himself, for his misgivings were growing. The house hulked before him like a fat, grey gentleman sitting for his portrait, ignoring his presence. Smoke was rising from the chimneys. The shutters were open. The family was here. Now he must announce himself to them.

There was nobody at the front of the building, where two short flights of steps led up to the door. Only two great, fat angel-faces, carved above the stone lintel, looked down upon him. Their faces were streaked with discoloration, and on one plump cheek there hung a trail of bird-dropping, exactly as if the face had wept a filthy tear that morning, and no one had bothered to wipe it away.

Rain had begun to fall, out of the yellow-grey sky. It was falling in grey veils that misted all the hills. It damped his shoulders, and ran wet-cold fingers into the cracks between his gloves and sleeves. He jumped from his horse at the very foot of the steps. Of course there was no one to take the reins.

'Stay,' he told it. And then, as it looked reproachful: '*Stay*, damn you!'

Up the steps he went, leaping in his great riding boots, two and three at a time. At the door he removed the plumed hussar's cap from his head, unbuttoned his greatcoat to show his green-and-white cavalry uniform, and hammered with his cold fist at the boards of the door.

He waited. After a while he beat upon it again.

He was about to knock a third time when he heard footsteps.

They came (clip, clip, clip,) across a stone floor within. He waited for the door to open. It did not. Whoever it was must be hovering just inside, as if they could not really believe they had heard knocking, or that a man could be out here, sodden and shivering waiting to be admitted.

Impatiently, he banged on the wood once more.

It opened immediately, onto a shadowy hall with high ceilings. A short man in a frock coat and a powdered wig stood in the doorway.

'I am Captain Michel Wéry.'

When that brought no response, Wéry added: 'Please tell the Knight that I have come to see him. I am a friend of his son Albrecht. I have the gravest possible news.'

The servant stood blinking at him. He wore no livery, so he must rank highly among the house staff. He would already have understood that Wéry was a foreigner. Now, behind that toad-like face, he was trying to decide what to do. Wéry did not seem to fit into any of the convenient categories of persons known and unknown, admissible and inadmissible, that a servant of this house was accustomed to dealing with. The enslaved mind needed cues, clues of standing in the orders of the privileged, before it could select the routine to follow.

'I am Captain Michel Wéry, of the Regiment of Hussars of His Highness the Prince-Bishop of Erzberg. I wish to see the Knight at once.'

Hussars. He jerked the lapel of his greatcoat to show his white, braided tunic and the green fur-lined jacket that hung from his shoulder. And he stared at the little man with all the haughtiness he could muster.

After all, no officer was admitted to the Prince's hussars unless all four of his grandparents at least had their own noble pedigree. (Or unless, for some mysterious reason, he enjoyed the *especial* favour of the Prince.)

It should have been enough. Surely it should have been. But he saw the servant's brow furrow more deeply.

'The Knight does not receive visitors,' the man said. His voice was plaintive as if he felt that any gentleman from Erzberg, even a foreign one, should have known better than to put him in such a dilemma.

'It is most urgent,' Wéry insisted. 'It concerns his son.'

The servant licked his lips. 'I will see if the Lady is able to receive you.'

The Lady? The wife? The mother?

Lady Adelsheim! She was famous for her wit, and her force-fulness. Even in the camps of the hussars Wéry heard about her. He had no wish to meet her. He would infinitely have preferred to deliver his news to a man, who in the crisis would act with a man's restraint. What was the matter with Albrecht's father?

36

This might be so much more difficult. 'Will the Knight not . . . ?' he began.

Plainly, from the servant's look, the Knight would not.

'Very good,' Wéry said in resignation. 'If you would please announce me.'

The servant was still standing in the doorway. He was waiting for something. After a moment Wéry realized what it must be.

'I do not have a card,' he said. He saw the man's eyebrows shoot up.

'I have told you my name and my business,' he snarled. 'Show me in!'

And he was shown in, to a large, elaborately tiled hall with pillars and an elusive smell. He stamped gracelessly across it in the wake of the frock coat. His agitation was growing, and because of it he had become angry as well – angry at his own posturing and the other man's deference.

Man was born free! he thought, as he handed over his coat, hat and gloves. And no race exhibited their chains with more pride than the Germans; and no German more than a servant! They had their brains, as well as their sense of status, from their masters, and would never think for themselves. So ask, and they would refuse you; but demand, and they would obey. Try showing them that you considered them an equal, speak informally, joke with them, and you would be met with blank, affronted looks. Call them 'Citizen' and they would be horrified!

The servant opened the door to a small waiting-parlour to one side of the hall.

And there He was.

There he was: Albrecht von Adelsheim, in a full-length portrait to one side of an empty fireplace. In that unremarkable little room he seemed to glow from the dark canvas.

His stance was formal, his uniform so neat and white it might never have seen a day's campaign. But it was the true Albrecht. His big, liquid smile was on his lips, beaming into the room. His eyes shone with laughter. They mocked the vain insistence of portraiture that its subjects should show poise and calm. And his eyes were on Wéry as he came through the door, as if he had just laughed that laugh and said – as he had done so many times – *Hey, Michel!*

'*Hey, Michel, did you ever look at someone? No, but truly look?*'

Or: '*Hey, Michel! Still in bed, you hound?*'

Oh yes! When he had been half-dead with sleep and drink and misery: '*Hey, Michel! Still in bed, you hound? Mother of God, you look worse than when we pulled you out of the river! You can swim in water, my friend, but it's harder to swim in wine. It's the wine that swims in you, ha ha . . . !*

'*. . . Listen to me. I said* listen *to me . . . Citizen Wéry! You will please stand to attention! I am about to recite your precious Rights of Man. Very well then, you may* lie *to attention. Hands by your sides, sir – not over your ears. Ready? "The aim of every political association is the preservation of the natural and imprescriptible Rights of Man. These rights are Liberty, Property, Safety and Resistance to Oppression." Am I correct? Good. So where* does it say *you have the right to* lie down *when I am talking to you . . . ?*'

Oh, that laugh! And the punch to the shoulder that had made all men equal. Whenever things had been at their worst – hunger, sickness, mud, some stupid quarrel about fodder in the horse-lines, then: *Hey, you fellows!*

Hey, Michel!

The voice was fading. It dwindled in his mind as the surprise of the portrait receded. He was looking at paint, and that was all: just a thin layer of paint on canvas, spread there by an artist cunning enough to catch the spirit of his subject, even as he observed all the formalities expected of him. And now the artist was gone, and the man he had painted was gone too.

Wéry turned his back on the portrait. He spoke to the air.

'My horse needs attention.'

The servant bowed and withdrew.

III
Fall of an Empire

Maria von Adelsheim was happy – happier than she had been for a long time, because there was peace at last, and her brother would come home.

She was sitting on one of the long settees in the library of the house at Adelsheim. At her back a great window let in all the light that the dull day would allow. Around her, bookshelves reached up to the high ceiling. Over her petticoats she wore the grey-green dress that her mother had chosen for her that morning. Its skirts spread widely around her. Her hair was piled and powdered, and there was powder on her skin, for she and her mother were receiving a caller today.

Maria did not give a fig for the caller – the elderly, fat, black-clad, self-satisfied Carl Joseph Baron von und zu Löhm, who had travelled out to Adelsheim to pay court to Mother because of Mother's influence with her cousin, the Canon Rother-Konisrat. But Maria did not have to entertain him herself. Her task was to look decorative, and to read aloud to her mother's pet poet, Icht, because there must be poetry in the air before Mother would breathe it.

Lady Adelsheim was at her desk, a tiny figure dressed in warm pinks, which stood out artfully beside the greens that she had picked for Maria to wear. Her hair, like Maria's, was powdered white and piled high above her head; there were letters before her and a pen in her hand. She was discussing religion and politics with the Baron Löhm. The Baron understood well the kind of talk that best pleased his hostess. Even so, he did not have her undivided attention. For Maria knew her mother was also following her reading, and might choose to correct her at any moment. At the same time she was directing her secretary, Müller, in undertones. And in a second or two she would turn to deal with fat, old, frock-coated Tieschen, who had bustled in from the front door with something he needed to tell her.

Löhm, Icht, Maria, Müller and Tieschen: Lady Adelsheim dealt with them all, and all at once, as though she were the Emperor in Vienna surrounded by the ambassadors of Powers and Princes, by subject aristocracies and even lowly citizens of the Empire, all demanding attention. She dealt with Maria in French (which she considered the superior language), with Löhm in French laced with Latin, with Müller and Tieschen in German, and with Icht in either French or German depending on the subject, because Icht's poetry was written in German and she would adopt that language whenever she was telling him how she thought he might improve it.

Thus (in French): 'My dear Löhm, you astonish me. One would think you and your kind would usurp the very place of the Church!'

'I will not deny, my Lady,' said the Baron, 'that to teach men to be holy and good, in their own interests, is the aim of Christianity itself. But these days the promotion of virtue is actually hindered by the structures that were created in its name . . .'

(Lady Adelsheim simultaneously, in an undertone and in German, 'No, the letter from Holz, Müller, I told you so quite clearly . . .')

'. . . not within a generation, to be sure, but far more surely than by feats of arms. *Tantae molis erat Romanam condere gentem.* Long before the first Pope took his seat, the ancients were hewing their own paths to virtue, as you will know.'

'I believe they hewed a very maze, my Lord. *Quot homines tot sententiae.* For the whole truth was not revealed to them . . .'

And Maria, reading aloud in French, emulated the voice of a man, '*Sing me your song.*' And in the plaintive tones of a woman who loved, she answered, '*I sing. But you do not hear me!*'

'Maria,' said her mother immediately, 'even for a heathen concubine, that is too much. Icht will tell you that you must maintain a certain distance from the work even as you appreciate it.'

'Oh indeed,' said Icht, the poet, who was sitting bolt upright in his seat because he could never let his spine touch the back of a chair in Lady Adelsheim's presence. 'Indeed, my Lady. And yet it is a work of passion, there is no doubt of that. Some passion must be allowed.'

'Passion impedes the mind,' said Mother. 'It is not possible to be truly virtuous if one is also passionate. Maria knows that quite well. Baron, you contrive to sound most reasonable. Yet the Abbé Barruel will have it that your kind were secretly responsible for the Revolution itself. Am I to suppose that this was an error?'

'*I sing,*' Maria read, '*but you do not hear me.*'

'You have read that already,' said Mother. '*I* heard it quite distinctly.'

'It is an error of the Abbé, no doubt, my Lady,' said Baron Löhm. 'Although you will forgive me if I do not wholly understand what you mean by "my kind".'

'Pish! You know quite well what I mean. You are an *Illuminatus* and a freemason. A most terrible man indeed. The church abominates you and all your like.'

'If you perceive this, my Lady,' said Löhm, looking more satisfied than ever, 'then doubtless you will also have perceived that an *Illuminatus* is not in fact a freemason.'

'I have perceived that they are the same thing, only worse,' said Lady Adelsheim, with a brilliant smile. And: '*Ja, Tieschen*?'

Tieschen did not speak at once, but took a step forward and bent to whisper in her ear. And because he did so, everyone else stopped saying what they were saying and craned to listen. Tieschen finished. There was a moment of stillness.

'Impossible,' said Lady Adelsheim.

'My Lady, he did say it was urgent, and most grave . . .'

'Quite impossible, Tieschen. I am occupied, as you must surely know. He must come back another time, or write. Continue, Maria. I am sure Icht is most interested.'

Maria lifted her book again, holding it up to make the most of the sullen light from the window behind her. Despite the grey skies and the tap of the rain on the windows, her spirits were high. This was one of her favourite pieces: an allegory composed of a dialogue between a prince and his concubine, set in some far Arabian land where the air was warm and scented, where clothes were light and the flesh beneath them throbbed with the blood of desire. It was a favourite because Albrecht had introduced it to her the last time he had been home, pointing out the references to the power of liberty and the impending death of tyranny, which pleased both her and him. It reminded her of him now, so that she even imagined that the face of the Prince in the story was his, and that she herself was the concubine, who in another time and place might have thrilled with love for him.

And soon they would be seeing him again. He was well. They knew he was well, because they had just had a letter from him – one of those letters that had come every few weeks during the long months of waiting, strengthening her and reassuring her like lamps on a dark journey, to tell them all the ridiculous things that had been happening to him in his regiment on the Rhine, or wherever the campaigns had taken him. And at last there was peace! Although Maria was sorry that the war should have ended in defeat, she was glad that it was over. She suspected it had never been necessary. It had taken him away. Last year, when the French had marched deep into Germany, it had even driven the family into exile in Bohemia, to find refuge on the estates of their distant cousin Count Effenpanz. And while Adelsheim had survived in their absence, many other estates and families had suffered. Now it was over, and Albrecht would come home at last.

That was what lit her heart, as she sat in the library with the cold fingers of the rain tapping at the window behind her; and the piece she was reading reminded her of it, in case she could possibly have forgotten.

'*Scatter roses!*' she ordered, in the voice of the Prince. And as the concubine: '*But you do not see them!*'

'Tieschen,' said Mother once more. 'I have said that it is impossible.' And Tieschen left to deliver her sentence to whomever it was that had been applying to her.

By chance, Maria caught the Baron's expression. He seemed more satisfied still. Of course he would not have welcomed another demand on his hostess's attention. And yet his brow had also lifted a fraction in surprise. Lady Adelsheim would normally have accepted any caller she thought capable of intelligent conversation, and of appreciating her intelligence when she bestowed it on them. The Baron, Illuminatus (or not), abominated by the church (or not), was wondering what this particular caller had done to offend.

So did Maria, a little.

For a moment Wéry could not believe he had heard correctly.

'But – but did you not give her my message? I must speak with her about her son!'

A frown flickered on the servant's face. Perhaps he did understand that this stranger had something to say about young Albrecht, who was away with the Prince-Bishop's little army. But it plainly could not matter any more, because the Lady had said he must leave.

'I regret, sir, that the Lady is not able to receive you today.'

'Then I must speak with the Knight.'

'The Knight does not receive visitors.'

And there he stood, like a fat old sheep in the track, too stupid to do anything but bleat the same old bleat in the face of a world that was changing.

'I do not believe you can have delivered my message correctly!'

'Indeed I did, sir. But the Lady is not able to receive you.'

'Why in Heaven not? I have come all the way from Erzberg, and with very important news. What is the matter – is she sick?'

'Sir!'

If the Lady of the house was not able to receive visitors, it seemed, that was enough. It was not permitted to ask why. Wéry towered over the small servant. He was nervous and angry. He had come leagues to be here, when his duty lay somewhere else. He was not going to start a brawl in this house, but . . .

He puffed his cheeks to show his frustration.

'Very well,' he said. 'Very well. Please have my coat and gloves brought to me. And let the stable bring my horse to the door.'

The little servant turned impassively, strode to the foot of the stairs and clapped his hands to summon help. And Wéry stepped lightly into the hall behind him. One, two, three paces were all he needed. He was heading down the corridor opposite, from which the man had come.

'Sir!'

'Don't be a fool!' he snarled over his shoulder, and shook the fellow's hand from his arm. *Clop, clop, clop* went his heels on the wooden floor, echoing along the walls like the guns of invading armies.

At the end of the corridor a door was half-open, and a woman's voice murmured from beyond.

The etiquette of Lady Adelsheim's salon did not permit Maria or Icht to take part in conversations between Lady Adelsheim and someone like the Baron, but it did permit the Baron to step down and join in whatever was going on between his hostess and the lesser persons present. Now he was offering them his views on the famous romantic writers of the day, referring largely to *The Sorrows of Young Werther* for examples to support his argument.

'. . . So are we to suppose that passion – a passion so great that the possessor of it ultimately destroys himself – should be in some sense held up for admiration? Surely this is beyond any reason? And if we admire it, do we not deny the faculty of reason in ourselves?'

'But my dear Löhm, to go – as you say – "beyond reason" is precisely what the man Goethe and his fellows would do! For them Reason is a cage to the spirit. If you do not appreciate that you cannot appreciate what they have achieved.'

'You said yourself, my Lady, that it is necessary to maintain a certain distance even as you appreciate.'

'And so I do. I remain within reason, and beyond reason, at the same time. It is merely a matter of existing in two places at once. Continue, Maria. Perhaps Klopstock – it is Klopstock, is it not? – has some further light for us. Although in truth I find allegory in all forms most tedious.'

Maria dutifully returned to the point at which Baron Löhm had interrupted her.

'*My love!*' she read in the concubine's voice. '*Your steed neighs to carry you to battle. And yet your heart trembles. What is it you see? A spirit of the dead?*' And in the Prince's voice she replied. '*Not a spirit of the dead, but . . .*'

'But a hussar!' interjected Lady Adelsheim, in a tone of mock wonder.

Maria looked up.

Standing in the doorway was a tall man, a complete stranger, in the uniform of a captain in the Prince-bishop's hussars.

He was indeed very tall, and he had that leanness about him – the hollowness of the neck, the prominence of the cheekbones – that Maria associated with men who had been on the campaigns, where food always seemed to be so scarce. His shoulders and upper spine stooped a little, as if he were forever having to bend to hear what people shorter than he were saying. His eyes were dark, his brows bushy, his nose long and blunt – there was something of the raptor in his look. His forehead was round and high, and might have been creeping higher still into the beginnings of baldness. His hair was light brown, unpowdered, and cut short.

Fat old Tieschen in his frock coat was at the man's elbow, looking agitated.

'I am astonished,' said Lady Adelsheim, still in French. 'Is this a hussar officer?'

A lady, on introduction to a gentleman, should offer him her hand. The gentleman should take it and bow over it as if to kiss it, although his lips must not actually touch her skin or glove. The gentleman might then be introduced to any other company present, and conversation might proceed, upon any topic that society considered suitable.

Mother had not offered her hand. She was looking at the newcomer as if he were an unexpected diversion, such as an owl flown in from the woods or a bailiff come to report on a disagreeable matter from one of the estates. And under her gaze the man did indeed seem to feel out of place – even flustered.

Of course, thought Maria. This must be the caller whom Mother had said she would not see. And he had made his way in despite that! Goodness!

'Madame, I beg your pardon for this intrusion,' said the newcomer, bowing. He spoke French – native French, and his voice was surprisingly soft for a man who looked so gaunt. 'I do not know if my message was correctly reported to you. I am Capt—'

'It is not an intrusion at all, sir,' said Mother. 'I believe a hussar is exactly the thing we most wanted at this moment.'

'Madame, I . . .'

'No, come, sir. We are discussing heroism, and hussars are heroes to a man – or so I am assured. You are a hero I hope, sir?'

'I . . . I am a staff officer, madame,' said the man in surprise.

'No, sir, you will not be modest. I will not allow it. See there,

48

Baron. A hero stands before you. You should question him. Demand why it is that Reason, which may make Man a god, must yet be an encumbrance to any hero of romance or tragedy.'

Again the tall man tried to speak. But he missed his chance and it was gone.

'No doubt, dear Löhm, you will tell me that, had our heroes been possessed of more capacity for thought, they should have been more successful in this wretched war than they were,' said Lady Adelsheim. 'But to be a hero, these days, is to be a slave to passion, I believe. It is merely a question of which passion one is slave to. Which passion are you slave to, Captain? Is it anger? I declare that you look as if you might be angry. Pray be unheroic for a moment, Captain, and control it. Maria, you must continue. I am sure that Icht is most interested.'

The tall man was indeed becoming angry. He had understood that he was being made a plaything. His cheeks were going crimson as he stood there.

Why *had* he come?

'Maria?' Mother repeated. 'Are you dreaming, child?'

'*What is it you see?*' Maria read quickly. '*A spirit of the dead?*' And in the Prince's voice she answered herself, '*Not a spirit of the dead, but the dreadful spirit of Liberty. Where is the power that . . .*'

'Observe, Baron,' Mother was saying. 'Our hero has perceived a heroine, and is now rapt in a vision of beauty.'

Maria's tongue stumbled. '*The power that — that can hurl it back into the depths from which it came?*' She was cringing inwardly, for her own sake and for the sake of the man standing in the door- way. Really, this was outrageous! What must he think? '*Who will dare . . .*'

'No, Maria. I believe our hero must now read the Prince, and you the woman only. Pass him the book. There is not another copy, I believe. I hope not. It is a most inferior work . . .'

'*Madame!*' the man exclaimed.

No one spoke to Mother like that! Maria froze.

She froze in the act of offering the book to the stranger, with her finger marking the place and her face forming a reassuring smile. She felt that smile fix itself on her face, as though her muscles were suddenly a mask that was no longer a part of her.

'Madame,' said the newcomer tightly. 'I think you will permit me to tell you that your son is dead.'

'This is impossible.'

Mother did not even seem to pause over his words.

Maria was still looking up at the man, still holding out the book to him, and trying to smile at him because he and she were to read aloud together and be teased and criticized for it, and – and . . .

As if in a dream she could see nothing but his face, his hawk-like profile as he glowered down at Mother. She saw it very clearly. There was a tiny spot of light reflected where his shining forehead rounded back to his hairline. She had been going to do something – say something or give him something – but she could not remember what. Inside her something was screaming *Alba!* And something was answering: *Impossible.* She felt as if she had swayed and almost fallen, and had only been saved by the sound of mother's voice, firm and decided, pushing her back into balance.

The room restored itself. The world was the same. Icht was still sitting bolt upright in his chair. Both he and Baron Löhm looked aghast. Over by the press Müller, the secretary, was on his hands and knees. He was surrounded by letters that he must have just let drop on the floor.

'I – wish it were not so,' the man was saying. 'But I must assure you . . .'

Oh Mother Mary, no! His words were like the opening of a great, dark pit in the floor, swallowing her and all the house with it.

Surely, no!

Alba!

'You meant my son Albrecht, I suppose,' said Mother.

'I do. And I regret to tell you . . .'

'I had thought it would be some such story,' she said calmly. 'No, it is ridiculous. We have only just had news of him, and he is well. And now there is no more of this stupid fighting. That is all. Maria, finish your reading please. Really it is inexcusable that you have not.'

Maria realized that she was still holding out the book. She withdrew it. Her finger was on the place, but the lines had no meaning. Her mind was clinging to her mother's words. It was not true. Albrecht had sent them a letter. It had reached them after news of the peace . . .

What had been the date on his letter? Oh saints, please . . .

'Madame,' said the newcomer earnestly. 'I do not know when your news came to you. But it is my painful duty to tell you that there was an action on the twenty-third of April against the enemy . . .'

'*Any* news of import would have come to me from either his servant or his commanding officer,' Mother said, overriding him. 'Either would have informed me instantly, I assure you.'

'I regret, madame, that both his servant and his commanding officer are also . . .'

'But you change your story, sir! What, has there been a massacre, now? After the war is over? I do not credit it . . .'

'Madame!' exclaimed the man once again. 'I would not bring you news that I knew to be false. Least of all news such as this . . .'

'Again you contradict me, sir,' said Mother wearily. 'Must I give you lessons in manners, too?'

Manners? thought Maria dazedly. Now?

Mother – let him speak, for God's sake!

Mother would not. She was stopping him, preventing him, denying him in any way she could. And the man was just saying the same thing, over and over, because it was the only thing he could say.

Because it was the truth.

It was true. Alba was dead.

He was dead!

'I suppose this is a prank,' Lady Adelsheim said. 'If so, it is a very poor one.'

Maria gripped the book, hard. *Mother!* her mind shrieked *Stop it!*

'Mother . . .' she murmured aloud.

'A very poor prank of his. He is always doing such things – letting us think he is in some trouble and then producing himself safe and well a few days later.'

'Mother . . .' said Maria again, more urgently.

'My Lady . . .' said the Baron, agonized.

'It is *most* selfish of him!' said Mother, overriding both of them. 'Indeed it is *nonsense*! I will not listen to it.'

'But you will hear me, please, all the same!' cried the man, angrily. 'It is my duty to tell you that it is true!'

She stared at him, and he stared back.

'And,' he added more slowly, 'I grieve deeply at it, for while he lived he counted me a friend.'

Mother's mouth parted in her pale face. 'Ridiculous,' she said deliberately. 'It is quite ridiculous.'

But now her voice shook as she said it.

'Indeed, Madame,' the man said grimly. 'Quite ridiculous. That any son of yours should make a friend of me.'

In the horrible, horrible silence he bowed, and turned to Tieschen.

'I suppose you may now escort me from the house.'

Tieschen hesitated, looking to his mistress for a sign that the interview was at an end. But the newcomer would wait no longer. He stalked out of the door and down the corridor towards the hall.

Mother put her hands on the desk in front of her and looked at them for a moment. Her head bowed.

Then, abruptly, she was rising from her place, small and shaking. Maria, released by her movement, was up and reaching for her. Mother turned up to her a face that was not Mother's, but like a bad wax image of it, twisted and working with appalling things. The mouth was open. A series of high sounds came from it, like the whimpers of a tortured lapdog. Maria caught her by the sleeves. Icht, murmuring helplessly, tried to take the other arm. Between them, the creature that was Mother writhed and began to shriek.

'Tieschen!' called Maria desperately. 'Tieschen!'

Tieschen had gone after the invader. But Müller was there, and Löhm was there, and neither were any more use than Icht. Mother screamed and screamed, and tried to push them away.

And Maria clung to her sleeve, with her own heart crumbling within her, and thought that she would never, ever trust her mother again.

Wéry stalked down the corridor, raging. His boots clattered on the flooring and the short, high-pitched cries of the woman were in his ears.

He had done it badly. They had *made* him do it badly. They had not wanted to hear him. They had sat there, playing games with him, to prevent him saying what he had come to say, because if he did not say it, it could not be true.

So he had blurted it out. He had shouted it at them: *He's dead!* What else could he have done?

There was an action on the twenty-third of April. What did that mean to a woman whose son had been torn apart by cannon-fire?

They had looked at him as if he had fired the guns himself.

The corridor was very short – far shorter than it had seemed when he had forced his way down it a few minutes before. The cries pursued him. Here was the hall, and the foot of the empty stair. Albrecht had always climbed stairs two at a time. Perhaps these were the ones on which he had begun, running across the floor and pounding loudly up them, yelling to the house as he went. He would never climb these again.

The frock-coated servant had not followed. He must have been called back by the daughter. No matter. No one was going to trouble themselves if Wéry let himself out.

But he needed his coat! His hat and gloves, which they had taken from him at the door! He could hardly go riding off into the rain without them. There was not a gulden in his purse with which to replace them.

He was going to have to hover in the hall, like a leper or a ghoul, until someone who knew what he had said and done in the house came, tight-lipped, to assist him.

God! Why was it so difficult to come and go in this place?

Opening off the hall was the waiting-parlour. Someone was in there. He stalked in, and found a servant. The fellow was on his hands and knees, blowing on a fire he had just kindled in the hearth. He looked up as Wéry stalked in. His teeth were bared like a rat's.

'Would you please fetch . . .' Wéry began.

There was another man in the room.

A tall, heavily-built figure had been standing at the window, looking out at the late, wet afternoon. Now the man turned to stare at him. His face was lined and fleshy. He wore a white wig, a long square-cut coat with large elaborate cuffs and a richly-embroidered waistcoat. He glowered at Wéry from under heavy brows.

Wéry looked into the face of the master of the house.

This was the mysterious Imperial Knight himself, August von Adelsheim. This was the Prince of this tiny state in the heart of the Empire. His word was as good as law on the soil of Adelsheim, and might well be heard in Erzberg, too. And Wéry had just offended his wife and family as deeply as it was possible to do.

But . . .

The wig on the great head was slightly askew.

The rich clothes were impeccable, yet the face seemed to have retreated from them. It was as if they were somehow worn by some other body, and the mind had nothing to do with it.

Drunk? No, not drunk . . .

55

There was no surprise on the Knight's face, as he turned and found a stranger in his house. There were so many strangers, the eyes said. Some they knew, but hardly remembered from where. Others they might not know, but that did not mean that they had not met before.

Wéry stared at the man before him, and the creature of Empire stared back, and did not understand.

A shrill cry echoed down the library corridor.

'They have killed their King,' said the man sombrely.

'The – the French, sir?' stammered Wéry.

It was more than four years since Louis XVI had gone to the guillotine.

The man frowned, as though this answer was probably correct but not what he had been expecting or hoping for.

'Yes,' he said eventually. 'On the cross. They nailed him.'

He bowed his head. A dribble of spit rolled from the corner of his mouth and down his cheek. He seemed unaware of it.

'It will rain now,' he muttered.

The Knight of Adelsheim was demented. Albrecht had never told him that.

'I think it is passing, sir,' said Wéry, carefully.

Dear God, just let him get to the door and he would go without hat, coat or gloves! He would fetch his own horse from the stables if need be!

The man nodded, and looked at the patterned rug on the floor. He paid Wéry no more attention. After a moment Wéry counted himself dismissed, and turned for the door again. But it was too late.

Crossing the hallway in a rustle of skirts was the young woman who had been reading aloud in the library. The little frock-coated servant was at her elbow. She stopped in the doorway when she saw Wéry. Then she looked past him to the man at the window.

'Father!' she cried. The man mumbled.

The daughter glared suddenly at Wéry. 'You have not told him, too!' she exclaimed.

Wéry bowed. 'I have not.'

She did not seem mollified. Again, she spoke past him. 'Father. Please would you come? Mother needs you.'

The Knight frowned, and mumbled again. The girl swept past Wéry and took her father by the arm.

'Please come, Father. It is – it is very important.'

The man growled, but allowed himself to be led to the door. Wéry backed away to make room for them, and bumped against a chair. They ignored him. But again the daughter stopped, as though she had remembered something. She looked back at Wéry.

'Would you forgive us, sir?' she said. 'For a few moments. I should like to speak with you.'

Wéry, aching to be gone from the house, could only bow once more.

And she left, shepherding her father along by the arm, down corridors that echoed to a woman's grief.

IV
The Wounded Hand

He paced wretchedly up and down. He was grateful for the fire, which the servant had made up for the master of the house before both had been called away. But otherwise there was nothing to recommend that little room. The carpet and wallpaper, the elderly chairs and settee, were all shades of pale green, which seemed almost grey in the light of the window. Everything was dusted and clean up to the height that a man could reach, but above that smudges appeared on the wall and cobwebs hung in the corners of the ceiling. There were cracks in the ceiling plaster, high above his head.

He paced, aware of these things, but aware above all of the fine features of his friend in the portrait, smiling down on him. The hand of the artist had diminished the stomach to a gentle curve: flattering, for Albrecht had been definitely fat ('plump as an onion', as he himself had said). And the skin was unnaturally white, Wéry thought – almost as white as the uniform, as if the artist had had some premonition of the man's death. But the eyes were still alive. Tolerant and amused, they followed him around the room: him, the man who had wrecked this home.

'Father has a good heart, and mother a great wit. I declare it must be impossible to combine such virtues in the same measure into one person. There would not be room! And Franz is a dear, and Maria

delightful. Tell me, Michel, was there ever anyone more blessed than I?'

Voices passed in the hall, sighing, 'Such a want of sympathy! Shameful, that you should have been told in such a manner!' Outside, a carriage was at the door. The little round man in black, the Baron, was taking his leave. 'My sincere condolences . . . a dreadful loss . . . Really it is a tragedy that the finest should be taken . . . ' The answering murmur must have been the daughter's voice. He heard them pass through the door, saw through the window the carriage drive away, and heard again the daughter's footsteps as she returned to the house. He thought she would come into the room now, but voices called her from up the stairs, and she answered and went after them.

He was left waiting, like a dog in its kennel.

Damn it!

His hand clenched in a fist before him. Then he swore. *Such a want of sympathy! Shameful!* God damn it! Aristocrats!

Albrecht was dead. And with Albrecht dead it was more obvious than ever what the rest of them were. Privileged, undeserving, mincing, *blind*! Blind to their faults; blind even to the end that stared them in the face! The world was changing, and they did not know it. They were finished, and yet they tutted about *sympathy*!

And he was shackled to them. Yes, like a dog. A dog that was useful, so long as it did not think to bark for itself!

From the portrait the mocking eyes looked down on him.

'Hey, Michel! Old Blinkers wants to see you. I think he's decided to like you. He says any man who can be that rude to his face must have something honest about him. He's got ideas for you – things you might do for us, if you're willing. And he's going to write to the Prince and have him offer you a commission – a commission, mind you – in the glorious *regiments of Erzberg. You must take it, Michel! It will be rare fun to have a rebel and a democrat in our ranks. The more we can get, the better, I say.'*

A rebel and a democrat. Something in Albrecht had transcended all politics, so that it had been possible to like and respect – even love – a man who should have been an enemy. Now the man was lost; and he was a dog; and his leash was held by men with hearts as corrupt as a row of month-old corpses.

God damn, damn, damn, *damn! Damn them all to hell!*

A voice sobbed. It was his. He shook his fists, not knowing what he was doing. He jammed his right hand into his mouth and bit upon it. He bit hard, hard to make the pain come. Something gave, and there was blood on his tongue. Warm, salty . . .

He drew a long, shaky breath, and looked at what he had done. The marks of his teeth were livid, white and red. He had broken the skin in two places, below the first finger joint and at the base of the thumb. Blood, bright red and fresh, was beginning to trickle across his hand. It hurt.

Stupid. But . . .

On the blotched skin there were the other, older marks, dull and pale beside the new wounds. The same teeth, the same rage. Different causes, and so many of them to do with his own failures. He could no longer remember which he had done when. There had been the time he had heard that the French had fired on crowds in Brussels; the time he had heard of the annexation; the time when, drunk on the Rhine, he had remembered his own words in Paris. The white scars overlapped one another, blending into one, gnawing rage.

Wéry knew himself to be sane. He knew that aristocracy must

be destroyed. The Catholic Church, as it was constituted, must be destroyed. But the French republic had to be destroyed first, and most completely of all. If it could not be destroyed, it must be opposed and opposed and opposed, with every weapon available. It must be opposed because of the tyrannies it had set up in the Lowlands, and now in the Rhineland, which had so corrupted the republican causes there that the people would welcome their former imperial overlords in relief if the Empire were ever able to return. It must be opposed because so long as it existed, with its string of crimes around its neck, all the old order of Europe – all these mincing aristocrats with their manners and quarterings – might point to it and say, '*See what comes of democracy!*'

Agh!

That was why he fought for the powers that had once been his enemies. Only when the slate was wiped clean could their fate be considered again.

He knew himself to be sane, but he could explain himself to no one. Even Albrecht had laughed at him gently. And so many times he had drawn his own blood, since the first night that he had bitten his hand and wept in the winey cellars of Paris.

Stupid!

What passion are you slave to, Captain?

He was bleeding now. If he was not quick he would leave stains on the carpet, on top of everything else he had done. His handkerchief was not the cleanest, but . . .

He was still trying to knot it one-handed when he heard a step and the rustle of skirts approaching again. The door opened. The sister of Albrecht entered the room. Quickly he hid hand behind his back, keeping the rag in place with his thumb, and bowed. As he did so a voice somewhere in the house called, 'Maria!'

'Sir,' she said to him. 'I beg you to forgive me for my delay.'
She offered him her hand.

He hesitated. Of course he must take her hand with his right, and his right was bleeding, wrapped in a dirty handkerchief behind his back.

She saw his hesitation and frowned.

Cursing to himself, he snatched at her hand with his left and bowed over it awkwardly, as if he were unschooled and performing the courtesy for the first time. He straightened in time to catch the look that flickered across her face. And his anger rose in him again, like vomit. God *damn* all aristocrats!

In the corridors someone was still calling 'Maria', but she ignored it. She nodded to him to sit, and they settled opposite one another before the fire.

'I regret, sir,' she said, 'that we have not treated you with the courtesy that we should have done.'

'For my part,' he replied gruffly, 'I regret what I have had to tell you. I also regret that I – was not permitted to give you the news in a manner more fitting.'

'It was unfortunate, sir,' she said.

(Unfortunate! And that little frown at his words 'I was not permitted'!)

'Unfortunate indeed,' he said, his tone hardening. 'Although – if you wish to treat me with courtesy – perhaps I should say that I prefer not to be called "Sir". "Captain" will do.'

If they would be aristocrats, then he would be a revolutionary. And in Paris no one called another *Monsieur* now.

Her eyes widened. She was astonished – astonished, and also angry. And still she did not understand, because she never could. She would imagine that she had offered him a courtesy, and the chance to start again as if that ugly scene in the library had never happened. Now he had flung it in her face.

'*Sir*,' she said deliberately. 'I believe . . .'

And then she hesitated, with her colour rising and her tongue lost for words. He glared at her, daring her to rebuke him. The thought niggled at him that perhaps he had gone too far. Perhaps he had. But he would not show it. And in a few moments, now, he would be leaving. He would take his hat, cloak, gloves and be gone; and he would never look back.

'Sir,' she began again. 'I think it is the custom, in any house or place . . .'

But she had to break off again, dropping her eyes and tightening her jaw in frustration. For with another plaintive cry of 'Maria' the caller from the corridors shambled in to join them.

He was a young man, perhaps a few years older than either Albrecht or his sister, with the same fine face that Wéry was coming to associate with Adelsheim. He wore a fashionable coat of dark blue buttoned down to his waist, complemented by yellow trousers and a white open-necked shirt. Oblivious to the anger around him, he leaned on the mantelpiece. His face was a picture of woe.

'She doesn't like me any more,' he said to the flames.

His sister glanced up at him and sighed. 'She is upset, Franz,' she said. And looking at Wéry she added, 'I believe we all are.'

Surprised, Wéry swallowed. He managed a curt nod in reply. Then he remembered to rise to his feet, out of courtesy to the newcomer.

The man's face had fallen further, as if he had just remembered why everyone was miserable today. 'I want to go riding,' he said.

Riding? thought Wéry.

'It will be dark soon, Franz,' said his sister.

'But I want to go riding!' said the man, kicking at the fender.

I want. I want. This must be Franz, the older brother, the heir to the Knight. And with his brother dead, and his mother in hysterics, he could do no more than march in on his sister and say *I want*, as if he were a child!

Indeed, Wéry saw, he was very much a child, although in an adult's body. Like his father, he must be afflicted in his mind. *Father has a good heart . . . Franz is a dear.* Albrecht had never said that his family had an inherited condition. In all the words he had let fall, in all his dreamy fondness for his house and family, he had never spoken of this. And yet his brother was a poor, stupid fellow who at this moment could no more grasp the thoughts or feelings of those around him than – than . . .

. . . than he himself, Michel Wéry, who was so wrapped in himself that he could be rude to a family that had lost its last sane son?

The thought hit him so hard that he grunted aloud.

'You should not ride in the dark,' the sister was saying. 'It is not safe. And the horses have been ridden today already. But – but why not go down to the stable anyway, and talk to them? They will like that, won't they?'

Misery sat on Franz's face.

'They will like to see you, Franz,' she said, coaxing.

He frowned, and curled his lower lip. 'Can I go now?'

'So long as the stable-boy is there with you. You know that, don't you?'

'Yes,' said Franz. 'Yes. And can I have Dominus? Alba won't want him any more, will he?'

'Oh Franz . . .'

64

Dominus, Wéry realized, would be Albrecht's horse.

'I'm – I'm sure you can, Franz. We'll speak to Mother when she is feeling better, shall we? Now *do* go and see they are all right.'

'Yes, yes.'

The heir of Adelsheim left at last. His feet clattered across the hall, suddenly eager at the thought of a new horse. He had never even looked at Wéry, standing beside him in the room.

There was silence as Wéry lowered himself into his seat.

'Lady Maria,' he said formally. 'I must beg your pardon. I have spoken very badly today. I – I do not know what is the matter with me.'

(Dear God! What kind of man behaved as he had done when bringing news of a death to a house? He could scarcely have been more offensive – or more ridiculous – if he had started to sing the *Marseillaise*!)

She sighed. 'You have hurt your hand,' she said.

He looked down. He was still holding the handkerchief around it, pinning it into place with his thumb. A trickle of blood had escaped the inefficient bandage and run down one finger.

'It is nothing,' he said, embarrassed.

'You must show me.'

He almost put his hand behind his back again. But after what had passed between them, he could not refuse. He held it out, and allowed her to remove the handkerchief. His skin throbbed and felt hot, and the touch of her fingers was cool as she turned his wrist gently to see what he had done.

The bite-marks were plain. There was no disguising what they were.

'Why did you do this?' she murmured.

'I – was upset. As you said.'

'With Mother?'

'No. Well, yes. But also with myself, you see. I . . .'

Someone was crossing the hall. She looked up.

'Hans!' she called.

The rat-faced servant, caught as he hurried from somewhere to somewhere else about the house, looked in through the door.

'The gentleman has hurt himself,' she said. 'Please bring water and a clean bandage.'

The man Hans hurried away to juggle this with whatever other errand he had been sent on.

She released his hand. He grimaced. 'I am not normally this stupid,' he said.

But she would have seen the other marks, the old white scars. She would know that it was not the first time.

'What makes you so angry?'

He gave a helpless gesture with his good hand. 'Many things.' He smiled, ruefully. 'Your mother was right about that. It is a weakness I have.'

He added, 'I was a revolutionary once,' as if that might explain something.

'I have been told so. You are Captain Michel Wéry, are you not? That was the name you gave at the door.'

'Yes.'

It was the first sign that any of them knew who he was.

'My brother wrote so much about you. Yours is an exceptional story.'

He nodded. Suddenly, he felt relieved – relieved that someone in this house had at last acknowledged his link with Albrecht, and therefore his right to have come to them. And triggered by his relief, he felt also an urge to explain himself. He wanted her to understand why he, a sane, thinking and compassionate man, could have been moved to behave as he had done in her home. If he could do that, he might also be relieved of his shame at the things he had said here.

But she had not come to listen to him speak of himself.

'What seems to me to have been most exceptional, Lady Maria,' he said, 'was the generosity of an Erzberg officer who made an enemy into a friend.'

When she did not answer, he added, 'I may say that your brother saw fit to call me "Michel".'

She nodded, slowly. But she did not answer, because at that moment the servant Hans reappeared with a bowl and rags. Wéry held out his hand to be cleaned and dressed. As he watched the little man fussing over his marks he was aware of the woman beside him.

He was very strongly aware of her, sitting there, studying him with eyes that might have been her brother's. '*Hey, Michel! Have you ever looked at somebody? No, I mean, truly looked at them? Look at old crook Bannermann there, dishing out the schnapps ration. Go on, look your hardest. Tell me his past, his hopes, his fears, if you see them. And I'll tell you if I think you're right . . .*'

What did she see?

An unlovely thing, surely: a story of so many failures that they might almost have been crimes. He winced inwardly. And he realized that he had committed yet another offence, even as he had tried to undo his earlier one. Of course no woman in her position could call him 'Michel', whether at the first meeting or at their fifty-first. It must always be 'sir' or 'Captain' or 'Count' or what-have-you. It must always be that polite, protected distance. Her brother had been free to condescend – free to step out of his aristocratic skin into that of a petty gentleman and revolutionary; free, even, to imagine himself as a fat and corrupt quartermaster's assistant, if the whim took him. For her, it would never be allowed.

He risked a quick glance from the corner of his eye – quick, and away at once, as though his attention had never left the dressing of his hand.

That was Albrecht's Maria, there: his sister, of whom he had spoken often. Strange! His stories had been of a mischievous childhood – of shared adventures, tree-climbing, stealing sweet-meats and smuggling hurt wild animals into the house. He had talked of a laughing, witty little sprite, who had stolen his spurs so that he could not be cruel to the horses. Wéry had never imagined this solemn figure, pitched abruptly into the world of full adulthood. He had never been told how she could address idiot brothers and rude strangers with a patience that neither deserved.

Tell me her past, her hopes, her fears . . .

He stole another glance. She was no longer watching him. She was waiting, with her eyes on the fire. So now he could look at her, spying on her from the corner of his eye, while keeping his chin pointed firmly at the servant who was dressing his hand.

In profile her face had the same delicacy about the nose and eyes as those of her mother and brothers, although there was a slight heaviness to her jaw, he thought, that dulled the effect. She was taller than her mother by a head, but the muted colours she wore, in contrast to Lady Adelsheim's bold pinks, had made her almost invisible when he had first stepped into the library. Now that he looked more closely he saw that the dress was old, a little short for her, and the lace that trimmed the skirts and sleeves was tinged with yellow. An orange-gold ribbon drooped where the overdress joined across her breasts. Her skin was powdered, and so was her hair – piled and powdered as her mother's had been. At another time, Wéry thought, looking at her would have been pleasing enough – although he would also have liked to have seen her wearing the new classical styles of France, with her hair left its natural dark colour and done in ringlets.

But before all that, she should have been happy.

She was doomed from birth: doomed into her narrow degree, here in this house between that lightning-witted mother and her father and brother who had no wits at all. All her growing life she must have watched Adelsheim decay: debts and misfortunes, exacerbated by the tolls of war. Now, without warning, she was mourning a loved brother who should have lived. And the hopes of her house were in ruins around her, and she herself must be the last asset left: the marriageable daughter who could offer to her husband the Adelsheim pedigree – the full sixteen quarterings on the coat of arms, which would open so many doors among the exclusive aristocratic castes of the Empire. Wéry had an idea that her hand had already been claimed by some cousin.

Perhaps marriage would change her life for the better. Who knew?

The servant rose, and Wéry remembered to thank the little man as he departed. Now they could both look at one another. And now he saw, as if for the first time, the heaviness of shock in her eyes – the shock that he had brought to her. The white powder on her cheeks was still pure and unmarked. Soon, when the world would permit her privacy, it would be tracked with the tears she held inside her. He could do nothing for her, except to make her misery complete.

'We had thought him safe,' she said.

She sounded very tired.

'The last we had from him was a letter that reached us only late last month, almost the same day as news of the peace. He said nothing was happening and that it was all very dull. Then he told us about driving pigs through a Cravatier officer's tent.'

Wéry smiled grimly. 'Yes, he did. The Cravatiers were not pleased with us.'

'Was it a duel, then?'

'A duel? No.'

How little they had grasped of what he had said to them!

'It was the French,' he said. 'They crossed the Rhine the day after his letter was sent.'

He drew breath. 'They were in great strength, and they had a new commander, Hoche. We suffered losses, and fell back. Albrecht was unhurt, then, because his battalion was not engaged. We joined the retreat towards Frankfurt.'

(Retreat! How could he describe the chaos – the orders that came from the Imperial headquarters, urging them to do this, do that – and none of it either possible or meaningful? Some regiments refused to obey commands. Others were not supposed to be where they were, or, when you reached them, proved to be nothing but a handful of men with a banner. Officers shot at their own men, and men murdered their officers and left their bodies by the road.)

'Hoche pressed us hard. We were very nearly trapped. We were at risk of being cut off and caught with the rest of the Imperial army. But the Erzberg commanders saw that if we could gain the crossings at Hersheim we would have a safe road home – for ourselves and maybe for the rest of the army too. So they changed route.'

She was listening, but she did not look at him as he spoke. She had gone back to watching the embers as if she could follow there the last acts of her brother and his friends, as if she could see the small, massed columns, many-legged, marching into the fire.

'The French reached the crossings first – only a battalion, with some guns, sent ahead of their main body to cut us off. But they were digging earthworks, and of course they could have been reinforced at any moment. Count Balcke-Horneswerden ordered the infantry to attack. They had to cross the open ground down to the banks, wade the river and climb the far side, with the enemy's cannon firing all the time. Some of the men lost their nerve and tried to shelter under the far bank. Albrecht rode into the water to encourage them. That was when he was struck – by canister, I think . . .'

Now she stirred.

'Canister?'

'A case of musket-balls, about so big.' He made a round with his hands. 'It is fired from cannon at close range, to kill many people at once . . .'

She was looking at his fingers, measuring their circle with her eye. He could see she was trying to imagine the weight of the shot. She was picturing how they might smash into a man's body. He saw her bite her lip.

'You said – his servant also died,' she said.

'I am sorry. Yes.'

'We will have to tell his family how.'

'It was shot from the same battery. He was trying to reach your brother.'

'Then – my brother was still alive?'

'The men he was rallying pulled him to the bank. They were able to bring him in when the enemy position was overrun. But – the surgeons could not help him.'

There was no point in trying to explain the dilemmas of the surgeons, working into the night on whomever they thought they might save while more and more shattered men were laid around them.

'Was he in much pain?'

(Don't lie. It will hurt her worse if you lie, and she sees it.)

'I fear he must have been. But it would not have been for long.'

'Were you there?'

'No.'

She looked away.

'I had been sent to the Imperial headquarters to inform them of what the Erzberg troops were doing,' he said. 'I did not return to the camp until that evening, carrying news of the armistice. When I heard he had been wounded, I went straight to the surgeons' tents. But he was already . . .'

He broke off. She had put her hand to her mouth in a sudden gesture. Her lips had formed a silent 'Oh!' Her pale skin now seemed white in the gathering evening.

Heavens! Was she about to faint?

'Was it really that close?' she asked, in a voice that almost cracked. 'He need only have lived one more day?'

'I fear that is true.'

'So – it was needless, then! It should not have happened!'

It should not have happened. That was true, of course. That was the devil of it. Wéry spread his hands, helplessly.

'Our attack, or theirs?' he said. 'We all knew the negotiations had started. But nothing might have come of it. And one side cannot stop fighting if the other does not.'

She was not satisfied. Of course she was not . . .

But once again they were interrupted. Once again he must climb to his feet. Standing in the doorway was a lady in middle age, with close brown hair and a dress rather duller and less elaborate than the girl at Wéry's side. She did not seem to be a servant – there was no air of officiousness or function about her – but there was a diffidence in the way she held herself which said that she was not a full member of the family either.

'Anna!' exclaimed the girl.

'Forgive me, my dear. She is asking for you again.'

'Oh – dear Virgin!' Maria groaned.

But in a moment she gripped the arms of her chair. 'Yes, of course,' she said. 'I will come. Anna, this is Captain Wéry. You remember, in Alba's letters. . . Captain, let me introduce to you Madame Anna Poppenstahl, who has been a lifelong friend and companion to my mother, and even more than that to my brothers and me.'

Anna Poppenstahl, thought Wéry, bowing over the woman's hand. So this shy, plain creature was the beloved Anna, Albrecht's governess.

And this was the woman who, all unknowing, had been the link of fate that had brought him to Erzberg: to Albrecht, to his commission, to his place in the struggle against France. '*My cousin was his governess,*' Maximilian had said in the dusk of the ramparts of Mainz. '*She still lives in their house.*'

73

She still did.

'Madame,' he said. 'It is a sad day, and nothing will change that. Nevertheless, I am glad to have met you. I made the acquaintance of your cousins, the Jürichs, in Mainz some years ago. I owe them a debt of gratitude to this day.'

Madame Poppenstahl's face was drawn, and her fingers worked together as she stood before them. She bobbed at his words, but did not answer him.

'Maria,' she said anxiously. 'Please.'

'Yes, yes. At once. Perhaps you would be so good as to remain with Captain Wéry until . . .'

Wéry read the exchange of glances. The governess was distracted and unwilling: the shy product of a sheltered life. Strange captains, even ones who claimed the acquaintance of her cousins, were more than she knew how to deal with. And the daughter was also distracted, and yet felt herself to be in sole charge of the house. She was determined, even now, that their guest should be shown some courtesy.

Beyond the thick clouds, the sun must be low. It was more than a league, by narrow and twisting paths, to the nearest inn in Erzberg territory. His presence here was already an embarrassment. If he remained another hour, they might even feel obliged to invite him to stay the night. And what would Lady Adelsheim say in the morning, when she discovered that such an unwelcome visitor had sheltered under her roof?

He had done enough harm here.

'You are good,' he said bowing. 'But time does not permit me to stay. If word could be passed to the stables for my horse, I will make no further demands of you.'

'It is you who are good, Captain,' said the sister. 'It is indeed a terrible day.'

'If there is anything more I can do, please name it.'

'I believe . . . I do not know if I ask in the right quarter. But I believe that my mother might expect a letter from His Highness.'

His Highness? The Prince-Bishop?

She must have seen his surprise.

'He is godfather to all of us,' she explained.

No doubt he was – and to the sons and daughters of half the gentle houses within twenty leagues of Erzberg! And that was the problem.

'I fear so many families have suffered in this last action that the Prince may not yet have been able to write to them all.'

He saw her face change. 'We had not heard,' she said.

'It was kept secret to begin with.'

'Then – our loss has been greater than I understood.'

'Indeed, Lady Maria.'

Indeed.

'Nevertheless,' he said, 'I will see that the Prince's secretaries are reminded. And if there is ever any other way in which I may be of service, I beg that you will ask it.'

They walked the few paces to the door together. And with each step he took Wéry felt that their talk was incomplete. Something more could or should be said to make the silence between them a little more whole. He racked his brains for it. Nothing came. Death was unanswerable. The man should not have died, and he had done.

On the steps he turned to her, and tried again.

'If I may say one thing more to you, it is that it was an honour and a privilege to be acquainted with your brother. I know he loved this house, and he loved his family. And also he loved his friends. These were the things he died for. And if you have nothing to die for, you have no reason to live. I truly believe this.'

She hesitated. Perhaps she tried to smile. But all she could say was: 'You must look after your hand.'

'I will. Indeed,' he lied, 'it has stopped hurting already.'

V
Written in Grief

Then he was gone, the messenger of Death. Maria watched him as he rode down the track towards the village. She could see him, huddled in his greatcoat under the rain showers, but she could demand no more of him – not one word more of explanation, apology, compassion, nor any of the million things she needed and that would never be enough. She was left in the confines of the world she knew, which was now so horribly changed.

She turned and entered the house.

Once, years ago, Albrecht had taken her to an ants' nest he had found. He had lifted the great stone that had covered it. She had watched curiously as the little creatures scurried to and fro in their tunnels, some with eggs in their jaws, some apparently aimless, and all frantic with the catastrophe that had suddenly laid them bare.

Albrecht had been going to stir them up with a stick for her, but out of pity for the ants she had stopped him. 'I suppose you are right,' he had sighed. 'It is a city, for them. One would have to have a horribly important reason to destroy a city.'

Carefully he had put the stone back in its place.

Now the memory of all that hurrying and scurrying flooded back to her. The house echoed with unusual noises. People

77

bustled when they should have walked in calm. Servants came to her for orders, which they had never done before while Mother was at home. She told them to prepare supper at the usual hour, not because she felt any appetite, but to give them something to do. Icht, who had been banished by Mother in a fit of weeping, came to take his leave of her instead. Franz wanted to tell her that Dominus had known him and liked him and would she please tell Mother so? And everyone was anxious that, when things righted themselves, they should not be blamed for whatever their part had been in what had happened.

'. . . It was not – really, Lady Maria, it was not my fault that he went to the library! I gave him my lady's message *most* distinctly. I told him – I told him very firmly, Lady Maria – that she was not to be disturbed. But he tricked me, Lady Maria. He sent me for his hat and gloves. So it was not my fault that he did not withdraw as he should have done . . .'

'It is no matter, Tieschen,' she had said to him, as he followed her all the way along the corridor, pleading at her elbow. 'I will see that Mother knows.'

And then she was sucked upstairs to where the great queen ant herself lay, curled on her side on the canopied bed. Mother's face was grey and her arms were clutched tightly around herself. Her shoulders were hard as wood, unyielding to Maria's reluctant embrace. Between bouts of weeping she was blaming all the world.

'. . . That *insufferable* man! Why did he come here? Why did he think he could speak to me so?'

'He was a friend of Albrecht's, Mother. He thought we should know what had happened.'

'It should not have happened! He was always too selfish!'

'There, there,' Father mumbled, looking gloomily at the floor as if the cause of all this trouble lay somewhere at his feet.

'We must not blame him, Mother. It was the French. They did it. He was leading his men . . .'

'*Monkeys!* That wretched d'Erles! We have all been ruined for the sake of one lazy, brainless godson!'

'I meant the French army, Mother . . .'

'But was not Albrecht *also* his godson?' Mother cried. 'It is a crime! He should have made peace years ago. Others did!'

'He' now was no longer Albrecht, nor his friend Captain Wéry. Nor was it the famously dissolute Comte d'Erles, the French émigré who had taken shelter under the wing of his godfather the Prince-Bishop of Erzberg. 'He' was now the Prince-Bishop himself! And who would she blame next? The Pope, perhaps? Maria gripped the back of a chair, and her knuckles were white.

'We must be strong,' she said desperately. 'He would want us to be.'

'That's all very well,' Mother muttered. 'But you did not love him as I did.'

That evening she sat at her mother's desk, alone at last. She was alone, with the grey tides of grief that had been pulling at her heart for hours.

The desktop was covered with the letters Mother had been writing when the news came. Here was the one to the bailiff Holz, on the Niederwald estate. Here was another, addressed to the cantonal court: the body that the local Imperial Knights had elected to oversee their dealings with each other, since no one else below the Emperor and the Imperial courts had the right.

Mother had been telling them imperiously, and yet again, that whatever else Grandfather's creditors might have a claim to, they had no right to her own personal incomes, which had been settled on her by the Rother family at her marriage.

And this one was to the Canon Rother-Konisrat himself, listing at great length – and some imagination – all of Franz's virtues; for Mother had lately decided that Franz could not after all be the one to carry on the Adelsheim line, and must be found some position in the church, even perhaps a canonry, so that he might have an income to maintain him when Albrecht came home to be the heir.

All these letters should have been completed, copied, sealed and directed by now. On a normal evening they would have been stacked in a neat pile on the desk waiting for dispatch. Instead they lay scattered across the board like fallen leaves, and their words spoke only to the air. Across the room the long-case clock ticked, marching on and on into the night like a soldier obeying his last command. Everything else had stopped, as if a sudden curse had put all the affairs of Adelsheim into an enchanted sleep.

And if ever Adelsheim woke again, everything would have changed. Certainly Franz could not enter the priesthood now. Somehow he must marry and have sons after all, or the last estates of Adelsheim would pass out of the line altogether. Because Alba would never come home.

And Mother lay upstairs, wrecked on her bed, with Father still sitting beside her, mumbling aimless comforts now and again. She would not come down tonight. Perhaps she would lie there, grey-faced and weeping intermittently, for the rest of her life.

She deserved to!

Had she thought she could will Albrecht into coming home

safe? She had made them all so sure that he would! And now she would blame everybody, everybody and everything, because he would not. She would even blame Maria, perhaps, sensing that her daughter had not believed strongly enough that he would return. As if it had been through some flaw in the wall of will that the enemy had come to rob him of his life!

You did not love him as I did.

Furious, Maria swept her mother's letters aside. The leather desktop, shiny, with all its familiar stains, looked up at her. For a moment she stared at it, unseeing. Then her fingers found more paper. They picked up the pen. She dipped it, and began to write:

Sirs,
Today I have heard the news of my brother's death at the hands of French soldiers near Hersheim.
I well remember how, when we first heard the news of your Revolution, my brother and I rejoiced together. It seemed to us a wonderful thing that a state should order itself according to the principles of reason and equality, rather than of privilege. Although we ourselves were privileged, we swore to each other that we would gladly exchange . . .

Already her fingers had begun to tremble. She put the pen carefully into its stand. There was a lump in her throat, and the emptiness in her chest seemed to weigh within her. Breathing was difficult. No, not difficult, but it had become a task that the body was no longer doing by itself. Now her mind was aware of it, and she must think about it to make it happen. Now, even living was an effort of will.

She drew breath, and heard the sob in it. She wondered if she was about to weep. And she thought that she would. Just for these few moments, at last, she would close her eyes to the world and weep, and cling to the thought of her brother, as if his ghost had come to be with her one last time.

She had been dancing, here in the library, eighteen months ago. There had been no partner but the lighted candle that she held in both hands, no music but her own low humming, and no audience except Alba, lying on the settee by the window with the heels of his boots propped up on the arm.

He had lost much of his plumpness in the campaigns. His uniform no longer fitted well. His neck had been scrawny, his nose no longer just fine but sharp, and pointed straight up at the ceiling. But he had still been alive, still Alba, just as if he always would be. And she had danced before him.

She had danced, feeling both very grown up and rather mystical, because she had felt the world was changing and that the changes might yet sweep everything she had known away. One-two-three, one-two-three, she had been thinking, and turn and back and one-two-three . . .

'I have been waiting for you to explain what you are doing with that candle,' he had said (speaking German as he always did with her, in defiance of Mother's rules). 'Will you not oblige me?'

'I'm dancing with it.'

'I can see that. Nero fiddled while Rome burned, and now you dance while the Empire totters. But it is more usual to dance with a gentleman, if one is present. And if the gentleman is not present, or does not please you, it is usual to dance with a chair. I believe you are about to set your dress on fire.'

'Then the Empire shall totter while I burn,' Maria had said, as she turned in a figure, counted and turned again. 'But I may not dance this dance with a man, nor with a chair. It must be with a lamp or a candle. The candle should have a hood and this one does not. Do not bleat, brother. I am being careful.'

'What dance is this, if men may not dance it?'

'It is the Lightstep. And it's your fault we dance it, because you and all your friends are away, and there are too few gentlemen to go around. So the Countess said that if we could not dance with the gentlemen, we should dance with each other. And she had some of the May-dances adapted for the ballroom. This is one of them.'

'I imagine the Countess was not sorry to surround herself with beautiful young girls.'

'Of course. But for the most part we do not mind her. And we prefer to dance with her than not to dance at all. In the Lightstep, the candle is the man. And the dance is a charm to bring him back to us.'

After a turn and another figure, because he did not ask, she had said: 'I'm dancing for you.'

She should not have told him. Of course it ruined the charm, if you let them know who it was for. And so his enemies had taken him, on the last day of the war, and they had left Adelsheim a shell.

She sat looking at her half-written page, fighting the thought that there might have been something she could have done, some prayer she might have said, that would have brought him back. Somehow she had failed.

You did not love him as I did. Perhaps, if she had loved him even more . . .

83

'You must bear with Mother, if you can,' said the ghost from the settee.

'I do not believe she wishes me to bear with her,' said the ghost of the younger Maria, still turning in her dance with the candle held before her.

'Fate has dealt her a hard hand, to have a mind like hers and yet be married to Father.'

'Father has a good heart. Even she admits that. I am sure a good heart is more in the eyes of God than any quickness of wit. She will marry *me* to Cousin Julius, Alba. I cannot think Father would have permitted it if his mind had been whole.'

'Can you not? A marriage to any Rother, even Julius, would assure you of wealth and position.'

'Julius is too young, and sickly. I shall spend a long engagement, year in and year out. And I shall spend it waiting to hear if my husband-to-be has in fact died. And listening to Mother in the meanwhile. I declare I am as oppressed as any poor peasant, and I long for my own revolution.'

. . . endless sequence of bloody acts and murders that you have committed, in your own country and in ours, horrified us, as it has horrified all the world. And now you have continued your murderous attacks even as your plenipotentiaries discussed peace, and indeed it has been represented to me that the action in which my brother died took place on the very day that news of the armistice reached the camps. Thus it seems that it was unnecessary, wasteful, an act of barbarity and nothing more. I do not know how to describe to you the virtues of the man that has been lost. I believe it no exaggeration to say that his gentleness and compassion approached that of our Saviour himself . . .

Was it too much to compare him with the Lord? Would they sneer when they read it, these men who knew no respect for priest or altar? But surely it was the truth. Everyone had thought the same about him. Even Michel Wéry seemed to have loved him (or why would he have come all the way here, a stranger, knowing that everyone else in Erzberg was too bemused by their losses to think of poor Adelsheim?). Even a man who had once been an enemy.

'You should meet my friend Michel,' said Albrecht from the settee. 'You would find him intriguing.'

'Michel?' repeated the younger Maria with a laugh. 'You write so much about him! Michel this, Michel that. What has become of him now?'

'He is still going off from time to time, trying to get himself killed. And thankfully the Lord keeps sparing him. Did I tell you the Prince has made him a hussar?'

'My Goodness!'

'My Goodness indeed. The hussars were pink with fury. I think His Highness must have wanted to spite them. But in truth he is attached not to the regiment but to Balcke-Horneswerden's staff. He spends half his time carrying messages for us, and the other half off seeing all sorts of strange people who have no love for Privilege, but who have come to have even less for the Liberty and Equality that France has brought them. He has become a sort of spy. I wonder if he feels the irony of it.'

An enemy and a spy, thought Maria. A fanatic, too. You never told me about his hands. Yet still you could make him your friend.

Truly we are wretched, yet in our wretchedness we are only one case among a legion who cry out because of what you have done. Therefore, sirs, I bring before you the loss of my brother, and of all those other innocent and worthy men, on both sides, who became victims of this act, though it be the least of all the acts you have committed. They are the innocent that you have condemned. And I beg you to pray to Our Lady for pardon, if indeed you pray at all; and I shall pray for pardon that I cannot pardon you.

Written in grief,

Maria Constanze Elisabeth von Adelsheim

Blot her mother's ink dry. Envelope it, and seal it with her mother's wax. Do not think on scruples. For now, and for however long it might be, *she* was the mistress in Adelsheim. While Mother wept and heaped her blame aimlessly around Christendom, she would speak with Adelsheim's voice. She would bring the guilt home.

Then, as her pen hovered over the envelope, she hesitated.

For with whom, exactly, did the guilt lie?

She knew very well whom she was addressing – those faceless men of France whose insanities had brought all this to pass. But she needed to point her finger at just one, or at most a few, of all that nation. She wanted to pin him, or them, with her words, as a duellist who had backed his opponent to the wall now skewered him with one fast thrust. And whom exactly did she mean? The soldiers, accused, would turn and point to their officers, the officers to their general, their general to his masters in Paris. And the masters would say, 'Yes, we did have a part, but it was also because of . . .' and they would point in other directions. And so it would go on, and on. The guilt – the one black guilt – would be broken into little pieces, like a Host at Mass, and passed out to a thousand, ten thousand, mouths that would swallow it in little black crumbs, and then it would be gone. To whom should she speak?

Her pen wavered, and she put it down. Then she picked it up again, frowning. There would be someone. Someone stood concealed, in the heart of that great diffuse conspiracy that had killed him. She needed only to think a little.

Perhaps it should go to Paris. She should address the so-called 'Directory' who were the masters of France at least in name. But how, if so, was she to reach them? There would be no post yet, working across the Rhine. And she could hardly dispatch one of the servants to ride all the way to Paris – even if she was the only one in the house left in their right mind.

In the end she wrote a single line upon the envelope. 'To M. the General Hoche, Commander of the French Army at Wetzlar.'

Let their creature in Germany receive her blame, for France and all its works. It was enough. And Wetzlar was only twenty leagues away, in Nassau, this side of the Rhine. It was much more likely to get there safely. She did not know the proper form for addressing a general of a republic that neither the Emperor nor her father recognized. However, she thought, the man himself probably did not know it either.

'You must introduce me to your Michel,' said the younger Maria, as she lifted her candle in the final, graceful movement of the dance.

On the settee the ghost stirred.

'Introduce you?' it murmured. 'Perhaps. But will you love him or hate him? I cannot predict.'

PART III:
THE FEARFUL CITY

June—October 1797

VI
The Gallant in
Mourning

A man walked down the main Saint Simeon Street in the walled city of Erzberg. His name was Karl von Uhnen, and he was the son of an Imperial Knight.

The first and most important truth about the Uhnens, known to all those who were aware of such things, was that the Knight's grandfather had entered into a misalliance. Moved by nothing more than love, he had married a woman of no pedigree. And he had bequeathed the consequences to his house. Now the Uhnen family shield bore only twelve quarterings, rather than a full sixteen. And although the Knight had wealth and wit and influence, although he had secured posts for himself at the Prince-Bishop's court and a commission in the Prince-Bishop's hussars for his son, nevertheless certain doors in Erzberg and the Empire – canonries, and positions in exclusive church foundations, would remain closed to him and his family for at least another generation.

For that reason, the Knight had said to his son, it was all the more necessary that one should conduct oneself at all times in a manner fitting to the blood. And Karl von Uhnen did, to the best of his ability.

He was a handsome young man, with liquid brown eyes. His usual expression was thoughtful and almost melancholy, as if he were trying to compose a poem and had got stuck half-way through. He had looked exactly like this the day he had had to sit at the head of his troop under French cannon fire, and had seen twenty of his men and horses killed in a quarter of an hour. He had looked the same, only perhaps a little more melancholy, as the ravages of campaigning had put holes in his boots, lice in his hair, and had ripped his immaculately-tailored uniforms to rags. At each return to Erzberg he had righted all deficiencies as swiftly as he could. Now, a month after the peace, he was again dressed in crisp white uniform and an extravagantly braided tunic, with his green jacket, lined with black fur, slung just *so* from his shoulder. He had even managed to grow his hair back long enough to tie it into a queue at the neck and into the elaborate braids that hung before each ear, which were a mark of the hussars in peace and which every hussar had cut off while in the field to help keep themselves free of vermin.

He was acting against orders. He was showing his uniform in town on a day when every man in the Prince's little army was supposed to be keeping indoors. The mob was out – a paid mob, hired by the Canon Rother-Konisrat, the head of the peace party in Erzberg. Yesterday they had chased and stoned two infantry officers who had tried to approach the Saint Christopher Chapel. They had pursued a baron of the war party across the New Bridge, and pulled two of his footmen off his coach, beaten them and thrown them into the river. And in the night a man had been mistaken for someone else by drunken vigilantes, and had been knifed to death in a gutter.

The mood in the town had swung heavily against the army as the scale of the losses at Hersheim had filtered through. Citizens who might have shrugged their shoulders at the death of a few mercenaries or sad émigrés had also lost sons. Apprentices who had once gaped at smart white uniforms had lost all respect. Now jeers and mocking songs sounded outside barrack walls. The army, fuming, stayed behind barred doors. And Captain Karl von Uhnen of the hussars walked in the streets, with his plumed cap on his head and his uniform plain to see.

He was not a stupid man. He knew there might be trouble. He had even left his valet behind, preferring to run an extra risk himself rather than bring his servant into danger. But his motives felt compelling, and he thought that he could handle it.

Mob or no mob, he calculated, his best chance of reaching the Saint Christopher Chapel was to make his approach as boldly as possible. He would march quickly (but not too quickly) down the Saint Simeon street, confident under the eyes that fell on him, and be past them before they could wonder what exactly he had to be confident about. His hand rested lightly on the hilt of his sword. His boots clumped purposefully on the cobbles, accompanied by the jingle of his brightly polished spurs. So far, it was going well.

He had reckoned without the crowds. It was a feast day – of which there were many in Erzberg's calendar. The guilds had closed their workshops. Journeymen who had followed their holy relics in procession that morning now swarmed around tables set out in the streets. They had tuned their fiddles, knocked the bungs off kegs and were beginning their celebrations. Even the broad Saint Simeon was thronged and difficult to pass. Von Uhnen came to a halt in a little square outside a guild chapel. The far exit was completely blocked by gangs of festive Ironworkers. Short of shouldering his way through (which he supposed would be unwise as well as undignified), there was no way forward. He hesitated, uncertain what to do.

Men were already looking his way. In a moment they would start to think about him. Haughtily, he lifted his eyes to the rooftops as if none of it was any of his business. At that moment a step sounded behind him. A hand caught his arm.

'Take your hat off,' a voice hissed.

'What?'

Beside him on the cobbles stood Wéry – bare-headed, and swathed in a greatcoat on this mild day. He was glaring at Uhnen.

'Take the thing off!' he said urgently. 'Hide that damned plume!'

He was too late. In a doorway a man, a fat, well-to-do shop-keeper of some sort, broke off from speaking with his neighbour. For a moment he glared at the hussars. Then he hissed.

More heads turned.

'This way,' Wéry grunted, jerking his head at the nearest alley. 'Don't run.'

'What?'

Von Uhnen stood scowling in the open, and everyone was looking at them.

'*This way!*'

Wéry turned on his heel to lead the stranded aristocrat off down a narrow, foul-smelling street. Von Uhnen hurried after him, with the awkward strut of one who must make more haste than dignity should allow.

Wéry checked his shoulder. They had not been followed. Not yet. Round a corner . . . He caught Uhnen by the sleeve again.

'*Now* run!'

His urgency seized the other man and drove them along together. Encumbered with their swords and uniforms, they stumbled along in the tight maze of medieval streets and filthy little courtyards where the river men and journeymen and apprentices of the city lived. The alleys were so narrow that their boots splashed in the open sewers that ran down the middle of them. The mean buildings of the Riverside Quarter stooped over them like huge old widows in shabby clothes. They passed the dark doorways and windows. *Don't look in!* Wéry thought. They were no safer here than they had been in the crowds. Stray cats stared at them and flitted from their path. The walls rang with unseen voices, calling and singing and already the worse for drink. There were shouts behind them. Was that a mob forming?

Run!

A mob could whip itself up in minutes. Wéry had seen it in Paris. There had been days, then, when sewers like this had run with blood.

(God, yes! An evening of September mist, with a chill in the air that brought out the smells; the lanterns and braziers around a big-walled prison, and a rumour of a crowd inside; and women laughing on the street corner while at their feet the sewer had flowed red-brown in the yellow lamplight with the blood of hundreds of murdered men and women, mingled with the filth of the city!)

He had seen it. And what they *did* to the corpses!

They broke out into a cobbled square of tall, stepped-gable buildings, all painted in bright colours and decorated with friezes. There was a fountain here, raised on steps, and an air of quiet and prosperity, as fragile as a bubble. Just a score of paces away, down another narrow street, they could glimpse the teeming Saint Simeon again. There was no sound of pursuit.

The two men struggled to catch their breath, glaring at one another.

'What are you doing here?' said Uhnen, panting.

'The same as you,' said Wéry curtly. 'But *I* know how to do it.'

'Do you? Then you may oblige me by doing it somewhere else.'

Von Uhnen was not one of Wéry's regular persecutors in the regiment. Normally he would just have ignored the upstart foreigner who had been so bafflingly favoured by the Prince. If the hussars, and all the rest of the world, were going to ruin, that only made it the more important to conduct oneself according to the standards of one's station.

But now he had been accosted by this same upstart and man-handled in the streets. He had been dragged off through the alleys without a shred of poise or dignity. And he was not ready to admit that it had been necessary to get his beautifully-polished boots covered with sewer-filth. He glanced disdainfully down Wéry's coat and uniform, showing with his eyes that he knew they had come from a tailor more accustomed to fitting infantry-men than hussars, that they had been purchased on Albrecht von Adelsheim's credit, and that neither Adelsheim nor Wéry had yet managed to repay the full amount. And, what was more, there was a patch on one elbow, yet Wéry had no other uniform more presentable than this.

In Uhnen's eyes, of course, this final offence was far the most heinous.

Wéry, for his part, had been planning to make his way carefully and unobtrusively down from the hussar barracks to the waterside, with his plumed hussar's cap under his arm and his coat around him. Now he had put himself into harm's way for a dandified, ungrateful aristocrat who would have deserved the beating or lynching that would have been his in a minute if he had not been rescued there and then.

And *why* was Uhnen out? Couldn't the brainless son of a horse have stayed indoors as he had been told?

They looked at each other, wordless and furious.

Von Uhnen was about to turn away when something else occurred to him.

'It was you who went to the Adelsheim house, wasn't it?'

'Yes,' said Wéry. And thought: *What's it to you?*

'I heard about that. It was not proper.'

'You mean I should have waited until somebody else remembered?'

'I'd have done it.'

'Then why didn't you?'

Von Uhnen looked at him, coldly. 'It's none of your concern.'

'I suppose not. And I suppose how – or whether – you get to the Saint Christopher Chapel is none of my concern either?'

'No, it's not.'

Von Uhnen turned his head and peered down the short alley to the Saint Simeon street. People were moving up and down over there, clattering, calling, cheerfully carrying on with their festivities. No mob was after *them* today.

'I'll tell you, all the same,' said Wéry, as the gallant hesitated. 'You won't get to the Saint Christopher at all. No one in uniform will.'

No one in uniform would reach the Saint Christopher chapel. For in the chapel, in a lead-lined coffin that was surrounded by candles and heavy incense, lay the month-old remains of Albrecht von Adelsheim. At the plea of Lady Adelsheim, the Canon Rother-Konisrat had sent his men to gather his young cousin from the battlefield and bring him up the Vater to his home. And

97

before the dead man reached his last resting-place, they had laid him in the Saint Christopher Chapel near the city waterside, so that the great and good of Erzberg might come to acknowledge the price of war. But no army officer, or any of the war party less than the Prince himself, was being permitted to approach the coffin. For it was in the Canon's script that they should be ashamed to show their faces while the coffin lay in their town. And his cudgels were out for any that did.

Von Uhnen watched the crowds passing in the Saint Simeon. A man's voice was singing, loudly and laden with drink. The song was a bawdy one. There was no threat in the words (to a man, at least). All the same . . .

'What were you going to do then?' he said at last.

'Come with me,' said Wéry, with a certain grim satisfaction, 'and I'll show you.'

VII
The Count in the Coffee House

The Vater flowed from north to south through Erzberg. On the eastern bank lay the medieval city, clustered around the cathedral on its low rise. On the western, lifted above the town on a high hill, stood the citadel and the Celesterburg palace. City and citadel were linked by the Old Bridge, which plodded out across the river on ancient piers of stone, bearing the traffic of the Saint Simeon on its narrow back. A hundred and fifty yards downstream the New Bridge crossed in bolder arches to serve the modern Saint Emil quarter, where the houses of the rich clustered under the shadow of the citadel.

Wéry and Uhnen hurried across the New Bridge together. To their right, beyond the Old Bridge, they could glimpse the Saint Christopher Chapel and the small square before its doors. There were figures there – loitering, it seemed, with no purpose at all in the summer evening. Some appeared to hold sticks or cudgels, which they carried with a nonchalant air as if they were gentlemen at croquet. It was late afternoon, and the square was in shadow. The clothes of the watchers looked as dark as funeral colours under the gilding sky.

The two officers crossed to a cobbled wharf. Here, standing among the broad fronts of the Saint Emil quarter, was the Coffee House Stocke, a solid, square building with elaborate wall-paintings, lights in its windows and a raucous babble indoors.

Wéry liked the Stocke. He liked it because of the people who came here – merchants and tradesmen, craftsmen and entertainers: outflows from the Saint Emil, the Celesterburg, the wharfs and workshops across the water. He liked to think the battered notice at the doorpost declaring 'All men equal under this roof' a true revolutionary sentiment, and not merely a reaction to the strict hierarchies of the city guilds. There were pamphlets and papers scattered on the tables; and even though their editors all complied slavishly with the requirements of the Prince's censors, there were often items of interest to be found in them. And while most of the nobility (including Uhnen – to judge by his reaction as they entered) preferred to drink and play in the ordered calm of their clubs, it was occasionally possible to see some thick-skinned son of an Imperial Knight here, smoking his clay pipe within a yard of a bargee who was doing the same.

The Stocke reeked, of course. But what of that?

Inside, the air fumed with tobacco smoke. The roof-beams were so low that both men had to stoop. The chatter was so loud that the woman who took their fee had to shout her banal greetings at them. Men were getting up, sidling between the tables and the wooden partitions, going out or sitting down again. A party of musicians were arguing over a score and making notes in the margins. Another group, barge-captains perhaps, were playing at cards. Over the low fire hung the coffee-pot, and before it were clay jugs, clay pipes, a bookshelf and an unlaced boot. There was a bible on the bookshelf, and also a row of locked frames containing drops and powdered medicines advertised to cure diseases of the skin, toothache, cough and pox. There was a tiny carved wooden shrine, painted in bright blue and gold, with the face of the Virgin smiling gently into the room.

'Hey, Wéry!' called a voice through the din. 'Over here!'

From beyond the farthest of the wooden partitions an arm waved – a flash of white uniform. Wéry made his way through the babble, balancing two mugs of coffee and stooping as he went. Three faces watched him as he approached. The one who had waved them over was Heiss, a Captain in the Dürwald battalion and aide to the army commander, Field Marshal Count Balcke-Horneswerden. He was a small, slightly-built little cockerel of a man, with bristling grey hair and moustaches and popping, bloodshot eyes, who grinned as they came up.

'How the devil are you, man? I thought you'd never make it! God damn! Who's this? Von Uhnen? What the hell are you doing here?'

'I . . .' began Uhnen. And he stopped.

He had seen who else was seated at the table.

Massive in the space between bench and table, like an elephant crammed into a pigsty, was Balcke-Horneswerden himself. He was a fat-chested giant, with bulging cheeks and a heavy jaw. He had removed his wig, which was on the table beside his coffee. His high, shaved head narrowed at the crown like the point of a pear. His eyes were black and his face red from the warmth of the room. He glowered at the newcomers as if they were late on parade, and poorly turned out at that.

This was the senior field officer of the small Erzberg army, a Knight himself, and a drinking companion of the Prince. The court of Erzberg, which delighted in wit and classical allusions, nicknamed him 'The Colossus', because of his great size and because a French cannon-ball had left one of his legs forever

101

planted in the soil on the west bank of the Rhine. But to his men, from the lesser colonels down to the cursing infantrymen, he was 'Old Blinkers', who looked neither right nor left but went straight up the middle.

And the man beside him . . .

Adhelmar Fernhausen-Loos was a young, wan-looking aristocrat with lazy eyes. A thin smile draped itself across his face as he lifted one hand in greeting to Uhnen. *Yes, it's me*, his expression seemed to say. *Droll, isn't it?*

Fernhausen wore the uniform of a major of the Fapps battalion, but he had not marched with his unit in years. Nor, to Wéry's knowledge, had his duties ever taken him beyond the walls of Erzberg. He was the second private secretary of the Prince himself. There were very few men in Erzberg who knew the mind of their ruler better.

Von Uhnen seated himself slowly on the bench, watching them. Wéry could sense a hurried reassessment going on behind his poetic face.

Balcke and Fernhausen: two men of the Prince's closest circle. It was as if the ghostly presence of the Prince himself were sitting in the reeking coffee house with them. Indeed, the Prince *must* be with them in some sense, for although Balcke might conceivably have visited the coffee house on his own account, Fernhausen would never have dreamed of spending time here if he were off-duty.

The Prince: his wills and whims ran through his palace corridors and out into the city, carried on the lips of hurrying subordinates who would preface every demand with the words '*His Highness has asked . . . He has said . . . He expects . . .*' as if the mere reference to the man were an incantation that would guarantee compliance. And very often it did. The Prince's favour mattered. Many posts and positions were in his gift, which would allow the fortunate recipient to drink in some measure from the trough of Erzberg's revenues. His disfavour mattered too: even the most influential of Imperial Knights might be dismissed or exiled at his word. His lesser subjects might face imprisonment or worse. And in the orbit of his personality the normal rules of caste and order might be bent, to some degree, so that men of different backgrounds and persuasions might nevertheless make common cause for some end that the Prince thought good.

And now Uhnen would be realizing that it had been Wéry, the upstart, the foreigner, who had brought these men of the Prince to this place.

'Delightful place you have found for us, Wéry,' Fernhausen said airily. 'The coffee, too. Delightful. I feel inclined for another cup. May I trouble you?'

'Don't you move a muscle for him, Wéry! Let the Fapps fop get it himself,' said Heiss, (who must have known that Fernhausen, crammed into the corner beyond Balcke, could no more have squeezed past the Count than he would have dared ask the mountainous man to move.) 'And how the devil are you? Are they treating you properly, those fine cavalry officers?'

'Well enough,' lied Wéry. 'They let me get on with what I have to do.'

'Damned right!' said Heiss. 'See that you do, Uhnen. I know you fancy lot. If a man's a shade light on his quarterings you treat him as if he's got two heads. But Wéry's different, yes? He's a comrade in arms.'

'I know that,' said Uhnen stiffly.

Heiss was not from a family of Imperial Knights. He was of

103

the service nobility, who held their title from the Prince, by virtue of the offices they performed. And at this moment Uhnen was less inclined than ever to accept lectures from an inferior.

'Damned right,' growled Heiss. 'What are you doing here anyway? I thought that old woman Altmantz had locked all his hussars up for the day.'

'Perhaps he did. But I seem to have come, all the same.'

'I know what it is. It's the girl again. You think you'll curry favour with her by paying your respects in the teeth of orders and the mob, that's what. Look at this, Fernhausen! You spout your damned poetry, but here's the true romantic. Last June he spent his leave riding secretly off all the way to Bohemia to go down on one knee to Adelsheim's sister. And for what? She showed him the door, poor fellow.'

'Adelsheim's sister?' repeated Wéry, surprised.

'And do you know,' said Uhnen coldly, 'I could instead have spent it frequenting Madame Charlotte's, as others do? How is she, dear Heiss?'

'Anyway you've left it damned late, both of you. It's nearly . . .' Heiss pulled out a watch and chain. 'Damn! I think my watch has stopped.'

'It hasn't,' said Fernhausen. 'But it's only five minutes since you last looked at it.'

There was an air of tension about the table. It told in Fernhausen's drawl, in Balcke's silence, in the oaths that peppered Heiss's speech. Balcke's coffee had barely been touched. Heiss's had been drained to the last drop. They were like men in a little fortress: a redoubt of coffee and tobacco smoke. The babble and smells of the place drew around them like a cloak, warm and reassuring. But the walls were thin. One step out through the door again, and it would be night. And the night was smelling blood.

Wéry realized that his heart was still beating hard, even though it must have been a quarter of an hour since Uhnen and he had run through the alleys together.

(Quarter of an hour? Half an hour? Time did strange things on the brink of action. No wonder Heiss kept looking at his watch!)

'So Wéry took pity on you and brought you to us,' said Fernhausen. 'Like Virgil guiding Dante through the Inferno?'

'A little like that,' said Uhnen stiffly. 'And now I seem to have stumbled on a conspiracy. Am I to be admitted to it?'

Everyone looked at Balcke.

'Yes, you can come along,' said Balcke gruffly. 'Two or three more will make no difference. But you're to keep your mouth shut afterwards.'

'We wait here until the family moves the body,' said Heiss, lowering his voice. 'My coachman's watching outside. He'll tell us when. Rother's people will take the coffin back downriver to Hohenwitz to give them the shortest overland route to Adelsheim. So their barge will pass under the bridges.'

'And?' He looked at Balcke.

Balcke said nothing.

'And there will be a gesture,' finished Fernhausen. 'From the army. And I'm to come along as a bit of comfort from His Highness. It's rather neat, in fact.'

'So he's going to side with the army after all?' said Uhnen. 'I must say, I thought he'd . . .'

'Yes and no, of course,' said Fernhausen. 'Insofar as this is a matter between the city and the army, the Prince will have no part in it. But it is not just that. Canon Rother wants to show his strength in the city, because . . . well, we need not go into it too much. But it suits the Prince to demonstrate that the Canon, and the peace party, are not as strong as they think they are. And he doesn't like mobs.'

Mobs. Wéry looked at his hands.

'. . . Rother's in the pay of the French,' Heiss was saying. 'That's what it is! First they start agitation in the city – the peace party, republicans, Illuminati and whatnot – and then they march in. That's what they've just done to Venice, isn't it? Hoche is camped at Wetzlar. He could be on us in three days, if he has a mind . . .'

Each of them had their reason to be here, thought Wéry. And each man's reason might seem quaint, or even crazy, to the others, set beside the risk they would run.

Take Heiss, now distracting himself and others with conspiracy theories about the enemy within. Why should a good and rather stupid man put himself in the way of a disgraceful death? Heiss was here because Balcke was here: out of dog-like, unthinking loyalty. Neither of them saw anything strange about that.

So why was Balcke here? Because he, more than anyone in Erzberg, represented the army. It was the army, in the first instance, that was Canon Rother's target. So Balcke and his colonels would lock up their men for safety. But *he* must meet the coffin, and its hangers-on, because it was unthinkable that the army could not salute the passing of one of its own. For Balcke, it was a matter of honour, like standing under cannon fire.

And Fernhausen, who was not stupid and was no man's dog, was here because of politics: because his Prince wished the army to understand that he had not abandoned it altogether.

For these things, they would each risk being torn bloodily apart.

'But what about the peace?' protested Uhnen. 'Won't the French be packing up and going home now? And anyway, the Emperor won't abandon us. He's said so.'

And Uhnen was here for love! The fact had slipped out so naturally that Wéry had barely felt surprised by it. Now he knew he was astonished. Under that distant, elegant exterior, it seemed, beat a passion as strong as any man's – strong enough to have brought this aristocrat out onto the mob-ridden streets. And he was surprised, too, that he should find it so disturbing that Uhnen's love was for the sister of Albrecht von Adelsheim: for the woman whose cool fingers had held his own bleeding hand.

So why then was *he* here, Michel Wéry, waiting for the chance to court death to see a dead man's coffin? Not for Balcke-Horneswerden (although he could respect a man, even an aristocrat, who chose his subordinates for their merits rather than their connections). Nor was it for Maria von Adelsheim. The memory of her was strong, but he would not have thought of doing such a thing for her sake. Of course it had been his own proposal that had brought him here. It was his own plan, and there-fore he should be part of it. But he would not have put it forward if he had not wanted to come in the first place. And Albrecht, for all that he had been, was gone. He could not sit up in his coffin, laugh and shake a friend's hand. What was it for, then?

How did it bring the defeat of France any closer?

'. . . The Emperor has Bonaparte's heel on his windpipe,' said Heiss. 'And why should he risk any more for Germany? Where were the Princes when it started to get rough? Prussia made peace. So did Bavaria, Wurttemberg, Baden, Kassel . . .'

'Much good it's done Kassel—'

'—They dropped like ripe plums, one after the other!'

'*We* didn't.'

'Damn right. And do you think Hoche will forget that?'

Why do they chatter? Wéry flexed his fingers below the table, and caught Balcke's eye. The big man was saying nothing. He was sitting with his coffee still untouched before him. He was waiting. They all were. Heiss was looking at his watch again. What was Time doing? *Come on!*

'My dear Heiss,' said Fernhausen loftily. 'Allow me to correct you on one point. Our illustrious Canon Rother may be many things. He may even be an Illuminatus, as you suggest. But he is no more in league with the French than are you.'

'He's the damnedest, slipperiest, most opportunistic bastard in the whole of the Chapter,' said Heiss, thrusting his watch angrily back into his pocket. 'And that's saying a lot! And he's got a whole string of others dancing with him now: Löhm, Jenz, Machting, and now the Adelsheims. Damn, but I hate to see a good man's death used this way . . .'

'Lady Adelsheim is Rother's cousin, of course. So in one sense they've always . . .'

'Wait a moment,' said Balcke.

The chatter stopped at once.

'I want to hear what Wéry has to say.'

His eyes were fixed on Wéry like a pair of muskets.

'Go on, Wéry. What do you think of all this? What are you hearing on these clever little trips of yours?'

They had all turned to look at him. Heiss had his elbows on the table, and there were tiny beads of sweat on his forehead. Von Uhnen's expression was mournful, as if he were expecting to hear of the death of a relative. Even Fernhausen, behind his blank expression, had paused to pay attention.

Wéry had meant to stay out of this. But . . .

'The French won't leave Wetzlar,' he said flatly. 'Not until there's a treaty with the Emperor. Maybe not even then.'

'Sure of that?'

'Yes.'

Balcke's face hardened at the thought of eighty thousand French soldiers camped within three days of his city.

'And?' he prompted.

Wéry shrugged. 'The Prince is exposed. He's still harbouring French émigrés – d'Erles and his party. Never forget how much Paris fears the émigré. That, more than anything, was why they went to war in '92. Moreover he's a churchman, and loyal to the Emperor, so they hate him. And he's small, so they despise him, too.'

With Balcke, it was best to be direct.

'Well,' grunted the Count at length. 'That's why we keep you, I suppose. To tell us what we need to hear.'

'I'll say something else, if I may.'

'That I won't like? Go on.'

'Squabbling makes you smaller still.'

'What do you mean?'

(What did he mean? And with the cudgels gathered on the far side of the river? Dear Mother of God!)

'You're at it all the time!' he said harshly. 'If it's not fighting Rother and the peace party, it's fighting the Ingolstadt set: the Ultramontanists and all those clergy who still live in the Middle Ages. Or you are chasing stories of Illuminati. Or it's the Jews. Meanwhile your guilds are at each other's throats, and at the same time they band together to hound any unlicensed trader who tries to make a new start. It goes from top to bottom of the city . . .'

He glanced sideways, and caught Heiss's agonized expression. And yes, of course it was impertinent. And naïve. But damn it, they could all be dead in an hour! Why not say what he *felt*?

'Now see here, Wéry,' rumbled Balcke, leaning forward. 'I know what this looks like to you. Little boys pushing at each other in their sandcastle while the tide comes in, you think. You'd like us all to line up in a nice straight line and fight the French to the last man. Well, I'd like that too. But the little boys have knives, Wéry. And so what's a boy to do, do you think? Let the other boy stab first, I suppose? Is that how you did it in the Brabant?'

'In Brabant I watched a cause fall apart,' Wéry exclaimed. 'I saw it in Paris and Mainz too. Why should I see it here?'

'Because we're damned human, and that's what you've got to work with!' roared Balcke, reddening as he thumped the table. 'There's little I can do about Canon Rother. And there's damn all I can do about the Ingolstadt set! The Ingolstadt stuff is *church* politics . . .' He wagged a finger at Wéry. 'It's been going for twenty years or more, back into the old Prince's time. Whenever we tried to reform anything – education, the prayer service, taxation, you name it – the Ingolstadt set fought us tooth and nail. "Saving the religion" they call it. They were bigots. They still are. But when we started on the monasteries – that's when it got really poisonous. We were hitting their pockets, then. And no one forgets. That's why the Prince goes so canny now. What can you do about that, hey?'

Think of Old Blinkers as a cart on a slope, Albrecht had once said.

110

Once he starts moving, it's absolutely clear where he's going to go. And you'd better not be in the way.

And here he was, in the way. His jaw tightened, but he would not drop his eyes.

'I've been wondering, Wéry,' said Fernhausen (still in that maddening drawl). 'Is that why you keep so close to Bergesrode? Or is it just that you both loathe the French?'

'Bergesrode?' said Uhnen in surprise.

'Oh yes,' said Fernhausen. He leaned back, enjoying the group's attention again. 'Oh yes, Bergesrode. His Highness's *principal* private secretary, and full initiate of the Ingolstadt set. Our – ah – former revolutionary friend here is quite a favourite with my priestly colleague. Can you imagine it?'

Von Uhnen was surprised.

'I'd have thought you would loathe everything he stood for!' he said, addressing Wéry directly for the first time since they had entered the coffee-house.

'I do. Believe me, I do.'

Slavery of the mind. Blind obedience to Rome. Yes of course he loathed that. And once the defeat of France had been secured, he would be as pleased as Balcke to see Bergesrode and the Ingolstadt swept away. He would do it himself, if he could.

And then . . . then it would be the turn of the very men he sat with. These aristocrats, well-meaning perhaps, thinking themselves reformists, but blind, blind and selfish and tyrannical in their privileges. If they could not be brought to step down into equality, in the end they too must go.

Von Uhnen gave him a long look, as if he had guessed at the thoughts that had chased through Wéry's mind.

111

'Well then, my Virgil,' he murmured. 'You may have to watch your step after all.'

'That's right!' exclaimed Heiss. 'See here, Wéry. I like you. Never mind what you were or what you think of us. I like you because you work hard and you don't pretend to be what you're not. But Bergesrode is a bad case. He'd be a Jesuit if they hadn't been banned. So mind where you put your feet. And don't go playing games when you shouldn't!'

'I must say,' added Fernhausen. 'I've been surprised that someone with your past could become so close to a representative of the – ah, what did you say? – "those of the clergy who still live in the Middle Ages". Yes, very apt.'

'I am to report to Bergesrode, and so I do,' said Wéry bluntly. 'But yes, he and I agree about the French. The Prince thinks the same.'

'Well, we can all do *that*,' said Heiss. 'Apart from Rother and his crew . . .'

He broke off, looking over Wéry's shoulder. 'Ah, at last!'

'Thank God! At last!'

A man – a servant in a brown cloak – stood in the doorway to the coffee house, beckoning urgently.

VIII
The Bridge and the Barge

They rose from the table in a clatter. 'Careful now,' said Balcke. 'Coats, and not too much hurry. We'll not be thanked for making a mess of this.'

Balcke walked with a stick, leaning on Heiss's arm. His artificial leg, shaped to fit into his boot, clumped as they made their way out into the late evening. Above them the Celesterburg palace bulked high and black against the afterglow of sunset. The river was lined with lights. The man in the brown cloak was some twenty paces ahead of them, at the New Bridge. He was still beckoning. With Balcke moving ponderously in their midst, the officers made their way over to join him.

'There, sir,' said the man, hoarsely.

'Thank you, Peter,' said Heiss. 'Fetch the coach now, please.'

Over on the far side of the river, a long musket-shot upstream, a small crowd had appeared at the doors of the Saint Christopher Chapel. The doors were open. There were lanterns there. Men were bringing something out from inside, carried high on their shoulders. That must be the coffin. And the men around it would be Canon Rother's own servants.

Nearer, at the quay, a narrow barge was moored: a dark bulk among the deep shadows of the riverside, waiting to take the dead man home to his family.

A whistle broke out from the Saint Christopher square. Men were moving there – black shadows against the glare of a brazier. Wéry saw one stroll a few paces, hands apparently in his pockets, to take a better look at the party at the church doors. Then he turned and called. Others were coming, striding forward. There were sticks and cudgels among them. And the crowd was growing. More figures were running across the square and out of the Saint Simeon Street. From the crown of the New Bridge the officers watched them.

'Paid mob,' muttered Heiss. 'All the signs of it, I'd say. And they've spent half of it on drink already.'

'If they see us, it could be ugly.'

'Best be ready to move smartly when they come our way.'

At the centre of the crowd the coffin moved. It moved like one of the medieval relics that the guilds brought out of their chapels on a saint's day to parade through the streets. The crowd gathered around it, following reverently as if the thing was sacred indeed. Many had removed their hats.

They have killed their King, thought Wéry suddenly. *On the cross. They nailed him.*

And that was Albrecht in there, in that box. It seemed to Wéry an obscenity that Albrecht, of all men, should be the one they used to make their point. The living man had been worth so much. Why should his remains be surrounded with this mock pomp and the artificial extravagances of grief?

The coffin moved, at the pace of the holy, and paused at the water's edge. There were men standing in the barge, reaching to lift it down. There it went, safely, silently onto the deck. The shadows of the quay seemed to push slowly out into the river as the barge parted from the bank. A streak of water opened between it and the quay, and the barge was out into the stream, drifting down towards the bridges. On the wharf the mob crowded to the very edge.

'Adelsheim!' called several voices. 'God bless Adelsheim!'

But further back, at the edges of the crowd, others called, 'Down with the Warmongers!' And, 'Give us back our children!'

They were following the barge along the bank. Some were running ahead to the Old Bridge to take up position there. Feet sounded, hurrying down the cobbles, coming closer. The clamour of the crowd was growing.

In a moment they would think of the New Bridge, too.

The barge emerged silently from the middle arch of the Old Bridge, folding its oars for long seconds to pass between the pillars of stone. Above it men crowded and yelled at the parapet. One had climbed up and was standing balanced there, waving his arms like a mad black clown. The barge came on. Feet were running again on the waterside, keeping pace with it, down towards the New Bridge where the officers waited.

'Bishop! Hey, Bishop! Give us back our children!'

'They're coming!' gasped Heiss.

'Stand fast,' said Balcke.

Wéry clenched his teeth. There were figures at the end of the bridge, approaching.

'You!' cried a drunken voice suddenly. 'You there! What are you doing?'

'Steady,' said Balcke.

Balcke and Fernhausen were at the parapet, ignoring the mob. They had thrown their coats back, and their white uniforms gleamed clearly in the dusk. The barge was coming on, holding its position to shoot the second bridge. Wéry could see the shapes

115

upon it – the steersman, standing clear at the stern; the heads and shoulders of oarsmen; a small group of people in the centre of the barge, around a long shape that must have been the coffin itself.

'Now,' said Balcke, and lifted his hand in a slow salute. Fernhausen bent outwards over the parapet. What seemed to be a large glove or gauntlet dangled from his fingers.

'You!' yelled the drunken voice, approaching along the bridge. 'You! Stand! And say your business!'

'They are – ah – rather close,' murmured Uhnen in his ear. 'Shouldn't we . . . ?'

'Wait,' said Wéry, tightly. His eyes were on the river, but his ears were following the footfalls coming along the bridge. Not yet, not yet. The longer they could delay it . . .

'Hey! You!' said the voice, a few paces from his ear.

'Wéry!' hissed Uhnen. 'Shouldn't we . . . ?'

'Yes. Now.'

Hand to hilt. Metal rasping in the night. The curved blade, heavy before him, pointed along the bridge at the shadow-men advancing!

'Stay back, there!' he cried.

'Stay back!' echoed Uhnen, also with his sword drawn.

'Ho there! Help here! Help!' The voice was louder still, full of rage and the lust for a fight. More feet came running. As yet there were only a handful of men on the bridge, but in a moment . . .

'The infantry will retire,' said Balcke calmly. Fernhausen was already turning away from the parapet. His hands were empty. Whatever he was holding had been dropped into the barge, still passing under the arch. Balcke placed his arm on Heiss's shoulder and began to lumber back towards the Saint Emil side.

Damn! thought Wéry. *That leg!*

He should have thought of it. That leg, and the swift-footed mob on their heels! Why hadn't he foreseen this?

How the devil were they going to get out of here?

Von Uhnen was gone. Wéry was on his own. The approaching men were desperately close.

He drew himself up to his full height. 'Keep your distance!' he cried.

'You bastard!' a figure screamed at him. 'You murderer!'

Beyond them, shapes and figures hurried on down the quay, yelling and calling after the barge. And at his back he could hear the slow clump, clump of Balcke's leg, still too near – much too near. He could hear the gasp of the Count's breath. Where was that damned coach?

'Keep back!' he roared again.

'Ho there,' called a voice from the far bank. 'On the bridge! On the bridge!'

'Wéry!' That was Uhnen, from somewhere behind him. He could not look round. The men were sidling closer. Three of them, and another close behind. Cudgels. He could not see their faces. They were enslaved minds, not men but guildsmen, and he cursed them.

'The first one dies!' he bellowed, pointing his sword. 'The first one!'

(Clump, clump, clump, receding. And the rattle of a coachwheel on the Saint Emil wharf. Not yet, not yet . . .)

Glances shot between the men. 'Get him!' cried one.

But none of them wanted to be the first. Behind them other men had stooped to prise up cobbles. That was the danger.

'Wéry!' (Von Uhnen again, close behind him now.)

'Back,' muttered Wéry. 'Step by step . . .'

117

Swords drawn, facing their enemy, the two hussars retreated across the bridge. Stones flew at them out of the night. One struck Wéry on his left shoulder. He barely felt it. A voice was yelling *Come on! Come on!* But whether it was calling to him or to the crowd he did not know. Behind him he could hear the steady plod-plod of the wooden leg; and the rising noise of hooves and wheels approaching across the square.

'Hey, Wéry! Uhnen! Smartly, now!'

'Run!' said Wéry. He turned and bolted. Ahead of him Uhnen was running, too. Cries pursued them. There was a coach wheeling slowly in the space before the coffee house. Heiss was helping Balcke inside. Von Uhnen was almost there. Wéry fled for his life across the short cobbled space and gained the door. He grasped it, stepped up, and swayed, because the coach was still moving. A few paces away, men emerging from the coffee house had paused to watch, as if pursuers and pursued were a gang of street-artists performing in the hope of a casual gulden or two.

Hands reached and pulled him inwards. He tumbled over white-uniformed knees and heard someone swear.

'Mind that sword!'

'All right! I've got it. Now drive, Peter! Drive!'

Wéry fought his way to a seat in the corner. Von Uhnen was struggling in to a place opposite him. A whip cracked. The carriage was picking up pace – to a fast walk, to a trot. Wéry twisted to look out through the small window. A man was running alongside the coach, gasping, cursing. For an instant, in the gleam of some lamp, Wéry saw his face – narrow and dark and twisted, looking up at him with the mouth open and a mad gleam of white around the eyes. He was dressed like a journeyman, with a battered hat jammed down over a sparse fringe of hair. 'You bastard!' he screamed up at Wéry. 'Come back!' He was trying to gain the carriage step. Wéry braced himself for a punch. But the carriage was faster. The man was falling away, still running wildly, howling after them, losing ground. The horses broke into a canter. The pursuit was lost in the darkness.

In the river beyond, the barge was a hundred paces downstream. Most of the mob was still on the far bank. They had begun to gather around a large, stone building on the waterfront. Clear above the babble Wéry heard the breaking of glass. He drew his head in.

'We're away,' he said. 'But they've started to attack the custom house.'

'Drink in their bellies and Rother's gold in their pockets,' said Heiss. 'They weren't going to go home without having some fun first. Damn, but that was well done, Wéry. They'd be playing cat's cradle with our guts now, if you hadn't been the rearguard.'

Balcke said nothing.

'It was – a little exciting,' said Uhnen. 'I'm glad I was part of it. What was it you let fall, Fernhausen?'

'The Prince's glove,' said Fernhausen, in the same affected drawl he had used in the coffee house. 'From his right hand. Because the army is his right hand, you see. I saw an oarsman pick it up, so it landed well enough. That was the only thing I was worried about.'

'Will they know what it is?'

'Maybe, maybe not. We'll put it about, as soon as we can. That will wipe the smirk off Rother's face, won't it? He wanted someone to end up looking a fool, and it's going to be him.'

'Clever!'

'Not bad, as it has turned out. I must say I had my doubts

when Wéry first suggested it. But we were all in a flummox up at the palace, and the Prince declaring that if we didn't come up with something by noon he would have the troops clear the wharfs after all. And *that* would have been delightful, wouldn't it?'

'Wéry suggested it?' said Uhnen, looking at him in surprise.

Wéry shrugged.

'So,' said Uhnen. 'Not only Virgil, but Ulysses too! And Horatius on the bridge. Truly, my friend, I had no notion.'

'I want to stop at the bend,' said Balcke.

Heiss relayed the instructions to the driver. The coach slowed as it began to follow the long, looping road that wound up towards the gates of the citadel, and to the Celesterburg palace. At the first turning, it halted. They clambered out.

The road was unlit. They stood part-way up a shadowed hillside, in the living night air. Above them the crags rose and rose to the walls of the citadel and the Celesterburg, gleaming with lights. Below them was the mass of the city, with more lights in its squares and on street corners. From somewhere faint strains of music rose to their ears. The black bars of the bridges stood out clearly against the pale river, but it was too far to see if anyone was moving down there now. The river wandered away to the south, between dark banks. A long cannon-shot downstream there was a speck drifting on its pale surface. The barge.

'Well, there he goes,' said Balcke. 'Carrying our sins with him.'

There was something regretful in his voice, as if the cart of his personality had checked its career for once and, against all natural laws, had rolled a little back up the hill to look at something it had run over. It was strange, too, thought Wéry, that he had stopped the carriage here for one more look, after all he had risked for his salute on the bridge. It was not like him.

It had been Balcke's order that had sent Albrecht and his men into the cannon fire. Maybe it was not just for his precious army and its honour that the Count had gone down to the bridge this night.

But halting the carriage had given Wéry a chance that he would not otherwise have had – a chance to say a last goodbye himself. And he could linger over it. There had not been time on the bridge. There was time now, in the cool air of the hillside, looking at the diminishing barge and thinking, Goodbye, goodbye. He tried to remember the man as he should be remembered. The face and the laughter and the friendship – '*Hey, Michel, have you ever looked at somebody?*' – why was it so hard to recall them, as the eye fought to keep that dwindling black point in view on the dull surface of the river? He tried to rebuild the face in his mind – those mocking eyes, the fluid lips and teeth – and the man behind it, who had spoken truth in the disguise of a clown. '*Hey, Michel . . .*' '*Hey, Michel . . .*' Was he gone already? No, there he was still. Just.

For long moments Wéry watched that black speck moving imperceptibly away, until it melded into the greyness of the Vater and left him with nothing.

Nothing. He stood in the colourless night, and the cold wind. There was nothing at all, now, except a purpose.

He drew a long breath. Then he brought his right hand across to touch his heart.

A friend was gone. But also a distraction. Now, in his loss, the way was open to pursue the struggle all the more. That was how he must think of it.

From now on, all his mind and all his strength must be spent on the fight against the French republic. Come peace, come war, that was all he had to do. Without question, without turning aside. He would eat and sleep only to sustain himself in it. He would speak only to further it. He would spend his life doing it; and his dying, too. He would march into hell for it, if he had to.

Friendship was distraction. There must be no more of it. Love was corrosion. When the world was gone to the devil, even these things became the devil's tools. The devil would lie, cheat, find any way or weakness that he could to turn a man aside. Only hatred, as hard and sharp as steel, served the purpose now. Only through purity of purpose could the world be changed.

'Come on,' said Fernhausen. 'We had best go up and report how it went.'

They climbed into the carriage and resumed their journey up to the Celesterburg. The road curled beneath the fortress-palace. The ramparts towered over them, blacker than the night, lined with silent guns. The carriage slowed for the last slope. The walls flung back the flat rattle of the wheels, bloodless and spiteful. They rounded the northeast point of the citadel and approached the gate. The vast bastions spread to left and right about them, like the arms of a monstrous mother stretched wide to welcome her children home.

IX
The Letter from Wetzlar

Lady Adelsheim, Maria and Franz were in Adelsheim to receive Albrecht's body when it arrived. They remained there for the summer. But in September, when most noble families moved from their estates to the city once more, they did the same. In Erzberg, the season was beginning.

The season was beginning, but Maria was not to dance. She was not to look gay. She was not to join her friends in the ballroom. She was to sit demurely in the salons and drawing rooms, let the society of Erzberg see her, and let them remember that Albrecht had been lost. There would be no picnics or soirées or trips to the theatre. Her marriage to young Julius Rother-Konisrat was postponed until the spring. Mourning for her brother, Lady Adelsheim said, was more important than all these things.

And day after day, she must wear black.

Do not pout, Maria. It is the least you can do for him. Be thankful after all that you did not love him as I did.

Lady Adelsheim still admitted poets and philosophers to her house in the Saint Emil quarter. But other notables of Erzberg came more often, especially her cousin Canon Rother-Konisrat and his hangers-on. And they shook their heads and spoke in low voices in the intervals between music being played or poetry read to the room.

123

'How sad the times are! Oh, nothing can equal your loss, my dear. But did you know Lady Reisecken has also . . .'

'. . . Did you see d'Erles and his émigré friends at the Canon's soirée yesterday? I swear that half of them were drunk before they arrived! Fresh from some gambling-house, I suppose. I imagine they had left this one in ruins, too . . .'

'Really, it is shameful, after we have suffered for them . . .'

'. . . Oh, the Prince is quite persuaded that I must have my lease,' said Lady Jenz-Hohenwitz. 'He has said so. But the palace never produces it. I believe that villain Gianovi is to blame. It is impossible to trust Italians.'

'Indeed,' Mother said. 'Oh, indeed. Who could possibly trust an Italian with the running of the state?'

'Oh, Constanze. Really!'

'My dear, I have only repeated what you said . . .'

Not even Mother would criticize the Prince aloud. It was always easier and safer to speak against the army, or against the foreign-born First Minister. But Lady Adelsheim would not let the others forget that behind all the organs of the little state stood the one man who was responsible for them all, and whom she blamed most for the death of her son.

The Saint Emil quarter had been built within the last hundred years. The streets were all paved, and the houses were broad-fronted, broad-windowed, and most stood apart from one another with small gardens about them. The Adelsheim house, which had come into the family with Lady Adelsheim's marriage, was decorated with busts of classic figures, reliefs and elaborate lintels above each window. On the lowest floor were the working rooms. On the first, reached by steps from the street, were the main reception rooms. Above these were the main bedrooms, and also Lady Adelsheim's study, and the little room on the other side of the landing which served as a library. The library was walled with bookcases that rose from floor to ceiling, and the bookcases were crammed with leather-bound volumes, most of which had been bought by Lady Adelsheim from the incomes settled on her by the Rother family. There was little colour in the room to relieve the relentless browns of the book-spines, and if it had not been for the big, square, six-paned window it would have been a dark place indeed. The only pieces of furniture in the room were a chair and a settee, and only on the settee, placed under the window, was it possible to read without a light.

Maria was on the settee, and in a state of rebellion.

To 'improve her mind' that morning, Mother had given her the house copy of Kant's *Perpetual Peace*. Maria had leafed through it, and found that it was a short, dry work, full of prescriptions for a world without war. It was exactly the sort of thing that interested Mother these days. It was exactly the sort of thing that did not interest Maria.

Maria did not want a world without war. She wanted Albrecht back. If she could not have Albrecht back, she did not want anything. Most certainly she did not want Kant, whom Mother called 'The Sage of Königsberg'. Maria half-remembered that there had been a time when it had been supposed that Kant would meet with the Frenchman Sieyès, and that between them the two great thinkers would resolve the differences between their peoples. But no meeting had happened. Perhaps the two men had sensed that no resolution was possible. Perhaps they, too, had swallowed their crumbs of guilt for Alba's death.

She was wondering whether she was ready to read his letters again.

He had written to her many times in the years when they were parted. She had saved every letter, carrying them with her even to the family's brief exile in Bohemia and back again. They were here in Erzberg now, in a chest in her room on the top floor, tied in a great bundle with ribbon. She had not touched them since the news had come. But she had promised herself that she would – one day, when she was strong enough to look at his words once more. She was not sure that she was, yet. She could imagine herself climbing to her room, opening the chest, and then, as her fingers touched the ribbon, hesitating at last. She feared the emotion she might feel on reading them. And she feared disappointment if, in the numbness of loss, she felt nothing after all.

So she had not gone to her room. Not yet. She sat in the library, turning *Perpetual Peace* in her hands without opening the pages.

She was still sitting there when a footstep sounded on the stairs. It was Dietrich, the house master, climbing up from the floor below. She heard him stop when he reached the landing.

'What is it, Dietrich?' she called softly.

He shuffled to the library door.

'A caller, Lady Maria.'

'For me?'

More hesitation. So yes, it was for her. But Dietrich had been wondering whether he should consult Mother about it first. Mother was writing letters in her study on the opposite side of the landing, just a few paces away. She would certainly assume that she should be consulted about any caller for her daughter whose admission to the house was not absolutely straightforward. Even so, Dietrich was not eager to interrupt her. He knew she would immediately think of several more things that he should be doing or should have done by now.

A caller for her; and one about whom Dietrich felt it might be necessary to consult first. Maria's mind jumped to a conclusion.

'Is it Captain von Uhnen, Dietrich?'

(Poor Karl! She had not spoken with him in a year, since he had ridden all the way to Bohemia on his leave to go down on his knees to her in the orangery of the chateau at Effenpanz. *Sir, you force me to remind you of certain facts. My marriage is agreed upon, and waits only for a suitable time. I am gratified by the sentiments you express, but there is no possibility that I could entertain them.* Of course there was not, neither then or now. But she still hated to think that she had hurt him so.)

'No, Lady Maria.'

'Who?'

'A captain, yes . . . But he's foreign.'

Foreign?

She was puzzled. She could think of no foreign captain in Erzberg who might conceivably call on her. Unless . . .

'Captain Wéry, then?' (Surely not!)

'No, Lady Maria.'

He hesitated again. She looked her question at him.

'It was Lang, I think, Lady Maria . . . Or – or Lander . . .'

'You may show him in, Dietrich,' she said firmly. 'Whoever he is.'

If it had been Wéry, she would have had to decline – however reluctantly. Mother would never have permitted that man to enter her house again. Mother might say that it was wrong to admit this stranger too – especially since he did not seem to carry a card, and his name was so unmemorable that Dietrich had forgotten it on his way up the stairs! But Maria was happy to be distracted. The grey spirit of Kant only encouraged her towards revolt.

'Up here, Lady Maria?'

'Is Father in the salon?'

'Yes, Lady Maria.'

Father would be napping at this hour.

'Then yes – up here, please.'

She picked up her book, but did not read. Her ears followed Dietrich's slow progress down the stairs; the murmured conversation at the door; and then more steps on the stairs – this time the double beat of two sets of feet climbing towards the library. She put aside her book, and composed herself.

'Captain Lanard, of the Army of France,' said Dietrich woodenly.

If a monster with two heads had leaped through the door, Maria could not have been more surprised. She stared at the young man in the blue uniform who stepped in, carrying his hat under his arm.

He was a little under medium height, with dark hair pulled back into a neat queue, and dark, arching brows that marked the paleness of his skin with the same emphasis as a beauty spot. His features were delicate, and his eyes, a clear blue-grey, showed surprise when he saw her.

He bowed. 'Pardon me. I asked to be admitted to Lady Maria von Adelsheim. Am I correct that you are she?'

'You are correct, sir . . .' she said, recovering herself. 'My mother, the Lady Constanze von Adelsheim, is in the house. If your business is in fact with her . . .'

'On the contrary. I believe you are the author of a letter which reached my General early this summer. Is it correct?'

Letter?

The letter she had written! That had been months ago!

'I have been charged to bring you his reply,' he said.

There was a paper in his hands, held out towards her. She stared at it.

'Please,' he said formally.

She took it. The direction read: 'To Maria Constanze Elisabeth von Adelsheim, residing in Erzberg or Adelsheim'.

Her first, almost childish reaction, was to glance past him out at the landing. Just a few paces away, behind the study door, Mother was sitting at her desk with her pen in her hand. Mother could hear any loud noise from where she sat. She might even know there was a caller in the house.

Maria had never told her about the letter she had written the day the news about Albrecht came.

And then she recalled herself. What Mother would say did not matter. Surely it did not, beside the letter in her hands. This letter, which Alba's killers had sent her! And she thought fleetingly that she had not expected any reply, that she did not need one, and that really it would be best in many ways if she could dispose of it quickly and have this unwanted visitor leave her as soon as possible. She stared at the letter in her fingers, and her heart was numb.

She did not believe what she was holding. She did not want to open it, to read what the murderers had written to her.

'Please,' she murmured. 'Sit for a moment.'

There was no device upon the seal. She broke it. There was a single page, with only a few lines of writing upon it.

Madame,

Your appeal has reached me. According to the senior surviving officer of the 2nd battalion of the 16th demi-brigade of the line, a parley was sent to inform the Erzberg troops of the armistice before the action at Hersheim began. This was rejected by the Erzberg commander. The 2nd battalion was then obliged to defend itself.

Words cannot describe the regret I too feel at the loss of life that ensued.

Lazare Hoche

'Thank you,' Maria said, speaking rather quickly as she folded the letter. 'I am grateful at least to have had some acknowledgement at last, and I thank you for bringing it. I hope your journey was not difficult . . ..'

She broke off, and looked at the page again. She had not been expecting any reply at all. Yet now that she had one she was angry at how short and inadequate it was. *Your appeal has reached me.* She had not been appealing to him. She had been telling him . . .

. . . *a parley was sent to inform the Erzberg troops of the armistice* . . .

She stared at the sentence – the one sentence in that short letter that meant anything – while the world turned silently on its head around her.

. . . *a parley was sent to inform the Erzberg troops of the armistice before the action at Hersheim began* . . .

She opened her mouth.

'Your General wishes to absolve himself from the blame,' she said.

'He is telling the truth, my Lady.'

'No doubt he is telling me what he has been told, and what he chooses to believe. But why should he have been told the truth? This officer . . .' she looked at the paper again. 'This officer of the second battalion – is he to be relied upon?'

There was a slight hesitation. 'I believe so, my lady.'

'You know him?'

'I do indeed. He is myself.'

She looked up, into the blue-grey gaze from that pale face. He was smiling ruefully, as if being the officer in question was a misfortune, but not one that he could apologize for. She saw again how his dark brows arched above his face, and she wondered for an instant if there was not something evil about them.

He was one of the men who had killed Albrecht.

They had sent her one of the men who killed him!

And . . .

How could they do this?

How could he *smile* at her?

'Does it please you, sir,' she said, 'to – to confront the sister of a man for whose death you are responsible?' She knew that her voice was shaking.

He frowned slightly, but as if he were puzzled rather than angry.

'I hardly know how to answer you, my Lady.'

'You have nothing to say?'

'To the contrary. There are so many things that I might say that I do not know where to begin. I might say I regret your brother's death – along with all those hundreds of others, French and

131

German, who died with him. It was an unnecessary affair. I might say that my commanding officer, who was a good man and now is dead, tried everything in his power to prevent it, as I did everything that was in mine. I might say that nevertheless your brother and his friends – or at least their commanding officers – were doing everything in their power to kill *me* at the time. I do not know if any of these things excuse me in your eyes, my Lady, but since you ask, I feel that I must state them.'

'I see.'

She did not see. All she saw was Albrecht's death.

Oh, she understood that he was saying that he was not guilty. He was saying that his side had tried to stop the battle. That was what he had told his General. That was why he had been sent to her . . .

Of course they would say that. She should not believe them just because they said it.

But . . .

That smile. It was not really a smile. It was the cast of his face, which turned up his mouth at the corners and arched his brows over his eyes, so that he seemed forever to be smiling in private amusement at all the folly of the world that he saw. She should not have accused him so.

'There was a parley?'

She heard her question as if it had been asked by someone else.

'I carried it myself.'

'With – with whom did you parley?'

'There were many officers on your side. But I recall the commander was a Marshal Balcke – a big man, with a wooden leg.'

132

Balcke! Count Balcke-Horneswerden – the 'Colossus!'

She shook her head as if to clear it of her mounting confusion. 'I . . . know of him, of course. I am not acquainted with him myself . . .' Her words sounded defensive, self excusing . . .

No one had said this before! No one had ever breathed the thought that the Erzberg commanders had been *told* the war was over!

'You are prepared to swear this?' she insisted.

Uncertainty flickered across the fine features.

'I do not know when or to whom you would wish me to swear. My orders are to bring you my General's letter and to answer any questions you may have with it.'

New thoughts started at his words, like game birds from cover. To whom should he swear? Why, to anyone who had lost . . . to all of Erzberg, if possible! Was it possible? But – but this should not be one family's secret. It should be known! They could have spared hundreds of lives. And they had rejected it!

If it were true.

A sunbeam fell through the salon window, warming the black cloth over her knee and glinting on the letters of the book at her hand: *Perpetual Peace – A Philosophical Sketch*, they said. And Maria's eye saw the gleam and her skin felt the sun: and her mind staggered with the sense of huge lies shifting in the fabric of Erzberg.

Mother had been right. If this were true, then she had been right and Maria wrong. The blame lay here, with people she had moved among all her life – people whom Albrecht and all the others had trusted. It had still to be brought home.

It was a horrible, deadening thought. And all the world had turned around.

'But sir, this is important! Indeed it is most important! You may not know ... There has been much concern over the conduct of our officers in the last days of the campaign. If what you say is true – it is indeed a matter of ... of great importance.'

'I understand. But I am not my own master. My General has recently assumed new responsibilities in Germany, and requires me back at his headquarters as soon as possible.'

'I beg you, sir, at least ...'

At least to speak with Mother.

She was going to have to tell Mother.

She was going to have to walk over to Mother's room, knock at the door, and tell her that there was a French officer in the house. She was going to have to tell her what he had to say. And she would have to confess why the officer had come.

She was going to have to. It was too important to hide it. It was the truth about what had happened to Albrecht.

And now she was a child again. An image rose before her eyes, of her mother's face, and how it would change as she tried to explain that, from her mother's desk and without her mother's knowledge, she, Maria, had dared to address herself to the most powerful men in France ...

She saw that the man was watching her.

'Your ... your General has been kind, sir.'

He shrugged. 'I will not say yours was the first such letter that he has received. And he has been much distracted by the affairs of the Republic this summer. Nevertheless when he read it, he was moved. He had us turning on our heads at the headquarters for forty-eight hours together. Erzberg this, Erzberg that. He wanted to know everything about your state. Some things we reported to him amused him. Others did not. I may tell you that this is not the only letter that we have delivered within Erzberg today.'

'I . . . it is not truly our state, sir, but . . .'

She wanted to stop, and educate him in the relationships between the bishopric and the families of Free Imperial Knights who congregated within and around it. She wanted to postpone the interview that she knew was waiting for her in the study. She knew her own cowardice, and despised herself for it. And so, angrily, she pursed her lips and rose.

'No, please remain!' she said, as he made to copy her. 'I am going to announce you to my mother. She must hear what you have to say.'

Even so, she paused in the doorway.

'Your manners are excellent, sir. Nevertheless, perhaps I should say that my mother is sometimes disposed to tease. She is fond of sparring, and likes it best if her callers respond in kind. Of course you will have to judge how far you may go. But . . .'

(She was reckless now, because of all the storms that were coming. And if she was to serve this man up to Mother, it was only fair that she should arm him as well.)

'. . . but if she becomes overbearing, you may try addressing her as "Citizen." Although I have no idea what will happen if you do.'

'Very good,' he said.

Suddenly his face broke into a real smile, amused and conspiratorial at the same time. 'Very good, Citizen Maria.'

Maria tried to smile too. And with a sinking feeling in her heart, she crossed the landing to knock at her mother's door.

X
The Prince

He had expected it: the urgent summons.

The message from the palace read: *Be at the north-east bastion of the citadel at five o'clock. Make it seem that you are there by chance.* It reached Wéry in his barracks at a quarter past four.

He came at once, and on foot, hurrying through a blustery wind that flung specks of dust against skin and into the eye. Above him the clouds were white-grey, high and moving quickly. People jostled him in the streets, and he jostled brusquely back. Angry voices called after him. But no one had been paid to chase soldiers this week. He reached the citadel gates out of breath but unmolested. The guard saluted as he passed in. The Celesterburg was brave with flags upon this windy day.

The bastion was one of four that encased the palace, pointing outwards like the arms of a star. It was a vast diamond of sloping stone walls, coated with turf. Along the top of its ramparts a row of cannon dominated the town. On the east wall of the bastion, grouped around one of the guns, were a number of men in white uniforms. Wéry eyed them carefully as he approached.

It was not unusual to find groups of supposedly senior officers drifting around the palace with the appearance of nothing to do. Erzberg had many more generals, colonels and majors than its army could usefully employ. There were extravagantly-uniformed officers of the life guard. There were inspectors of infantry, cavalry, artillery and militia. Then there were the aides to the inspectors and the aides to the generals and colonels, all in their big tricorn hats and red sashes and glittering orders, and none of them did or were expected to do anything except to draw their pay, which was the reason they had gained their appointments in the first place. And of course they were all Knights or lesser nobility to a man.

But *this* gathering did seem unusual. Or at least, it was unusual at such a time and place.

There was Balcke-Horneswerden, standing like a great statue at the parapet.

At his feet – on his hands and knees, even, and appearing to inspect the carriage of one of the cannon – was Baron Altmantz, the colonel of the hussar regiment and nominally Wéry's own commanding officer.

These two were the only ones of Knightly rank present. Then there was the colonel of the Fapps battalion, a mortal enemy of Balcke's but effective in the field.

As for the others – well, Knuds, the commander of the citadel, was also a colonel. But Skatt-Hesse there was only the senior major of the Erzberg battalion. He had three senior officers over him in the regimental chain of command; and yet when the rations got short and the roads got muddy it always seemed to be Skatt-Hesse who was left in charge.

And standing a little by himself, looking deeply embarrassed, was a captain of the field artillery, who had no claim to nobility at all, but who knew more than any man in Erzberg how to get the best from an eight-pounder.

Who had called them here? Not Balcke. Balcke might have

called the artilleryman to a conference, but he would never have included the Fapps colonel if he could have helped it. Nevertheless someone had chosen them all. Someone had gone down the lists of officers with a hard, cold eye, hunting through the layers of waste and corruption for those on whom the system rested. Wéry could almost hear a passionless voice, saying '*Him . . . Not him, he's a fool . . . So is he. We'll have the Major. Yes, and make sure Wéry is there . . .*' He could guess, too, who it had been: Bergesrode, the black-clad priest who was first secretary to the Prince.

And each had had the same message. The north-east bastion at five o'clock. And make it seem by chance.

'No good, no good,' clucked Baron Altmantz, prodding with his fingers at the wood of one of the cannon's wheels. 'One shot, and it will go, you see.'

'Stick to your horse-parades, and let a man do his job,' said Knuds. 'We overhaul them every summer.'

'Time for another one, then,' said the Fapps colonel. 'But I'd not like to be the man who fires this, whatever shape the carriage is in.' His fingers stroked the row of Latin numerals that humped vaguely across the barrel above the touch-hole. 'Sixteen thirty-two. The middle of the great war. Probably hasn't been let off since.'

'We test them, too,' growled the citadel commander.

The infantry colonel had moved to peer along the line of the barrel and out over the city.

'With shot?' he said incredulously.

'We drag them round to the west rampart and fire into the hillside. That is, we do it when His Highness's Treasury allows us the powder.'

'A miracle!' said the infantry colonel. But whether he meant the common-sense of the garrison or the occasional generosity of His Highness's Treasury was not clear.

Baron Altmantz got painfully to his feet, dusting his knees. He looked up and saw Wéry.

What, him too? his expression said.

The hussars had been outraged by Wéry's attachment to their unit. Altmantz in particular, who was not only colonel but who had also provided at his own expense the men, horses and uniforms for two full troops of the regiment, felt he should have been consulted. But he had been powerless in the face of His Highness's whim. All he could do was ignore the new officer as far as possible. And whenever this did not work he would affect to be mystified as to why Wéry existed or what services he performed.

He turned his shoulder and joined the collected brains of the army of Erzberg, brooding over the single gun.

'So what's up?' asked Balcke, dropping all pretence. 'Does anyone know? Something to do with you, is it, Wéry?'

'I sent a report up this morning, sir. It may be that.'

'Hah! Thought so.'

'Is that right?' said the Fapps colonel. 'I was sure it would be those Frenchmen who came in yesterday.'

'French?' said Knuds, astounded.

'A gaggle of them arrived in the city yesterday, bold as you please. I'd not like to guess what they wanted, but I doubt if it was good news for us.'

'Surprised they didn't get lynched in the streets.'

'The city's too hot against us to be bothered with a real enemy.'

'And who do you suppose . . .'

'Ah, the army!' said an affable voice behind them.

Wéry turned. They all did.

It was a tall gentleman in a buff coat and white wig. He was heavily built, but given his height he was not fat by the standards of Erzberg society. His face was fleshy, and his nose blunt like an owl's beak. His pale eyes beamed at the gathering as if they were a favourite dish that his cook had whipped unexpectedly out of a hidden kitchen.

The officers came to attention. Wéry, standing a little behind them, did the same.

'I was walking the ramparts between my appointments,' said the gentleman in the buff coat. 'It was just a sudden whim I had. Really, they let me have so little air during the day, you know.'

At the gentleman's elbow was the black robed, craggy-faced figure of Bergesrode.

'And what brings such a distinguished group of officers to these walls?'

The colonels hesitated. Then Knuds, still at attention, said, 'Inspection, Your Highness,' as if it were perfectly normal that a field marshal, three colonels, a major and a couple of captains should mount the sort of inspection that was usually left to a sergeant.

'Commendable,' beamed the Prince-Bishop of Erzberg. 'Commendable! No, come, gentlemen, we are all colleagues. Let us be at ease together. Continue your work and share your conclusions with me. I shall play truant from my duties to assist you with yours.' His smile took in all of them, and he nodded agreeably to Wéry, whom he seemed to recognize without difficulty.

The colonels looked sidelong at one another. They were wondering at all the play-acting. Could the Prince not even be seen to consult his officers any more?

After a moment the citadel commander, gruffly, began to speak about the armament on the walls, repeating much of what he had said earlier. Wéry sidled closer. The Prince looked like some genial and indulgent uncle, listening to a favourite nephew recite his piece.

But the questions he asked . . .

'How much powder is there in the city . . . ?

'Dear me. And how long would that last, if the guns were firing all day . . . ?

'How many trained gunners are there . . . ?

'Very well, so how long will it take to train more?'

'Six weeks, Your Highness. About six weeks,' said Knuds, beginning to look uncomfortable.

'That right, Grasse?' interjected Balcke.

'Um . . . If it's just to crew a gun in a fixed position, I'd say less, sir,' said the artilleryman. 'But to captain it, manage the charges, lay, elevate – three months at least. And it needs plenty of live firing. As much as . . .'

'It's gun captains we need,' growled Balcke.

Knuds's left shoulder seemed to shrug involuntarily.

'If only it had been possible for the Treasury to have allowed us . . .' he ventured.

'Of course,' sighed the Prince. 'Really, they are so unreasonable! And how is the mood of the men?'

'Excellent, Your Highness,' said Balcke stiffly. 'It is excellent.'

The Prince's smile broadened. 'Come, my dear Colossus. I am no despot. I think you may be frank with me.'

Balcke hesitated. 'Show them an enemy, Your Highness, and they will do their duty.'

'Oh, I am sure of it. And the militias, what of them?'

Again the officers hesitated.

First the guns, then morale, and now the militia – the half-trained bands of countrymen who would fulfil secondary tasks for the army in time of war, and who in a last resort might be called on to man the defences.

Where was all this leading?

'Your Highness must of course address that question to the inspectors of militia.'

'I believe that I shall. And I believe that the inspectors will tell me that the mood of the militias, too, is excellent. However, let us suppose that I were to command that the militias take to the field beside the – ah – *regular* army. What would you gentlemen, as experienced soldiers, advise me to expect?'

'The country militias should be well enough,' said Altmantz, after a moment's pause. 'Put a peasant behind a plough or behind a musket, it's the same thing. He'll keep it pointing straight ahead. But I'd not like to arm the guilds.'

'Not with the city in the mood it is at present,' grunted Balcke. 'We'd have to be desperate, or damned fools.'

'You are right, of course you are right,' said the Prince, nodding his head sorrowfully. 'The mood of the city is most uncertain. Indeed it is not inconceivable that, should certain events occur, the question of keeping order may arise again . . .'

Keeping order. Wéry saw the words register on the officers' faces. 'Keeping order' must mean martial law. And the Prince would only do that if there were more riots. Or a siege.

142

The officers looked at each other. Martial law? A siege? In time of peace?

Balcke cleared his throat.

'The men would do their duty, Your Highness. As we have said.'

The Prince swung his owlish face to the others. There were grunts that might have been assent. His gaze fell last upon Wéry.

'Ah, Captain,' said the Prince. 'It is a pleasure to see such a hard-working officer in the open air. Are you also part of this inspection?'

'Er, I believe so, Your Highness.'

'Excellent. I found your recent report most interesting, Captain. Have you by any chance shared it with your fellow inspectors?'

'Er, no, not yet, Your Highness.'

Bergesrode had strictly forbidden him to pass anything to any-one outside the Prince's office.

'Perhaps you would do so.'

Everyone was looking at him. And they were beginning to guess now.

'It will be recalled that Hoche had withdrawn a part of his Army of the Sambre-et-Meuse from Germany,' he began. 'Our understanding was that an expedition to Ireland was contemplated . . .'

The Prince nodded, encouragingly.

'. . . It now appears that this expedition has been aborted. The troops who were to take part in it are on their way back to Germany. What is more, Hoche himself, although recently appointed Minister of War in Paris, has given up the post and has also returned to Germany.'

'Indeed,' said the Prince. 'A remarkable move. One would have thought that the star of the Republic had plunged suddenly into disgrace, were it not for the other elements you drew to our attention. Continue, Captain.'

'The Army of the Sambre-et-Meuse is to be united with the Army of the Rhine in a new army, the Army of Germany, and Hoche is to be in command.'

'Plainly there has been something of a change of plans in Paris,' said the Prince. 'The French forces in Germany are to be reorganized and returned to full strength. Intriguing. Mystifying, one might say. You had a theory, Captain. You put it rather elegantly, I thought. Please share it with these gentlemen.'

'I think Paris must be planning to enforce its will on some party in Germany,' finished Wéry.

'And I am inclined to agree with you. For I have been graced with a letter from the vigorous General Hoche, in which he demands many things.'

Someone drew breath. And suddenly the things that had puzzled them – the clandestine meeting, the questions about the defences and militia – had fallen into place.

'Dear Virgin!' exclaimed the Fapps colonel. 'Is it *us* they are coming for?'

'That depends on exactly what he is demanding, doesn't it?' said Balcke.

The Count and the Prince looked at one another, and the Prince smiled broadly. For a moment Wéry sensed a tussle in the air between them.

'Things,' said the Prince, 'that he may well imagine I will find difficult to grant him. And I do.'

There was a long pause.

The army of Erzberg consisted of three infantry battalions, two squadrons of hussars, a handful of ceremonial life guards, some dragoons employed on frontier duties, and a battery of field artillery. At full strength it would have numbered some three and a half thousand men. After the recent campaign, and the fight at Hersheim, it was of course no longer at full strength.

At Wéry's last estimate the Army of the Sambre-et-Meuse had nearly eighty thousand effectives, counting the troops who had been dispatched for the expedition to Ireland, and who now appeared to be returning. The Army of the Rhine was smaller, but not by much. It would also have to watch the Emperor's garrisons at Mainz and Frankfurt, but that made no difference. Uniting the two commands would give Hoche all the freedom of action that he needed.

And the Erzberg's defences were hardly defences at all: one line of bastioned walls, a ditch, and the citadel. No outworks. Nothing to compare with the massive fortifications Wéry remembered at Mainz, which had held the Imperial force for four months.

And not enough powder. Or time. Or men to captain the guns.

'We are in a serious situation, gentlemen,' said the Prince.

No one answered him.

Beyond the ring, another man entered the bastion.

Wéry recognized the newcomer at once, from the largeness of his head upon his delicate body, and from his long nose and pink cheeks. It was Gianovi, the First Minister of Erzberg, strutting purposefully towards them. He had no coat, despite the wind, but bright white silk breeches and a dark blue velvet doublet, which would have been better off indoors on such a day.

Following Wéry's glance, Bergesrode looked over his shoulder.

'Highness,' he murmured at his master's elbow.

The Prince turned. He showed no surprise. Instead his face broke once more into that expression of gourmand's glee that he had worn on greeting the army officers.

'Ah, the First Minister! Dear me – does this mean that I am late, after all?'

The First Minister bowed.

'Your pardon, Highness,' he said smoothly. 'I have not checked my watch. If you are late, then I am also. I had – a sudden whim – to take the air before the Privy Council meets.'

His voice had a light accent, and his tone took it for granted that any meeting between the Prince and the army would of course include the First Minister as well. The officers stood rigid, hiding behind wooden expressions. But the Prince showed no surprise at this arrival in the middle of his council of war.

'Indeed? Indeed? We are of like mind this morning. Good! And I have come upon an inspection of the defences, Gianovi. These gentlemen tell me many things I find fascinating.'

Gianovi eyed the officers with a little smile. He held his huge head a little on one side, and with his long nose and pink cheeks he reminded Wéry of a jay on a fence, watching a snail and wondering if it were good to eat.

'I imagine they have been instructing you in what steps are necessary to breach the walls, Highness.'

'I do not believe we discussed that, no.'

'It surprises me,' said the First Minister in a tone of no great surprise. 'I should have thought it was the first – indeed the only – step that we would require of the army in our current position.'

'Our current position?' said the Prince, as if it had been the last thing on his mind.

'I believe the letter from General Hoche requires us, as well as expelling forthwith from the city all who – ahem – plot against the Republic, to make breaches in the walls of both the citadel and the town, as evidence of our goodwill. Of course,' he added, 'I have not yet seen this letter, but I believe it is quite specific . . .'

From the expression on Bergesrode's face, the First Minister must have quoted it almost verbatim.

'Of course you are right,' said the Prince. 'We must consider our options.'

'We might very well consider our options,' said the First Minister briskly, 'supposing we had more than one.'

The Prince frowned. But he did not rebuke his servant for his tone.

'We shall appeal to the Circle, of course.'

'Of course, Your Highness. And I am sure our neighbours will listen politely. The representatives of Ansbach and Bayreuth will then apply to Berlin for instructions. Those instructions will take time to come, but we can imagine what they will be. The other Protestant princes will wait for Berlin to reject us, and will then do the same. So, I imagine, will some of the Catholic counties. I did happen – quite by chance – to speak with the delegate from Bamberg this afternoon, who told me in confidence that he would seek instructions to press for the Circle to offer help. In the case of his state, he believes, this would mean money. The delegates from Eichstatt and the cantons will no doubt say similar things . . .'

'I did think,' sighed the Prince, 'that my cousin Bamberg might send a musket or two.'

'Not one state in the Circle will offer troops, because not one state believes that we or they could possibly resist if – in an entirely imaginary situation, which I am sure no sane man, least of all a Prince who is father of his people, would contemplate – if General Hoche and his legions were provoked into descending upon us.'

His bright little eyes swept the row of officers as if to suggest that it was they, rather than the Prince, who must be responsible for the insanity that he had come hurrying to the bastion to prevent.

The officers glared back at him.

'And the Emperor?' said the Prince, unperturbed. 'After all, he has pledged to us that the integrity of the German body will be maintained.'

Gianovi bowed. 'Your Highness is accurate. We shall of course appeal to Vienna. We may at the same time enquire precisely what His Imperial Majesty intended by the words "integrity" and "German body" which seem so curiously open to interpretation. I am sure His Imperial Majesty will consider our case – when he can tear his mind from his negotiations with France. But we must be prepared for the possibility that he may be slower than we would wish to return to armed confrontation, and may perhaps require a greater cause even than the fate of Erzberg before he does so.'

'You may be right, my dear Gianovi,' mused the Prince. 'We are almost helpless, it seems, in the face of the French phenomenon. Although . . .'

And he looked away into the air, as if he were addressing no one in particular, and contemplated only the passing of the seasons.

'. . . Although I have wondered of late whether our helpless-ness, and that of the Empire and of all the crowned heads of Christendom, is not so much a lack of means, but of will . . .

'And whether, if that were the case, it might not be possible for the will of Christendom to be recovered by some example, be it never so small, from amongst the ranks of princes.'

Gianovi spread his hands.

'But if *will* were all, Highness,' he said carefully, 'we might have achieved many things that we have not. We would now have a printed German prayer book in your territories, and cultivation of clover, not to speak of emancipation of the serfs, reform of the monasteries, a broadening of the university curriculum, taxation of the nobility and many other right and just things that you have sought over the years. Alas, we sometimes meet with a will that is countervailing, armed with force that is − in this case − overwhelming.'

Once more, as if to underline his point, he ran his eye over the row of sullen officers. Someone muttered, angrily. But no one contradicted him.

Wéry counted to three. Still no one else spoke.

And so he did.

'You are right, Your Highness.'

There was a sharp, warning look on Gianovi's face. But the Prince beamed and nodded his head, as if it were perfectly natural that the most junior man present might have something to say.

'Do speak, Captain. We are all friends here. Although I cannot promise you that the First Minister will suffer you to be as brisk with his notions as he is with mine.'

'It *is* a matter of will,' Wéry said. 'The French themselves have proved that. In '93, they were opposed by every power in

Christendom. Yet they were not overwhelmed because the Republic had the will to demand of its people things that we all would have thought impossible. They conscripted their fighting men *en masse*. Even women fought for a while. All experience was that such armies were too big, and must swiftly starve, disperse, and beggar the state that raised them. And maybe they did. But still they kept fighting. In the end it was the will of the Princes that failed.'

'An interesting parable. I have thought of this too. Is it our conclusion, then, that to fight this Republic we must become more like it?'

Wéry looked into the watery blue of the Prince's eyes. It was as if the affable voice had spoken his deepest, darkest thought.

'No, sir!' he said emphatically.

'I agree we must not. *Justum et tenacem propositi virum*. But you are saying we should be ready to do things that habit informs us against.'

'Yes, Your Highness. Exactly.'

'I beg the Captain's pardon,' said Gianovi. 'But my wits are slow this morning. He says "exactly". But I do not see exactly. When Hoche has marched upon us, knocked down our walls with his guns (since we were so disobliging that we did not do it ourselves at his request) and proposes to accept the surrender of the city, what *exactly* are these things that we should do?'

'One does not have to surrender simply because the walls are breached,' said Wéry.

'That's right,' said Balcke. He sounded surprised. 'You stand fast, they have to take you down man by man.'

'So,' said Gianovi. 'If I have understood, we have – in our imaginations – defied the ultimatum, manned the walls, seen them breached by our enemies and are now fighting street by street while the city burns, the women are dragged from the cellars and the children hoisted on bayonets. Very good. I have two questions. One. Shall this course lead to victory? I doubt it, but perhaps our young friend could explain. Two. Even if it led, improbably, to victory, would it be worth it? The issue for which we would burn our city is simply this: whether a certain foreign nobleman – dear to our hearts, if not endearing in his ways – should be permitted to remain here. General Hoche claims that d'Erles and his party are agitating and arming against Paris. Well. I suppose d'Erles and his friends have a pistol or two between them and would remember how to load one if only they could stay sober for long enough. I do not imagine that he is so pressed for other havens that he would actually wish to remain here during the unpleasantness itself. That is beside the point. But let us suppose that after all is done, the Comte d'Erles is able to return freely to our smoking ruins, as we are dragging our dead from the rubble. Shall we hold ourselves vindicated when his gilt coach rolls by?'

The gaze of the Prince swung from one side to the other. How deftly he had removed himself from the argument! Now it was a joust between the First Minister and the army, with the Prince waiting to award the laurels to the victor.

'Let me propose your answer, gentlemen,' said Gianovi. 'For I believe I do understand you. You will say that it is not for our dear d'Erles, or even for the city, that we are concerned. For the sake of Christendom, the church, virtue, truth, the French phenomenon must be defied. No matter that the phenomenon cannot be defeated. By defiance, even by sacrifice, you propose to set an example that others may follow. I admit it is not inconceivable that you may succeed – although history does not encourage me to believe that you will. The ruins of Heidelberg have stood for a hundred years, and what of that? It is a rallying cry for a few bourgeois scholars who dream of a German nation that does not exist. Nevertheless, the virtue that flows to you from your ancestors demands this. Am I correct?'

'If you mean it's a matter of honour,' grated Balcke. 'Then yes, I'd say you've understood. Just about.'

'Honour, yes. Dear me. Honour. I had forgotten,' sighed Gianovi. 'Honour lies in fulfilling obligations. The Prince has an obligation to his godson d'Erles, granted. It is for His Highness, and not for you gentlemen, to judge whether the baptismal oaths he has made should extend to sheltering d'Erles in the city when the most powerful force in Germany demands his removal. He has higher obligations, too, you would say. Although such obligations are curiously difficult to define, let alone fulfil.

'But His Highness has yet more obligations: to the Cathedral Chapter, who elected him; to the Estates, through whom his territories are run; and to the thousands of his subjects who live in the city where you would make your stand. These are obligations he *can* fulfil. Should he not consider these too?'

He waved his arm over the battlements at the tiles and chimneypots and wreaths of blown smoke below. The town looked quiet this morning, subdued under the bluster of the wind. A barge drifted below the New Bridge, heading for some port downstream. A cart clattered distantly on the cobbles. There were people moving in the streets. Away on the roof of the great cathedral, which rose like a second citadel on its hill in the heart of the city, tiny figures moved like ants on a small scaffolding around one of the lesser spires.

Think, cursed Wéry to himself. *Think!* None of the other officers could debate with this man. He was too quick, too clever. And none of them, not even Balcke, was yet ready to commit themselves to the Prince's logic – not for a fight against odds of twenty or forty to one. But Wéry had lived his life by the same logic. He knew what the Prince had been saying, and what he was looking for from the rest of them. If only he could find the words to say it himself!

And yet, as he stared out over the city, all the arguments seemed weak. Gianovi had stated them and dismissed them. And the things Wéry had said already sounded foolish now – not because they were foolish, but because of the way he had said them. He looked at the scaffolding on the spires, and his mind, unbidden, conjured a vision of the burnt towers of the cathedral at Mainz. In his confusion he could not help wondering whether there was scaffolding around those too, at that moment. And if so, what did it mean?

'In any event, this is idle talk,' said Gianovi. 'There has been a development, Your Highness.'

'Indeed?'

'The Canon Rother-Konisrat has sought an audience with you, which he hopes will be granted as soon as the Privy Council has finished. It seems that he has heard some story from his cousin Lady Adelsheim that Your Highness's officers declined a truce, immediately before the action at Hersheim.'

'Really! Which officers?'

'The officer named in the story is present, Your Highness,' Gianovi said, inclining his head towards Balcke.

The Prince looked down at the little First Minister, and his face was set like stone.

153

'I do not doubt, of course, that there has been some exaggeration in the telling . . .' said Gianovi, with an apologetic smile.

'Dear, dear,' murmured the Prince. 'Has there been, my dear Colossus?'

Balcke's face was red. 'There's not a word of truth in it, Your Highness,' he said.

'. . . Nevertheless,' continued Gianovi smoothly, 'I believe we can all appreciate that, given the current mood of the city, this rumour would be enough to make any call to arms most inadvisable.'

'You believe the guilds would not respond.'

'I believe they would respond with alacrity, Highness. I believe they would be clamouring at the doors of the armouries. But I fear that, when the doors opened, the direction in which they employed their arms might be less than helpful to us.'

There was a short, thick silence. Balcke stood like an oak in the middle of the group, and no one met his eye.

After a moment, the First Minister continued: 'In the circumstances, I have felt it necessary to indicate to Canon Rother that Your Highness may consent to the War Commission conducting an inquiry into events at Hersheim.'

'I see,' said the Prince. 'And shall I?'

'I suspect the – ah – *will* of the Chapter, and of the estates and city, may brook nothing else, Your Highness.'

'I see.'

'And in the meantime I am sure the army will consider itself employed in obliging the French in the matter of the city wall.'

The First Minister ran his eye once more down the line of uniformed men. No one answered him. He turned away.

'Your Highness.'

'Indeed, indeed. We are interrupting these gentlemen in their work. And the Privy Council must be waiting. Let us return to our duties.'

The officers stood to attention. The Prince smiled, and turned to pace down the bastion wall with the First Minister at his side and Bergesrode shadowing them, a few paces behind. Gianovi was speaking to his master, but the wind bore his words away. There was no way of telling whether the Prince was nodding to some pleasantry, or to some earnest warning about the dangerous men they were leaving.

'Blow up the walls!' exclaimed someone. 'Is he in the pay of the French, that man?'

'No city, no nice nest for Gianovi,' grumbled someone else. 'I never could stand foreigners in the service.'

'Hum!' exclaimed the hussar colonel angrily.

'Dammit, Altmantz. I didn't mean your man here. Good stuff that, Wéry. Well done.'

Silence fell again as the officers contemplated their defeat. The Prince and his First Minister were diminishing along the bastion wall. Still the big man was listening, the small one speaking, waving his hands like a conjurer.

'That about Hersheim,' ventured Knuds. 'Damned awkward, at this time.'

'Propaganda,' said Altmantz. 'They're sowing dissension.'

'I've a bottle of brandy on my table, if you fellows wish,' said Knuds.

'First sensible thing anyone's said today . . .'

'Not for me,' said Balcke abruptly, and stalked off.

There were embarrassed looks among the colonels. Altmantz cleared his throat.

'Coming, Wéry?' he asked. 'Something to cool that hot head of yours?'

Wéry shook his head. He was speechless with anger. The uppermost thought in his mind was: how was it *possible*?

'Hey, Wéry? Are you dreaming, man?'

'I – I don't know if I will be able to, sir,' said Wéry.

Bergesrode had dropped back behind the Prince and the First Minister. He was looking over his shoulder, jerking his head.

'What's the matter?'

'I think I am about to be dismissed.'

XI
The Priest

Dismissed?

He would have dismissed himself, for sure.

He would have torn up his commission in his own face, yelling, '*Idiot! Fool! Half-baked ideas!*'

'*You had the chance, and ruined it!*'

He had had the chance – exactly the chance he had prayed for. Now that it had vanished, he could see it so clearly: the chance to step up from the endless, meaningless drudgery of spy work to strike a real blow! A city armed and defiant! A fight to the bitter end! The Prince had been willing to listen. He had even given Wéry the cue. And then they had all been out-talked by the quick-tongued First Minister. The army had been made to look foolish. Balcke was declared a villain, fit only to be investigated. And what Wéry hated most of all was that his own wits had been slower than Gianovi's.

Politics!

He understood, dimly, that the other officers were not displeased with him. Balcke had even backed him. Altmantz, who normally averted his eyes at the sight of Wéry, was now almost friendly. But that was beside the point. What they thought did not matter. They did not see things as clearly as he. Bergesrode did. Bergesrode, who had prepared the Prince for this meeting and had made sure Wéry was included, would understand that he had failed. Now Bergesrode was waiting for him.

The face of the priest was like weathered sandstone, hard and lined and pitted. His thick, dark brows sloped naturally, so that he was forever frowning. The smudges beneath his eyes matched his brows so perfectly that they might have been reflections in some pool. All four dark marks slanted towards the bridge of his nose, as if they were the remains of a diagonal, ashen cross that dour saints had traced there at his birth, to show that the child was one of their own. His hair was black and his priest's robe was black, and he never wore anything else.

'Well?' said Bergesrode.

'I said what I believed to be true,' Wéry replied stiffly. 'I still believe it.'

'I don't mean that. Your report about Hoche. Can he rely on it?'

'Oh.' Wéry gathered his thoughts. 'Yes, I believe so.'

'I need more than that.'

When Wéry hesitated, he said, 'Come on. We can talk as we walk. But I cannot be left behind.' He turned to follow his master.

'You want to know the sources?' Wéry said, hurrying to keep up.

'Tell me no more than you need to. But yes.'

'There is a merchant in Kassel, who has contracts to supply one of the French divisions. There are two peddlers. There is also a money-lender whose clients include French officers.'

'A Jew?' Bergesrode looked at him sharply.

'Does it matter? Their officers visit him, eat with him, get drunk and talk.'

(With Bergesrode, as with Balcke. Keep to the truth, short and

158

direct. Loathe his every instinct, churchman and aristocrat, but loathe in silence. On the one point that mattered most, they were agreed.)

Bergesrode walked a pace or two, brooding. At length he shrugged. 'The end justifies the means. So this is chit-chat among the officers at Wetzlar. Is that all?'

'I have confirmation from the Rhine.'

'Who do you have beyond the Rhine?'

'I will not say.' And as Bergesrode opened his mouth, Wéry cut in again. 'He is not doing it for the Prince's gold. I do not owe you his rank or name.'

'I have to trust what you say he says,' snapped Bergesrode. 'I have to advise the Prince to trust it too.'

'He can be trusted. The difficulty is bringing his news back to Erzberg.'

'And how do you do that?'

'So far, by crossing the Rhine myself.'

'You could have been arrested!'

'I have not been.'

'Yet. But if you carry on with that we will lose you. You must not go into French-held territory again. You must think of a better way.'

'I'm trying to!'

And that was weakness, that outburst: weakness shown to Bergesrode, who knew no weakness. Wéry was still struggling to adjust, still wondering why there had been no word about dismissal or even reprimand. Perhaps the question of dismissal had never crossed Bergesrode's mind. A chance had been lost – what of it? Continue, with the tools that you have. Discard them only if you think you can find better ones.

In some ways Wéry wished he could be more like Bergesrode himself.

But what a chance it had been!

So, no dismissal. Or not yet. Perhaps the Prince, strolling ahead of them with Gianovi at his side, would remember him at some point in the weeks ahead and pronounce his sentence then. In the meantime, he must continue.

'Very good,' said Bergesrode. 'But from now on you must double your efforts. You must watch Hoche like a hawk. We need his correspondence, his plans, his preparations – anything you can learn about his intentions. If he is going to move against us, we need as much warning as you can give.'

'I understand,' said Wéry, sorting in his mind the possible from the impossible among Bergesrode's demands.

(Hoche's plans? As well whistle for the moon.)

(Correspondence? Well, if there were a corrupt clerk, and the money to bribe him with. But could he find either?)

No. It would be counting tents, watching wagon-loads, listening to what Bergesrode called the chit-chat, sorting fact from rumour. No army, not even the French, could move anywhere without some sign of stirring.

They turned the corner of the palace. The Prince and First Minister were some fifty paces ahead of them, approaching the gate to the inner courtyard. A coach, rolling out of the archway, stopped at the sight of the pair. Its occupant, a long, languid young man in a yellow coat, climbed out of the carriage to accost them.

'D'Erles,' murmured Bergesrode. 'Our *causus belli.*'

'Do you need to join them?'

Bergesrode shook his head. 'Let the First Minister catch it,

160

whatever it is. It will serve him for forcing himself in on a meeting to which he was not invited. In any case, with d'Erles it will be about his lodgings or his allowance. It won't be high policy.'

'I'm surprised he doesn't ask the Countess.'

Bergesrode glanced at him coldly. Wéry shrugged. No one would admit to him that the Countess Wilhelmina Pancak-Schönberg – the huge and brainless noblewoman who dominated the Prince's court – was the Prince's mistress. But what other explanation for her influence could there be? And she doted on the handsome d'Erles. It galled Wéry to think that his final confrontation with Paris might come about not for the sake of Freedom, or Truth, but because an eccentric female aristocrat was besotted with a feckless, self-centred, exploitative young man whom France had every right to hate.

Bergesrode watched the group ahead of them. After a moment he said, 'There will be agitators.'

'Agitators?'

'Republican agents. Illuminati. Sent to foment discontent here.'

Wéry shrugged again. 'If I hear anything, of course I will report it. But they won't be in Wetzlar. They'll be in the city.'

'Then *look* in the city.'

'Isn't that for the city police . . .'

'Yes, and for you, too. This is important. The Illuminati are the danger. They are the ones who controlled the Revolution. Abbé Barruel had proved it. Never forget that.'

Wéry shook his head. He had helped to organize a revolution himself, in Brabant. He had walked in Paris in the heady days of '92, and early '93 when Louis XVI had gone to the guillotine. Not once had he come across any sign that anyone professing to

161

be an Illuminatus (or freemason or Martinist or Rosicrucian, for that matter) had secretly steered events to their conclusion. Not once had he even thought of them, until he had come to take service in the Empire where the vast and fearful Catholic Church still held sway, peering at the signs of its destruction and seeking its enemies in the shadows.

Control the Revolution? No one had controlled it at all. That was how it had become what it had become.

And in any case, how was he, a foreigner and barely a gentleman, to penetrate the political salons and lodges of Erzberg and learn their secrets?

'The French messengers that came yesterday went into the city too,' said Bergesrode. 'We know one of them called at a house in the Saint Emil quarter. That's where this story about Balcke will have come from. And this morning a crowd pelted the coach of one of the d'Erles party . . .'

'Do you think it's true, that story about Balcke?'

'Weren't you there?'

'Not at the action itself.'

'That may be very lucky for you. If it is true, Balcke is finished and so is anyone who was with him. We will find out. At the same time we will stop this leakage into and out of the city. It is ridiculous that French messengers can come and go where they please before we are aware of it. From now on, passports will only be issued or countersigned by the Prince's office or by the First Minister. The Prince has signed a decree to that effect. Stop a moment.'

They stood under the shadow of the Celesterburg arch, looking in to the courtyard. Half-way across the cobbles the Prince was making his way slowly towards the palace steps, now surrounded by a small crowd of notables vying for his attention.

'Best we do not let too many people see us talking,' murmured Bergesrode. 'He doesn't want it known that we are consulting the army at present.'

'I need passports for myself and my couriers. How am I to get them if . . .'

'Come and see me when you need them.'

'Your antechamber is too damned crowded . . .'

'That is blasphemy, Wéry.'

'. . . Whenever I go up there, I find half of Erzberg waiting for you or the Prince. And they can hear every word we say!'

'You don't come early enough. Come at dawn. I'll give you a pass for the side door.' He caught Wéry's look. 'Oh we'll be there. Don't worry. But come ready to talk about the Illuminati. Also, I want to know more about these ideas of yours.'

'Which ones?'

'What you said out there, on the bastion. He liked that.'

Wéry stared at him. 'You think he would do it?'

'That's as may be.'

'Didn't he decide it was impossible?'

'The only thing he will have decided this morning will be that he has even fewer competent officers than he thought he had. And the only thing we can be sure of is that *if* the French come, it will not be that fool Knuds who will be commanding in the citadel! Nothing else is certain. That's why your work matters. And your ideas.'

With a nod of dismissal, he set out across the palace courtyard. His black robes blew around him as he hurried in the wake of his master.

XII
In the Barrack Room

The colonels had dispersed by the time Wéry returned to the commandant's house. So he took his leave of Knuds and departed from the citadel on foot. He walked slowly down the looping road from the citadel to the bridges. His boots roused little dry dust-clouds for the wind to fling in eddies and disperse over the hillside. His thoughts flew with them, and alighted nowhere.

Politics!

The nasty, little, petty-minded politics of Erzberg: Gianovi against Balcke; Canon Rother against the army; little boys in their sandcastles. Little boys with knives. *Balcke is finished.* That was a swift judgement. That was exactly what might be expected from someone who had not been with the army in those last days! And if there were few competent officers in the army of Erzberg, there would be one less when Balcke was gone. Wéry would be sorry. Balcke had been the first to take him seriously.

Bergesrode would not be sorry. He was one of the Ingolstadt set, and the Ingolstadt set hated Balcke, just as they hated Gianovi and anyone they suspected of swaying the Prince towards reform of Erzberg's ancient customs and institutions. The Prince kept Bergesrode in his office as a balance to his other advisers. So the lethal bickering penetrated right to the heart of the Prince's government. Squabbling makes you smaller. And paranoia makes you smaller still. *Come ready to talk about the Illuminati.* Hah. Rubbish. The obsession of a sick and backward-looking church . . .

Squabbling, and paranoia, and impossible demands. Find Illuminati in the city. Bring us the plans of Hoche. Stay out of French-held territory. (But yes, he must find a safe courier to and from the Rhine. Somehow, he must.)

And your ideas.

Because the French would come. Now or later, whether they evicted d'Erles or not, one day the French would come. There could be no real peace with such an enemy. His pulses beat with the thought of it.

Ideas, ideas. His idea was to fight. To oppose the French with a will that exceeded even their own. But Bergesrode knew that. The question he was asking was: how?

Defence had to have depth. When one line was breached, there must be another behind it, and another behind that, so that no attack could gain momentum. A serious fortress should be surrounded with lines of outworks and redoubts. But Erzberg could not be made into a fortress. That would take months, and vast sums of money. The French would be alert to it at once. They could be outside the walls in days.

So what could be done?

Build further lines within the walls? Pitch the fight inside the city?

He paused on the Old Bridge, looking out across the quays. The riverside was crowded. His eye rested on the folk loading barges, wheeling barrows, passing in the street. Glances were thrown in his direction, and a few frowns, but there were no hisses for a hussar officer this morning. They did not know about Balcke and Hersheim, yet. Nor did they know that this particular hussar was pondering a murderous fight for the city. It should be written on his face, like a mark of Cain. *Fighting street by street while the city burns, the women are dragged from the cellars and the children hoisted on bayonets.* Yes, all that. All that would happen, here on these chattering wharves in the breezy air. Once you have made the attackers fight their way in, they will show you no mercy.

And this was the voice of the enemy. It had been voiced in good faith – supposing Gianovi was capable of good faith – but it was the enemy nonetheless. *Look at them, pity them. And for their sakes, do not oppose me.* It was distraction. It was lies. The enemy offered every excuse for weakness. But truth was only truth if you were prepared to die for it.

And, he thought, it could be done.

They could fight for these streets. Look at the Coffee House Stocke, there. Or at this merchant's house, four-square at the end of the Old Bridge. Beneath its elaborate friezes of vines and fat cherubs, these were good stone walls. Put loopholes in them, put oak shutters on those broad windows, and it would be a small fortress. No one could cross the river this way until it was taken.

Look at the Saint Christopher Chapel. A cannon in its door-way could sweep the length of the wharves . . .

It needed determination. Not fear. Fear was the corruption that had consumed the Republic: fear of émigrés, fear of the mob, fear of the Powers and fear of each other. No cause of *his* must go that way. To do this – not just to contemplate it, but to carry it all the way through – Erzberg's leaders would be tested to the very limits of their will.

And it needed arms, powder and shot. Level eyes and level heads. Steady hands on the muskets. The defence would show no mercy either. And when they came on, with their banners and their bayonets – *Bang! Bang! Damn you, bang!* And the smoke clearing and the bodies writhing on the cobbles. And they would have learned, in Paris. They would have learned the price of betrayal!

His fists shook. His jaw was clenched. And he stood there, lost in his vision at the parapet of the Old Bridge, until his ear began to pick up again the clatter of the people on the wharves. The wind gusted, flapping his tunic, and his eye saw the brown swirl of the river once more.

It could be done, he thought. That was what he would tell Bergesrode at dawn tomorrow. It could be done if there was the will. And if they came.

He left the bridge. Moving swiftly now, he began to make his way upstream, skirting the narrow, gated street which was the city's Jewish ghetto, into the northern districts of the city. As he went he looked left and right, noting strong buildings, avenues of fire, killing grounds. There were many, he found – so many ways and places in which an attacker could be made to suffer.

Why in heaven's name did cities bother with walls at all?

It was in this frame of mind, intense and agitated, that he reached the Saint Lucia barracks where the hussars were quartered. He was moving so fast that he did not acknowledge the sentry's salute. He barely heard what the man had said to him. He had walked on five paces under the archway before his brain caught up with his ears.

'What? What did you say?'

'There's callers for you, sir.'

'Callers?'

'Two gentlewomen, sir.'

Gentlewomen! What in heaven . . . ?

'For me? You are sure?'

'Asked for you by name, sir.'

It must have been business of some sort. Here in Erzberg, no gentlewoman would call on an officer in his barracks for any other reason. But he could not think what business one could have with him, or indeed which, if any, of his scarce acquaintances in the city it could possibly have been.

'Did they leave a card?'

'They're still here.'

Still here!

Gentlewomen waiting in a barracks? God above, what kind of business could this be?

'Where are they?' he asked urgently.

'Don't exactly know, sir. Officers' quarters, I suppose.'

They were in the long room in the officers' block: two women in brown habits with their skirts spread wide on the stained and faded settees on which the bachelor officers would lounge and drink wine in the evenings. One he recognized instantly – it was Madame Poppenstahl, whom he had last seen in the little waiting room at Adelsheim. The other wore a veil. A black dress peeped out from under her habit. It was almost certainly one of the Adelsheim women – the daughter, he guessed, from her height. But with the veil and the dim light he could not be sure.

'And here he is,' cried Altmantz, looking up from an armchair. 'The lost sheep returns. Well, boy? Still got your commission, I hope?'

'Fortunately, sir, yes,' gasped Wéry. 'Ladies, I am at your service.

And I regret – I bitterly regret – that you have had to wait for me. If I had known, of course I would have been here at once.'

'It is no fault of yours, sir,' said Madame Poppenstahl, as he bent over her hand. She turned, perhaps a little awkwardly, to his superior officer. 'And Baron . . .'

The colonel raised an eyebrow. Women like Madame Poppenstahl did not normally dismiss barons who had condescended to wait upon them.

'Baron, you have been most kind,' said the woman behind the veil. And it was indeed Maria von Adelsheim.

'Well,' said the Baron, gallantly levering himself to his feet. 'It – it has been a pleasure, but I have matters to attend to. I'll leave him to your mercies.'

'Sir . . .' began Wéry.

'Think nothing of it, boy,' said Altmantz. 'Only tell me what it was about afterwards if you can. I'm all agog.'

He left them, with the forced cheerfulness of a man who knew he was not in control of events in his house, and therefore behaved as if all events that occurred exactly suited him. The sound of his boots clattered away on the wooden boards and Wéry was alone with the two women.

They were alone, in the room where up to a dozen young unmarried men would sit of an evening, drinking and smoking and roaring at one another. There was dust in the air, ashes in the hearth, the smell of wood smoke and tobacco smoke and spilled wine. On a sideboard stood a row of decanters, full, half-full and near-empty. The furniture was shabby. Here and there the fabrics were torn, as if by some undisciplined cat. But it was no cat that had ripped the upholstery and picked at the carpet so. They were the marks of spurs.

'By your leave, ladies,' he said, feeling embarrassed by their surroundings, but also helpless. There was nowhere else in the barracks to take these two unexpected visitors. He perched on the edge of a settee that had been visibly deformed by generations of drunken hussars sprawling there and tipping bottles into their mouths.

He waited. Madame Poppenstahl was preparing to speak. Wéry understood that she was to do the talking, and also that she was not quite sure how to begin. He stole a glance at the woman in the veil, but he saw there only poise and silence. The outline of the face showed dimly behind the dark material.

What were they doing here?

'Once again,' he said, 'I truly regret that I was not here to receive you.'

'It is no fault of yours, sir,' said Madame Poppenstahl. 'But it was not possible for us, finding you away, to go and return tomorrow. Therefore we were obliged to wait.'

'I see,' said Wéry, blankly.

'We wish,' said Madame Poppenstahl, 'to acquire a passport.'

'A passport!'

'For a foreign gentleman to remain a month within the city. He will be travelling on private business and therefore it would be best if he had papers from our own authorities.'

Madame Poppenstahl looked at him, as though hoping she had said all that was necessary by way of explanation.

'But – but it is no part of my duties to issue passports,' said Wéry, baffled. 'You would have to apply to . . .' He hesitated.

There was a new decree, Bergesrode had said. He struggled to remember the details. 'I believe . . . You now have to go to the office of the Prince, or the First Minister.'

'Alas, sir. Enquiries have already been made on our behalf in these quarters. We understand that it is impossible.'

Were they so innocent, these women?

'It should be perfectly possible. If the clerks in the palace have said it is not, it will only be because they were waiting for a bribe.'

Madame Poppenstahl's hands shifted in her lap. 'Sir, Lady Adelsheim has said most strictly that we should pay no bribes to the palace officials.'

Wéry could imagine Lady Adelsheim's opinions of the officials of Erzberg. For the most part, he shared them. He eased back a little in his chair and thought what advice he might give.

'A family of the Adelsheims' standing . . . Perhaps you should approach Gianovi himself?'

'Lady Adelsheim has said that we must not ask favours of Gianovi under any circumstances.'

Really!

'Why not?'

'She will not have it, sir. She says . . . She has no liking for him.'

He sensed her delicacy. The thing that would offend the knightly families of Erzberg most about Gianovi was that he was not one of them. He was a foreigner, ennobled by grace and not by birth. He owed no loyalty to any faction within Erzberg other than to the man who had employed him. And the same, at a much lesser level, was true for Wéry. There was no doubt that Lady Adelsheim would have her views on lowly and foreign-born army officers as well. If she had thought that her emissaries might approach him, she would have forbidden that too. But she had not.

'Who is it you want a passport for?'

'A Major Jean-Marie Lanard.'

'An émigré, madame? I do not know him.'

'He is an officer of the Army of the French Republic.'

'*What!*'

No wonder they had not been able to get what they wanted! Madame Poppenstahl returned his look with a frail defiance.

'But what you ask is most difficult,' said Wéry slowly.

Difficult? It was madness! Allow a revolutionary officer back into Erzberg? If there were even a possibility that the Prince would resist Hoche's demands?

He could feel the eyes of the veiled girl on him. He did not want to disappoint her. He very much did not want to. But really, it was best to be honest.

'I should explain . . .' he said. 'There is great alarm in the palace about the possibility that republican agitators may enter the city. I doubt if anyone less than the Prince would willingly sanction such a letter at this time.'

'We had understood, Captain, that you had become an aide to the Prince.'

Great heavens! They expected him to get the passport for them!

And they were not so innocent after all, were they? Clearly they knew he was not just a hussar officer. They knew he came and went from the Prince's offices. That was why they had come to him.

'That is accurate. But I fear that His Highness would hardly seek my advice on a matter such as this.'

Madame Poppenstahl was disappointed, but she was not put off. Some power greater than her natural diffidence was pushing her on.

'Truly not? I wonder if you do yourself justice, sir.' She shifted once more, awkwardly.

And then, as if she was not quite sure whether she meant what she was saying, she went on, 'Lady Adelsheim has said we were not to offer any rewards to the *palace* officials . . .'

Her voice trailed away as she saw Wéry's face change.

He could feel the muscles in his cheeks, set like stone. He was glaring at her, and he knew it, and could not help it. And yes, she was just a plain-thinking woman, trying to play palace games that she did not know how to play. Yes, this was probably the first time she had ever offered a bribe in her life. Yes, Erzberg was riddled with corruption. Of course it was.

But damn it! To have picked *him*! To think that he was as warped as they were – these princing, mincing aristocrats who thought themselves so *fine* and everyone else so base, and they did not see, because they could not allow themselves to see, how close on the precipice they trod!

Finished! he wanted to scream. *You're finished, all of you! And be damned to you all and good riddance!*

If he spoke, he would not contain himself. They would have to leave, and would never be able to support his presence again. And he nearly spoke. He nearly damned them both. And perhaps the only thing that kept him from speaking was the memory of the Adelsheim library, of what he had said there and by the fireside, and of how even so he had been forgiven.

At last there was a sigh, and the hands of the other woman lifted to put back her veil. The face of Maria von Adelsheim looked out at him from under it.

'I should be grateful if you would address me – Captain.'

He nodded grimly.

173

'You are rightly outraged, Captain, because we have approached you as if you were a palace time-server, and not as a gentleman and friend of my brother. I see now that it was very wrong of us. I can only plead that we have suffered so much disappointment in this today that on coming to you we have failed to give our suit the consideration it warranted. We are most abjectly sorry.'

For a child of an Imperial Knight to speak so to a commoner was not just unusual in Erzberg. It was almost unknown. Even in his rage he could see that.

He found his voice, at last. 'Do not – please do not think on it. I know how things are done in the palace. It was – I will not say it was a natural mistake but . . . It is better that we do not think on it.'

Her face was very pale, but her voice was steadier than his. 'You are merciful, Captain, and more so than we deserve. Truly we see so often that a victim becomes a villain. Yet we never imagine we will act so ourselves. Now Anna and I, thinking only that we were victims of tyranny, have committed villainy in our turn. I am ashamed. I wish you to know it.'

Tyranny? He frowned in incomprehension.

'Oh yes!' she said, exasperated. 'How is it that we are brought to wait in the Saint Lucia barracks, attempting to bribe one of the few men in Erzberg who cannot be bribed? I will tell you. It is because we dare not return to our tyrant and tell her that what she wills cannot be achieved!'

'Maria . . .' said Poppenstahl nervously.

'I know, Anna. I am being indiscreet and I should not be. But I would not wish the Captain to think that we do this to amuse ourselves! You have lived under tyranny, Captain. Have you ever lived under such as we? There is no guillotine in Adelsheim, no wheel, no hurdle, no flogging-stake. And yet I swear to you that we tremble at a word. "Anna, dear, we will need a passport. Go and get one, and don't allow any nonsense from those *wretched* people at the palace." So. Although even our cousin the Canon Rother said it would be impossible, nevertheless poor Anna must go, and must succeed, because my mother wills it. Do you see it, Captain? I wonder if you do.'

'Yes,' he said slowly. 'I see it.'

So they had been at their wits' end, trying to satisfy the monstrous Lady Adelsheim. Indeed, he could imagine it. It had been a rather good imitation of Lady Adelsheim's manner. He had recognized it at once.

At the same time he recognized something else – something suddenly and painfully familiar.

'*Hey, Michel! Behold me! I am the Emperor Leopold. Tremble, you fellows . . .*'

Were they all mimics, in the Adelsheim house?

'Yes,' he said. 'I do see it. Although – and I know you did not intend this – but I think that I saw your brother too.'

Her eyes widened in surprise. 'Alba?' Then she dropped them. 'Truly sir, I – I did not know I was so poor an actor.'

He waited, but she did not look up.

'I did not say that you were,' he said gently.

'No, but Albrecht . . .' Her brow furrowed.

He saw the grief on her face. He felt it in the way she fumbled for words. And he felt, too, how the name stirred in the mud of his own heart. For a moment he cursed himself. Yet he had not been able to help speaking of him.

'He did not *command*,' she said at length. 'It was more that he

175

inspired us. At least he was so to me. Even if it was the most ridiculous thing . . .'

She lifted her chin and looked at him again. And suddenly her face lit up in boyish exuberance.

'Maria,' she cried mannishly, swinging her elbows in a pantomime of someone in a hurry. 'Hey, Maria! Attend to me this instant – I have a notion! Maria, you *must* attend. It is of the utmost importance. It is *squirrels*, Maria! Such beauty, such grace – nothing surpasses them! We will go out and catch a hundred, Maria. And we will have the kitchens place them in a dish, with pastry on top. And then we will invite the Machtings and the Jenzes to dinner, and when Father puts the knife in the pie – out they will come, hoppity hoppity all over the table and down the hall! Will it not be the merriest thing?

'And so,' she finished, dropping back into her normal voice, 'so I must spend a long day in the woods with him, he up the trees, and I with a long-handled net waiting on the ground, and we did not catch one! Was he not so? Anna, do say.'

'Oh, he was very merry, dear, all the time.'

'Captain?'

'Yes,' said Wéry, smiling. 'Yes, he was.' A strange imp was stirring inside him. 'But also . . .'

A gentleman in conversation with a lady should not remove his eyes from her.

He certainly should not lie back full length on his battered settee.

He could not *possibly* lift his feet, booted and spurred and muddy, and prop them crossed one over the other, on the settee's sagging arm, as if no lady were present and he himself were a hundred miles away, in another time, inhabiting another body.

'Michel,' he said languidly, staring at the ceiling.

(His voice was too husky. That was nerves. Pause, and strengthen it.)

'Behold me, Michel . . .' (pause) '. . . I am furniture' (pause) '. . . and I am content.'

He could sense her leaning forward to watch him. Would she be shocked by what he was doing? Dear Heaven! What *was* he doing, imitating her dead brother for her?

But there was nothing for it now.

'I am becoming,' he went on, 'Joinery. Yes, I feel sure of it. And cloth – a little threadbare perhaps. And better yet . . .' He smacked his lips with luxurious delight and whispered, *'Woodworm!'*

She laughed.

She laughed, surprised, delighted, and the sound burst over him like applause. He felt elated. He felt a power growing in him. It was years since he had played this sort of game. But once there had been a time . . .

'Oh!' she cried. 'But was it not exact, Anna? Was he not just so? Captain, you have a talent! I declare it might have been himself.'

'He was the nearest I had to a confessor for four years,' said Wéry apologetically, as he righted himself. 'As to the passport . . .' he frowned in thought.

'Oh no! Do not let us think of it. But tell me – was he drunk when he said that?'

'Why, I do not recall,' lied Wéry.

'Then he was, I swear it! Were you, too? Were you drunk with him often?'

'Maria!' said Poppenstahl warningly.

'Oh no, Anna. The Captain will forgive us, I am sure. You do not mind, do you, Captain?'

177

There was no malice in her. Greed perhaps, for something of her brother that she could never have shared, but no malice.

'What I *do* recall,' said Wéry, 'was that he might be most merciless if I were – a little ill – of a morning.' He chuckled. 'He would visit me in my sickbed, stamp up and down, recite the Rights of Man at me, until I was fairly driven to get up and chase him away. "War on the cranium, peace to the corpus," he called it. You know the saying of Chamfort? "War on the castles" and so forth?'

'And you drove pigs through the tents of other officers together.'

'Well, I may have helped, but . . .'

'What villains you were!'

'Ah, but did he tell you about the bear?'

'Bear? No! What bear was this?'

'A dancing bear. A poor creature. Its master brought it to the camp with a halter around its neck and played on a drum for it to dance to. We watched. And then suddenly your brother said, "Aha! But now comes the deluge!" And he pushed the man into the ring, and said, "Now you, sir, will dance!" and he took the drum and gave it to the bear!'

'No!'

She was laughing aloud. And so was he.

'And – and the bear could not hold the stick. So he sat down with it, and put one arm around its shoulders . . .' He hugged an imaginary bear with one arm. 'And with the other hand he took the bear's paw and the stick and played the drum for it. And he cried to us, "Make the villain dance!" And someone drew his sabre, and the fellow danced, and – and the bear . . .'

He tried to imitate the bewildered look of the bear, watching the stick bounce up and down on the drum, and the girl laughed, and could not stop laughing, and he was laughing too at the memory. '. . . And at the end he – he p-paid the bear!'

And he did the bear's face again, looking at the purse in its paw, and the girl laughed again, and he was laughing too, and weeping a hot tear from his eye. And it hurt.

And it was good – unimaginably good. It was healing, like a massage of muscles that had gone stiff and cold for years.

'But – but was it not dangerous? The bear!'

'Very! I was sweating for him. But he was like that, was he not? Danger, and a joke, and something serious too. He meant it as a parable – an allegory of revolution. And I did not agree, for no man of any station is an animal, and we argued over it afterwards. But also we laughed. We laughed for days . . .'

'Maria,' said Madame Poppenstahl more urgently. 'Really I think we must not detain the Captain . . .'

He saw the older woman's look, and understood.

They were being too familiar. *She* was being too familiar with him. And yet he too was greedy for her company now. Greedy for more of this. He did not want her to go.

'The – ah – the passport,' he said.

'Oh no, Captain,' the girl exclaimed. 'You must not think of it. We did wrong to ask you!'

'It may be possible,' he said. 'I do not know but . . .'

He had their attention again.

'This officer you require it for. He is not here already, in the city, is he?'

'He has returned to Wetzlar to attend his General,' she said soberly. 'But he has undertaken to my mother that he will seek leave to come back, if we can obtain the permissions.'

'For what purpose?'

She hesitated for a moment. 'It may not be a purpose of which you approve, Captain. But I feel bound to be frank with you. He is the officer who carried the French parley to our troops before the action at Hersheim. We wish him to testify at an inquiry of the War Commission, for which we have petitioned. It is for my brother's sake. And for the other men who died.'

He let out a long breath.

This was impossible. He was supposed to be on watch for agitators. How could he help admit to the city a man whose word, true or false, could do more damage than a hundred rabble-rousers? And the man would be given an opportunity to speak against Balcke-Horneswerden – to do him as much damage as possible. If he owed anything to anyone living in Erzberg, it was surely to Balcke.

And yet he had already let her believe that he would help.

'You . . . want this very much, do you not?' he murmured.

She looked at him, considering. She had said he must not think of it. Now she must decide whether she would truly ask it of him.

'Yes,' she said slowly. 'Yes I do.'

'May I know why?'

'I – I believe I have already said . . .'

Words rose within him – words that he would never normally have considered, and had not known were true.

'Lady Maria,' he said. 'I am a man who hates. I know it. It is not good – although I believe that reason is with me. But I know how treacherous hate is. It does not admit – cannot admit – that there is reason, or good, or honour, in the one we hate. I do not ask you to tell me your thoughts. But I do ask that you consider why you want this man to come here.'

She looked at him levelly. 'You are . . . most frank, Captain. Tell me. Whom do you suppose that I may hate?'

'Perhaps it is Count Balcke-Horneswerden.'

'Oh,' she said, as if she had thought he would name someone else.

She considered it. Perhaps she nodded, slightly. But at length she said, 'What we seek is the truth about why my brother died, Captain. That is all.'

He spread his hands. 'So. Whose truth do you mean?'

'I do not believe there is more than one truth. To say otherwise is to be like Pilate, who demanded "what is truth?" of the Lord Our Saviour.'

'I have always felt that he had a point,' said Wéry.

He might also say that the various political factions in the city would all seek to use any testimony given to the Commission for their own purposes. But she would know that. He could guess how she might answer him . . .

In the end, she was here before him. He could not refuse her.

'Very well,' he said. 'You will have to remind me of your officer's name.'

'Major Jean-Marie Lanard.'

He repeated it to himself. Then he nodded. 'I will do what I can. At present, that will be nothing. In a week or a fortnight, it is likely that the Prince's decree will be less rigorously implemented, and there may be a chance. No, my ladies. Please remember, you have said that your Major Lanard has gone to assume other duties. He will not be free of those quickly and therefore it is best that we take our time.'

'Captain . . . I am grateful. And if there is anything we may do for you, I beg that you will name it.'

I beg that you will name it. He must have said those very words to her, on the steps at Adelsheim.

'I do not think . . .'

Suddenly he frowned. A thought had occurred. He looked at Anna Poppenstahl. 'Your relatives beyond the Rhine, madame. Do you have news of them?'

She blinked at the question. 'I have indeed. Although I fear their condition is a wretched one. My cousin Ludwig is well, but his state is much reduced by the war. The impositions of the French army are far heavier than any he had to endure from his former ruler. And his nephew Maximilian is not well, for he had high hopes of the Revolution when it began, and is much afflicted by how it has turned out . . .'

He listened, understanding that Madame Poppenstahl, although wishing him no particular ill-will, was determined to return the conversation to the ordinary polite gossip that was the only intimacy permissible with single young men such as him. And as he listened he tried hard not to betray that he already knew as much and more of Ludwig and Maximilian Jürich as she did. They would guess of course. Was this wise? He was not dicing with someone's honour, now, but with lives.

'Terrible!' he murmured. 'How you must wish to comfort them.'

'It is my earnest wish to visit them as soon as I may,' said the simple woman. 'When Lady Adelsheim is able to release me.'

'I see. But in the meantime are you able to correspond with your cousins, and perhaps send them little luxuries that they cannot now obtain in their territory?'

Madame Poppenstahl shook her head sadly.

'Letters may pass, although they may be opened. But not

goods, unless they are stoutly accompanied. I declare the soldiers will steal anything bigger than a thimble.'

'Indeed,' sighed Wéry.

Of course letters were opened. That did not worry him. No censor or spy would make anything of the communications he was thinking of – so long as their destination could be disguised.

Maria von Adelsheim was watching him very closely. Had she already guessed what he was going to propose?

'Well,' he said, and acted a light laugh. 'If by chance you should open your letters and find within them something that is not after all for you, perhaps you would forward it on to me?'

'Why, I do not know how . . .' began the woman dubiously.

'Anna . . .' said the girl, and laid her hand on her chaperon's arm.

She had not taken her eyes off Wéry's face. She was weighing his words. She would be wondering what these letters were, that somehow could not come to him directly: these letters for an "aide" to the Prince. And she must be able to make guesses. She had understood what he was asking.

'So, Captain. We make something of a devil's bargain, I think,' she said at last.

'A fearful city is full of devils,' said Wéry. 'Let us try to be honest devils with one another.'

'Maria!' said Poppenstahl, alarmed at last.

Maria von Adelsheim was still watching him. She was trying to read the future in his face. Now she must decide.

'How will they know that they may pass these packages to us?' she asked.

'The next time you write to the Jürichs, send a man you can trust. Let him use my name in the hearing of the household. It will be enough.'

It crossed his mind that if he were truly being an 'honest' devil, he should speak to them more about the dangers – the possibility that if something went wrong their man might be arrested, imprisoned, interrogated, executed. But it would not do to frighten them. It would not do to have Poppenstahl running to Lady Adelsheim about the wild plan into which her daughter was entering. So long as the courier knew no more than he had told them, and did no more than he had said, it should be well.

'And for my part,' he said, 'I vow to you that I will do my best to obtain what you want. If it proves impossible, then I think it is better that none of us remember what has passed between us.'

'I hope – and believe – that it will prove possible, Captain. And we will do as you ask. No, Anna, I am sure this is the right thing. We will tell Mother that a nameless gentleman has undertaken to provide the passport in a few weeks' time, when the clerks will be less conscientious about this decree. All that he requires is that we be discreet. It is the best that we can hope for.'

'Now, Captain,' she went on, with a sudden brightness in her tone. 'I wish to trespass a moment more upon your courtesy. Tell me, for I have been longing to know, how you find this city as a home from home?'

I wish to trespass a moment more. That meant: *After this topic I will leave.* She had begun the ritual politenesses of departure. He was sorry. He did not want her to go. Ordinarily he had little time for small talk. Now, in her presence, he wished that he could fascinate, sparkle, juggle a dozen witticisms and conjure back that delighted laughter, so that she might stay a little longer.

'I grow fond of it,' he said. 'It is more fortunate in its weather than Brussels or Paris. The people are kind, the ladies clever as well as beautiful . . .' This last was an attempt to win another smile from her, but she made no sign. '. . . In their dancing as well as their looks,' he stumbled on. 'At the Prince's ball early this summer I saw a dance performed by the ladies alone. It reminded me very much of my home in the countryside of Brabant, which was where I last saw such a thing. I hope we will see more of it this season.'

'Oh, you mean the Lightstep?' she asked.

'I believe that was its name here, yes. In Brabant it was one of the May dances. The country women dance it as a charm . . .' He broke off, realizing that it would probably not be delicate to say what the charm was supposed to do.

She was looking at him. There was a mischievous smile on her lips. 'That is strange,' she said. 'For so do we.'

His heart thumped. Anna Poppenstahl, loudly clearing her throat, might never have existed.

'And it is apt, is it not?' she went on. 'To play with a man, after all, is to play with fire.'

'So . . . so it is sometimes said. Although I have felt it apt in another way. A dance has moves. It is a process. The dancers turn this way, turn that, but the end is already determined. The end of a courtship is of course not determined, but there is nevertheless an inevitability about it. The partners are expected to surrender to one another. If they do not, the onlookers would say that the courtship had gone wrong.'

Her eyes watched him pick his way along the very fringes of the impermissible. Why had he not seen before how pale they were? (*Hey, Michel – have you ever looked at somebody?*) They were pale and blue and clear. And why had he thought her jaw too heavy? It was beautiful and full, curving to the throat. He was

185

beginning to blush. He knew it. 'Shall I . . .' he stammered. 'Er . . . Shall I see you dance it soon?'

Her eyes dropped at once. 'When I am out of mourning, of course.'

'Oh.' *Idiot! Damned idiot!* 'Of course. Forgive me.'

'There is nothing to forgive,' she sighed.

Her eyes strayed around the barrack room, recalling to her where she was, and why. 'Captain, you have been most kind . . .'

And now she was rising, and he was rising with her.

The women stopped in the door for Poppenstahl to rearrange Maria's cape. Poppenstahl bustled anxiously about her charge, as if by folding and patting the thing neatly enough into shape she might erase any trace of the conversation they had just had, with all its unfortunate trespasses. The girl exclaimed, 'It is all right, Anna. Really it is quite warm enough . . .' mingling amusement and exasperation. And Wéry remembered Albrecht's hand on his own shoulder, that first evening in Balcke's quarters, and his own voice gasping, '*I'm all right, I'm all right*' as he stood still dripping with Rhine water among the ring of officers.

He felt no resentment towards Poppenstahl. She was only doing her duty as she should. He could even be sorry, now, that he had become angry with her at all. There was no harm in the woman, and much good. The very clumsiness with which she had offered her bribe showed that. And whatever influence the mother had had in the education of the young Albrecht and Maria, it would not be to Lady Adelsheim that they owed whatever humanity they had learned in their childhoods.

He followed them to the doorway and stood there as they stepped out into the sunlight of the yard. And for an instant the girl looked back, and caught his eye. She was smiling as she dropped her veil.

I'm a fool, he thought.

A fool, he thought again, as he paced the room where she had spent all those minutes in his company. And he was a traitor, too, to all the men who counted him a comrade.

He did not feel foolish. He felt . . . *light*. Lucky, perhaps: as if some hope or opportunity had opened somewhere, even if he could not quite think what it was or why his circumstances could suddenly be so much more promising than they appeared to be. His mind grappled cheerfully with the impossibilities of extracting a passport for an enemy officer from the palace. And – heaven willing – he might even have solved the problem of communicating with the Rhineland. A devil's bargain. Yes, but a good one, surely . . .

Baron Altmantz put his head around the door, learned that it had been 'about her brother mostly' and left muttering, 'Yes, of course, a good man. Such a waste . . .'

At last Wéry made his way up to his office. It was a narrow room of bare and dusty boards. The walls were plain whitewash. There were two small windows, a fireplace and the doorway to an even smaller room where he slept. The only furniture was his desk, his chair, and the cabinet in which he kept his unimportant papers.

The only decoration was a painting of the head of Christ, in agony upon the cross. It was small, in a plain frame, but in that sparsely-furnished room with the white walls the image jumped forcefully to the eye of anyone who came in.

In coarse strokes the artist had shown a face twisted in horrible pain. The mouth hung open in a silent howl, missing teeth and dribbling a dark fluid. The eyes rolled, and the whites showed strongly whenever the light outside began to fail. Wéry did not need telling that the artist had seen death for himself, or knew what it was to suffer agony. It was stamped on the canvas for anyone to see.

He walked up to it and peered at it closely. The background showed a landscape, peopled with allegorical figures, none of which seemed at all remarkable beside the tormented head. He studied them carefully, but in vain. There was nothing there that he had not found already.

XIII
Ways and Means

The rustle of paper, the scratch of a pen, were loud in the Prince's antechamber at dawn.

'This is your promotion to Major,' said Bergesrode tersely, holding out a letter.

'Congratulations,' added Fernhausen.

Wéry raised an eyebrow. 'Promotion? For one report?'

Less than half the captains in the hussar regiment would ever reach the rank of Major. Those that did would mostly be in their forties.

'No,' said Bergesrode. 'It's because he likes officers who think more about what they do than about who they are. And we've too few.'

'Thank you.'

'Don't thank me. If you must thank anyone, thank yourself. He's had his eye on you for a while.'

Wéry took the letter, opened it, and glanced down the page. He was conscious of the two secretaries watching him, in the fading glow of their lamps and the growing light from the windows. He was conscious, too, of the silent, closed doors to the inner room where the Prince himself had his office. It was a strange feeling, to think that he could rise from his place, walk over and throw open the doors to reveal the man who had elevated him, there at his desk.

It would be perfectly possible. It was only a matter of will and muscle. He had heard that the walls and ceilings of the Prince's chamber were covered with a great *trompe l'œil* painting of Heaven. It was supposed to be famous. He was curious to see what it looked like, and what the Prince looked like too, heavy-eyed in the early morning with scattered papers before him.

And yet he could not do it. All the barriers of thought and habit and expectation, in his own mind and in those of the men before him, kept him fast in his chair, and his eyes on the paper before him.

The commission was lengthy, flowery, and as full of un-necessary words as Erzberg's army was of unnecessary officers. It did not make him feel any different.

'Thank you,' he said at length. 'I have just one question.'

'What is it?'

'Does a major in His Highness's service merit a clerk . . . ? No, it matters!' he insisted, reading the secretaries' expressions. 'I am spending too much time copying reports. It is keeping me from important work. And there must be someone to receive them and pass them on if I am occupied.'

'We have a hundred clerks,' sighed Fernhausen. 'The problem is to find the right one.'

The problem was to find a clerk who would work, who could understand what was important and yet would not blab about it, who would not drink or gamble. Anyone that good would be jealously guarded by the man he was already working for.

'I had thought, if we could not find the right man at once, that I might borrow one from the Office of the First Minister to begin with,' said Wéry gently. 'For one or two days a week, only. He could attend to his normal duties the rest of the time.'

The idea had come in the small hours of the night. Rather than try to persuade a man in Gianovi's office to give him a passport, why not persuade someone else to give him the man? Then the clerk could be in one office one day, in another the next, and no one would notice or care which papers he signed where. Only let him have a week to learn to know the fellow and then . . .

The two secretaries were looking at each other doubtfully. But they would rather pick a fight with the First Minister than part with one of their own.

'We'll do our best,' said Bergesrode.

'Thank you.'

If it did not work, he would have to try something else.

'I only said we would do our best. Now, important matters. What do you know about this coup in Paris?'

'Coup? Nothing at all. Has there been one?'

Bergesrode's mouth twitched in a rare sign of amusement. He enjoyed knowing more than his intelligence officer. 'The news came in overnight. A General Augereau took his troops into the city. Two of the Directory have been purged.'

'Have they! Which ones?'

'Barthélemy has been arrested. And Carnot has fled across the Rhine.'

'Has he!'

'Well? What does it mean?'

(What did it mean? It could mean a thousand things!)

'Are they more likely to attack us, or less?'

Wéry eased himself back in his chair. A coup by the army, against the Directors of France? In the past such news would have filled him with excitement. The fall of the Girondins he had thought would be the beginning of the end. Then Thermidor, and the fall of Robespierre – surely, this time, it would be the beginning of the end! But there had been so many twists and turns in France over the years. There was an awful stability in the way the Revolution devoured its leaders. He could no longer believe in a dawn that rose from Paris.

'Augereau is Bonaparte's man – or was, in Italy,' he mused.

'So?'

'It is hard to say. Yes, I suppose it makes an attack more likely.'

'Do not suppose. Find out! It's what we keep you for, isn't it?'

Bergesrode was glaring at him. Any congratulation in the priest's manner had vanished. They were back to the cold stare, the atmosphere of demand and urgency that surrounded the man like the air he breathed.

'I'll do my best,' said Wéry smoothly, borrowing Bergesrode's phrase from moments before. 'But . . . as you know, I came to talk about other matters.'

'About the Illuminati?'

Wéry shrugged. He was no more ready to talk about the Illuminati than he was to talk about coups. If the Prince's treasury could not afford the cost of an agent in Paris, he was damned if he was going to spend what it could afford on agents in Erzberg.

'About the defence of the city, principally.'

'Very well, tell me.'

'It is possible – with enough determination.'

'Tell me how.'

The priest's eyes betrayed not a wink of emotion as Wéry outlined the enormity of what must be done.

Lady Adelsheim, surrounded in the green satin of her dress that

192

spread widely upon the settee, broke off from her other conversation to stare at her daughter.

'Anna – to Mainz?' she repeated.

'She is much concerned, Mother,' said Maria humbly. 'It would be a kindness to let her go.'

'She has not spoken to me of it.'

Behind Lady Adelsheim, the poet Icht stood patiently at the fireplace, waiting for her attention to swing back to him.

'Of course she will not, Mother. You know Anna. And if we press her of course she will deny it. But it is plain, nonetheless. You yourself have remarked,' she went on, appealing with her eyes to Icht, 'how much she is anxious to visit her cousins, if only there were truly peace.'

'I recall it, my Lady,' said Icht dutifully.

'I recall it too,' said Lady Adelsheim. 'I was speaking with the Knight von Uhnen in this very room. My purpose was to expose the perfidy of the Emperor and the Prince concerning the status of the Rhineland. But that question is not settled yet. Besides, Maria, so long as you are here in Erzberg you must have a companion. You are too wilful, and too ready to forget you are in mourning.'

Her brow arched as she spoke, as if it were only too *pitifully* obvious that Maria was more interested in winning freedom for herself than in relieving Anna's concerns.

Maria dropped her eyes, feigning confusion.

'Icht?' said Mother, resuming her other conversation.

'Oh, I agree with you, my Lady. The chief fault of the Lutherans is that they do not admit private confession. Therefore they throw too much on the conscience of the individual.'

'Precisely what I said,' said Mother.

'Perhaps, then,' murmured Maria. 'Perhaps it would be best if I were to accompany Anna when she goes. I – would be willing to, Mother.'

'Really! Why this?'

'She is . . . dear to me. I knew I would miss her when she went.' Maria knew that she must talk as if it were absolutely settled that Anna should go and that the only question remaining was how Anna was to chaperon her at the same time. 'And it would keep me occupied, Mother.'

'I do not see how. There is almost no one left, west of the Rhine.'

Maria hesitated.

'I think there must be some people left, Mother,' she said. 'Indeed we know that Anna's cousins are there, and they cannot be the only ones!'

'You are impertinent, Maria. Of course I meant that there is no one of quality there – for the very good reason that they all seem to have fled to us! I do not doubt that Anna's cousins are honest enough, but they are not of our rank. In any case you will find little frivolity in the poor Rhineland at present. Although . . .' She put her head on one side and looked penetratingly at her daughter. 'Although for that reason it might be good for you, indeed. You are too wont to run simpering to the young men.'

'Indeed I do not think so, Mother!'

'Oh, you may say it. Perhaps you even believe it. But I saw you today at the levee, looking and looking among them. Whoever it was you were seeking was not there. Was it that man Wéry perhaps? Now he is Major Wéry, we understand! Really! So swift a promotion, one dreads to think what the man will yet become!

It was very improper of you to have called on him in his barracks, Maria, and thoughtless for the memory of Albrecht too.'

'Indeed, Mother, it is not true . . .'

(How had she known? Dear Virgin – how had she known?)

'Not true? I may sometimes be mistaken, but I do not think so.' And with that she turned back to Icht and in almost the same breath she said, 'Yet I do not see why confession must be made to a priest.'

'My Lady! Absolution is a sacrament and must be properly administered.'

'Indeed it must. But one does not need to be a member of the Guild of Ironworkers to have the *ability* to work iron. One needs to be a member only so that other members will permit one to do so. Why must one be a member of the priesthood to be able to hear confession? I am sure I could do as well as any of them.'

She looked back to Maria and lifted an inquiring eyebrow.

'Mother,' said Maria, rallying from her surprise. 'It is true that I accompanied Anna to the hussar barracks. You will recall that you asked Anna to obtain a passport for Major Lanard. And we did not know which way to turn . . .'

'Many women, and all men, may be led,' said her mother simply. 'Anna is no different. It would be a simple thing to speak of Wéry in such a way as to make her think she should go to him. That is plain. You are learning to direct others. It is what I expect of you . . .'

Johann, one of the footmen had entered softly. Lady Adelsheim waved him forward with one finger even as she continued speaking.

'. . . But the ends to which you manage them should not be your own gratification. We have serious business to attend to. This morning I am awaiting . . .' she examined the card that Johann produced for her. 'Löhm!' she cried. 'And behold, he is here.'

'He claims he has an appointment with you, my Lady.'

'Indeed he has,' said Lady Adelsheim. 'But he must wait a moment longer, while I find some papers. We have finished, Maria. You may go now.'

'Am I then to accompany Anna, mother?'

'I have not yet said that she should go. I do not see how your father could afford it at present. But yes, when she does, I believe you should.'

Maria found she was shaken – trembling, even – as she closed the door of her mother's study. How had Mother known about the visit to the barracks? Anna had promised she would not speak of it. Anna did not break her promises willingly, whatever misgivings she might have.

No, it would have come from the coachman or possibly gossip from someone acquainted with the hussars. But that she should have found out so quickly! Sometimes her ability to detect the thoughts of others was like witchcraft.

Tell me. Whom do you suppose that I may hate?

Yesterday Michel Wéry had looked her in the eye and talked of hatred. In that instant she had assumed he was talking of Mother. He had not been. Yet even so he too seemed to have read her thoughts. He had recognized in her something she had barely known herself, and had spoken to it. It had been strange, and awful.

Did she hate Balcke-Horneswerden? She supposed so. She could hate anyone who robbed her of Albrecht.

You did not love him as I did!

196

But she had not been defeated, this time. Not altogether. Mother had said that 'when' Anna went, Maria would go too. Of course Mother had not yet consented to think about when 'when' might be. She would make difficulties about money and such until she had decided for herself that it was necessary. And she would be suspicious if Maria approached her again. So Anna would have to be coaxed (and coached) into doing it. That would take time. Maria did not know how much time she had.

Because it would have to be Anna. There was no 'man she could trust' in the house. Not in her mother's house, with Mother sitting over them all like a great spider, eight-eyed and casting web after web until nothing could move without bringing her scuttling down the threads to pounce on whatever was going on. None of the servants were safe. The only person she could trust, and who could have a reason to go, was Anna. And because the journey might be difficult, and possibly dangerous despite the peace, Maria herself would have to go too. She could not let Anna go alone.

But how ridiculous of Mother to accuse her so! ('Simpering to the young men' indeed!)

Yes, she had been looking for someone at Lady Jenz's levee. Yes, it had in fact been Major Wéry she had been looking for. Now that she had realized that she herself must go to the Rhine, she needed to hear much more about whom she was going to and what the difficulties might be. Distances, documents, what to take and what to leave behind – she needed to know these things. Was this not good reason – even if one she could never confess to Mother?

And why should she not talk more with him about Alba and their adventures together? They had been close companions for four years – four years that had been lost to her when Alba had been away from home and which she could now never recover. All the things they had done, like the tale of the dancing bear – had there been anything more like that? What else could he have told her?

Why had he not been there? Did he never attend levees or balls at all? If he did not, their meetings would be few indeed.

She felt her heart sink at the thought.

But then, all the more reason to make the most of what meetings there might be. And never mind what Mother said of it afterwards! She remembered his eyes on her, in that shabby barracks room where the light had fallen sideways upon his face and left half of it in darkness. She thought how he had glared when Anna had offered her bribe. He had dismissed it without hesitation. He had not even stopped to calculate what kind of bribe the meagre purses of Adelsheim could have afforded him. As an émigré and a revolutionary, probably he had no money at all.

Handsome? No, he was not handsome, but who cared for that? So much the better for him. Good looks always seemed to make men idiots, just as money only made them feckless. Nor did he have 'quality' as mother reckoned it – four quarterings or more. But he had a quality of his own, strange and angry, like a black vulture that had alighted on a branch as she passed, and through some wild magic had spoken to her. She saw that very clearly.

With a new firmness in her step now, she went in search of Anna.

XIV
Vulture

Wéry was twenty leagues from Erzberg, in a land still devastated from the war. He sat on his horse in the ruins of a great half-timbered farmhouse. Barn and byre and house had all been one building, as imposing as a moderate church, rising for four storeys within the great pitched roof. But the roof had fallen in fire, leaving blackened stumps of rafters naked to the air. The byre had collapsed altogether, and most of the end-wall with it. Weeds and brambles grew among the wreckage.

From this hiding-place Wéry looked out to a far hill-top, crowned with a wood. In the fields below the wood a group of peasants, tiny with the distance, were hand-pulling a plough through the soil. They would be hand-pulling it because there were no oxen left here, no mules or donkeys and certainly no horses. Anything so useful had been lost a year or more ago. Now, months after the peace, there was still not the money to replace them. So the peasants harnessed their wives and children to the plough, and scratched as best they could in the sparse greens of the fallow.

Twice in the last few years French armies had advanced this way from the Rhine, and twice retreated. And as they had passed they had taken the beasts from the field, food and possessions from the villagers, even the timbers from the barns. Waters still ran here, birds sang and trees grew, but in all other senses it was desert, dotted with the skeletons of buildings and hamlets where half the huts were empty.

Wéry was watching for news that they would come for a third time.

There was a new regime in Paris. Directors had been expelled, royalist sympathizers purged. Was there a change of French plans for Erzberg? No one knew.

And Hoche was dead, suddenly, of some sickness. There was to be another commander in Germany now. Again, what did it mean? Erzberg seethed with war rumours. Canons argued with the Prince in the cathedral chapter. Bergesrode fumed and demanded answers that Wéry could not give him. And away beyond that hill-top where the human plough-team laboured was the road to Wetzlar, headquarters of a French army tens of thousands strong.

Wéry waited. He was not expecting to see the heads of enemy columns yet. Not yet, even though the French when they moved could move faster than many an opposing general thought possible. There would be some sign first – some news or rumour or fact that would warn him they were about to march. That was what he was waiting for.

On the far side of the valley, a brightly-coloured cart was trundling slowly down the line of a track that dropped from the wood to the valley floor.

It was a curious sight, on this grieving landscape. The side-panels were painted a light blue, outlined in yellow, and covered (Wéry knew, although he could not see them from this distance) with lively figures of flowers and trumpeters and gypsy girls. It had a brash, unforced cheerfulness, which seemed to shout that from now on everything was going to get better and better, and soon there would be prosperity again.

Curious, but Wéry had been expecting it. He knew that a certain pedlar, Tomas Kranz, worked along these roads, into and out of Giessen, into and out of Wetzlar. Kranz painted his cart in bright colours so that he could be seen from far off by anyone who had a little money, and who might drop what they were doing to come and pick over the goods that he carried. Wéry saw him now and waited for him. There was a purse at his waist for Tomas Kranz, and also a bottle of brandy in his saddlebags. Kranz liked brandy. And he should be carrying more than pans and leather straps today.

He should be carrying news: facts, gossip, maybe columns of figures, written on scraps of paper and disguised as some random act of book-keeping. He should be carrying all the bits and pieces that he and others had managed to gather from their perilous associations with the French occupiers. It might be a mass of contradictory information, meaningless without other clues that Kranz and his fellows had been unable to hit upon. It might all point in one direction. Or, buried among it, in some drunken officer's tittle-tattle, there might be some gem that would make sense of all the hints and rumours that had reached Erzberg so far.

Soon he would know.

But as his eye followed the slow progress of the cart down the hill, Wéry felt a sense of detachment. Soon he would speak with Kranz, but not yet. In the meantime the French, Bergesrode and his demands, Kranz and his answers – there was nothing to be done about any of them. They were like a great, thick coat of thoughts, which he had worn for a long time and which, at the moment of seeing the cart, he had understood at last were not part of his skin. He could peel them off, if he chose, and lay them aside. He could put on other thoughts that lay waiting in the cupboards of his mind. Watching that blue-and-yellow cart as it lumped and rocked its way to the ford, he could actually wish that it were not after all a cart, carrying a brave, cross-grained, self-pleased, snuffling little man, but that instead it would be the carriage of a lady. And that it would draw up on the roadside by the barn where he waited and Maria von Adelsheim would lean from the window and call to him.

And they could walk together by the stream down there, with the chaperon a good distance back, and talk together. They could talk for hours. (Heavens, what would he say? What could he say of himself that might interest her? But surely he would think of something.)

It was a bittersweet thought, because he knew it was impossible. There was no chance that he might be permitted to meet her, except in some great ballroom where all officers were commanded to attend, and where a thousand eyes would be watching who met with whom, and for how long. And yet he preferred to play with it, as if it were a candle-flame – even to burn himself with it a little, rather than to consign it to nothingness. He wondered, if the idea about the packages worked, whether he might pass his own letters to her along with those that went and came from the Rhine. But the woman Poppenstahl would surely be alert for that (she might be simple, but she could not be *that* simple). And even if letters could reach the hand he intended them for, what could they say? And what would she think?

Hopeless, of course. Quite hopeless. And if he did not shake off these thoughts soon they would simply torture him.

Still, he was not sorry to be thinking them.

The cart was moving slowly. It had come perhaps a third of the way down the slope. The plough-team was moving even more slowly. The increase of the patch of tilled earth, the diminishing of the fallow, was all but imperceptible.

There was plenty of time to dream.

Then another movement caught Wéry's eye.

A party of horsemen had appeared where the road emerged from the far wood. He could not see how many there were. Nor could he see their uniforms, because in this cold, wet autumn all soldiers wore coats or cloaks, and all coats or cloaks swiftly became a muddy grey or brown.

But he did not have to see their uniforms – not here, within a few leagues of Wetzlar. He leaned forward in his saddle, feeling a cold prickling at his wrists and throat. He swore softly.

Enemy!

The horsemen came on down the road. They seemed in no hurry but they made up ground easily on the slow-moving cart. The cart did not change its pace. Kranz might not know they were behind him. Or maybe he did know, but knew also that the very worst thing he could do would be to attempt flight. He could not out-distance them. He would be carrying papers, letters from French unit commanders, permitting him to do his trade in their lines. He would have to rely on those, and hope that the patrol had some other reason to be out here.

Wéry watched, helpless. The horsemen closed up on the cart. From this distance, he could hear nothing. But all at once, and without fuss, the cart had stopped, a couple of hundred yards short of the stream. The horsemen surrounded it. There would be questions now. Kranz would be producing papers. He might even be starting his salesman's patter – *belts and buckles, Captain. Belts and buckles and handkerchiefs, and there's no soldier alive who has too many of those. See for yourself. I only carry the best. Silks, Citizens? Presents for the girls? Take them to the house of Madame Herder in Giessen and say I sent you* . . . Kranz was good. He'd delight in earning a coin or two from the French, under the very nose of his spymaster. He . . .

A small puff of smoke sprouted among the men and horses. Wéry did not hear the shot.

Nothing seemed to happen for a few moments.

Then, lazily, the cart turned in its tracks. It began to make its way uphill, even more slowly than it had descended. The horsemen gathered behind it and followed. Maybe they were laughing to one another. Wéry thought there was now a man standing in the back of the cart, picking over Kranz's bales and stores as the little caravan went bump, bump, bump back up towards the ridge from which they had all emerged.

In the field, the people at the plough had halted. Two of them stood, gazing down at the road. Two others sat in the furrows, glad of any chance for a rest. But the ploughman himself was running downhill, across the fallow, to the roadside where the cart had been halted. Screwing up his eyes, Wéry thought he could see something lying there. At this distance, it only looked like a small pile of rags.

And that was all Kranz would be now.

Wéry swore savagely.

He swore because he had lost a man, a good and lucky man, who suddenly had not been good or lucky enough.

He swore because he had lost the information – all that information! All the answers he had been hoping for! And he had

had to watch it happen! (Damn it – he had been sitting here day-dreaming while they came and stole his man's life from under his nose! If he had been alert, perhaps . . .)

He swore because he did not *know*. He did not know whether what he had seen was a casual murder, for the sake of the purse and a cartload of goods, a score settled by men who thought they had been cheated, or an assassination of a man known by the French to be a spy.

And if they had known he was a spy, what else did they know? What about the other agents – were they safe? Who had betrayed Kranz? What else had been betrayed?

And what was he to do?

You must not go into French-held territory, Bergesrode had said. Up here in Nassau, "French-held territory" was wherever the French went. And the French went where they liked. The danger grew the nearer he came to Wetzlar. And it would double if the French were breaking his ring as he sat here.

The best thing to do – the wise thing to do – would be to lie low, wait nearby, and see who got out.

But he could not sit still! However sensible it might be, it was not the way he was made. There were men over there who might be warned. They had information – possibly vital information – that he needed. Kranz might have been carrying something on his body. Had the soldiers searched it? Had they found something, and recognized it for what it was?

There must be no dreaming now. No distractions. He had been dreaming a moment ago and the enemy had punished him for it. Now he must catch up.

He watched the soldiers disappear into the distant trees. Then he urged his mount towards the doors of the barn that concealed him. Just before he emerged from hiding, he held the horse back for a moment. That cold pricking was running up and down his wrists again. He could feel his own pulse beginning to drum the beats of action.

The soldiers could not have known he was here. If they had known, they would simply have delayed their pounce, to catch him as well.

But they might suspect that Kranz had been due to meet someone. Eyes might well be watching now, from the cover of the far wood, to see if anyone else came to the body.

He swallowed. He studied the line of trees carefully. Nothing showed. But of course, if they suspected something, nothing would be allowed to show.

After a little thought, he turned his horse again, and made his way out to the back of the barn.

He was still going to cross over. He was going to find his agents, if they were alive. And first, he would go to the body. But he would come at it the long way round, so that he might see any watchers before they saw him.

He was going to circle.

XV
The Gathering

On an evening in early October, Lady Adelsheim stood in black in the house in the Saint Emil quarter. 'So, sir,' she cried. 'His Highness now supposes that he might be a general himself. Is it true?'

The gaunt Knight von Uhnen, a member of the War Commission and Colonel-Inspector of Militia, bowed and kissed her hand. 'It is true that he pays more attention to the army than is generally realized,' he said.

'Then I declare I am mad,' said Lady Adelsheim. 'For one of us must be, and I am sure that it could not be His Highness.'

'Ha, ha, my Lady,' said the Knight, and presented the young man beside him. 'You know my son, of course.'

'Of course. Why, Karl, how handsome you look tonight. How very dashing.'

Instead of his hussar uniform, Karl von Uhnen was wearing a suit of a modern French cut, in buff and blue. His hair was unpowdered and tied in a queue. It was a calculated, casual look, as if he were still in the country rather than on the fringes of the court. With his clothes and youth he stood out sharply among the small array of embroidered gentlemen in their wigs and silk breeches who posed for the attention of the ladies in the room.

'Oh, this fashion is very well, very well,' the older Uhnen said.

'Not a creature under fifty will wear anything else, I hear. But for that reason I am exempt, you see.' With another bow he made his way past her into the high and gilded drawing room where the Knight August von Adelsheim, arrayed in his majestic velvet doublet and decked out in his great wig, had been placed on a settee near the fire.

Maria sat beside her father. She kept her hand on his arm to remind him that she was there with him, and also that he was where he was supposed to be and should not start wandering around while the guests gathered. She saw the Knight von Uhnen approach. Beyond him yet more faces were appearing in the doorway – Baron von und zu Löhm, and a friend, she thought.

'My dear August,' said the Knight von Uhnen. 'It is good to see you in health.'

He bowed his head as he spoke. He had wealth, wit, influence – many things that Father had not. Like Father, Uhnen had 'immediacy': he had no lord but the Emperor himself. But Father had the sixteen quarterings on his coat of arms, and so the Knight's tone bestowed the respect that was due. Father mumbled something in reply. He gave the Knight his hand, but did not look up.

The Knight peered down at his host, waiting to see if there would be some further acknowledgement. When there was not, he said, 'My dear,' to Maria, bending briefly over her hand, and passed on with the glassy smile of a man who had escaped without embarrassment from the company of the exalted but unfortunate Adelsheim.

'. . . Now, cousin,' cried Lady Adelsheim at the door. 'You owe me your wig, sir. Where is it?'

His Excellency the Canon Rother-Konisrat was a tall man,

with the face and figure of a plump crane. He wore soft pinks and greys, and bowed low to his female cousin as if he were not, after all, one of the most important men in Erzberg.

'Pardon me, dear Constanze,' he said mildly. 'But for the time being I believe I still have a use for it.'

'No, sir, this I will not have! This man,' she said, addressing a wider group, 'having failed to obtain for me a passport for my Frenchman, staked his wig that I could do no better. And lo! With a flick of my fingers, it is done. Now I shall have his wig for my wall too.'

'It has come, has it?'

'It was in my hands at noon today. Your wig, sir, or you shall be a knave.'

'If you will permit it to me to cover my embarrassment tonight,' said the Canon with another bow, 'I shall send it to you in the morning.'

Anna Poppenstahl was sitting by herself against the wall, with a drawn look on her face. Anyone who saw her, thought Maria, would know at once that it had taken something more than a flick of Mother's fingers to have the passport delivered anonymously to their door. (Why had she ever allowed poor Anna to be involved in this?) But no one seemed to notice. Mother was convinced that, whatever Anna and Maria had done, and whoever they had gone to, the precious passport had come entirely because she herself had said that it should. And her conviction was so strong that it carried the room – Canon Rother included. They fawned on her in her triumph.

'The master-stroke was to find the Frenchman at all,' said the Baron von und zu Löhm. 'Who would have thought it possible?'

'Baron, you know I have looked for understanding all my life.

209

And it is to be found in the most unexpected places. It was obvious to me that lies were being told about Hersheim. To confront lies, you need witnesses. I simply asked myself, if all *our* officers were suborned, where else might a witness be found? And now he will come to Erzberg, whatever His Highness's creatures think.'

'You have routed them all, my Lady.'

'I knew that I would.'

'I am agog to see him,' said the Knight von Uhnen, rejoining the central group. 'A genuine revolutionary! Is it true that he addressed you as "Citizen", my Lady? Will he parade up the Saint Simeon in a liberty cap and bare feet, do you think?'

'I judge him to be as gallant a gentleman as his station allows,' said Lady Adelsheim. 'And that when we are more acquainted with him we will all see how great a folly this war has been.'

'Indeed, indeed,' murmured the gallant gentlemen in the room, every one of whom, Maria thought, had fled like startled pigeons each time Captain Lanard and his comrades had marched east from the Rhine.

Karl von Uhnen managed to prise himself free from two of the ladies, who had been quizzing him on his dress, and made his way over to Maria's settee.

'I am delighted to see you, sir,' he said, taking Father's hand. 'I hope it is well with you.'

Father said something indistinct, but again he did not look up. Maria spied a dribble from his mouth cutting a track through the powder on his chin. She leaned across and patted it dry with a handkerchief, trying to disguise the damage.

'Lady Maria?' said Karl von Uhnen to her, with a slight bow.

'Of course,' she said, and gave him her hand.

He settled himself on a stool on her other side.

There was the slightest awkwardness in his manner. Apart from greetings exchanged in passing, and his formal condolences for Albrecht's death, they had barely spoken in a year. The memory of that awful scene in the orangery at Effenpanz still lingered between them. '*Sir, you force me to remind you of certain facts . . .*'

Nevertheless she had been hoping that he would come, and not only because he could be pleasant company when circumstances were right. There was a further reason why she needed him this evening.

'I admire your suit, sir,' she said, falling into the light, teasing tones of mannered conversation. 'Did you don it to attract some poor woman's attention?'

'If I must be a rebel, I shall be one in my own way. But really, it is very comfortable. I think I shall dispense with this queue, and let my hair fall to the collar like a true revolutionary.'

'You should! You would be a sensation. And it will give the town something to talk about, other than sickening itself with war and politics.'

'Indeed. Although I suspect this company has stomach to sicken itself some more.' He was looking around the room. Löhm, Jenz-Hohenwitz, Machting-Altstein-Borckstein – almost every notable present was identified with the peace party in Erzberg. There was not one senior officer, not one escapee from the occupied territories, nor was there anyone remotely connected with the Ingolstadt set. Two groups had formed, one speaking in low voices around Canon Rother, a few feet away. Another surrounded Mother on the far side of the room.

'Kant?' exclaimed Mother. 'I am *most* disappointed. A man with many gifts, but his perceptions are too narrow. No, sir. I have

211

read his writings eagerly, following like a disciple wherever he led. I have declared his critiques to be genius. I have even tutored my own daughter in them. And then what? I find he would discourage the interest of women in things of the mind! It is base treachery, sir, and you cannot defend him!'

'On the contrary,' cried a jovial voice. 'I shall now defend him with my life!'

'What, sir? This, in my house?'

'My Lady. If we men are not to have the exclusive advantage of education, however would we remain *your* equal?'

'Aha! Ha-ha!' cried other men around the pair.

'. . . Erzberg to suffer as Frankfurt and Mainz suffered,' Canon Rother was saying. 'Bombardment! Can you imagine? Only perhaps for us it would be worse.'

'It *must* be avoided.' said someone else. 'It is madness to put one spoiled godchild above the wellbeing of a city . . .'

Karl von Uhnen bent to whisper in her ear. 'A very distinct gathering,' he breathed. 'I wonder that even we were included.'

'I believe my mother feels you are kindred spirits, or should be.'

He shrugged. 'Maybe, maybe not. Father is a strange old dog. I don't think he'll sit up to beg for anyone. I had thought we were to hear music, not talk politics.'

'You shall certainly hear music, sir. Mother has obtained a new quartet by Haydn, which Meister Holz and his fellows will perform for us after dinner.'

'But this is excellent! A new Haydn, did you say?'

'I understand it has not been performed in Erzberg before this. However, I am sure there will be politics too. I believe Löhm in particular has some notions he wishes to introduce to the gentlemen.'

'Oh Merciful Muses!'

'. . . Let me enter the lists on education,' cried Baron Löhm. '*Atque inter silvas Academi quaerere verum.* Education, I hold, should promote virtue over vice everywhere. It must be our goal to replace the politics of self-interest and self-advancement with Education. And there is no better education than the personal instruction of those who are themselves men of virtue. I say "men" of virtue, my Lady,' he added, bowing. 'But for example only. Of course the same could be achieved among women, if any could be found to follow your lead. And maybe you have already begun, with your daughter and others?'

'Quite, Baron,' said Mother dryly. 'But perhaps this is the moment for you to introduce your guest more widely.'

'Gentlemen – and ladies,' said the Baron. 'This is Doctor Heinrich Sorge, who is secretary of the "Heribert" Reading Club in Nuremberg. He is a man of great understanding. I have had the benefit of a long correspondence with him over the years, and I know of no better mind in Germany – save yours, my Lady,' he added as an afterthought.

Doctor Sorge was a small man, almost a twin of the Baron for height. But whereas the Baron, in his white wig and dark embroidered velvet, looked almost as round as he was tall, Sorge was thin in face and mouth and body. His suit was plain brown, such as a merchant or university professor might wear to Holy Mass on a Sunday. He shifted a little and pursed his lips while all the company stared at him.

'Doctor Sorge has come to educate us,' said Lady Adelsheim. 'He has a very special understanding of worldly government.'

'My Lady,' said Sorge, in clipped tones. 'I did explain to the Baron that the size of the company would limit what I might be able to reveal . . .'

213

'Of course. But you should have no fear of us. Dietrich – the doors.'

The house servants flung open the double doors that led into the next room. Chairs were arranged in a rough circle before the hearth there.

'If the gentlemen would follow me,' said Canon Rother.

Every man in the room, except for Maria's father and the younger Uhnen, trooped through. Maria noticed that Doctor Sorge hung to the rear of the group, and she was close enough to hear him say to the Baron, 'It would be better if the servants are not admitted.'

'As well part cripples from their sticks,' murmured the Baron. 'But this house is safe, do not worry.'

'Who was that curious fellow?' said Karl von Uhnen, who had kept his seat despite the invitation.

'A doctor from Nuremberg, I believe,' said Maria off-handedly. She had her own guesses about the sort of man that Löhm might wish to introduce to his friends. The Baron was notorious for his dabblings in freemasonry and other such societies. But she knew, too, that in Erzberg it was best not to let the tongue wag too much about such things. 'I expect he has some very wise ideas to propose. Will you not join them?'

'I don't think I shall,' said Karl von Uhnen, after a show of indecision. 'It's certain to be dull. What was that about cripples indeed? Hasn't Löhm as many servants as any of us?'

'His heart may lean after his words,' said Maria with a smile. 'But indeed it is far ahead of his habits. Now you must forgive me.'

She rose to her feet, for now she was hostess to those who remained.

Three women were left in the room – wives who had accompanied their husbands to the gathering. Maria approached and respectfully suggested a table of cards.

'Why,' cried the Lady Jenz-Hohenwitz, looking sharply around. 'Is Lady Adelsheim not to be with us?'

'She will return in a very short time, I am sure,' said Maria, with the most charming smile she could contrive. Of course Mother had slipped out to join the men in their discussions, and would neither rejoin the ladies nor care what they thought of it.

'Well! I think it is very bad of her!'

'Oh come, my dear,' said Lady Machting-Altstein-Borckstein, sallying to the rescue. 'We all know our dear Constanze. Let us not embarrass the poor girl. Cards would be very pleasant, I believe.'

Lady Jenz declared once again that it was very bad. Nevertheless she allowed herself to be manoeuvred to a card table, with an ill grace. She must have suspected all along that her hostess would abandon her that evening. No doubt she would have liked to break with convention herself, but she knew – and perhaps this was what truly rankled with her – that she had neither the wit nor the character to imitate Lady Adelsheim without seeming ridiculous.

To be truly free, Maria thought, one must free oneself early, and live so ever after. There was no hope now for Lady Jenz, who had ambled placidly within the hedges of convention all her life.

Maria should have taken the fourth hand herself. It would have been proper. But instead she summoned Anna to the table with her eyes, and partnered her with the good-humoured Lady Machting. Father was still on the settee, Karl von Uhnen on the stool, and the space that she had abandoned lay between them. When she looked more closely she realized that Father was asleep. So for the moment she was indeed free – at least within the confines of the drawing room. She could entertain herself as she chose. And she chose her entertainment with a purpose.

Karl was craning round at the double doors. He must be wondering what was brewing in there. He looked back and raised an eyebrow at her.

'Perhaps you, too, would enjoy a hand of cards, sir?' she asked.

'Gladly,' he said.

'We are watching, you two love-birds,' said Lady Machting, from her seat at the card table. 'You must behave yourselves!'

Karl frowned. Maria smiled. She meant her smile as a challenge. She did not want Karl to follow the other men. He could be pleasant company for her. But better still, he had a convenient habit of playing for high stakes.

She signed to Dietrich for another table and pack. They came, with the automatic efficiency of a cripple's stick clicking into place to support another stride. She settled to her place.

'A gulden to a point?' she suggested.

'That makes it worth the play,' he agreed.

The room had fallen quiet. Beyond the double doors a voice was speaking, but in tones so low that there was no hope of hearing what was said. Cards were already flicking to and fro on the other table. She returned her attention to the young man opposite her. She would start by shocking him a little.

'I am to go to Mainz next week,' she said.

'Are you!'

'Indeed. And beyond it into the occupied territory. Anna is visiting her cousins there.'

She had allowed Mother to exult over the passport for an hour. Then she had sent Anna in to see her, equipped with the latest letter from the Jürichs. In less than five minutes Lady Adelsheim had given her consent. House servants who had scurried to prepare these rooms today, would be scurrying to engage a coach, horses, additional trunks and travelling gear tomorrow.

Provided that there was money. Not even in her triumph had Mother slackened her grip on the purse. Funds for the journey must come from Anna's and Maria's allowances. These were not adequate, whatever Mother might think. And Maria knew that if she went begging to Mother for money now she would only risk having the precious consent withdrawn again. There would have to be another way.

A gulden a point . . .

She must not think about losing.

'This is — most adventurous!'

'I own that I am more nervous than I expected.'

'I must say that I wonder whether it is wise.'

She looked at him sharply.

He shrugged. 'Oh! No, I meant only that the Emperor has not yet concluded his peace with France. The fate of the Rhineland is not yet clear. Anything may yet happen.'

'That is no concern of ours,' she said firmly.

'Mainz . . . From all I have heard, I am glad I had no part in that affair.'

Affair? thought Maria.

Oh, he meant the siege. Why was everyone so obsessed with sieges at the moment? Come, Karl. You should pay attention to *me*, now, since I have been so good as to put myself in your way for the evening!

His eyes had swung to the window. From the street below came the sounds of a cart passing. Voices called cheerfully, with words that did not quite carry. The sounds reminded Maria how many people there were in the houses around her. And beyond this street there were a hundred others in Erzberg, where people passed and called and dined in their houses while the dusk grew outside: people, people all around them, and every one of them striving, like her, to love, laugh, live and be a little bit free. And still Karl stared at the window, as if he thought to see a cannon-ball crashing inward in a cloud of dust and plaster.

And rumours thickened around the presence of d'Erles and the other émigrés. The men talked of sieges. Mother's criticism of the Prince just now had been far louder and sharper than ever before. Then they all retreated to inner rooms and spoke behind closed doors.

She suppressed her thoughts, and waited.

At last Karl looked back, and with a smile he said, 'Nevertheless, a siege may be instructive.'

'How so?'

'Why, it shows that if you are persistent in the pursuit of your objective, in the end you may be met with surrender.' And he smiled more broadly at her.

(So, he was bold now! But this was better than gloom. She had business to do here. And she would use every advantage she could to get what she needed.)

'Surrender?' she responded, lingering on the word. 'Why do you insist upon surrender? Will you not treat with your foe upon even terms?'

'That depends on whether the objective may be so obtained. But the greater the prize, the greater you must expect the struggle to be. I think of Troy, with the beautiful Helen as the reward . . .'

'I believe it is your lead, sir,' she said brightly.

A gulden a point was enough to keep their minds on the play. But while he was reckoning the score she teased him by looking away across the room, allowing him to throw glance after glance at her in a vain effort to catch her eye.

He held out the cards to her. His fingers lay upon them in such a way that she might, if she wished, brush them with hers as she took the pack from him. And she looked at them for a moment, with her head cocked on one side, and then carefully took them without touching him, but with an air that said that *next* time, perhaps, she might choose to do so.

She dealt. She gathered her cards and studied them. It was a difficult hand.

There was nothing she could discard without risk. And yet she must discard. The diamonds were the least likely to help her. They must go. After that, what?

Resolutely she threw away her hearts and drew five more cards. Her hand was a cloud of the black suits. Very well.

'I have a point of six,' she said.

'Good,' came the reply.

Nothing else was good. Not her tierce, not her three queens. Both were overpowered by his hand. Then, when it came to the tricks, she made only her six clubs and the ace of spades. After that his red suits swept her hand away. The score was nearly even, but she should have done better. Now it was his turn to have the advantage.

'My heart suit conquered,' he said. 'I am encouraged.'

'You should not be,' she murmured.

'If a man's hearts are true in his hand, then perhaps the heart in his breast is true also. I wonder if it is the same with a woman. Or do they always prefer the diamonds?'

She frowned.

'Sir, my suits were black,' she said.

'But they will not be so forever.'

'Sir,' she said, quite sharply. 'I shall play as I wish.'

And cut, and deal. And declare, play, and then there would be more banter. Card-play was like a dance. It had the same inevitability. Both went through prescribed figures, turn in, turn out . . . Who was it who had said to her that a dance was like a courtship? It was apt. Although she remembered that the dance they had been speaking of was the Lightstep. In the Lightstep there was no partner, only a candle – an undisclosed hope in the hand. Now she remembered who it had been: Michel Wéry.

Something in her heart kicked at the thought.

Something kicked, and she saw that she was in chains. She might dream of travels, or of handsome young men. She might even dream, as suddenly she longed to, of someone low-born, unpolished and deadly, who dealt in secret things and would deal with her. Yet after every night's dreaming she would wake to find herself the possession of a fine house, able to come and go only at the behest of others, and destined to be wed to poor, pathetic cousin Julius. She might win little victories in her drawing room, but she was no more free to move outside it than a dancer was free to alter the dance.

And she was not winning. She knew she was the better player, and that in the long run she would come out ahead of Karl. But the game turned on luck and now, just when she needed it, the luck was not good. The hands held no promise. She must throw away cards that were valuable and the cards she drew were not the ones she wanted. The score was mounting. The Rhine was getting further away. And still she smiled brightly and flashed her eyes at him and kept up the little bouts of banter, while she waited for the luck to change.

Another hand ended. She looked up. She saw Karl watching her. And she saw what she was doing to him.

His mild brown eyes were fixed on her. They were pleading with her, just as they had last summer in the orangery at Effenpanz when he had gone down on his knees to her on the blue-and-white tiled floor. '*You must allow me to say this . . . I adore you, Maria. I cannot think of anything else. Sometimes I do not even remember to eat . . .*' It had been painful to hear him. It was painful to see him now. His feelings had not changed. Why in Heaven had she expected them to? And because she was flirting with him, he was beginning to hope once more. In a moment, in a murmur, he would tell her so.

Oh, there would be no need to approach Mother to fund her losses to Karl. (Losses! There, she had thought it now. Adieu, the Rhine!) He would allow her all the time she asked for to pay her debt. He would never mention it. He would carry it all his life, if she allowed it, and absolve her of it on his deathbed. It would always be there between them, like the words she had spoken at Effenpanz. And in his eyes the nobility with which he endured it would only strengthen his right to her. It would be a reproach to her, a final, unanswerable argument why she should turn to him at last.

How could she have been so blind?

He had caught her look. He was leaning forward. She dropped her eyes.

'May I say something?' he said, in a low voice.

'Not yet,' she said, holding up her hand and looking hard at her cards.

A weak pretence. She had won herself only seconds. In an instant she must look up again, and he would speak.

And then rescue came. Father woke on the settee. He heaved himself upright and looked around, making a slight grumbling noise in his throat like a sleepy, embroidered bear. His eyes wandered dully around the room, absorbing the lights, the servants, the party of women. He had no memory of the gathering. He was wondering what they were all doing here.

He saw her, and his face split into a beam of childish pleasure.

It warmed her like the sun, that smile. It told her, whatever she did and whoever she disappointed, that the biggest, kindest and most important man left in her life loved her, and was pleased that she was near.

Then he saw what she was doing.

'Cards!' he said.

'It is piquet, Father,' she said. 'Do you wish to play? If so, you must take my hand. I am losing; you must come to my aid.'

Karl von Uhnen looked startled. She smiled a hostess's smile that fixed him in his seat, and rose smoothly to let her father lever himself into her place.

'The gentleman is a very good player, Father,' she murmured.

'Is he? So, so. My major?'

'You are minor, father. And the gentleman approaches his hundred.'

'Ah.'

Dutifully, Karl picked up his cards. If the woman he adored

required him to play with her demented father, then he would play, whatever came of it. She saw him glance across, and register that the old gentleman could at least still hold his hand straight. Then he looked up expectantly at her, standing behind her father's chair. Perhaps he thought she would give the old man hints. She would do nothing of the kind.

It only needed the luck to change. If it was set on dogging Maria all evening, might it not smile on Father instead? Of course there was no reason why it should. But Luck and Reason were enemies after all . . .

Karl exchanged only four cards. Father took the remaining four. They went through the declarations, Father rumbling his answers, 'Not good . . . Good . . . Not good . . .' and proceeded to the play. Maria watched Karl's face as the tricks fell. She saw him understand that, addled or not, there was still a part of his host's mind that knew the game.

Indeed he knew. He brooded over his cards like Jove looking down from Olympus. His eyes never left them, even when he spoke. His big fingers moved as if of their own will, playing the cards *flick, flick, flick* with barely a pause between. And his score lengthened, and the tricks lined up before him. Maria let her fingers rest upon his shoulder, and watched.

And she loved him. She loved to see him like this, with his mind ruling the things that it could still rule. He had woken when she needed him, like some ancient knight from an enchanted sleep in a cave. And although so much had been lost, and so much had turned to bitterness, he was still her champion – a champion she had almost forgotten – ready to rise and do battle for her in a world that was altogether changed.

An hour later Uhnen's face was white. He had won just one

game to Father's five. His fingers shook slightly as he added up the score. At a gulden a point, that made . . .

In the room beyond the double doors a muffled chatter arose. A chair was pushed back. Someone in there laughed – a high, giggling sound.

'Father,' Maria said, putting her hand under his arm. 'They are coming out. We must be ready to lead them into dinner.'

Father rose laboriously to his feet. Karl rose too. 'This has been – most instructive,' he said, with a rueful look at the score. 'I fear I must give you a note in hand for this, sir. But I shall gladly bring it tomorrow . . .'

'You may bring it to me,' murmured Maria. She did not feel triumphant. If anything she felt a little ashamed. But she had her drawing-room victory. Now the orders would indeed be given, the servants would scurry, the wheels of a carriage would roll, because the Uhnen family would bear the costs of her trip to the Rhine.

Karl leaned forward and spoke in a low voice. 'I shall do that gladly. And perhaps when I come, I may be permitted some time to speak with you alone?'

There was an earnest look in his eyes. Her heart sank.

'That may depend upon what you wish to say,' she said, so softly that he could barely have heard her.

He hesitated. 'I must speak as my heart dictates,' he said.

'And so must I. But I can offer you no change.'

His jaw tightened. Abruptly he looked at his shoes.

Father had already forgotten the game. His eyes were roving the room. He was seeing it all again as new – the ladies, the lights, the footmen, the sudden crowd of brightly-clad gentlemen now debouching through the double doors into the room, chattering and tittering at their own wit. He looked lost, lost in his own house.

'Are we going down, boy?' he asked suddenly, speaking from the corner of his mouth. 'Are we going down?'

'I – I pray not, sir,' said Karl, and his voice was hoarse.

'Pray then,' growled Father. 'Pray.' He fixed his eyes on the carpet. 'Damn if I didn't see her last night, all in her long gown and the head of a dog where her face should have been . . .'

Karl too was looking at the carpet, and in the candlelight his eye shimmered with moisture. And Maria cursed herself bitterly. For she knew she had given him hope, and then she had cheated him. She felt that she could weep too – for him, for herself, and above all for Father and for the brief glow that had lit his mind and was gone.

XVI
A Word

'Aux armes, citoyens,' said Wéry boldly, as he marched into his office.

Asmus, the new clerk, looked up from the one desk they had to share.

'Guerre aux châteaux!' he replied.

'Paix aux chaumières,' trumpeted Wéry, and flung his coat into a corner.

'Et sois mon frère, ou je te tue,' said Asmus wryly, gathering his papers and rising from his place. 'I like that one especially, citizen.'

'Thank you, citizen,' said Wéry. He picked his hussar's cap off a dusty shelf and balanced it on his head. Ponderously he took his seat. 'Now, Asmus, I am uniformed, at my desk, in my barracks. I am an officer of the Prince and of the Empire once more. And so?'

'For God and Emperor, *sir*!'

'The Divine Order! And shall we yield the Rhineland?'

'The integrity of the German body must be maintained!' cried Asmus, raising a defiant fist to the ceiling.

'Exactly. We may shout for revolution, but we fight for integrity and order. That is our contradiction. And underlying our contradiction is the deeper truth, from which all things spring. And it is?'

'You said it was "Fuck the French", sir.'

Wéry's brow furrowed. 'I thought we decided that was too broad. Was it not to be "A Plague on Paris" or "Damn the Directory"?'

'You said, sir, that "Damn the Directory" was insufficiently poetic.'

'You are right. I did,' Wéry sighed. 'Even to be a poet, one has to lie a little.'

Asmus was a young man, with long, brown hair so thin that the white of his scalp showed through it. He was capable, spoke some French and had a dry sense of humour that made working with him a pleasure. He had not seemed to mind being taken for days at a time from his prestigious and presumably lucrative work in the First Minister's offices. Best of all, he could think. He had opinions on philosophy, politics and the personalities of Erzberg, and was more than ready to share them.

It was he, for example, who had finally explained to Wéry that the Countess Wilhelmina Pancak-Schönberg (whom everyone called simply 'the Countess') was not only the Prince-Bishop's mistress but also his aunt. Wéry had been wondering why his fellow officers would joke freely in his hearing about the Countess's fondness for young women but would fall quickly silent if he referred to her relations with the Prince. Now at last he understood. Incest as well as fornication! It was too much for Erzberg to admit to the outsider.

Wéry had warmed to Asmus from that moment. He had warmed further when he found that Asmus was willing to take part in some of the joke-rituals that Albrecht von Adelsheim had invented, such as the 'Slogans of Contradiction', in which the participants shouted the rallying-cries of opposite sides with increasing fervour. Altogether he was far more valuable than any promotion. The only sadness was that he might soon be with-drawn because Wéry had, after all, so little for him to do.

'You had better make the most of him while you can,' Fernhausen had said ruefully. 'Gianovi nearly had a fit when he heard we were after the fellow. He may even try to raise it with the Prince.' It had sounded, then, as if Asmus's recall might arrive any day. But September had given way to October and still Asmus came down to the barracks twice a week to take his place in Wéry's office. Perhaps Gianovi's influence had declined. Indeed it must have done if his notoriously busy staff could be depleted for the sake of an intelligence officer who struggled to gather any intelligence!

'How was the mission, sir?'

Wéry sighed again. 'Kranz is dead. French dragoons did it.'

'Oh!'

Asmus was shocked. His hand made a curious movement, searching the air behind him. It was reaching for a chair for his body to sink into. But there was no spare chair in the office, which had only recently had to accommodate two men rather than one.

'Because he worked for us, sir?'

'No knowing. Robbery, grudge, assassination – it could have been any or all. The others are all right. Of course they are scared now, which means they will be less likely than ever to stick their necks out because we ask it.'

'I see.' Asmus thought for a moment more. 'And is there news?'

That was the question. That was what every man in Erzberg, from the Prince downwards, wanted to know. And Erzberg would pass quickly enough over the loss of a hired man, so long as there was news. Wéry had done the same himself, in those moments after he had seen the cold-hearted puff of pistol smoke across the valley. It was just that he knew now what the news amounted to.

'Not much. Comings and goings. If anything, there's been a slight reduction in the strength at Wetzlar – another demi-brigade posted back across the Rhine. They still have plenty of force if they want to move. There's no sign of an increase in supplies, but that doesn't mean anything because we know the French don't believe in supplies when they are in a hurry. They will need more artillery but otherwise they can come and get us when they want.'

Asmus had drawn pen and paper to himself across the desk, but his nib did not touch the sheet. He looked up, 'So – no change?'

'Dress it up to make it look as though we've been busy. We *have* been busy, after all. But yes, that's the message.'

'Who is the source?'

Wéry hesitated. If he let it be known that he had been skulking around Wetzlar himself, scratching on doors and whistling at windows, there would be another difficult interview with Bergesrode. Just the thought of it made him feel tired.

'For the purposes of the report, you say that Kranz told it to me while he was dying in my arms.'

'You want me to say that he is dead?'

'Yes, of course.'

'If I do, the Treasury will cut his pay from our funds.'

Wéry groaned. (Erzberg, Erzberg! Lose a man but keep the money. And pocket it if you can! But Asmus was right. That was exactly how the palace functionaries thought.)

'He's dead in the Prince's service. Let him have a line of ink.'

'Yes, sir.'

'Now, what's been happening here?'

Asmus shrugged. 'There have been more demands from the French about the d'Erles party.'

'Telling us the émigrés have got to leave, and the walls must be blown up, and if we don't do it ourselves they will come and do it for us?'

'Exactly. I must say . . .' Asmus was fiddling with his pen in a rare sign of agitation. 'I cannot understand why His Highness does not just send d'Erles away! Can it really be that the Countess is so fond of this wastrel?'

'That's up to His Highness,' said Wéry. 'If there's a fight, we fight. That's all.'

'Yes, indeed. But . . .'

But Asmus was right. Whether out of love for his godchild, devotion to his mistress or loathing for the Republic, the Prince was playing a terrible gamble with his state.

'What does the Chapter say?'

Asmus glanced out of the window in the direction of the cathedral. The light was going early today.

'They were to meet this evening,' he said. 'Very soon, now, I imagine. Many of them are against him. Perhaps most. And there's an extraordinary meeting of the Estates tomorrow.'

'Maybe they will haul His Highness back.'

'Maybe.'

Maybe, maybe. But they did not know. No one knew. Would the French move now? Would they wait until spring? Would they do nothing but threaten? Wéry was the only one who could tell them. And at present he could not. His agents in Nassau were frightened and resentful. All they wanted to do was hibernate. That only left the Rhine, if anything useful could be gathered there. And if the messages could get through.

'Did that passport go to the address I gave you?' he asked.

Asmus looked at him.

'Yes.'

'There was no trouble about it?'

'None yet, sir.'

'Good.'

If she kept her promise. How long? Perhaps a man was already on his way to the Jürichs. Would there be something waiting for him? Probably not, because they would not expect him. So they would have to keep him there, or send one of their own when they did have something. How long then? No knowing.

Damn it, again he did not *know*!

'The War Commission has appointed the panel to investigate Count Balcke-Horneswerden,' said Asmus.

'Have they?'

He had not told Asmus there was a link between the passport and the investigation. Asmus must have guessed. But he had asked no questions yet.

'They are Steinau-Zoll, the Canon Inquisitor, Canon Rother-Konisrat, and the Knight von Uhnen.'

'Ho,' said Wéry, thoughtfully.

So Balcke-Horneswerden was to be investigated by one clever man from the Ingolstadt set, one clever man from the peace party – its leader in fact – and the mercurial Uhnen, whose son might be a hussar, but who could not safely be associated with any faction. They would be armed with hindsight, knowing that the action at Hersheim had been useless. There had been no need to

231

save the army, because peace had already dawned when Balcke had ordered the attack. And if that Frenchman ever appeared before them, Steinau and Rother at least would be happy to take his word over Balcke's. That might be enough to tie the noose.

Wéry shifted uncomfortably. He did not like to think he might be responsible for Balcke's dismissal. Balcke had helped him in the past. There was no denying that. And if the French came in force, Erzberg would need Balcke a thousand times over.

The sooner they got news of the French advance, the better then! There would be no time for inquiries after that. And no place for a French witness either! Damn it . . .

'Take the seat,' he grumbled. 'I'm getting changed.'

He retreated into his narrow bedroom, got rid of his mud-spattered civilian disguise, and pulled on his hussar's tunic and trousers. His thoughts would not leave him alone.

The Chapter was meeting this evening. Perhaps it had already begun. He tried to picture the Prince and the Canons – including Canons Rother and Steinau – all speaking in those soft voices of war. The Prince was relying on the reports Wéry had given him.

There had been nothing new for weeks!

Back in the office the light was going fast. He stalked around the room, ignoring Asmus, who was busy at the desk inventing who-knew-what to justify both their salaries. On the wall the white eyes of the dying Christ rolled grotesquely in the gloom.

He peered out of the window at the gathering evening, and tried to decide whether the barracks should be another strong point in his plan for the defence of the city. It had thick walls, and a good open square where troops could be ordered or stores piled. But it was overlooked by the onion-dome of the Saint

Lucia church. Any defence would have to hold the church as well. And if the church was a strong point, why bother with the barracks? Manpower would be limited, after all.

The less warning of attack, the less manpower there would be. Damn it! He could not just sit here!

'I am going out,' he said. 'Get that report written up, will you?'

'Yes, sir,' said Asmus, still writing.

'And get yourself a lamp, for God's sake. It's nearly dark already.'

'Yes, sir.'

It was indeed nearly dark, and the mist was coming off the river in a thick, cold smoke that filled the lower streets. For all that, there seemed to be more people about than was normal for the hour. Men passed him, striding swiftly, hurrying to some house or friend or gathering that he could not guess at. Others hung in doorways or at street corners, murmuring to one another or listening to someone holding forth by the light of a lantern. They glanced at him as he strode by in the shadows like a rumour of war. A man spoke to him. It was a question, but because of the accent he did not catch it. He stared at the fellow, who stared back at him, holding out a pamphlet. There were a stack of other pamphlets under the man's arm. He saw the man realize that he was an officer, start, and draw back even as he put out his hand to take the sheet. Then the pamphleteer was scurrying away in the mist, leaving him standing arm outstretched, fingers empty.

Five years before, in Brussels, in Paris, he had taken pamphlets like that one eagerly. He had even written some of them. Now he was on the other side. He took off his plumed cap and drew his coat around him as he went, hiding his uniform as far

233

as he could. And he walked among them, like a hidden enemy.

Enemy? No, not enemy. This was not revolution in the air. It was fever. Fear. He caught the words *Prince* and *émigré* and *Chapter* again and again. People were pressing each other for news. Anyone who could be imagined to know what was happening inside the Chapter meeting was being called over, to exchange rumour and counter-rumour. Wéry heard the phrase *the French have demanded* . . . but whatever it was they were supposed to have demanded was lost in the noise of someone coughing up fog. He heard the word *siege* uttered like the hiss of a snake in a thicket.

He stopped in the little square of Saint Lucia and the church loomed down at him, lightless and silent. It was broad-fronted, with a high tower, small windows and walls of stoutly-built stone. It stood corner-wise on to the street opposite. Cannon fire from down there would be deflected by the angle of the walls. The other streets onto the square were narrow and twisted. Any guns firing up those would have to be positioned so close that the crews would be at risk from sharpshooters in the spire. You could post watchmen up there. You could loophole the walls. The place could be a little redoubt, as long as men were determined to hold it. And as long as they had powder and shot. When that ran out the defenders would have to retreat or die like rats in a trap.

And how could you retreat from here? You would have to have allies on the rooftops. The rooftops would be important. So would the sewers. Where did the sewers run?

He paced on down the narrow streets, fighting his battle in his mind. The mist thickened, warning him of smoke. The enemy would fire the town. That would clear the rooftops of any of his sharpshooters who were downwind. It would also make it impossible to breathe in cellars, where people would be hiding, and in the sewers too. What could the defence do about that? Could they soak the timbers of every house in town with river water? Which way would the wind be blowing?

There were people ahead of him. There was a noticeable drift among them, in the same direction that he was going – uphill towards the cathedral. Probably there was already a crowd assembling outside the Chapter House, waiting for news. He might go and join them – he might at least hear how things stood, if there were announcements after the meeting ended. But if it ended badly, and the crowd found a uniformed man in its midst, it might become dangerous. He would do better to go back to the barracks.

He did not want to. All he could do in the barracks was fret. Here in the street he could at least have ideas. This guildhall now . . . Look beyond the carved gilt wood gleaming in the lantern light over the door. See the windows, commanding the alley opposite. See the French skirmishers cowering for shelter under the fire from its roof. See them scuttling for doorways, leaving a comrade writhing in the smoke! Then they would regroup and attack the door. Bayonets and musket butts. Yet . . .

Stand fast. That was the answer. Make them take you down man by man. The Lie loved weakness. It loved to whisper of the cost. Never listen. Never surrender. Never, never, never – no matter what the odds or the changing causes, *never* surrender. Only that way would it have any meaning at all.

A carriage was coming up the street behind him. Its wheels clattered loudly on the cobbles, and the sound echoed from the walls of the overhanging buildings. People were squeezing to the side of the street to be out of its way. The horse had nearly reached him. He pressed himself into a doorway and let the thing by, vaguely recognizing the device on the bodywork from somewhere. He felt the street-muck spatter from its wheels against his boots, and then it was past him. He stepped out from the doorway to follow.

A man's voice sounded from the carriage, and it stopped. As he came up with it again, a door opened and a pale face showed from inside.

'That you, Wéry?'

It was Uhnen. He was drunk.

'It's me.'

'My Virgil. Where're you going? Climb in. I'll have you there in a minute.'

'I'm just taking the air.'

'Climb in. You're a good fellow. I want to talk with you.'

Reluctantly, Wéry climbed into the leather-smelling interior. There was almost no light. There was no one else in the carriage.

'Drive on,' said Uhnen to his coachman.

The carriage lurched into motion again.

'Where are we going?' asked Wéry.

'Nowhere much,' said Uhnen, lolling on the other seat. 'I think I was going to try the Hotel Markburg next, but it doesn't matter. We can go anywhere you like.'

'What's the matter?'

'Oh.' Von Uhnen waved his hand dismissively. 'She doesn't want me.'

She?

'Told me so yesterday, over cards.'

She would be Maria von Adelsheim, of course. (What had she

236

done about his messages? Surely someone should have gone for them by now!)

'I thought she was already betrothed,' Wéry said.

'Oh, she is. I don't see it should matter . . . Well, why should it? He's a boy, and anyway he barely leaves his rooms from one year to the next! What sort of a match is that? It's ridiculous . . . I tell you what, Wéry. I lay it on that mother of hers. It's her way of keeping Maria with her as long as possible. That, and spite because they made *her* marry an idiot. Ruin it for everyone else. That's what she's doing . . .'

'I'm sorry to hear it,' said Wéry stiffly.

'I need to get drunk,' groaned Uhnen.

'You've done that already, haven't you?'

'Not half enough. We'll go down to the Markburg. I know them there. They'll see us right.'

Wéry doubted very much if he would be welcome at the Markburg, which was exclusively for families of Imperial Knights. And even if they turned a blind eye to his presence, he did not want to spend his evening nursing Uhnen's lovesick heart. Certainly not when Maria von Adelsheim was the cause! But Uhnen had been friendly since the affair at the bridge. Aristocrat he might be, but he did not deserve to be abandoned like this. Love was a great leveller, *and* a dangerous enemy.

And it was not as though he had much else to do! He only hoped that Asmus would have the sense to go home when he did not reappear.

'She *seemed* to like me very well,' groaned Uhnen.

'She may well do. But that doesn't mean everything.'

'And I've been protecting them! I could destroy them with a word. But I've not told her that. I won't.'

'Destroy Adelsheim? It would have to be a very powerful word.'

'Oh,' said Uhnen, with affected weariness. 'Illuminati.'

XVII
Alleys in the Mist

Even in his drunken nonchalance there was a tremor in his voice. *Illuminati.* Who had secretly inspired the Revolution? Who were determined to bring down the Mother Church? Had you never seen one? That only proved how clever they were.

Wéry said nothing. He had seen two revolutions without laying eyes on a single Illuminatus. Before coming to Erzberg he would have sworn with confidence that the Illuminati no longer existed, and that even if they did they were an irrelevance. And yet time and again the word was spoken here, with a conviction that sometimes shook his own.

'I could have told her how much she owes me,' said Uhnen absently. 'How much all her house owes me. Maybe I should . . .'

'It's probably just gossip.'

'That it is not! I was there!'

Wéry drew a long breath. For a moment he almost changed the subject. But then he said: 'You had better tell me about it.'

Von Uhnen looked at him, swaying slightly with the movement of the carriage.

'You're a good fellow, aren't you? You're my Virgil. You'll know how to treat this.'

Wéry said nothing. Von Uhnen knew that he reported to the palace. He would know, too, that the palace thought the

Illuminati were in league with the French. And yet he was still going to speak.

'There was a reception at the Adelsheim place last week . . .' Uhnen began.

'Which one?'

'The house in Saint Emil quarter.'

In the city. On the Prince's territory. That was unwise. But of course the Lady Adelsheim would think herself invulnerable.

'There was a funny little man there called Sorge. Lady Adelsheim said he had come to educate them all . . .'

'The name again – Sorge?'

'Doctor Sorge, of Nuremberg.'

Sorge. In German that meant *Worry*. Apt, and memorable too. Although Nuremberg, an Imperial city nestling in Bavarian territory, was not the first place he would have looked for French agents. Perhaps their reach was longer than he had thought.

'He came under the wing of Baron Löhm. The strange thing was, my father said, when they all sat down and started to talk, both the Baron and Sorge seemed to think that it was the Baron who was under Sorge's wing, and not the other way about . . .'

'Your father was there?'

'My father went into the meeting with them. I didn't. Most of this I had from Father. They were trying to seduce him, because he's on the inquiry into Hersheim. Of course that didn't work. But according to him, Löhm said there were Illuminati in half the cities in Germany. There are some in Nuremberg, some in Frankfurt, some in Cologne – I can't remember all the places. They recruit followers, and those followers recruit more followers, and so on until they've a great net of people in every state, influencing the government and what have you. Apparently they've even got someone here, in the palace. Highly placed. I had thought it was all rubbish but . . .'

'How high? A canon? An official?'

'Can't tell you. Sorge told him to stop blabbing, I think.'

Connections with the French; connections with an Illuminatus; opposition to the Prince; rumours that could have been *designed* to undermine the army; and now secret infiltration of the palace! What did the Adelsheims think they were doing?

God! And it was to Adelsheim that he had trusted the link with his contacts across the Rhine!

The coach rocked and clattered slowly over the cobbles. There was a sick feeling in Wéry's stomach. Steady, he thought. Steady.

Fears make nightmares of the smallest things. There did not need to be anything in this. The men in Lady Adelsheim's set were exactly the educated, bored, free-minded sort who might band into secret brotherhoods out of a vague philanthropy and a love of being mysterious. Canon Rother, in particular, was no French tool. His aim was clear enough: to foster enough disaffection with the Prince for the Chapter to appoint him coadjutor, to rule the city and state alongside his enemy. Why should any of this mean there was a conspiracy? When you hear them singing the Marseillaise in the city quarters, that's when you need to worry.

Nevertheless, it sounded as if the Adelsheims had been very unwise indeed.

'We're going to have to start again. And I'll need this written down. Can you come back to the barracks with me?'

'I don't want to go back to the barracks!'

'We cannot talk about this at the Markburg.'

'Then we'll talk about something else. I don't mind.'

'I could have a bottle brought to my rooms,' said Wéry, and groaned inwardly at himself.

'Make it one each, to start with,' said Uhnen promptly.

Then he seemed to hesitate. 'You're a good fellow, Wéry,' he said uncertainly. 'You'll do the right thing.'

'I don't know what I'll do,' said Wéry frankly. 'But let's hear it anyway.'

He was suddenly feeling very tired. And the coach had stopped again. Noises surrounded it. A crowd was pressing past in the narrow way.

'You'd think half the city was out,' mused Uhnen.

'Perhaps it is.'

A white uniform gleamed beyond the carriage window. A voice Wéry knew was calling urgently.

'Lanterns! Lanterns!'

Wéry looked out. There, standing in the roadside behind the coach, was the stocky figure of Heiss.

Heiss, like all the officers close to Balcke-Horneswerden, had acquired a hunted look in recent weeks. More and more of his colleagues seemed to think it bad luck to associate with him. He had become moody, unpredictable, prone to fits of temper and long silences. Now he cut a wild figure in the gloom. He was hatless, cloakless, and held a pistol pointed up at the sky. With his other hand he was gesturing to the crowd to gather around him.

'What's the matter?' called Wéry.

'Who's that?'

'Wéry, and I've got Uhnen with me.'

'Good man! Get down – we need you!'

In a city where officers were barely showing themselves by day, the crowd was rallying around Heiss like a ragged platoon.

242

Lanterns danced among them. A number of them held sticks. Drawn by the urgency of the voices, Wéry climbed out. Von Uhnen followed him.

'What the devil's going on?'

'Devil may be the word for it. There's saboteurs out. Fire-raisers. Someone's seen them, down on the quays!'

'Fire-raisers?'

'My brother saw them!' said a voice. 'Down there, by the Old Bridge!'

'I don't believe it!' said Wéry.

The mist was cold, and the wide-eyed faces pressed around him. Suddenly he was not so sure. He felt their fear, and his muscles stiffened with it. In the Chapter House, the city was debating war. But what if the French were already in the city? What if they struck first? That was what they were like. That was far more credible than any talk of Illuminati. You watched your front, and you watched your front; and then suddenly they were on you, round your flank and marching for your lines!

'I don't believe it,' he repeated lamely.

'That's what we're going to find out,' snapped Heiss. 'Come on!'

He led and they all followed him. Down the twisting streets they poured like a pack of hounds. Feet pounded and slipped upon the cobbles. Voices called. A head looked out of a first storey window and cried out a question.

'Fire-raisers!' they answered as they ran past. 'On the quay!'

All at once Heiss turned to his right and plunged down a narrow alley. Wéry hesitated. Then, as if swept up by the others who pushed past him, he followed. The ground was muddy beneath his boots. The alley stank and there was little light. Men hurried ahead of him, squeezed by the close walls into a thin straggle of ones and twos. Others panted behind, pressing him on with their pursuit. There was no time to look round.

'Hey, hold up!' came Uhnen's voice from far behind. 'Hey there!'

But the men ahead of him ran on. Wéry followed, caught by the fever of the hunt, and his duty melted into the mist behind them.

Down, turn, and on down. They were somewhere near the city's small Jewish ghetto, but he did not know where. They were heading towards the river, but where they would come on it he could not guess. Heiss must be aiming to strike the waterside as high as possible, so that his little force could then scour the length of the quays in one sweep. But for God's sake, what was it they had seen? A torch? A plume of smoke? How could you tell smoke from mist in this murk?

'Lights! LIGHTS!' roared Heiss from ahead. He was standing in an open space, looking back up the alley. Beyond him was the gleam of water. Three or four men joined him. One had a lantern. As Wéry arrived on the quay, gasping for breath, Heiss set off again, striding along the narrow wooden walkway that ran before the mean house-fronts of the Riverside Quarter. Wéry followed, a pace or two behind the others.

'No fires yet,' said someone.

'Keep your eyes open,' growled Heiss.

More men were reaching the quay behind them. But voices were still calling among the alleys above and to their left. Some were still making their way down. Some were already lost.

'Quietly, now!'

Thump, thumpety-thump! went a dozen boots upon the

walkway. *Ripple-ipple*, murmured the dark water. The mist blocked the far bank and the Celesterburg from sight. Squinting as he strode, Wéry could just make out the loom of the Old Bridge, barring the river. And the figure on the walkway thirty yards ahead of them, part-lit by a glow from a window. 'There!' he cried.

Others shouted at the same moment. The figure turned, looking their way. It wore a heavy cloak.

'You there!' cried Heiss.

The figure wavered, and seemed to back away.

'You there! Stand! Stand!'

There was a flash from Heiss's upraised hand, and the report of the pistol. The figure disappeared.

Wéry swore, and pushed past the others. For a few lonely seconds he was out and alone, with his boots thumping on the boards and his heart pounding, a cold, sick feeling in his guts like the river beneath his feet. Then he gained the stonework of the quay proper. What seemed to be a pile of cloths was lying there. But the pile had a foot, and an arm flung out of it. And a faint, keening noise came from it.

It was a man.

'Bring a light!' yelled Wéry. 'Bring it!'

The others gathered round. The lantern swung above the fallen man's face.

It was an elderly man – a Jew, from the beard and long locks. His eyes were open. His face, yellow in the lamp-light, was drawn in pain. His mouth moved, gasping. His right hand was groping for his left shoulder, where the dark cloth of his cloak was beginning to soak with blood. Wéry looked up into Heiss's horrified face.

'I challenged him,' Heiss gasped. 'He didn't stand.'

A wealthy Jew, on his way back to the ghetto before the gates locked for the night. And a mob had run up out of the darkness and shouted at him. Of course he had retreated. And . . .

'Eeeee – eeee,' the man whined. One hand clutched at the air near his wounded shoulder. His eyes were screwed up and his nose was a sharp yellow peak jutting up from his face against the shadows behind.

Wéry's knees were wet. He looked down at the dark pool that was growing around him, and already becoming sticky as it grew. His trousers were stained, irreparably.

'You – *idiot*!' he exclaimed.

Others had run up and were looking down at the wounded man. Von Uhnen was among them.

'There's a surgeon down by the New Bridge,' someone said.

'Help me lift him,' said Wéry.

They hung back. Lift a wounded man, and a Jew at that?

Wéry cursed them in French, as he struggled to get the man's bloody arm over his shoulder. The man cried out.

'Help me!'

It was Uhnen who stepped forward. Heiss had disappeared somewhere, eyes dazed and pistol dangling. The lantern swung in Wéry's eyes.

'Get out of my way,' he snarled, furious with all of them.

Saboteurs indeed!

'And run ahead,' he added. 'Rouse up that damned doctor, and get the bottle out of his lips!'

The wounded man shrieked.

'Now my man,' said Uhnen beside him. 'Don't you worry. We'll have you down to the doctor, and he'll set you right . . .'

Other hands were helping now, lifting the head, a trailing foot, anything they could touch or raise. It still seemed to Wéry that he had two thirds of the weight. His grip was not good, but because of the crowd around him he could not stop and adjust himself. He was hobbling down a foreign quayside, carrying a wounded Jew, with the son of an aristocrat on the other side and a crowd of war-scared murderers around him.

'You know,' gasped Uhnen with false cheerfulness. 'I went – through four years of campaign – never touched a wounded man. Always left the lads to do it. Sorry – about that, now.'

'You may yet get your fill of it,' grunted Wéry.

War, war. It was fear of the war that had sent them all running down the alleys after a rumour. They had gone charging off, like green troops into a forest. No wonder someone had got shot! And if he'd had the pistol, he might have fired too.

The lantern was waiting for them at a door downstream from the New Bridge. The doctor stood in his shirtsleeves in the hall-way. There was a scrum as the bearers rearranged themselves to carry the victim in. Relieved of the burden, Wéry sank exhausted to the cobbles. Von Uhnen felt unsteadily for the doorway, and disappeared inside. From within came the voices of children, one excited by the bustle, the other complaining her supper had been interrupted. Probably they had cleared the dining room table and dropped the wounded man straight onto it.

He should think about doctors. They would be needed, if the city were defended. How many were there? Half of them would want to leave if they thought a siege was coming. So there would have to be orders for the gate guards. That would be the very first thing.

Where should they set up the hospitals?

He was climbing wearily to his feet when he heard a further disturbance, this time from the New Bridge. More voices, another crowd. For a moment he wondered if they had been drawn by the shooting on the quays. But this hubbub was different. It had a lively and strangely festive sound. As he listened, a cheer broke out. Part of the crowd was crossing the New Bridge. Others, lanterns in hand, were coming down the quay-side towards him. Faces appeared at windows. Questions were called.

'It's peace!' someone in the crowd answered.

'Peace!' cried a man near Wéry. 'Hurrah!'

'Peace?' asked Wéry urgently. He seized one of the loudest shouters by the arm. 'What's happened? Tell me what's happened!'

'The French Count, sir. He went to the Chapter House while they were meeting. He forced his way in through the doors. And he walked up to His Highness on his throne, and went on his knees. And they all thought he would beg to stay, sir. But he begged that we should not fight for him. He said he would leave the city, because he would not see blood spilled in a place that had been so good to him!'

'His Highness wept, they say, and so did the Count . . .'

'Hurrah!'

'Damn me,' said a voice at his elbow. 'I would never have thought d'Erles had it in him.'

It was Uhnen, emerged from the doctor's house. He was carrying his purse in his hand, and had not stopped to lace it up.

'A surprise, certainly,' said Wéry hollowly.

'I suppose we will have to blow up the walls after all.'

'I suppose we will.'

And they would not loophole churches, dig up streets, set up makeshift hospitals or commandeer doctors – not this time. The Prince had surrendered.

At one or two places around the city, the bells of churches had begun to ring.

Wéry felt a great sense of weariness opening inside him. He did not want to think about the future. If he thought about it he might find there was nothing there. War that became peace in a burst of lanterns and cheering. What was real? Was any of it real? He did not know any more.

'I've settled here,' said Uhnen, finally putting his purse away. He sounded completely sober.

'The city justice next?'

'Not yet. It may be possible to buy off the man he's wounded. But I think we'll leave that to Heiss. He can send his factor to the Jewish elders in the morning.'

And so Heiss would be relieved of his sins. A sordid little act, to clear a man of his conscience. Wéry sighed.

'Very well. Let's get along to the barracks, write your story down, and then we can be finished with that, too.'

'What story?'

'What you were telling me in the coach.'

Von Uhnen hesitated.

'Forget about that,' he said. 'It was nothing.'

Wéry knew he should not be put off. But . . . he barely cared. He had not come to Erzberg to write grubby little reports on families he knew. In fact, he was no longer sure what he *had* come here for.

'Let's go back anyway,' he said. 'There are still those bottles we were going to share between us.'

'No. No thank you. I've finished for tonight.'

'Have you? I might have both then.'

PART IV:
THE HOUSE OF THE GREEN JUDGE

November 1797–January 1798

XVIII
The Plundered Land

On a mild November day Maria saw the Rhine.

It was a great, wide, grey river, flowing steadily northwards at a pace little faster than a man might walk. It seemed to move very gently, past flat fields of grass and plough land, past the gentle slopes freckled with trees and dotted with villages, past the purple, cloudlike shapes of the distant hills. It was a silent weight of water, untroubled by all the tilling and felling, the trading and bickering and blows of the humanity along its banks. Half the history of Christendom had been written on its shores, and it did not care.

On the far side, in a tumble of roofs and spires, was the city of Mainz, once seat of the most exalted Archbishop and Prince-Elector of the Empire, and Primate of all Germany. The six towered, red sandstone cathedral rose above the buildings of the upper town. The eastern towers were broken, and burned by fire. Other churches and buildings were also ruined. The quays of the waterfront were longer than those of Erzberg, but no more busy. And lines of huge, brown earthworks were visible where the old walls reached the river. Their great shapes dwarfed the buildings, even the cathedral. Altogether the place looked, Maria thought, like a crowd of sad and battered children huddling inside a giant's overcoat. She said so to Anna, who sighed.

'When I was last here they had not built those things,' she said. 'And the roofs were all whole. And all the south side of the city was a wonderful garden. Really it is such a shame that war should spoil so many things.'

The coach halted. More earthworks, with great, angled bastions, blocked the way ahead of them. There were soldiers on the gates, wearing the white uniforms of the Empire. Maria looked at them curiously, wondering if they were from some Hapsburg dominion like Austria or Bohemia or Croatia, for she knew that the Emperor had a garrison of his own troops in the town. But they spoke with the accents of the Rhine, and when they saw the seals of Erzberg on the passes they saluted without hesitation. Presumably they were troops of the long-fled Elector of Mainz; suffered to perform the gate-duties while the Emperor's own soldiers lurked within.

And where was the Elector now? Gone – vanished away to safer territories at the first coming of war. And the revolutionaries of Mainz, who had flourished briefly under the French occupation, were gone too. And all that was left were the soldiers, and the people of the town, the ruins, and the vast fortifications.

The coach lurched onwards, over the bridge, over the great, slow water. The bridge was built on boats that floated on the stream. Anna said this was so that the central spans could be removed and towed to the bank in the coldest weather, to prevent them from being smashed by the great floes of ice that would come drifting down the river. Maria's window looked downstream. On one side was the bank they were leaving, where the order of the Empire with all its intricate hierarchies still held. On the other was the fortress city, and beyond it the territory held by the French army. That land – she could see it clearly, fields, woods, hills and the city – seemed no different to the eastern bank. And yet there the hierarchies had been swept away. What did the territories of Mainz, Trier, Palatine, Cologne and all the rest mean now? What would become of all those years of history and self-understanding? Surely it was wrong that they should be erased, as though some monstrous teacher had wiped a slate clean! And yet the great, grey river rolled north between the two shores, and cared only for its search for the sea.

Their journey ended at an inn, in a crowded street where beggar-children yammered at the coach-steps and tall, surly men waded through them to lift down the baggage. The Adelsheim footmen cried out sharply that the luggage must be kept in sight. They had been armed with pistols for the journey, for fear of bandits or French marauders. One of them drew his and brandished it in the air.

'The poor people!' said Anna wearily, as she, Maria and the maids struggled out of the crowd into the haven of the inn.

But the innkeeper was anxious to please, and bowed, waving them into a low-ceilinged front room where tables were set. There was a fire here, and sitting before it was a lean gentleman in a wig, reading a newspaper. He looked up as they came in.

'Well, well!' he cried softly. 'Cousin Poppenstahl, at last!'

'*Ludi!*' shrieked Anna. She rushed forward to embrace him. He had barely time to rise from his seat before she flung her arms about him and jumped to kiss his cheek. Maria had never seen her so excited. And she felt that, whatever her own reasons for this adventure to the Rhine, it had been right to bring the two cousins back together. Watching as the pair parted, she thought there were even tears in Anna's eyes.

'Oh Ludi – let me look at you! You are so grey and your cheeks sunk – you have not been ill?'

'I?' said the gentleman mildly. 'No, I do not believe I have. Forgive me if I am not so young as I was six years ago.'

'Oh Ludi – no, *you* must forgive *me*. I am sure it has been a hard time for you. But we have brought you wines and sweet-meats and . . .'

'A wonderful range of cures for all ills indeed. But we should not talk of it here. Let your fellows see it is all safely stowed. And if we can whisk it past my French guests tomorrow, why, there will be a dinner party at my house in the evening and we shall all grow young again together.' His eyes went to Maria, and he bowed.

'Oh – Maria,' said Anna, remembering her etiquette at last. 'This is my cousin, Ludwig Jürich. Ludwig, this is the Lady Maria von Adelsheim, whose mother is so good as to let me be governess to her family.'

'Lady Maria,' said the man. 'A humble gentleman of the Rhine salutes you. And my house is yours, and all entertainment that I may offer you will be yours for as long as you are pleased to be with us.'

His speech, as he bent over her hand, was a model of polite deference, as a country gentleman should offer to a lady of superior rank. But then he straightened and looked down at her gravely. His eyes were very deep. For a moment she felt very young, and perhaps a little foolish, like a child with a guilty secret to hide. Many thoughts dashed into her head at once. One of them was that a gentleman should not stare at a lady of rank so. Another was that he was wondering why someone like her should have come to these distressed places. And yet another was that he had already guessed everything that she was thinking.

What was it he knew, that was so important in Erzberg?

'Sir,' she heard her own voice say. 'Your cousin is, in truth, more of an aunt to me than she is a governess. Therefore I beg that you treat me as one of your family too.'

'We shall be glad. And also I must offer my deepest condolences to you on the loss of your brother. I did know him, a little, and was grieved to hear that he was killed. I am sorry, too, that it has been so long before I have had the opportunity to say this to his sister.'

'Sir, you are good. And although it has been long, I feel the loss is still fresh. Therefore any words of condolence are fresh too. Indeed it is in some ways the memory of my brother that has impelled me to come.'

It was the memory of her brother, and of his friend in the barracks of Erzberg. But she would not say that yet.

The soldiers on the South Gate were Austrians and there were many more than there had been at the bridgehead. They looked closely at the papers, and asked questions of Cousin Ludwig, who answered patiently. When the coach was allowed to pass, Cousin Ludwig mounted his own horse and rode ahead with his groom. After a few hundred paces they made the coach halt again. Leaning out of her window Maria saw Cousin Ludwig take something from his groom's hand and pin it onto his hat. It was a green cockade. He unbuttoned his coat and flung it back, allowing his green tunic to show. Then he rode ahead on his own, the groom still signing for the coach to wait.

By a ramshackle set of buildings, a furlong ahead of them, another party of soldiers waited. It was hard to tell the colour of

257

their uniforms. Most of them were wearing greatcoats and blankets, and all were different browns and greys. A wisp of smoke rose from where some of them were cooking in the open.

Maria looked at them curiously. She knew that any soldiers on the road outside Mainz must be French. She saw Cousin Ludwig ride up to them and dismount. He seemed to show some papers of his own. After a while he and one of the soldiers went inside a hut.

She waited.

At long last Cousin Ludwig reappeared, mounted and rode back towards them. He spoke a few words to the coach driver, handed his horse to the groom, and then climbed into the coach, squeezing in to a corner beside the two maids. As the door closed, the team began to walk forward.

'It would be better to keep back from the windows, I think,' said Cousin Ludwig.

'Oh dear,' said Anna anxiously. 'Ought we not to draw the curtains too?'

'No. Let them see that they may see in if they wish to.'

The coach jolted slowly on its way. Maria sat back as far as she could. She was suddenly very aware of the frail shell of the coach-body around her, and aware too of Cousin Ludwig, sitting bolt upright by the coach door with his face all false calm and his fingers drumming lightly on his knee. No one said anything. The rattle of the wheels and the clod of hooves were loud in her ears and seemed to grow louder still. Beyond the window the grassy roadside rolled slowly backwards. The hummocks and puddles and bushes passed by, repeating and repeating themselves, mean-ing nothing. Then, for a few seconds, she was looking at something she could recognize: the remains of a formal avenue, all felled and overgrown, running to a ruined pavilion by a weedy pond. They were passing through the gardens of the vanished Elector, now all smashed and half buried by war. The men who had smashed and buried them were waiting for her on the road ahead.

She was going to them, rolling slowly into their arms with her coachful of hidden sweetmeats, her silks and purses, her friends and herself! Nothing could stop her. Nothing could save her, if she needed saving. Her hand lay on her lap, and she saw that her knuckles were white. And she suddenly felt that she had been sleepwalking for days, dreaming dreams of confidence and courage, and had only woken at last when it was too late, and there was no help, and no turning back.

How could this have happened to her?

And then, through the coach window, there was the grey-weathered wall of a building, and a man leaning against it. He was bare-headed, moustached and bearded, small and dark-skinned. Maria's heart bounced. She had a powerful impression of something dwarfish, as if the soldier had not marched from France but had crawled out with his fellows from legendary underworlds beneath the Rhine. He was smoking a pipe as he watched the coach pass by. His greatcoat was buttoned to his collar, but in places the buttons were missing. He passed out of sight.

Now she could see other men, sitting and standing, looking keenly at the windows. One of them seemed to see her. She would have shrunk back, if there had been anywhere to shrink to. A grin was spreading over his face as he was lost from view. A voice called something. It was French, but no French that Maria could understand. Someone laughed. But now the window showed her only grassy hummocks again. And they were still moving forward, deeper and deeper into the occupied Rhineland.

At last Cousin Ludwig sighed.

'That was well, then. The officer was a reasonable fellow.'

'Did you have to bribe him?' asked Anna.

'Of course. I would have paid him more if he could have escorted us. It would have saved us trouble if we had met any other soldiers. But unfortunately he could not leave his post.'

'Could he not have given us an escort anyway?'

'The men are not to be trusted without the officer.'

'They seemed so small!' murmured Maria, looking out of the window as if she could still see them, unkempt and dwarfish, lounging by the roadside.

Cousin Ludwig looked at her in some surprise. 'No smaller, I think, than many a beggar or peasant in Erzberg, Lady Maria. You may be used to your Prince's regiments, where men are – or were – recruited for their height. But France has swept its streets and furrows for fighting men, and placed them under arms in tens of thousands. And now France requires us to feed them. Alas, a soldier's appetite does not diminish according to his stature!'

'So many of the barns are ruined,' observed Anna, looking through the far window.

'Soldiers have great need of firewood,' said Cousin Ludwig. 'Surely you have seen the same on the other bank.'

'Yes, especially as we were passing Frankfurt. But not so many as this.'

'They have been here longer. Yet it is better now than it was. Last year they were following the farmers into the fields, digging up the potatoes that had been planted for seed. So at the harvest of course both farmer and soldier went hungry.'

'Senseless!'

'Quite so. The soldier, cold and starving, can think only of the moment. And his superiors are little better. Did they take horses and cattle in Adelsheim?'

'We were fortunate that they never came to Adelsheim,' said Maria. 'But the last time they marched into Germany they took many horses from the territories around Erzberg. Six hundred, I believe.'

'Six hundred!' murmured Cousin Ludwig. Maria guessed he must be more used to hearing figures in thousands. 'Well, I fear that of those six hundred very few may now be alive. They gather them in great herds and move them to places where they believe they can use them. And then they discover that in those places there is not enough hay to feed them. So they give them the straw from the roofs of thatched houses for a few weeks, and after that the animals begin to die. It is the same with the cattle. And of course if any of the animals is diseased, the whole herd will suffer – and all the land after that.'

'You seem well acquainted with their ways, sir.'

Very well acquainted, Maria thought. Did he have reasons other than idle curiosity for watching the movements of the armies?

He looked at her, mildly.

'I am a recruit of theirs,' he said.

'A recruit! For the soldiers?'

'Quite so. Until this summer, the occupiers sent their own commissioners to rule these territories. I need not bother you with the kind of men those commissioners were. I suspect that most of them were selected for this task because they could not be trusted with any other. In the end even the generals saw that they were successful only in arousing resentment. So the

261

much-lauded General Hoche hit upon the quite original and ingenious idea of requiring those who had served the former, despotic regimes to serve the liberating Republic in their former ranks and posts. I, as it happens, was a judge under the Elector. So I am again.'

'I believe you consider this ironic, sir.'

'Indeed I do. Nor am I over-fond of the green cloth my more enthusiastic colleagues adopt for their uniform – although it is sometimes a help in dealing with the soldiers. But perhaps it will not be for much longer. Now that Hoche is dead, the Directory considers his ideas capable of improvement. Once again we are to have a commissioner. What this means for my position and that of my colleagues, I cannot guess. Although I believe the new man is an Alsatian, and should therefore at least be competent in German. French is an elegant language for conversation, but to administer the law it is preferable to speak the language of the native dwellers.'

'Perhaps peace will come soon, and the lands will be restored to the Empire.'

'It is what we all pray for.'

He worked for the French, she thought, watching his profile against the coach window. He was their helper. What did that mean? Could he nevertheless be the man she was looking for? *What* was it that was to pass from Jürich to Adelsheim, and thence to Erzberg?

She did not know. She did not know who or what she was here for. She had had no chance to meet with Wéry before her departure. She had not dared to put messages into the hands of Adelsheim servants, or to risk another visit to his barracks herself.

Now she was wishing that she had done. She was west of the Rhine, in a country teeming with a savage soldiery. She had nothing to guide her.

And a wrong word might lead to something terrible: for herself, or worse, for Anna. It might even mean the death of the man she was looking for.

She was going to have to be very, very careful.

XIX
The Name

Cousin Ludwig's house was a square, pale villa on a low hill that was part-cloaked in oak trees. In the grey afternoon it had a plain, rather mournful look. Lights gleamed through the windows, but not many. The grass on the hillside was long, as if no flock had grazed there all autumn.

They were welcomed by Cousin Ludwig's wife, Emilia, a round-faced woman with a bright trill in her voice. She was probably some years younger than her husband and might in other times have been gay indeed. She bobbed deferentially to Maria and embraced Anna with a laugh. She laughed and embraced her again when the hampers were swayed down from the coach and carried in for the household to inspect the contents: pickles, pâtés, ox-tongue, wines, coffee, dried fruits and sweetmeats.

'Wonderful!' she cried. 'You clever things! How did you smuggle it all through?'

'Ludwig spoke to the soldiers, and all seemed to be well.'

'Oh!' Emilia looked at her husband. For a moment her smile had dropped. There was something like weariness in her eyes. 'I hope there was no risk, sir.'

'Not much,' said Cousin Ludwig. 'And there will be none at all if only we can dispose of it before our General hears of it. We shall have a dinner party tonight, my dear, if you are willing. Hofmeister will come, I am sure of it. So will Septe, if we can get a message to him before Vespers. I think also . . .'

'I have no cards, of course. It is difficult to get them.'

'Of course. But a message may be passed as easily by mouth. Shall we say eight o'clock? That will give our guests time to recover from their journey. And no word of our sudden good fortune. It is a dinner party in honour of our visitors. Let them suppose we have dug our last vegetables from the garden for the occasion.'

Maria was looking around her. The hallway was very bare, and the glimpses she had of the drawing room beyond were the same. There seemed to be no paintings on the walls, or curtains in the windows. The fire was lit, but the supply of logs beside it looked rather poor. The hall would have benefited from lamps and candles on this grey afternoon, but none were lit. She must not remark it. She must not, by one wrinkle of her forehead, let them see that she was used to more light and wealth and beauty than this. They would know anyway.

'Is Maximilian in the house?' asked Anna.

'Oh!' said Emilia. Once again she was looking at Ludwig, and the weariness was back in her eyes. 'You have not explained . . .'

'Not yet,' said Ludwig. 'There were many happier things to speak of. Anna, my dear, my nephew is in the house, but he rarely leaves his rooms.'

'Is he still unwell?'

'He is not unwell. In fact, he has never been unwell, in body. But he keeps to his rooms and will not willingly leave them.'

'He has been like this since the siege of Mainz,' said Emilia.

'Is it – is it possible to see him?' asked Anna, blinking anxiously.

'Normally, yes. If you wish I shall make arrangements.'

'Arrangements?' repeated Maria.

'He is perfectly safe,' said Cousin Ludwig. 'That is to say, he is not violent. But I prefer that his footman should be in attendance.'

'Come, my dear,' said Anna, rallying. 'Of course there is no need to worry.'

And everyone was smiling again. Smiling, bravely.

'Magnificent!' cried Father Septe, eyeing the long dining table on which were loaded the offerings from Erzberg.

'What our General would give to see this!' exclaimed Hofmeister, an elderly, stout gentleman in an old-fashioned wig and frock coat. 'Eh, Jürich, let us strike a blow for freedom tonight, hey?'

'For freedom, or for liberty?'

'Feed me like this, man, and you may report me as you like. Or Kaus can do it for you. Run to your masters, hey, Kaus – after you've eaten perhaps?'

The fourth man, a thin, hollow-eyed gentleman in green, smiled sadly. 'There is no prohibition, so far as I know, on enjoying a dinner in the Republic. It is not our business to wonder whence . . .'

'Republic? Republic, he says. Now sir, which republic is it today? Is it the Cisrhenian still? Or some other one? Is there to be another referendum? Please heaven, no! One exercise in democracy is enough! Did I tell you when they came up to make my village vote . . . ?'

'I believe you did . . .'

'Just four cowhands came forward, and none of them knew

where to sign, so the clerk had to do it for them! The rest of the village all shut their doors. So back the clerk came with a troop of French dragoons to explain it was the right of every free man to vote for the Republic, and vote they must. No, sir, not for the Elector. One does not elect Electors, ha ha! For the Republic – the Cisrhenian Republic, that not half of us have heard of and not a man among us can pronounce!'

'Gentlemen,' said Cousin Ludwig. 'I hope all differences may be put aside at my wife's table.'

'Oh, do not worry yourself, Jürich. Kaus and I know each other very well.'

'Very well,' sighed Kaus. 'If dear Hofmeister did not chide me about republics, I should fear he were ill. Though a more sensitive soul might spare me in my disappointment at the reluctance of my countrymen to see reason.'

'Reason!' cried Father Septe. 'Reason, he calls it!'

'Gentlemen,' said Ludwig, a little more firmly. 'The ladies are seated, and await us.'

At the ladies' end of the table Emilia Jürich sat with Anna on her left and Maria on her right, and Madame Hofmeister and Madame Kaus beyond them. Madame Hofmeister and Madame Kaus were Emilia's sisters, all with the same cheerful round faces. They rolled their eyes and shook their heads at the sparring of their husbands, but filled their own conversations with laughter. Maria wondered if there was not indeed something hysterical about their laughter, brought on by the imported food and drink, and the thought that one day – soon, God send! – the Empire and France would sign a treaty, the world would be at peace, and all the things now before them would be commonplace again.

Certainly they did not want to talk of politics or privation or war. But they were eager to hear Anna talk of Bohemia, where she and the Adelsheims had taken refuge with the funny old Count Effenpanz during the months when French armies had been marching deep into Germany. And they laughed with real delight when they heard that Count Effenpanz went about his rooms bald and wigless and had spent many hours trying to teach them all about his collection of butterflies. 'Bless him!' they cried.

Maria nodded and smiled through the conversation, ate and drank little, and listened. She liked the three sisters, but did not suppose that any of them could be the person she had come to find. Of the men present . . .

It would not be Hofmeister. He was too outspoken. He wore his heart on his sleeve, an enemy of the Republic and a supporter of his Prince. Perhaps it was Father Septe. He had a dark, square head, frowned a lot and looked more thoughtful than Hofmeister. But his sympathies, too, were obvious. He did not seem to be a man with anything to hide. And as a priest he would be under suspicion anyway. That left Cousin Ludwig, calm and moderate at the head of his table, and the lean-faced Kaus, who still believed in the republic. These looked more like men who could hide things, and who could deal in secrets. She would not have thought that Wéry would correspond with allies of the French. But perhaps their politics were only a pretence: one that a man like Kaus could feed carefully by permitting himself to be Hofmeister's butt?

It was no use guessing. She could not – dared not – approach anyone on the basis of a guess. She must make herself known, in a way that only the person she was looking for would understand. And there was only one thing that would do.

In a lull in the conversation at the men's end of the table, she broke gently into the talk around her and said the name 'Wéry'.

Instantly, it seemed, she was rewarded.

'Wéry!' echoed Hofmeister. 'Ay, there's a man I envy!'

'Who?' asked Kaus.

'Wéry. The Brabançon who came to us in Mainz. He warned us of French perfidy, and he was right. But no one listened to him – or to me either! You remember him, Jürich?'

Ludwig gazed at the man peaceably. 'I believe so. What of him?'

'Oh,' said Maria. 'We were talking of what it is to live for a while in another country, and I remarked that sometimes it is instructive to hear a foreigner speak of your own country to you. The things that impress them are often surprising. Major Wéry, I recall, mentioned a particular dance we do in Erzberg, for example.'

'Then I am sure you should teach it here,' said Cousin Ludwig. 'Dances that impress should not be kept a secret in Erzberg.'

'Oh!' said Maria. She waved her hand lightly as if to dismiss a compliment. Now that she had Wéry's scent, she did not want to lose it. 'But, sir,' she addressed Hofmeister. 'One sees so many exiles, and there is often something sad about them. Why would you envy this one?'

'Why? For his youth, and his lack of responsibilities, which allow him to do that which he most wishes, which is to curse and confront in arms this wretched barbarity that afflicts us and has betrayed us – I ask your pardon, brother Kaus, but so it is and so the night will tell you when you wake in the small hours. Wéry may make his stand freely, and reckon the likely cost only to his own bones and body. Would that I could do as he!'

'What sir!' cried Madame Kaus, with mock horror. 'Will you

269

leave us, leave my sister and her children, and go east to throw your body on the top of some rampart?'

'No, my dear,' said Hofmeister. 'It is this that I am saying. My heart is divided. But of course the greater part remains here, and here I remain, where I shall resist – forgive me again, brother Kaus – in such ways as I may. Let my General demand of me meat for his table and wine for his glass. Let his clerks requisition my saddle-leather. Let them call for the bells and the shoes and whatever they like. Let them levy – what is it up to now – fifteen million livres?'

'Twelve million,' said Ludwig.

'Twelve million livres, if you like. I shall send them the worst and least of what I have, and write them long wearying letters of poverty and injustice, and find for every Rhinelander and against every Frenchman that comes before me in my court. And I shall make believe that my pen is a musket and my desk a rampart east of the Rhine.'

'Very well,' said Kaus. 'But does this not hasten the moment when the army wearies of our administration and once again imposes its own?'

'Let them, sir,' said Hofmeister, and the redness of his face spoke of wine. 'It will be a relief to me!'

'I suggest that in this you indulge yourself still. The lot of the people would surely be worse.'

'The lot of the people, sir, would have been better if our Elector still sat in Mainz and we had all been let well alone! Hey, Jürich. Do you read your Bible these days? Come, tell me that you do.'

'For the most part I read the ancients,' said Ludwig. 'Especially when the air is bright and the news good. But yes, when the day darkens I find no consolation at the shrines of Reason. Then I will take myself to Scripture instead. I am sure that I am not alone in this.'

'Ay, sir, but the psalms – the *Misericordiam et judicium* – you have read it of late?'

'I believe I know it . . .'

'Read it, sir! The Archduke Charles – saints strengthen his brave young arm – would have us all read it! It is God's word, but also the word of the Archduke and his brother the Emperor to us here. *He that practices deceit will not dwell in my house; he that tells lies will not stand in my presence* . . . They shall not be suffered to remain, brother Kaus. Of that you may be certain!' He finished, flushed, leaning across the table to point his finger at the chest of the thin, green-clad man opposite him.

Kaus did not answer. He glared back at his brother-in-law.

'Gentlemen,' said Cousin Ludwig gently, rising to his feet. 'Let us remember that nights have dawns and wars have peace at the end of them. May ours not be far off.'

'Amen!' said his wife.

'And I think it is right that we drink a toast. To our guests, with our gratitude for what they have brought us, and for their presence most of all.'

'Our guests,' cried the women, and Septe. Someone clapped.

Ludwig remained standing. 'I have another to propose,' he said.

'Ah sir,' said Hofmeister. 'Now let us hear who you cleave to. The Elector or the Republic, I care not. But be bold. If you are not, I will name you a trimmer!'

'Indeed, I shall be bolder than you think, brother. My toast is to Germany.'

'Ho!' cried Hofmeister in surprise. 'And what may that mean?'

271

'I will drink to Germany, if I am allowed,' said Kaus, looking down at his fingers.

'Well . . .' said Hofmeister. 'Well, as you are my host – to Germany, then.'

'To Germany,' the diners repeated.

'To Germany,' said Maria. She had never drunk such a toast. But in that instant, in that place, the word had a meaning that she had not felt before. She had no very clear idea of what it was. She sensed a mass of neighbourhoods, spreading out from the place in which she stood: people, people and more people, unreachable and unembraceable. And it was only from here that she could see that they were all one – here in the huge shadow of something that they were not.

Later, when they gathered again in the bare and partly-furnished drawing room, Maria made sure that she spoke with each guest, contriving, by all her art and wit, with her rank, and with every device that she had ever seen employed in the salons of Erzberg, to be alone with them one after another, if only for moments. She dropped her fan for Septe, her handkerchief for Kaus. Each was returned to her gallantly, and without the scrap of paper she had been half-hoping for. No one gave her a sign, or hissed a rendezvous under the pretence of telling her some gossip. She finished the evening in the corner with Madame Kaus, listening to Hofmeister once again berating the woman's husband on the far side of the room.

'I suppose it is natural that the men should feel strongly,' she said in a low voice. 'But I hope that no ill-will comes of it.'

Madame Kaus looked at her. The laughter was gone from her face and in her eyes was the same weary look that she had seen in Emilia Jürich's. She put a hand on Maria's arm – perhaps it was to reassure both of them.

'I believe not,' she said in a low voice. 'For my sister's sake and mine, if not for their own. But it is hard. Hofmeister tries my husband sorely. It is unwise of him, as well as unkind. Oh, that wretched psalm! He *must* not speak like that. Sometimes I believe he is willing us to denounce him, as if that would prove him right about the evil of it all. And yet we are lucky, compared to so many. Have you seen your cousin Maximilian?' she asked Anna, who had joined them.

'I called on him in his room before dinner,' said Anna sadly. 'He knew me. Certainly he did. But I do not think he cared.'

'I am very sorry,' said Madame Kaus.

That night Maria dreamed. She was sitting in a dark room, in a house she knew quite well, but could not remember from where. Friends and members of her family came and went through the doors of the room. She was waiting for one of them to stop and say something to her: something important. But those that did speak to her only said that she should go on waiting, and others seemed to pass without paying her any attention. Gradually the comings and goings ceased. She watched the doors, and they did not open. And after a while she understood that she was alone. Everyone else had gone, and left her. And a great sense of desperation and urgency rose in her, for there was still something important, something very important, that she should know, and know soon. Terrible things would happen if she were not told quickly. But all the people who could tell her were gone.

Then, as the gloom deepened around the far corners of the room, she realized that not everyone had disappeared.

Somewhere on another storey, behind another door, there was someone else. And she and they were alone in the house together.

She woke, sick and urgent in the darkness. Her bedroom had two windows, but the night outside was very black. She could see almost nothing. The bedclothes, the little night noises, the very thickness of the air were all strange. She thought of the other people in the house, all asleep: Ludwig, the judge; his wife; his lunatic nephew; the servants, the horses, all around her. She thought of the leagues and leagues that lay between herself and home.

Why had she come? She longed to fly home at once, and be safe. But that was impossible. And the long, long journey to dawn seemed impossible, too.

She lay awake, and listened.

XX
The Breach

Major Jean-Marie Lanard, of the Army of the Republic of France, stood in the sunlit field below the walls of the city. He was dressed in an immaculate blue-and-white uniform and looked at the world with pale eyes and a permanent, slight smile upon his lips, as if he was amused by what he saw.

All the gaiety of Erzberg thronged around him. They had come, in their carriages and glittering cloths, with their bonnets and buckles and polished boots, to fete him as a society hero, and to watch the final surrender of the war party. They gathered in a long, chattering, brightly-coloured crowd in the mild October sun. Among them were a number – chiefly the young married men and women – who wore the new fashions that were emerging from France: simpler, country-style dresses for the ladies, with plumes of feathers in the hair. For the men, no powder, no wigs, no swords, and coats with no embroidery. Bobbing in the sea of tricorns, a dozen high-crowned, narrow-brimmed hats punched towards the sky.

Between the crowd and the moat a rope had been pegged at ankle-height, patrolled by grey-uniformed engineers who now and again called respectfully to persons at the front of the crowd to *move back, please, sir; move back*. The crowd obeyed, good-humouredly, and went on chatting, and the wind wavered over the bonnets and tall hats, teasing feathers and light veils and planting its cold kiss on a hundred wealthy cheeks.

An elderly engineer officer was watching the wall, shading his eyes with his hand. 'It will be any minute now, sirs,' he said.

'As it has been for the past quarter hour, I believe,' said the Frenchman cheerfully. 'But perhaps they have changed their minds after all, and are readying the guns instead.'

Someone near him laughed, nervously.

'Oh, I am serious, madame,' said Lanard. 'You should stand well away from me. You can never tell what these heroes will decide to do— Ah, no, I am mistaken. See there your signal, Captain.'

'That's it! That's it!' cried the engineer. At his nod the soldier beside him lifted a great pale flag and waved it in a wide arc above his head. On the point of the nearest bastion, another flag echoed it. The bearer, a tiny figure, disappeared.

Hundreds of eyes watched the wall. Nothing happened.

'Perhaps the powder . . .' began Lanard.

Smoke billowed in a thick, tight cloud below the ramparts. The line of the wall above it sagged gently, and disappeared in an uprush of dust and rubble. The great, rolling *boom!* reached the crowd, accompanied by the roar of tons of stone pouring down into the ditch.

'Oooh!' they cried, and some started clapping.

The cloud of dust hung, and hung, obscuring the wall. Slowly it parted. In the angle between two great bastions the neat lines of ramparts and glacis had been wrenched out, as if by a giant's fist, and rubble lay strewn all down the slope, choking the moat before them.

'Let peace reign!' cried a gentleman in the crowd importantly.

Wéry, standing a little aside among the engineers, did

not applaud. He had not taken his eyes off the Frenchman.

Since he's here, Bergesrode had said, you had better watch him. Make sure you know who he talks to, and what he says . . .

That, and a hard look, was all Bergesrode had said about the arrival of Major Lanard in the city. They did not seem to have guessed yet how the Frenchman had obtained his papers. And for the time being the palace was not going to risk uproar by revoking them. Perhaps the Prince had even decided that it suited him that the Inquiry should have such a witness.

Nevertheless, Bergesrode had sent him out here to be the palace eavesdropper. He would not be the only one. At this instant there were probably a dozen other ears of the Prince or Chapter or city police in the crowd, straining to hear what was said.

Wéry also had the impression that an intelligence office that produced no intelligence was suddenly worth rather less of Bergesrode's time than it had been. But at least they had not taken Asmus from him yet.

Lanard had not applauded or commented. His eyes ran over the damage to the wall, and over the two great bastions on either side of it. Any storming party that tried to gain the breach would still be subject to fire from left and right.

'Yes,' he said at length. 'A small hole.'

'We are constrained by the closeness of the houses on the inside of the wall, sir,' said the engineer quickly. 'But the same operation will be repeated on the citadel, as your authorities have requested.'

'On the east wall, no doubt?'

The east wall of the citadel faced over the town, and was the least exposed to any assault.

'It is the best for the purpose, sir.'

'Ah.'

The crowd was beginning to drift back to its carriages.

'You are coming to the levee, Major Lanard?' said a woman, who had ventured out into the fields in fine yellow silks. 'I insist that you should.'

'It is needless, madame,' said the Frenchman, with a bow and a smile. 'For my hostess has already insisted.'

'Wonderful! And how charming you are! I declare you are not at all what I expected.'

'From the cartoons I have seen,' sighed Lanard, 'I imagine you expected a monkey with bloody hands and the cap of liberty on its head. But there has been some poverty of understanding between my country and its neighbours of late.'

'It is all the fault of the Paris mob and the excesses they committed,' said a gentleman on the other side of him. 'Are you from Paris, Major?'

'I am from Poitou. But I have studied in Paris, and know its shortcomings.'

'Yes, we must take issue with you sir, for the sake of your countrymen. Come, is it not madness that descended upon your people? Such behaviour as no civilized nation should understand, or permit!'

'Indeed, sir,' said the Frenchman. 'Would that our folk were so contented as the Germans, who to please their lords would allow themselves to be sold to an English king to make battalions for his wars.'

'Aha! *Touché*, Baron, is it not?' cried the woman.

'Indeed, indeed. But you must beware of speaking too broadly, Major. That outrage was committed only in Hesse and Ansbach.

Not all princes comport themselves so towards their subjects.'

'I am well aware of it. Yours, I believe, is in some ways considered a model. And yet to be a prince at all – is that not to steal something from his subjects? Do not misunderstand me – I am not here to preach the Rights of Man. But these are ideas that long precede our revolution . . .'

'Of course, of course! You are speaking of Rousseau.'

'If you like . . .'

Wéry knew this was exactly the sort of conversation that Bergesrode would want him to report. But the crowd around the Frenchman was thick, and he had no wish to waste his energy burrowing through it. He had no stomach for this mission in any case. So far, he agreed with everything the speakers had said.

And now they were reaching the carriages, and the conversation was broken off, with both men promising that they would resume it as soon as they could. Wéry supposed that he should find out in which carriage the Frenchman rode, and who shared it with him, and so on. It was all useless information, yet if he reported less than other spies he would fall further from Bergesrode's favour.

But it was a bright day, perhaps the very last of the year, and what he most wanted to do was walk slowly back to his quarters and think of things that had nothing to do with intrigue, espionage, or the old, ugly memories that the sight of the Frenchman brought up within him.

A hand tapped him on the shoulder. He looked round into the face of Franz von Adelsheim.

A message? At last? But . . .

'M-mother wants you to come in our coach,' said the young man, whose gaze had already wandered away into the crowd.

Wéry did not know what to say. 'This is most unexpected.'

'The Frenchman wants it. He wants to meet you.'

The Frenchman? Yes, of course he was staying at the Adelsheim house.

'I think Mother was surprised, too,' said Franz, with the alarming clarity of the mentally affected.

'I . . . am most grateful, but . . .' He did not want to face the Frenchman. He did not want to face Lady Adelsheim, either.

'They're waiting for us,' said Franz and shambled off into the crowd.

And of course he could not refuse – not without giving mortal offence. And perhaps – just perhaps – this invitation had been arranged by Maria, so that she might pass something to him? (But under the nose of her mother and Lanard? Surely not!)

He hurried to keep up with Franz. 'Is your sister well?' he asked, falling in beside the young man. 'I have not seen her for some weeks.'

'Oh yes, I think so.'

Useless! Where was she?

But there was no more time to speak. They were at the door of the Adelsheim carriage – a closed coach, drawn by four black horses. Lady Adelsheim was inside, looking down at them. Two other women were already in the gig. One he recognized as Lady Machting, and the other he supposed must be the Machtings' daughter. There was no sign of Maria, or Madame Poppenstahl.

'My Lady,' he said.

'Major,' said Lady Adelsheim, coldly.

'I – er – trust your daughter is well?'

'She is quite well, sir,' said Lady Adelsheim. And she looked pointedly in another direction.

He climbed up to join them. Franz followed. The Frenchman was seated in the far corner. And Wéry found he must sit opposite him. The pale, amused eyes watched him as he struggled into his place. Wéry noted, too, that Lanard's uniform was that of a general's aide-de-camp. The man had risen since the day he stood with his infantrymen at Hersheim. No doubt it was the correspondence with the peace party in Erzberg that had drawn him to his masters' attention.

'Ah, the Brabançon!' said Lanard, who did not wait for an introduction. 'I have heard much of you.'

'I dare not think what you have heard, sir.'

'Many things. You are quite a swimmer, I understand. Now tell me, because we are all friends these days – how did you manage to pass out of a city under siege?'

How?

Wéry shifted, and tried to find a comfortable position. 'They say the Rhine is good to its children,' he said. 'Perhaps it adopted me.'

'Oh come! I am a soldier too. The river must have been the least of it. What of the walls, the patrols, the boats? A remarkable feat, and very subtle.'

Wéry smiled tightly.

'You will have had help, of course,' said Lanard. 'Perhaps you are reluctant to speak of that. But come – the city of Mainz is in Imperial hands again. No harm can come to your friends now. Nor do I wish them any. Is it not proper that men who have opposed one another in war may share their reminiscences in peace? Or are the Erzberg officers – I have had some experience of this, of course – still reluctant to believe in peace when it comes?'

Wéry smiled again and did not answer. The coachman called to the horses. Slowly the carriage began to move.

Lanard shrugged. 'Perhaps your friends are not as safe from us as I suppose them to be. Very well, we will speak no more of it.'

The carriage bumped and jolted on its way. It was one of a long train of vehicles snaking from the site of the breach around to the city gates. Every now and then it halted, waiting for the carriage in front to pick up speed again. The skirts of the three women took up four-fifths of the interior space. Lanard and Wéry were crammed into their corners with their knees against the doors. Even in this uncomfortable position the Frenchman seemed serene.

'All the city holds its breath for your testimony, Monsieur,' said Lady Machting.

'Then they may soon exercise their lungs again, my Lady. I understand the Commission desires to see me this afternoon, and also that Count Balcke has won the right to attend. I must say I did not think that I would meet that man again.'

'Indeed! Are you not nervous? You must stand no nonsense from the Inquisitor, sir. I have known Steinau for many years. He has his opinions but he is far from the worst of his set.'

'I believe the Canon Steinau is concerned to establish whether I am Christian. But I suspect it will be in my capacities to persuade him.'

'And will you also attend the Mass at the cathedral tomorrow, Monsieur?' asked the Machting girl.

'Naturally, Lady Elisabeth.' said Lanard. 'If you are to be of the party.'

'The Bach is a master of his profession, and must be heard.'

'Forgive me – the Bach?'

'The chapel-master. A relative of the great Bach.'

'Every prince must have his Bach,' said the Lady Adelsheim, in tones of mild scorn. 'As every cathedral must have its organ.'

'I fear I am no judge of music,' said Lanard. 'But I shall be delighted to see the cathedral. I have heard that the roof is a wonder.'

'The painted ceiling? Oh indeed! Do you admire such things?'

'Very much. It is curious in me, I know. But for me it is the highest of moments, to walk through a doorway and find, instead of a dull ceiling looming over my head — behold! One stands beneath a heaven.'

'Then,' said Lady Machting firmly, 'we must arrange a private audience for you with His Highness. For his office, it is said, is from floor to ceiling a depiction of Heaven, and widely admired!'

'So I have heard. But my Lady, supposing that you, with your infinite resource, were to obtain such an audience for me, it would be a sore trial indeed. For I doubt that it would be thought proper that my eyes should rove wall and ceiling while His Highness seeks to address me. Fortunate are those who have had the chance. Have you seen it, Major?'

'I?' said Wéry. 'No.'

'But are you not curious?'

'I confess I had not thought of it,' said Wéry coldly. 'I have seen the antechamber, but that room is often busy. If you look too much at the walls, you may miss your chance to be heard.'

'Ah yes. The offices of His Highness are often busy. And often to no purpose.'

'Quite so,' murmured the Lady Adelsheim.

'You do not agree, Major?' said Lanard. 'Yet it seems to me obvious. I understand that when my General Hoche returned to the Rhine in the summer, it was supposed in Erzberg that he was come to lead an advance on the city, and this was the cause of much excitement. Shall I discover to you the true reason?'

Wéry paused. 'If you wish,' he said.

'My General's return – in which I took part – was not an advance but a retreat. You will know there were political tensions in Paris over the summer. My General had been called by those who considered themselves faithful to the Revolution to come and set things right. The planned expedition to Ireland, of which you may have heard, was used as an excuse to move some of his force close to Paris. For a week or two he was lauded in the streets. He was Minister of War. He was the pillar of the government. But his enemies attacked him most viciously, and he sickened of it, resigned, and we withdrew our force as if defeated. That was all. Erzberg? We had opinions, to be sure, and I believe we communicated them to His Highness here. But our minds were in France, not Germany.'

'I see,' said Wéry, keeping his face as impassive as he could.

Was this true? If so, his report of the danger to Erzberg would have been false. His *interpretation* of it, to Bergesrode, to the Prince and the colonels on the battlements, would have been false. The one thing he thought he had achieved, the one blow he had struck, might be nothing at all – worse than nothing.

Could it be true? His faith in his work had fallen, but had it really fallen so far? From the corner of his eye he searched the Frenchman's face. Lanard was no longer looking at him, but away into the air.

'And then that ape Augereau went and did the deed anyway,'

sighed Lanard. 'Troops on the streets. Out with the royalists. Long live the Republic once more.'

Certainly there had been a coup in Paris. There would have been months of tension before that. Of course Hoche would have been caught up in it. Yes, it was plausible. It was more than plausible. It was absolutely the way things happened in Paris – except that Hoche had not spilled blood in pursuit of his ambition. He had left that to someone else. And out of that confusion he, Wéry, had spun a lie, and nearly sent the city into a hopeless war.

And *that* was the reason there was no news. That was why his message from the Rhine would not come! Because, seen from the Rhine, there had been nothing to report! There had been no movements, no preparations, nothing worth the risk of communicating across the river! All the sources from Wetzlar had told him nothing was happening. He had not believed them. And in the absence of the message from the Rhine, he had read only the most sinister possibilities.

Resign? Just let him get out of this coach, and he would resign at once!

'So – your General had a chance of greatness, and did not take it,' said Lady Machting. 'Did he regret it?'

'In truth I do not know, my Lady. For when I returned to Wetzlar he was already sick, and within a few days he was dead. His surgeon says it was a suffocating illness. I have heard others claim it was poison. On what evidence, I do not know. But I suspect that what you say is also close to the truth. Truly, for a few days, he could have been the Saviour of the Republic. Certainly he had that ambition. But he had not enough ambition to pay the price that would make it his. He was disappointed in himself, and disappointment sickens, I think.'

285

'I am so sorry,' said the Machting daughter. 'And I am sorry for you too, Major, for I suppose you had high hopes for him, and for yourself too.'

'You are right, Lady Elisabeth. But in the event, no, I would not have wished to see shooting in a city, or for him to have climbed to power over Parisian corpses. Nevertheless he is a loss. He leaves a young wife – a German lady, in fact – as well as those of us who knew him. Ah, there is no use regretting. But we lose generals too easily. Our heroes fall like wheat. And mostly it is our own fault.' The smile was back again, like a mask. 'Eighty-four we have sent to the guillotine since the war began. Perhaps, if he had not resigned, Hoche would have gone that way. Perhaps Augereau will yet – though I do not think so.'

'Eighty-four!' cried Lady Adelsheim. 'To say nothing of Louis d'Orleans, Madame Roland, Danton, Robespierre and all the rest. Truly, sir, I find that your Revolution consumes itself!'

'Almost as fast as it consumes everything about it,' murmured Wéry.

'Ah, that is the war,' said Lanard.

'War may be waged in different ways,' said Wéry. 'Imperial officers may be court-martialled if they allow their soldiers to plunder.'

He knew he was sounding graceless but he could not help it. The discovery of his failure – yet another failure – had shaken him.

'And yet I do not think they are altogether without sin. But if I, an officer of the Republic, am starving because the Republic cannot feed me, and if my soldiers bring me food that they have found, shall I eat it first and arrest them afterwards? Or shall I arrest them first and carry on starving? The miseries of the war lie at the door of those who incited it – Citizen Wéry.'

Wéry felt as if he had been stroked with a hot iron. *Those who incited it – Citizen Wéry*. Shadows tumbled into his head – ugly memories of Paris, and close, hot rooms crammed with faces, and his own voice speaking words that had then seemed so good. Was that what the man meant? What did he know?

Hadn't he done enough since, to bury all that behind him?

He glared at the Frenchman. The smile broadened.

'Now – if my Lady will forgive me, and since we are talking of such things, I must counter-attack. You, sir, were one of us. You were a rebel with Vonck in Brabant. You fought the Austrians at Turnhout. You were one of the international delegates who came to Paris. I *believe* you even addressed the Jacobin club on behalf of your countrymen – a thing I can hardly claim for myself. Now here you are, an obedient servant of the Empire, struggling – vainly I may say – to contain the forces of liberty that once you espoused. How were you suborned?'

'Suborned?'

God! He could wring the man's neck! Or at the very least, challenge him!

'Come,' said Lanard. 'I did not mean to insult you. To be corrupt is to be human, I think, and often preferable to the alternative. As I believe you saw "The Incorruptible" – Robespierre himself – it is a thing you too should understand.'

'Sir!' said Wéry. 'I think you presume on your status as a guest here!'

He fought to control himself, aware of the women in the coach, and of the eyes of Lady Adelsheim fixed on him in cold surprise.

'. . . But be that as it may,' he managed, 'I tell you that it is a

287

question not of whether I have been "suborned" or "corrupted", but of what has corrupted your revolution so far – so *very* far – that its word has proved utterly different from its deed, and that those who were most friendly to its ideals – and not I alone – should become its most constant enemies!'

'Ah, so it is anger,' said the Frenchman smoothly. 'My General too was an angry man, although not in your way. He used to bite his knuckles, sometimes. I see from the marks on your hand that you may know what that means. But when the time came for calm, he could be calm, and so he brought peace to the Vendée when no one else would have done . . .

'But let me make two observations, Wéry. First, to block your charge, let me answer that a revolution is made of many voices, and that many different things will be said before a course is decided upon. This is plain. But also – and here I turn your flank – that your view of us has led you to serve the very opposite of what I know you believed. Will you tell me that is not corruption?'

The carriage had passed the gates of the town. Now it turned to the right, heading back along the line of the wall towards the hussar barracks. A few minutes more, and this impossible conversation would be over. He had only to hold out.

'I believe,' he said, 'that it would be better if we did not speak about this further in this company. If, at another time, you choose to repeat your words . . .'

But now the counter–attack was supported with heavy artillery. For the Lady Adelsheim broke her silence at last.

'No, sir!' she exclaimed. 'I declare this is an interesting discussion after all! Since my cousin the Prince chooses to increase his power in the face of all good counsel, and then uses that power for war and misery, are not all who choose to serve him condemned with him?'

'My Lady,' said Wéry desperately. 'Another time I shall endeavour to satisfy you. But we have almost reached my quarters, and to answer you I must keep your carriage standing in the street longer than you may desire.'

'The carriage may drive around again,' said Lady Adelsheim. 'And it is inexcusable, Major, to dismiss yourself before I am finished. Come. You will no doubt tell me that you face a choice of two evils. But my son has been crushed between your evils, and I wish to ask you why any man should adhere to either.'

Wéry spread his hands, helplessly. He saw the coachman flick his whip gently, impelling the carriage on past the barrack gates. He knew Lady Adelsheim was watching him, preparing her next salvo. And the Frenchman was listening, with that maddening, amused smile on his face.

'My Lady,' he began. 'I too grieved and continue to grieve for the loss of your son, who was the first and best friend to me in all Erzberg . . .'

'Indeed? And you suppose this will excuse the choices you have made?'

'My Lady . . .'

XXI
The Maimed Colossus

News reached Erzberg that evening. A treaty had been signed at last between the Empire and the Republic.

No one seemed to know what the treaty contained. Everyone assumed that Liège and the Austrian territories in the Netherlands had been surrendered to France and that the French would withdraw in Italy. There was no word on how far the Emperor had honoured his pledge to 'the integrity of the German body', or what would happen to the Rhineland in particular. It was said that the French and Austrians would hold a congress at Rastatt with the princes of Germany to discuss the peace, but it was not clear what there was to discuss.

Bells were rung again in the city. Rumours hissed along the corridors of the Celesterburg palace. In the Saint Lucia barracks Wéry dismissed Asmus and went down to the coffee house Stocke, to comfort himself with stimulant and the smell of tobacco.

Heroes fell like wheat, he thought, staring into the little black pool of the cup before him. Still the world longed for the next to appear.

Hoche had been a hero to his people. He could have become a saviour, if he had been prepared to pay the price. But because the price was to be the blood of his own people he did not pay it.

Now they would wait for another saviour to come.

If Hoche could rise from grenadier to be Minister of War, if Bonaparte, a captain of artillery, could bring an empire to its knees, then *anything* was possible. He must remember that. Failures did not matter. Defeats were only to be overcome. What mattered was absolute, single-minded, purity of . . .

'There he is!'

A crowd of white uniforms surrounded him. Heiss was there, and with him was Skatt-Hesse of the Erzberg regiment, and a number of other captains and majors of infantry. Their expressions were ugly.

Heiss leaned forward, planting both hands flat on the table.

'That Frenchman. Is he a friend of yours?'

'Not in the least,' said Wéry coldly.

'Is he not, now? So why is the palace saying you were the one who requested his pass?'

The palace? God damn it!

Wéry looked into Heiss's red face. He wondered if the whole world was tumbling around his ears today.

'They're fools,' he said.

'Come, that won't do!' said Skatt-Hesse. 'That man damned well crucified the army this afternoon. Did you or did you not get them to let him in?'

The wood of the partition was hard against the back of his head, and his cheek muscles felt like wood, too.

'I did.'

'Damnation!' cried Heiss. 'Why in heaven?'

'Reasons of state.'

'Don't give me that! That's clerk's talk!'

'It is true, however. And I regret to tell you that I cannot say any more. If you doubt it, ask yourself why His Highness did not revoke the pass.'

Skatt-Hesse adopted a look of contempt.

'Well, he could hardly have done that after it had been issued, could he? Not with the Chapter and the Estates and the War Commission all panting to hear what the fellow said.'

'I cannot help what he had to say. But yes, I did help with his papers. That is all.'

'All!' roared Heiss. 'If they take that man's word over ours, we'll go down, and you know that! See here, Wéry. There've been times I thought pulling you out of the Rhine was the best thing we ever did. Now I wish we'd just pushed you straight back in. At least we'd have to deal with fewer *lies*!'

The others crowded in behind him.

'Did you feel fine, Wéry, riding in the Adelsheim carriage like a lickspittle?'

'You can be a knave or an idiot as you please, Wéry. But it has to be one or the other!'

'And don't talk to us about honour. If we hear any more we might be sick . . .'

'Enough,' said Skatt-Hesse coldly. 'Let's leave him.'

They turned and began to crowd back to the door of the coffee house. Wéry watched them. His cheeks were flaming. He saw the set of their shoulders, the shape of their ears, the lamp-light glinting on the brassy epaulettes. Their boots had a thin patina of the dust from the streets. And if he hesitated for an instant they would think him a coward.

'Gentlemen!' he called, keeping his voice as steady as he could.

Two or three of them turned at once. They had been expecting this. Their eyes were blank – masks of contempt. Wéry rose, awkwardly, in the narrow space between bench and table.

'Gentlemen,' he said, pitching his voice to carry clearly across the room. 'In the space of a minute you have called me, I think, a clerk, a lickspittle, an idiot, a knave, and a liar. Am I right?'

None of their faces changed. None of them would draw back from it.

'I am a foreigner and I have my views,' he continued. 'But I hold a commission from your Prince, and I think you will permit me the customary recourse. I am very much afraid that I am going to have to kill somebody.'

And he could not draw back either. He was committed. And he did not care. He only wanted to damage something, or somebody.

Still they were waiting for him. He drew breath.

'If you would please see that I am notified which of you . . .'

'That is enough, gentlemen,' said another voice.

From behind a wooden partition in the corner of the room rose the vast head and shoulders of the Count Balcke-Horneswerden.

He was wrapped in a heavy cloak, as if he were cold, and he was alone. Perhaps he too had been brooding by himself over a cooling cup of coffee all this while. But there was nothing mournful about him now. He leaned over the partition. His skin was dark and his eyes black as the mouths of cannon.

'Gather round,' he said softly. 'I do not wish to shout.'

They shuffled closer to him.

In the same low tone, a rumble that was almost a mutter, he said, 'Gentlemen are gentlemen wherever they go. But when they wear my Prince's uniform they are to be soldiers first and last. Their lives are at His Highness's disposal and no one else's. Does anyone disagree? No? Good. Now, I believe some question has arisen over the commitment of one of you. Let me settle it. His Highness has chosen Major Wéry to perform certain very exacting duties. It is our duty to support him as we may. If you ask me why His Highness has so chosen, I will tell you that he was so advised by myself . . .'

He paused, and took a fresh grip on the partition before him.

'I so advised His Highness because I believed Major Wéry would be useful to us in ways that no other man in Erzberg could. If asked today I would so advise again.

'And I would also advise that when the Pope, and the Emperor, every last prince in Germany, and every one of you, gentlemen, are ready to knuckle under to the French, this man Wéry will still be fighting them. This is my opinion, which you will please to value above your own.

'Now. You will have duties to attend to. If you think you have not, I can persuade you otherwise. Thank you. Wéry, wait a moment.'

The officers dispersed silently. Wéry was alone with the man he had betrayed. His body had locked itself into an attitude of rigid attention.

Balcke leaned his elbows on the partition.

'Now, Wéry. Just one question, and by God I want the truth. You said you brought that man here for reasons of state. Did the Prince tell you to do so?'

'No, sir.'

'Did he know, or did anyone close to him know, that you were going to bring the man here?'

'No, sir.'

Balcke let out his breath. 'If that's right, then I may beat this thing yet. So, you were playing one of your own little games, were you? I hope you're proud of yourself.'

'I'm not, sir. And I would like to apol—'

'*Don't* give me that! Don't make me think that after all you are one of these spineless, over-the-shoulder *back-lookers* who gets all tearful about what they've done! See here, Wéry. I'm as guilty as hell of the things they say I did. But the only thing I'll regret is that I didn't handle it differently when the story first came out in front of His Highness. I should have made a clean breast of it there on the bastion. But that damned Italian had my goat, and so I lied in my Prince's face. None of that changes the fact that the Prince needs me to make sure the army is there for him when it has to be. And he needs you to tip him the warning of when that time will be. So . . .' he said, jabbing a thick finger towards Wéry's face. '. . . You may make your nest in this city. You may even play your games if you have to. But you may *not* kill my officers. And you may *not* get yourself killed either. *Is that clear?*'

'Yes, sir.'

'Hah. You'll find staying alive harder than you think, after the things you said just now. My advice is, keep to the barracks, unless you have some specific and immediate duty that takes you outside. The hussars may not like you, but they won't like the other regiments picking fights with their uniform either. They'll close ranks around you, unless you give them a reason not to. You understand?'

'Yes, sir.'

'Good. And I'll make sure that old woman Altmantz understands too.'

His eyes held Wéry's for a long moment. Then, in a slightly altered tone, he said, 'Now, man, what's biting you?'

Wéry drew breath. Twice today he had almost challenged someone to a duel. It was as if something inside him was screaming to find a way out of what he was doing – even at the cost of death, wounding or disgrace.

'I – don't like this post, sir. And I don't think I'm doing it very well.'

'That's damned rubbish! You do good work.'

'I doubt if Bergesrode would agree with you, sir.'

'Bergesrode? Bergesrode didn't appoint you. The Prince did. He and I got drunk together and decided it would be a good idea. We still think it's a good idea. And I'll tell you, if you didn't realize, that Altmantz nearly resigned when we foisted you on his precious hussars. But I spoke with him and changed his mind for him. So don't worry about Bergesrode. If he's bothered, it'll be about something else. He's too close to the Ingolstadt set, that one. Ultramontanism, the ties of Rome, peg everything back to the Middle Ages – all that. A very uncomfortable position, when you've a man like His Highness as your master. And now there's no threat of war to bring the Ingolstadt set behind the Prince, of course they'll fall out. That's all it will be.'

'You may be right, sir.'

'You can be damned sure I'm right. I've known Erzberg all my life. Now take yourself off somewhere and be useful. And get them to send me some more coffee on your way out.'

XXII
The Madman's Easel

On a Sunday in the village of Knopsdorf, Father Septe spoke as usual from his pulpit. Because of events in the world, he said (referring to the Treaty, and the hope that the Rhineland would be restored to the Empire) it was more than ever necessary to be sure of the favour of the Almighty and his Saints. Therefore the good people of Knopsdorf must make their lives more pleasing in his sight and work for the restoration of the Church to its rightful place . . .

And so forth.

Maria, sitting at the front of the church with the Jürichs and Anna, thought no more of it than that it was a sermon such as she had heard a thousand times before. She felt she did well to listen to the end without yawning. She never dreamed that his words would lead to his arrest.

The family were at lunch some days later when men came running to the door. There were soldiers at Father Septe's house, they said. Emilia cried out in horror. Ludwig rose from the table, hurriedly brushing away crumbs, and called for his horse. Emilia fetched his cloak herself and threw it round his shoulders, begging him at the same time to be careful. Everyone fussed to and fro until he was out of the door. And when he was gone, no one felt like finishing their meal.

297

That afternoon, while they were all still waiting for news, Anna caught Maria in the little drawing room.

'My dear,' she said in a low voice. 'I wonder if we should not think when we mean to leave?'

'Leave, Anna? At a time like this? How could we?'

'Well, I cannot see how we can help them more than we have. And I must think of your safety.'

'I am sure all will be well, Anna,' said Maria determinedly. 'Ludwig has gone to speak with the soldiers. And whether it is well or not, we can help your cousins by being company to them in a difficult time. You know they are pleased to have us. And it has been a pleasure to be here. You cannot wish to say goodbye already.'

'My dear, of course it is a pleasure for me. And yet it is no pleasure to think of what *could* happen here. Also I know it is hard for dear Emilia. She is worrying about Christmas, so. She has so little to offer us.'

'Oh, perhaps we will not impose on them for Christmas. It will not be that long.'

'What will not be that long? You are surely not still waiting for some silly package? If there had been anything, it would have been given to us by now. Perhaps it has already gone, by another way. Really, I hope that no one here has anything to do with such things. It must be very dangerous.'

Dangerous indeed, thought Maria, when soldiers might march up and seize people without warning! Was that why there had been nothing – no messages, no signs, no urgent whispers in the dark? Was that why no one had called her aside or slipped a sealed packet into her hand? Because it was just too dangerous? Day had followed day, with frugal meals and little to do. And every day there was nothing.

Or was it that no message had ever existed, except in her imagination and that of Wéry? Was she here on a fool's errand, after all?

And how long could they remain safe?

Yet still she smiled in Anna's anxious face, and said Not Yet.

'I am sure you are right, Anna. Therefore let us enjoy our visit with a clear conscience. And yes, of course we cannot stay for ever. But in truth I think it would be wrong to think more of it now.'

For whatever her regrets, she was here, and any day might bring the answer to her riddle. She would tempt fate here a little longer. She could always wait a little longer, if she could get what she came for.

Ludwig returned some hours later, alone and dejected, to anxious cries from his wife. 'Dearest, are you all right? What happened? Did you find him? Is it well with him?'

'With Septe? I confess I do not know. The soldiers were gone when I came to his house. I followed, thinking to overtake them and speak with their officer. But as I was passing through Bringen I learned that they had set upon a man there, and killed him.'

'What – not Septe!'

'No, my dear. It was an unfortunate gentleman from Kaiserslautern whom they met on the road. He was possessed, it seems, of a silver watch, and would not part with it when they demanded it of him. Several of the Bringen folk saw it happen, and I have their accounts.'

'Horrible! Why do they act so? They are monsters!'

'They are men, which may be much the same thing. But I recalled that I, too, was carrying my watch, and that even if I did overtake them I could do little good to Septe and maybe some harm to myself, given the mood they were in.' He sighed. 'I shall write to the General on both counts, all the same. I suppose they have taken Septe because of what he said last Sunday. It was unwise of him to talk of the Empire and the restoration of the Church. Any ragged informer might have twisted such words to earn himself a coin.'

'They will deport him,' said Emilia sadly. 'They have done it before.'

'There is still hope, my dear, if I am quick. Lady Maria, I must beg your pardon most humbly. But I think it will not be possible for us all to ride out this afternoon. In fact, I believe that for the time being it would be wise if we all remained as close as possible to the house.'

'Of course, sir,' said Maria. 'We will do as you think best.'

'I am obliged to you,' he said.

She looked at him, and saw there the same polite calm that he had worn like a mask from the first day.

They could not ride out. They could walk only short distances from the house, for fear of falling in with ill-disciplined soldiers. And there was no town to go to, with Mainz in imperial hands and the French soldiers ringing it outside. There was very little to do. Maria took to the library in the mornings, to spare her hostess from entertaining her. Most of the shelves were empty – Ludwig Jürich had sold many of his books, to pay for some levy from the occupying forces – but there was still pen, ink and a little paper, and she could compose closely-written letters to her father, who of all the people at home was now the one she missed most. She included covering notes to Dietrich, asking him to be sure that the letters were read out to Father, and demanding reports on Father's health.

One bright December day, the shortage of paper forced her to finish her latest letter about an hour before noon. She rose to her feet, thinking that she might walk in the garden, which was pleasant enough, if she averted her eyes from the beds that were gone to ruin because the gardeners had vanished. She left the library and stepped into the corridor.

It was at that moment that a servant came out of a door to her left. He was a tall, sad-eyed man, in a livery doublet with a wig that did not fit him very well. She had seen him often about the house, and waiting on the family at table.

He stopped when he saw her, his hand in the act of closing the door. There were rooms beyond. She had not been in there.

She had not been in there because these were the doors to Maximilian's quarters.

Maria had grown accustomed to the idea that one of the Jürichs lived apart from the rest of the household, and was not seen. She took her cue from her hosts, for whom the thing was a part of their lives. She had heard them speak of him, two or three times, when he was demanding things that were not to be had, or that would have to be sought in the towns further down the Rhine. She was curious, but she had not asked about him directly because she felt that it might be indelicate. In a way, she supposed, it was not very different from how things were at home, with Father. Father could be unnerving for strangers, until you came to know him.

Only at night, when the fetters of reason loosened, might she turn in the darkness and think that a madman paced in the house in which she lay.

The servant was carrying a bowl of water, and had a towel over his shoulder. In the bowl were a razor and traces of lather.

He had been shaving the man in the room, and now had finished. So presumably the man would now be made presentable, as Father was made presentable every morning at home.

Normally, it was possible to see him, Cousin Ludwig had said.

Perhaps she should ask Cousin Ludwig first. He had said that there would be arrangements to be made.

But she had understood that those arrangements were simply to ensure that someone else was present. A footman would do. And here was a footman, arrested in the doorway, looking at her as though expecting her to say something. There was yet an hour to go before noon. And if she turned and walked away down the corridor, even to seek out Cousin Ludwig, it would be because she was afraid.

She took a step towards the footman.

'Is he . . . Is it possible to call on him?' she asked.

Wordlessly, as if this were exactly what he had been expecting, the man stepped back through the door. She followed.

She stood in a little room, almost a corridor. At the further end there was another door. The man knocked softly at it and went in, motioning her to stay where she was. She heard the soft murmur of voices from beyond. There was a faint smell in the air: tantalizingly familiar, and yet she could not identify it.

She waited. In the room there was a chair, a small chest, and little else. On one wall was a painting.

It was a painting of the head and shoulders of Christ, in his last agony upon the cross. Set upon a background of pastoral scenes, the dying face occupied almost half the canvas. It was painted crudely, with the flesh glowing yellow, as if someone close by was holding a lamp. The wounds of the thorns were a dirty brown-red; they looked foul and messy. The whites of the eyes showed huge. The mouth was open in a soundless cry of pain. Maria thought it a small obscenity that the Saviour should be shown with so many teeth missing.

The more she stared at the horrid thing, the more she hated it. It seemed to her that the man in the picture was not merely dying but *had died*. The face was as insensible to the agony stamped upon it as was a coin to its king's head.

She stared at it, and looked away. But she could not keep her eyes off it. Again they were drawn back to it: to that horrible portrait of pain.

What joy could there have been in making such a thing?

The servant reappeared in the doorway, beckoning. She followed him into a large, sunlit room. Instantly the smell was stronger. The air reeked with it, and she knew it. It was oil paint.

It was a big room, the twin of the dining room at the other end of the house. A range of long windows to her right and in the wall opposite let in the day.

Between the windows, and all around the walls, above and below one another, were paintings. And they were all the same. Each one showed the face of Christ, in agony on the cross. Fifty – a hundred – faces of the tortured man rolled their eyes on those walls: over and over again, in relentless, shadowy oils, the same howl of pain.

The artist himself was working at an easel in a corner of the room, where two windows gave him light. He had not looked up. He did not seem to have noticed her.

He was in his shirtsleeves, and his dark hair was tousled. Heavy brows frowned from his face at the painting in front of him. He resembled his uncle very little. After waiting a moment she walked over towards him. There had been a carpet in the room, but it was gone. Her feet sounded loudly on the wooden floor. Still he did not look up.

She stopped.

'I hope, sir, that I find you well,' she said.

The man paused. He looked not at her, but at the space in front of him. After a moment he went back to painting.

It was so rude that it was not rude.

Yes, she thought. Clearly it was better that this man did not take meals with the rest of the house.

'I'm well,' he said. His eyes followed the minute movements of the tip of his brush. After waiting for more, Maria stepped around to look over his shoulder.

There was the face of Christ again, starker than ever as it lolled on the plain canvas where no background had yet been coloured in. The brush was making tiny, pale strokes in the white of the left eye. The man leaned into his work. His body and hand and eye all were intent on the easel before him. She waited to see if he would explain what he was doing. But he did not. He ignored her and carried on.

'I am a visitor,' she said, speaking slowly and clearly, as though she was addressing her father. 'I came with your cousin Anna Poppenstahl.'

'Yes,' said the man. 'I know.'

A few strokes later he said, 'Hartmann.'

'Sir,' said the servant, still standing by the door with the bowl in his hand.

'I need more fine brushes.'

'Yes, sir.'

'You must get me some.'

'Yes, sir.'

304

There were many, many brushes on the table beside the painter. There were others littered around the room. Why did he want more? A paintbrush – even such a thing as a paintbrush – must be terribly expensive in the war-ravaged Rhineland. Surely Ludwig Jürich had better things on which to spend his money than more paintbrushes!

The servant, Hartmann, had remained by the door. He could not leave until she did. The painter had not noticed. But in a moment he would. And then what? Would he fly into a rage? The servant was in a difficult position. Perhaps she should leave. The man was not going to speak. She had seen him now. She understood the distress of the house. Why stay longer than she needed to?

The man went on painting. She stepped away from the easel and looked at some of the paintings on the wall.

They were not all exactly the same. She could pick out occasional slight differences between one face and another – in the light, in the fall of the hair, in a shadow applied too clumsily. There were different backgrounds too. They were mostly views of countryside, with hills and towns in the distance, with kings and legionaries and angels grouped in allegories in the mid-distance and tiny figures scurrying like ants across the landscapes behind them. But all interest in such details failed before the face. The face, and the agony of Christ.

She thought of all the bare walls of the house, stripped of paintings when Ludwig and Emilia had had to sell them. They had not chosen to replace what they had lost with any of these. Small wonder.

'Why have you done so many that are so like each other?' she asked.

Again that pause, as if his mind had to travel a long, long way back from where it had gone in order to answer.

'It's what you see that matters.'

'Thank you,' she said.

After a few moments more she stole out of the room. The servant followed, balancing his bowl in one hand while he closed the door. In the corridor she turned to him.

'Let me pay for his brushes,' she said.

The servant looked at her in surprise.

'Did he not instruct you to buy brushes?' she asked.

'He did, my Lady. I go to Koblenz for them.'

'Come, then. Your master has so many things to bear, and brushes must be expensive even when you can find them. Let me give these as a gift. And you can add some brighter colours, if you think he will use them. You may tell him they are from me.'

'Very good, my Lady.'

After that, she sought out her hostess and they walked together in the garden.

'He was always passionate, where Ludwig is moderate,' said Emilia. 'He joined the republicans in Mainz after the Elector fled. He had such high hopes for the new state. Of course, under the French the republicans split. There were purges. He found he could trust so few people. Ludwig went to the city to beg him to leave, but he would not. Then the Austrians and Prussians besieged the city. It was a terrible time for all of us, for Ludwig was trapped in the city with him, and so was Hofmeister. The danger to them was very great, for Ludwig and Hofmeister were former officials of the Elector, and if the republicans had found them they would have been driven out of the city to starve between the lines, as so many others did. So Maximilian was hiding them, and putting himself at risk of a treason charge. When surrender was near he and some friends tried to open negotiations with the Imperial force, but it was already too late. The French left the city, and the townspeople turned on the men who had brought them the republic. He would have been killed if Ludwig had not saved him.

'Think of it – to have had dreams that you could better the lot of your fellow men. And then to see everything you did corrupted and become crimes, until you are hunted by the very people you have sought to help! And of course what he paints now comes from the things he saw then.'

'He said to me "It's what you see that matters",' said Maria sombrely. 'I suppose he meant that it is what you *have* seen.'

'I suppose so.'

XXIII
The Scent of Danger

'Here,' said Bergesrode, in the antechamber at dawn. 'It's taken a while to emerge but you had better see how it went.' He passed some sheets of closely-written paper across his desk.

Wéry took them. They were a draft, with many corrections and notes in the margins. He did not recognize the writing. But the first page began: 'Testimony of Major Jean-Marie Lanard, formerly of the 16th Demi-Brigade of the Line of the so-called French Republic.' The words 'so-called French Republic' had been deleted and in their place the words 'country of France' had been inserted, written small between the lines.

Wéry glanced up at Bergesrode, surprised. But Bergesrode was already absorbed, or was pretending to be absorbed, in Wéry's own summary of the latest reports from around Wetzlar. Wéry looked down at the transcript again.

On being invited to proceed, Major Lanard stated that, in accordance with orders received in the course of the twenty-second of April, his company, together with two other companies of his battalion and a battery of field guns, marched through the night to occupy the ridge to the east of the bridge at Hersheim. This they achieved without encountering the enemy . . .

The words 'the enemy' had been deleted and in their place a note was added in the margin 'forces of the Empire'.

> . . . his company, stationed in the centre. While overseeing this manoeuvre, he received a further message to attend a meeting with his company commander and the commanders of the other companies, and of the battery. At this meeting he was informed of messages from his brigade headquarters with news of the Armistice at Loeben and orders to observe a ceasefire with [enemy] Imperial forces . . .

It went on, for page after page. Lanard must have been before the War Commission for the best part of the day. Wéry skipped forward, familiar with the details of the story but eager to see how the Frenchman had told it.

> . . . At ten o'clock the head of a column of [enemy] Imperial troops was sighted emerging from the woods on the opposite bank . . .

Such a sentence might have been dictated by any Imperial officer. It took a soldier to read beyond the bald words and know the horrible, crawling thrill at the sight of those distant uniforms. The enemy!

> . . . instructed to cross the river, under a flag of truce, to ensure that the commander of the force was aware of the ceasefire, and to establish his intentions.

At this point in the narrative there must have been an

interruption, for the next few lines were half-completed jottings in the clerk's hand, most of which appeared to have been written hurriedly and had subsequently been crossed out. Then there followed an exchange in which Lanard appeared to have played no part at all.

On being granted permission to address the Inquiry, Count Balcke-Horneswerden asserted that the testimony of Major Lanard could be given no credence. The Observation was made that Major Lanard had not yet said what had passed at the parley, and the Question was put to the Count: what grounds he had for his assertion. The Answer of Count Balcke-Horneswerden: that the word of an officer of the so-called Republic could not be trusted.

The Question was put: whether Count Balcke-Horneswerden would not believe the word of such an officer. The Answer. He would not.

The Question: whether this would be true, even if the officer brought Count Balcke-Horneswerden news that might be of very great importance to the men under his command. A further Question was put: whether Count Balcke-Horneswerden would, on receiving such news, take steps to find out whether it were true. The Answer of Count Balcke-Horneswerden: that the actions of the revolutionary forces and their government over a number of years made it plain that they did not recognize the concept of honour.

The Observation was made that this point had been considered by the Representatives of the War Commission before Major Lanard had been permitted to give his testimony. Major Lanard was invited to continue.

Wéry skipped on hurriedly down the page.

> ... that he had informed the senior Imperial officer, Count
> Balcke-Horneswerden, of the ceasefire, that he had repeated
> this several times, and that he had offered to return to his lines
> to bring back the message they had received from their
> brigade. To which Count Balcke-Horneswerden had replied
> that he should return to his lines and remain there.
>
> On being granted permission to address the Inquiry, Count
> Balcke-Horneswerden asserted ...

Poor Old Blinkers. All he had achieved had been to turn the
interrogation away from Lanard and onto himself. Wéry could
well picture the scene: the three inquisitors, the quick-witted
Frenchman, and Balcke, red-faced, battering vainly away at points
which the Inquiry had no intention of granting him. There was
no doubt who had come off worst.

And then, lower down:

> ... conference of French officers, at which one of the company
> commanders, a Major Bretonne, proposed to the senior
> officer that the 2nd Battalion should itself withdraw to a
> distance until the Imperial forces could be persuaded of the
> ceasefire. Major Lanard further stated that the French officers
> were still debating this possibility when the Imperial cannon
> opened fire. Major Lanard wished the Inquiry to record that
> Major Bretonne was subsequently killed in the action ...

Skatt-Hesse and the others had been right. The army had been
crucified.

'It looks bad,' he said, handing it back over the desk.

'Yes,' said Bergesrode shortly. There was a pause, as though he was waiting for Wéry to say something.

'Thank you for showing it to me.'

'I thought you should see it.' And then: 'So why did you do it?'

'Do what?'

'Bring that man here!'

So they had come to it, now.

'I did have a hand in the arrangements,' he said slowly. 'It was rather against my will. But the price was something we needed badly.'

'What?'

'A safe link to the Rhine.' He said it as stoutly as if he still believed, to the very heart of his heart, that Maria von Adelsheim could keep a promise.

Bergesrode's face hardened, as if nothing that could possibly come from the Rhine could have been worth allowing an officer of the revolution into Erzberg.

'The reports could be very valuable,' Wéry added.

'Yes?' said Bergesrode. And he slammed his desk and screamed, '*Where are they, then?*'

Wéry jumped. With another man he would have expected fits of rage, but not with Bergesrode. This was not Bergesrode. This was a wounded animal.

And he had nothing to say. There was no way he could defend himself. The reports had not come. He had gambled – gambled grotesquely – and lost. Was it dismissal, at last?

The two men glared at one another. The silence between them lengthened. Wéry sensed a struggle in Bergesrode's eyes as the priest mastered himself. He sensed exhaustion (Heaven knew

312

what hours the man slept!). He remembered what Balcke had said about the tensions between the Prince and the Ingolstadt set, and how Bergesrode might be affected. And none of that would help him now.

Bergesrode looked down at Wéry's report again. 'They are still reducing, then,' he said coldly.

'So it seems.'

'What does it mean?'

'For us, not much. It would be natural to pull some strength back across the Rhine – there must be an endless list of tasks for them to do. But what they have left is more than enough to move against us – supposing they have the guns.'

'And have they?'

'I don't know.'

'You don't know. That's always the answer, isn't it? Maybe this, maybe that, but we don't know. We just don't know. There is no information!'

'I'm doing what I can!' said Wéry. Now he wanted to scream. He wanted to shout back at Bergesrode – to demand how, since the Prince's Treasury could afford no more than a bare dozen informants scattered across middle Germany, he was to steal the secrets of high policy, and whether he was expected to measure each muzzle of every gun in the camps of the Armée d'Allemagne at the same time! And also why he should bother, since every report only provoked more questions! But it would be pointless, pointless . . .

'So this is the best you can do, is it? After what we – and you – have paid?'

The Frenchman again.

'I told you, I'm still . . .'

313

'Still waiting. So am I. And on the Illuminati? Nothing on them either, I suppose. This is not . . .'

'*Yes!*' Wéry exploded. 'Yes, I have had something on your precious Illuminati!'

'You have? What?'

Instantly Wéry regretted his words. 'It was an unconfirmed report,' he said.

'So you should confirm it. What did it say?'

'There was a meeting, in Erzberg,' said Wéry reluctantly. 'It was attended by an Illuminatus from Nuremberg, who may have been trying to recruit for his order. The report came from a man who was close to someone who attended the meeting.'

'When was this?'

'In October, when we all thought we were about to be attacked. There was no evidence of French involvement, so . . .'

'You should have reported this at once! Were there any Illuminati from Erzberg at the meeting?'

'The report did not say. But . . .'

'What?'

Wéry shook his head.

'But what?' insisted Bergesrode.

'A claim was made, apparently, that there is at least one Illuminatus in Erzberg, and that he is in the palace. That's all it is,' he said hastily. 'A claim. All of this is unconfirmed . . .'

'You have said that already!' Bergesrode snapped. 'I will be the judge of it. But I must know everything – who was at this meeting, where was it held, what was said. Names, above all. You had no right to keep this to yourself!'

'The name of the man from Nuremberg was Doctor Sorge,' said Wéry.

'Sorge,' repeated Bergesrode, making a note. 'Good. But who is this man in the palace?'

'We don't know. It was stated that he was highly placed, but how much credence . . .'

'I will be the judge of that. Who else attended the meeting?' His pen was poised.

Wéry squirmed inwardly. 'I – I will have to consult my notes. And perhaps re-interview the informant . . .'

Notes? He had none. Interview Uhnen again? Hardly. He was stalling for time. But what could he do with time, if he got it?

Slowly, Bergesrode put the pen down again. He put his hands together under his chin as if he were about to pray. His eyes never left Wéry.

'Very well,' he said at last. 'Let me have a proper report, as soon as possible. In the meantime I will see what can be found out about this Doctor Sorge. But this is not satisfactory, Wéry. His Highness expects better.'

He gathered papers from his pile and got to his feet. He must be about to go into the Prince with the morning's business. Wéry's report from Wetzlar remained on the desk.

'Will you show that to him?' asked Wéry, nodding towards it.

'There's nothing new there,' said Bergesrode curtly.

He walked to the inner door, knocked softly, and passed inside. For a moment Wéry glimpsed the rich blues of Heaven on the walls of the Prince's office, lit with the gold glory of the winter sunrise. Then the door closed, shutting them away from his sight. And he was left in the antechamber, with his fists clenched in anger.

He looked at them. He almost put them in his mouth. Then a sound behind him made him turn.

Fernhausen had entered, and was sitting nonchalantly on the edge of his desk. He was in his shirtsleeves. A month ago he would not even have unbuttoned his tunic in the antechamber. He had taken his time about reaching his desk this morning, too.

'He likes to be consulted, our priestly friend,' he said, with a little yawn. 'Especially about bringing revolutionaries into the city.'

Wéry let out a long breath. Instincts began to twitch in his head. Something was happening in the Prince's office. Here was the representative of the army, and the reformers, looking surer of himself while the secretary from the conservative clergy was sounding harassed. Some balance was shifting here, even as outside the palace the Ingolstadt set appeared to be on the point of bringing down the army's most senior officer.

'He was right, though,' Wéry confessed. 'I made a bargain. It may not have been a good one.'

'How very intriguing,' said Fernhausen. 'I have to tell you that the Prince was not pleased when he heard what you had done. But our priestly friend took your part. He told His Highness that we must be seen to give the War Commission all the help it needs. There was a bit of a drama between the two of them about it. His Highness thought that Bergesrode was carrying on the old feud on behalf of the Ingolstadt set; but it wasn't that. Bergesrode was protecting you. He's still hoping you'll strike gold somewhere, you see.'

'If I strike it anywhere, now, it will be on the Rhine.'

'Ah, the Rhine, the Rhine. Doesn't it seem strange that France and the Emperor can spend months agreeing a peace treaty, and yet no one seems to know what is to happen about the Rhine?

Worrying, for everyone. Did you know the Adelsheim daughter was over there?'

'What! In the Rhineland?'

'Oh yes. She's visiting the relatives of a friend, or some such. That's the story, anyway. I myself suspect that she's gone to hunt for some new French fashions.'

Wéry stared at him. Of all the things that had been said to him this morning . . .

'I didn't know,' he said hoarsely. 'I've been in the barracks for a fortnight.'

'Ah yes. I heard about that, too. So dull for you. But probably best to let tempers cool. Although in fact she went off at least a week before that. I had to sign the passports myself, because after your little coup Bergesrode insists that anything that looks or even smells as if it is anything to do with France has to be approved here. Are you going to challenge someone when you get the chance?'

'No.'

No of course he would not. That had all been weakness. None of that mattered now. But . . .

'That's good. It would upset my priestly colleague again, and he can be so tiresome.'

'I must go,' said Wéry. And he fled.

He fled down the long, soft-carpeted corridors of the Celesterburg, with his mind a daze of thoughts. She was in the Rhineland! Why? For him? A crazy thought! She was with the relatives of a friend. That must be the Jürichs. He must speak with her as soon as she returned. Maybe he could at least learn from her how things stood, and why there had been no news. But when would she return? And how would he manage to see her if she did?

Why hadn't she spoken to him before going?

Because she could not. Because she was the child of aristocrats, chaperoned and supervised and tied to the round of balls and levees and soirées that he loathed. He had engaged her as a go-between, and had never thought that a noblewoman in Erzberg might have difficulty communicating with just whom she chose. So it was *his* fault! Damn, damn, damn! Now she had gone off into the very Rhineland itself, marching to the last order given like her brother to Hersheim! What a stupid thing to have happened!

Fernhausen was no fool. He must have guessed something, or why would he have mentioned her name? People were always guessing at what he was doing, and their guesses struck very close. He went busy, busy, busy like an ant, imagining that all the things he did were seen by him alone. All the time they were peering down on him, watching from all around. Could he never keep anything safe? If Erzberg guessed and gossiped, then the enemy might guess too, and might learn names that he did not want them to learn. And that could be dangerous: dangerous for the Jürichs. Dangerous, too, for her.

He thought of his man Kranz, and that distant puff of smoke. And his heart lurched, and he felt sick.

He had seen her twice – only twice in his whole life! He had trusted something important to her, had thought she had failed him, and had now discovered that she was being faithful to her promise after all. That was hardly enough . . .

Hardly enough to explain what he felt, as he hurried out into the palace courtyard, and sunlight burst around him.

He had only seen her twice. But she had been with him for such a long time – in Albrecht; in Albrecht's words of her, and of his home; in his thoughts after he himself had seen her, and since that day in the barrack room, in the tantalizing feeling, day in, day out, almost unnoticed beyond the horizons of his brain, that there was something more than he saw and did, something more to the world, there for him to wonder at the moment he could drag his mind from what it was doing!

The long windows of the palace, heavy-eyed with their carved sills and cornicing, looked down upon him, and told him she was beyond the Rhine.

There was nothing he could do to help. Messages would only increase the danger. He could warn the frontier dragoons to look out for her coach – for any coach – but that was all.

And he had, this very hour, promised Bergesrode a report on a conspiracy in the city. Bergesrode would not forget that. The report would have to be delivered. He could stall, delay, claim to be following up clues; but sooner or later he would have to deliver it. He would have to name names. One of the very few names he had was 'Adelsheim'.

XXIV
The Path from the - Liberty Tree

The Jürich household prepared for Christmas in a spirit of determined optimism. Maria and Anna sat together by a low fire one long, wet afternoon, and with two serving-maids to help them they made more garlands than Maria believed could possibly be necessary. Emilia Jürich came to join them, and exclaimed over how much they had done. She seemed happy, and pleased with herself, and eventually she said, 'Well, *I* have news. I own I have been concerned but it is going to be well. It is a great relief to me.'

'My dear! Please tell!' said Anna.

'No, Anna,' said Maria. 'Let us see if we can guess. It will be diverting. Let us guess, Emilia.'

'Very well. In twenty questions?'

'Indeed. And you must answer precisely, or it will not be fair.'

'Go on, then,' said Emilia, with her eyes sparkling.

'Is it an idea, or is it a thing that I may touch?'

'It is a thing you may touch – and indeed I hope you will.'

'No, you must give us no clues, Emilia, or it will be too easy.'

'I do not care. I love the thought and I want to share it with you. Indeed you are cruel to me, to put me off so!'

'Hug it to yourself a moment more. Is it alive?'

'It is – for now.'

'Is it . . . Oh, no. Anna dear, you should have a turn.'

Anna blinked. She looked at Emilia. 'Is it,' she asked slowly, 'something concerned with Christmas?'

'It is indeed. I am astonished you have not guessed it already.'

'It must be – ah, it must be some provision for Christmas,' said Maria. 'I know it has been weighing on you, and really it should not. Is it the Christmas lunch?'

'Ah yes!' said Emilia. 'But you must guess what!'

'Very well,' said Anna. 'Has it four legs or two?'

'It has eight!'

'Eight? There are more than one, then. Very well, are they flesh or fowl?'

'Flesh.'

'It is calf, is it?' cried Maria.

'Or pig?' said Anna.

'It is pig!' cried Emilia, and clapped her hands. 'My man Bauer has been hiding a sow and a litter of sucking pigs in the woods, and I knew nothing of it until today. But I am promised two, if they are not discovered and taken before next week. And he has been so clever and close with them that I do not think they will be. Oh, I am so relieved!'

'Oh, but well done!'

'Now let Christmas come,' said Emilia. 'For I am prepared.'

And Maria was glancing at Anna with a look that said *You see? I told you that it would all be well*. And Anna was pulling a rueful face as she understood that her last, late arguments had been swept away, and that they would indeed remain in the Rhineland for Christmas . . .

And that was when they heard the feet of many men approaching the door.

Crunch, crunch, coming closer, coming up the beaten drive-way to the door of the house! Boots and the clink of metal: a file of men, and there was nowhere else they could be coming to! The track led only to the door, to the house, to the people inside it. The women stared at each other in mounting horror.

'Oh, dear Mother of God!' whispered Emilia.

A voice outside called. The noises stopped. One of the maids looked out of the window.

'Soldiers!' she wailed.

Maria cursed her silently. Of course it was soldiers! What else could it be? And why couldn't the stupid girl remain calm?

Then the banging started. Someone was hammering at the door from outside. Footsteps were running in the house. There were servants in the hall, voices raised in consternation. Still the banging went on and on, and then stopped all at once as the door was opened. One of the servants protested. A man spoke German at him rapidly. And over it all another voice shouted.

'Jürich! Come out, Jürich!'

'Dear Mother of God,' whispered Emilia again, and her face was white.

Boots – many boots, clumping on the bare boards of the hall. They were in the house.

'Jürich!'

From somewhere, muffled, Ludwig's voice answered. A door banged open. A voice began to shout in German – a long stream of abuse, punctuated by fierce thumps as of a hammer on wood.

'Dear God – have they come to arrest him?'

'What are they doing?'

Maria listened to the loud, ranting voice. She could pick out some of the words: *Treacherous! Disloyal! Fanatic!* And the thumping – was that someone slamming his hand on a table? Was it? Or were they . . .

She was standing, staring at the door to the hall. She heard a man laugh softly out there, as the litany of rage went on and on.

Dear heaven, what were they doing? Were they arresting him? Were they beating him? Why? Was he, after all, the man whom she had been sent to meet? But why had he given her nothing?

And was it now too late?

She heard Ludwig try to answer. She heard him shouted down. She heard one of the maids begin to whimper with terror. Her nerve broke.

'Enough of this,' she muttered. She stepped for the door.

'Lady Maria – no, you must not!' cried Emilia.

'My dear – please!' exclaimed Anna in the same moment.

She ignored both of them. She flung the door open, and with her eyes blazing she marched down the short corridor to the hall.

The hall was crowded with men in shabby blue uniforms, with white cross-belts and cockaded hats. In a glance she saw again how short many of them were: short, but the muskets they carried were very long in that confined space, with cruel and rusting bayonets fixed to the barrels. She drew breath. The men smelled foul.

Someone had come with her. It was Emilia, putting her hand on her arm.

'Please!' she begged. 'You should not show yourself!'

They were already turning to look at her. She lifted her chin.

'What is going on here?' she demanded.

Eyes, moustaches, crossbelts. Cheeks grizzled with unkempt whiskers. How old was the man who stood there, feet away, staring at her? Forty? A haggard twenty-five? She could see the little lines around his eyes, the black gaps in his mouth where so many teeth were missing. His boots were not boots, she saw, but strips of filthy linen wrapped tightly around his feet. And his musket – the long and horrible musket that he held, with its rusted ramrod slung beneath the barrel, the point of the bayonet a bare inch from scoring the wall where she had rested her hand!

All their eyes were on her.

'What is going on here?' she repeated loudly. 'Who is in charge?'

'Please – do not trouble yourself, Lady Maria.'

It was Ludwig's voice!

She could not see him through the soldiers, but he must have come out of his office at the same time as she arrived in the hall.

'Really, it is nothing,' he called to her.

'Nothing!' she cried, at her most imperious and incredulous, as she swept the soldiers with her eyes. 'What kind of *nothing* is this?'

Perhaps she should not have said that. She saw them glower at her. Any one of them could drag her screaming through the door. Someone said something, in a voice she did not quite catch.

Three men pushed their way through the crowd: a French officer, a green-coated clerk, and Ludwig in his shirtsleeves, mopping his brow.

He looked unhurt. Thank God! He was unhurt!

'Please do not trouble yourself. It – it is a small matter,' Ludwig said, glancing at the officer and clerk. 'I have undertaken to see to it.'

The officer nodded curtly. 'Let us go,' he said to his men. 'We are finished here.'

Without a word more to his host he stalked out of the front

door. The German clerk and the soldiers followed him. Maria found she was holding her breath as they passed one by one through the doorway. She counted only nine of them. It had felt as though there had been fifty. When Ludwig closed the door softly after the last one, she let the air from her lungs in a long, shaking sigh.

'What was it?' cried Emilia, hugging Ludwig around the chest. 'Did they hit you? Oh my dear, I thought they would take you away!'

'They will not, while I am still useful to them,' murmured Ludwig. 'Do not distress yourself. I am not hurt – apart from some passing injury to my eardrums. I suspect our clerkly visitor will have done himself more damage simply by banging on my table. No, my dear. It is just that some fool has cut down the Liberty Tree in Knopsdorf. Our General is not pleased, it seems.'

'Not pleased!' Emilia was almost weeping. 'I thought the most terrible things!'

So did I, thought Maria, looking out of the hall window at the departing file of soldiers. So did I.

I thought they had come for me.

The Liberty Tree of Knopsdorf, the village nearest to the Jürich estate, had been a mere sapling, planted two years before to show the district's faith in equality, fraternity and the rights of man. But someone had come and cut it down in the night. No one seemed able to say who had done it, even though the sound of axe-blows in the small hours must have woken half-a-dozen households and everyone knew it had happened because Father Septe had been deported. French messengers and green-coated clerks stamped angrily into Ludwig Jürich's office again and again in the days after Christmas, and stamped angrily out again when he told them there was nothing he could do to find the culprit.

'They see it as their duty to liberate us,' he sighed at table. 'So if we cling to our princes they must necessarily liberate us by force. But I have told them we will plant it again tomorrow.'

'Yet it is meaningless!' cried Emilia. 'There is a treaty now. In a month or two the Elector will be restored, and the people will simply grub the tree up again.'

'Nothing is certain,' said Ludwig gently. 'In the meantime, we must do what we must do. At least the weather is mild. I do not believe you ladies will need your cloaks tomorrow.'

In fact, the next day was grey and windy. Maria certainly thought her cloak would have been a comfort. But Cousin Ludwig looked at the heavens, and declared so firmly that it was mild that she felt compelled to leave it behind. They took an open carriage down to the village, which was less than a mile away, and dismounted at the edge of a grassy space. A file of twenty French soldiers with their officer was drawn up at one side of it. They almost outnumbered the small crowd of villagers, gathering silently on the other. There were two other carriages there. One contained Kaus and his wife. The other held Madame Hofmeister. No one remarked that her husband had not come.

In the middle of the lawn was a round circle of freshly dug earth. Presumably this was the very spot where the liberty sapling had been murdered. Now it was gone, and its roots had been pulled from the ground, and on the grass beside the bare earth lay a new sapling, less than six feet long.

Cousin Ludwig nodded to a green-coated clerk who stood nearby. 'You may begin,' he said.

The French officer and the clerk came forward. The clerk took a paper from his pocket and, in a voice that barely carried to where Maria was standing, read an address that hailed the renewed advent of Liberty in Knopsdorf. The speech was in French. Looking at the dour faces of the crowd, Maria thought that less than half of them knew any French at all, and less than half of those would have been prepared to admit it.

Cousin Ludwig had been wrong, she thought, as she clutched her thin shawl around her shoulders. The day was proving very cold indeed.

The clerk finished. The French officer stepped forward and, speaking fairly and in rather good German, promised the friendship and support of the Republic to all who yearned to make themselves free. The Republic made war upon the castles, but would leave the cottages in peace. Silence greeted his words.

A peasant with a spade dug the soft earth away. Another lifted the sapling into the hole, and held it straight while the first firmed the earth back at its roots. The officer spoke a series of commands. The French soldiers lifted their muskets and fired them into the air. At another command the muskets returned to the salute. The officer waved his arm. Unaccompanied by music, voices straining in the open air, the soldiers sang.

Amour sacré de la Patrie, conduis, soutiens nos bras vengeurs.
Liberté, liberté chérie, combats avec tes défenseurs; combats avec
  tes défenseurs.
Sous nos drapeaux, que la victoire accoure à tes mâles accents;
Que tes ennemis expirants voient ton triomphe et notre gloire!

Aux armes, citoyens! Formez vos battaillons!
Marchons, marchons, qu'un sang impur
Abreuve nos sillons!

Beside her, Ludwig Jürich began to applaud. Clap, clap, clap went his hands, sounding alone until at last the ripple of clapping spread among the villagers. Then the ceremony was over. The French soldiers grouped in a huddle by themselves, glancing now and then at the people as they dispersed. The Kauses and Madame Hofmeister clustered with the Jürichs for a few words, and then climbed into their carriages.

'My dear, I think Anna is cold,' said Ludwig suddenly to Emilia. 'Do take her back in the carriage. I shall walk, for I need the air. Perhaps Lady Maria will accompany me?'

He bowed to her.

'Oh – but is Maria not cold too?' said Emilia.

'I shall be delighted,' declared Maria boldly. 'I shall only be cold if I stand still.'

They bundled Anna and Emilia, still protesting, into the carriage. Then she took Ludwig's arm and, followed by his servant, began to walk back up to the house.

They went in silence for the first hundred yards. At the edge of the little wood above the village, Ludwig stopped.

'I have been unpardonably overconfident,' he said. 'It is certainly cold! Heinrich, run up to the house and return as quickly as you can with a cloak for Lady Maria.'

The servant grunted and strode ahead.

'Quickly!' cried Ludwig.

The man broke into a run, and disappeared around the corner

of the wood. After a moment Ludwig returned his arm to Maria and they resumed their walk.

'I wonder if you are disappointed with my house,' Ludwig said suddenly.

'Oh, no! Indeed you must not think so! Your wife has striven so hard to make us comfortable that I own I am ashamed to have been the cause of so much trouble.'

'I am glad to hear you say it. But of course that is not what I meant.'

Maria paced beside him, looking down at the tussocks beneath her feet. She was alone with her host. No one could hear what they said. Only one man – the servant – even knew they were together.

'Sir,' she said. 'I imagine you are as much a patriot as I – which is to say that you never thought of patriotism until the world had forced it on you. I believe what you do to be for the good of the people of your district, and serves them better than any empty, prideful gesture that would surely bring the revenge of the French.'

'Thank you. In truth they love me very little for it, and less now that I have failed even to save poor Septe. Yet shall I abandon the path of Reason for the Romantic? Others have done so. But it seems to me only to be folly. Deliverance will come to us and to all Germany only through patience and faith. The summit of my ambition in this time is that I may yet prevent my brother-in-law Kaus from denouncing my brother-in-law Hofmeister. If I achieve this, I shall hold myself vindicated.'

'I believe you are too gloomy, sir!' she said, surprised that this aloof man should suddenly confide so much to her.

'About Kaus? It is, I think, almost inevitable. The occupiers

329

and their acolytes suspect everyone who held positions for the princes. And Hofmeister is not a silent man. If Kaus does not speak against him, he may fall under suspicion in his turn.'

They walked on in silence for a few paces.

'My house is under suspicion, too,' he said. 'As you will have observed the other day.'

'I am – sorry for it, sir.'

'I do not doubt that you are sorry. But if I may say so, I do not think you are surprised. You spoke a name at my table on your first night here, and I do not believe it was by chance. I am aware that the man you mentioned has visited my house in secret. He did not speak to me. Yet I can guess what it was that he wanted.

'I remember Wéry well. We talked much during the siege. There was, after all, little else to do. I was in hiding and he, although still trusted by the republicans, was reflecting on his experiences in Paris. He had once had a house and a small estate in Brabant, which he loved, and people, including more than one woman. He had locked all that away to dedicate himself to his cause. I remember thinking even then that I was not capable of so great a sacrifice. Nor am I yet. More and more I have come to see that it is better to love a few – or even only one – than it is to loathe an empire. So I hold Hofmeister to be justified by his love and duty to my sister-in-law, and not by his opinions. As for Wéry . . .

'You have lost a brother, Lady Maria. But you may at least honour him in his grave. Now you have seen my nephew Maximilian. You have seen the price my house pays every day for having dabbled in affairs far greater than we could control. I wonder if you can guess what I think of Wéry's demand that we

330

should renew our acquaintance with such things – and perhaps pay a price far greater.'

When Maria did not reply, he went on, 'I was expecting couriers – messengers in the night trying to tap at my windows. Indeed I have even wondered whether I might hand the next one over to the occupiers. But Wéry is a clever man, and also a subtle one.' He looked at Maria. 'He must know that I wish him to seek no more help from my house.'

'Sir,' she said, feeling her colour rising. 'I know Major Wéry, whom I believe to be a man of honour. As for the rest, insofar as I have understood it, I wish you to be assured I desire no harm to your house and will do whatever I can to avoid it.'

'I thank you, Lady Maria. And I do believe you have some affection for us. Therefore I believe that you will deliver the message I have given.'

He should *not* talk to her so! She was not a child or a witness in his court. Indeed, it was presumptuous of him. A man like him, even a judge, should show her father's daughter more respect!

But her instincts subsided. This was not a time to insist on her status. This was about life or death. She had come for a message, and finally it had been given to her. It was not what she had been expecting. It could hardly please Wéry. But . . .

'There is another matter,' said the green judge.

'Sir?'

'I am grateful to you for bringing my cousin to see us. But I now believe it would be very much better if you were to take her back to Erzberg as soon as possible.'

'Sir!'

Now she was astonished. A host did not – did *not* – tell his

331

guests when they were to leave, unless some great offence had been caused. She struggled for words.

'Sir, I assure you! Anna most desired to come to see you. She has desired it for a long time. I – I am simply accompanying her. It was to satisfy my mother, that is all.'

'Of course I believe that Anna has desired to visit us. But if I believed Anna was the arbiter of your stay I would have addressed myself to her. I do not. Recollect that I have known her a long time, and that I have also had the opportunity of observing you. And I know that you are capable of leading her in this direction or that, as it may suit you. She knows it too, of course. Yet she allows it because she loves you, and because it is simpler if she does not think too much herself.'

'You are unkind, sir!'

'My Lady, I am desperate. I would not speak so if I were not. And understand me. I do not know if you yet have that which you came for. But whether you have it or not, for your own sakes you *must* be gone. In these past days you will have observed that I have had a number of unpleasant visitors. Most of it was indeed about that wretched sapling we have just replaced. But I have also learned something of the plans of the new commissioner for the Rhineland. Neither Hofmeister nor I, nor any other figure from the time of the princes, will hold our positions for much longer. That is little surprise. The occupied lands are to be divided into departments, such as they employ for administration in France. Plainly, whatever we hoped, the occupation will not be ended soon. The French will stay.

'Moreover, the soldiers who were present today will not return to their billets. They will rejoin their column, and bivouac under canvas tonight near Mainz. Commanders do not make their soldiers change roofs for canvas without need. Some movement of troops is underway, this side of the Rhine. I firmly believe that if you are not across the Rhine by the time those movements are complete, you may find it hard to cross the Rhine at all.'

'You think we should leave.'

'For your comfort, but above all for your safety.'

Footsteps sounded on the path ahead. The servant Heinrich came into view, carrying a long white cloak that she did not recognize, and that must have belonged to Emilia Jürich. Ludwig hailed him, and the secret talk was over. As the man Heinrich arranged the cloth gingerly around her neck and shoulders, she shuddered.

She was cold, and shocked and angry. She was confused. She had been told that she could not have what she had come for, and had been given instead some vague words about soldiers marching up and down, which was supposed to be alarming. She had been told that she must leave. And she had been accused of manipulating Anna for her own ends – yes! No matter that Anna had *wanted* to come, and that all Maria had done was to make it possible. That was the worst of it.

It was the worst, because in her heart she knew it was true.

Back at the house, she could not settle. She did not join Emilia and Anna in the drawing room, although they sent to tell her that the fire was made up high and that they were sure she must be chilled to the bone. She paced her room, and the corridor, and into her room again, thinking. Her thoughts did not calm her. They made her angrier yet.

What she hated most was that he had discovered her. He had

known from the very first evening why she had come to the house. And he had watched her all the time.

Who had Michel Wéry spoken to, if not to Ludwig Jürich himself? Hofmeister? Kaus? Some unfortunate servant, who had since been dismissed?

And after weeks of waiting, she had nothing to show. That depressed her. How would he know how much thought, effort, patience this had demanded from her? He would think she had spent her time playing cards and word-games, and had come back as soon as she was bored.

Bored? She had been bored for weeks, in this hateful, depressing place! She had been bored, bewildered and frightened – yes, more frightened than she had ever been in her life! She had been pining for home, pining to see her father again, and yet staying here out of duty. And now she was being told to go – dismissed, like a poor cousin. *This* was not right! On this at least she should be the master! She was the daughter of a Knight of the Empire. *He* was a gentleman-judge, and a poor one at that. What was this talk of departments and billets and canvas? He would *not* tell her when she might stay or go. Nor would he decide when he would speak to her and when not!

She looked in the mirror. She saw herself, poised and imperious, and the arch of her brow was a cool command. She turned, and with the spirit of her mother rising in her, made her way downstairs to the corridor outside the judge's office.

Even as she knocked at the door she had not decided what she would say. She might tell him, scornfully, how much his hospitality lacked of what she expected, and therefore they would indeed leave his house – not because he wished it but because she did. Or she might tell him that she would leave when she pleased, and she pleased not to tell him when this would be. She was not sure which. She was sure only that she wanted the revenge of words.

There was no answer to her knock.

He was hiding from her. He was pretending that he was not there. He did not want to be trapped in his study, like a rat. She turned the handle and stepped in.

The room was empty.

It was a dark place, panelled and furnished with polished wood. Here too the pictures were gone from the walls and the carpet from the floor. There might have been a desk and presses once, but there were none now. Piles of paper, closely written, were stacked against the walls. On a rough table, placed beneath the one window, there were more papers. There was also a book.

Thinking, perhaps, that he had been called away somewhere, and that if she waited he might return, she walked softly to the table. The papers on the desk were letters and petitions. One that caught her eye begged, in ill-spelled, incoherent German, for His Honour to intercede with a certain French commander to remove his troops from their village, where everything including all livestock, hats, shoes, bed-linen and even neck scarves had now been taken by the soldiers, and the people feared starvation.

On the table beside it, in Ludwig's own hand, was the draft of a letter in French, likewise entreating that the troops should be moved on. But the page was incomplete, as if the judge had stopped in thought. (Moved on? Where, indeed, should the villainous soldiers to be moved on to? Which other village must suffer them now?)

Beside both papers was a Bible. It was open, as if Ludwig in his doubt had sought some counsel from Scripture. She lifted it, and read it.

The page could have given him little comfort.

Therefore when they were gathered together, Pilate said unto them, whom will ye that I will release unto you? Barabbas, or Jesus which is the Christ? For he knew that for envy they had delivered him.

When he was set down upon the judgement seat, his wife sent unto him, saying Have thou nothing to do with that innocent man: for I have suffered many things this day in a dream because of him.

But the chief priests and elders persuaded the multitude . . .

There was a sound behind her. She whirled, with the book in her hand.

It was not Ludwig. It was one of the footmen. It was the servant Hartmann. She had not seen him for weeks, since the demented Maximilian had sent him to Koblenz for brushes. He was looking in through the doorway.

They stared at each other for a long moment. The thought floated in Maria's mind that neither of them, neither she nor Hartmann, should be where they were, standing in the study of the master of the house, as if it were some waiting hall.

Hartmann's eyes had the same, quiet, mournful look that they always had. He held a plain package, wrapped in brown canvas, in his hand.

'You must take this with you,' he said softly. 'For your friend. He must have it as quickly as possible.'

She stared, unbelieving, at the package.

'Yes,' she said. 'Yes, at once.'

It felt very light when he handed it to her.

They left the room together, and she made her way upstairs to hide it in the folds of one of her dresses, which she then placed into her trunk. Then she added a few more things, folding them and placing them around the dress with the package. After a few minutes she rang for her maid and left her to get on with the packing, while she made her way downstairs to tell Anna and Emilia that, on the advice of Cousin Ludwig, they should prepare to leave as soon as possible the next day.

XXV
The Lost Border

Ludwig Jürich rode with them in the coach, just as he had done on their journey from Mainz the month before. And just as before, he got out and approached the French pickets outside the city on horseback. But once they were through to the gate he stopped and took off his hat.

'I should dearly like to pass one more evening with you, cousin,' he said to Anna. 'But I have decided that it would be better if I returned at once. I do not know what may happen in the space of the next day.'

'Oh you must,' said Anna at the coach window. 'I am sure Emilia is already anxious for you. And we will shift very well for ourselves tonight.'

'Sir,' said Maria, over Anna's shoulder. 'I shall always carry good memories of your house, and of the people in it.'

He bowed. 'And I wish you good speed to Erzberg. Only be sure that you start early in the morning.'

He placed his hat once more upon his head, turned his horse and rode away down the track, followed by his groom. Maria watched him go, riding with his shoulders straight and his head high, back towards the ragged pickets of his oppressors.

When he was set down upon the judgement seat, his wife sent unto him, saying Have thou nothing to do with that innocent man . . .

That line had followed her into her dreams.

'I was angry with him yesterday,' she said. 'When he told us we must go, I was angry. But he carries so much. Both he and Emilia do. Now I feel ashamed.'

'My dear, I knew there was something.'

There was indeed something. There was the package, concealed deep in her trunk, which Ludwig had been so anxious to prevent from leaving his house. And it had come, in the end, from one of his own servants. Strange how one always overlooked the servants! Even one who had a perfect excuse to travel up and down the Rhineland, hunting for impossible supplies for the madman in the long room. So she had defeated Cousin Ludwig after all. She was sad about that. It was inevitable, but it was also sad, like the theft of the golden apples from the gardens of the Hesperides.

Outside the guards had finished looking at their papers, and the coach lurched forward, on into the fortified city.

Having cheated her host in the one thing that mattered, Maria was anxious to keep faith with him in every other way possible. So she reminded Anna, before they went to bed, that they were to leave Mainz early the next day, and she gave orders to the servants and the grooms that the coach was to be ready to move at a good hour. And so they were up and watching things being loaded back into the coach before it was fully light. The streets were quiet. The other people in the inn were mostly still abed. It was cold, and Maria was glad when the landlord came out to tell them that their breakfast was set.

There was broth, very hot. Maria wanted something warm inside her, but she did not want to burn her tongue. She blew on it, and tried it. Then she waited a little longer, and tried it again. It was still too hot.

She was dipping her spoon into it hopefully for the third time when a kitchen boy came banging in through the front door. His face was pale and his eyes were staring.

'The Austrians!' he cried. 'Austrians're leaving!'

The landlord stopped in the act of putting more bread on the table. 'What? What's that?'

'Paul saw'm in the main street,' the boy cried. 'They're up and away, carts and all!'

The landlord swore. Other faces appeared in doorways, calling out to know what was happening. Half a dozen alarmed conversations broke out around the room.

Maria put down her spoon. 'If the garrison is leaving,' she said slowly to Anna. 'Then I think we should go too.'

Anna blinked at her.

'I'm sure it is nothing, dear,' she said. 'People say and hear all sorts of things, and then they become excited.'

Maria stared at Anna, who was looking firmly at her bowl. Somehow she had managed to begin eating it. The landlord had abandoned the table and run out into the street.

'Anna, I think we should go now.'

'After breakfast, of course. But it is silly to leave what the poor man has set for us.'

Eat your breakfast, dear, and don't fuss.

'Anna!' Maria thumped the table. 'Ludwig told us the French were moving their soldiers. He thought something was about to happen. He wanted to make sure we were away before it did. We must hurry!'

'You are too directive,' said Anna crossly. 'I do not wish to leave

340

without breakfast, and I certainly think you should not. It is not good for you.'

Shouts broke out in the street, urgent and alarmed. They brought Maria jumping to her feet.

'Oh, Mother of God! You cannot make me eat, you silly woman!'

The servants were staring at her, arrested in their meal by the sudden excitement. 'Ehrlich,' she called to the groom at the head. 'Ehrlich, we are going *now*. You can pocket the bread, but we must be on our way.'

The servants exploded from their table. A bench went over. Maria caught Ehrlich, who had the purse, and made him go and put money on the landlord's table for when he should return. The others hurried out to swarm around the coach and bring out the horses.

'Oh, very *well*!' exclaimed Anna and began to gather herself.

Still it seemed a long time, an agonizingly long time, before the team was hitched and the women were seated aboard the coach. It was fully light. The streets, which had been quiet before, were busy with people, not at their daily business of stalls and workshops, but hurrying along, crowding down towards the main street in search of whatever was happening. The coach followed along in the direction of the crowd, slowing to a crawl when the press of bodies grew too thick under the close, over-hanging house fronts.

'The French are at the west gate!' she heard someone exclaim.

'The French! The west gate!'

In the main street the press was thicker still. The carriage stopped. Leaning from her window, Maria saw a group of cavalrymen, part of the retreating garrison, forcing their way through the crowd a hundred yards ahead. People were calling to them, booing them, snatching at stirrups and begging them to remain. She saw one of the horsemen raise a hand. They had all raised their hands, and their hands were holding drawn swords. Under the threat of the steel the crowd gave back a little, and the horsemen moved on.

A cart had drawn up behind them. There was a family in it. The man at the head bellowed for room. Another wagon appeared further back. Other people were trying to leave the city. But they were all stuck, all stuck!

'Ehrlich,' she called, leaning as far out as she could and peering up to the driver's perch. She could see only his boot and the top of his tricorn hat. 'Ehrlich, for Heaven's sake move on.'

'I can't, my Lady.'

'You may have to use the whip,' she said.

She heard him mutter doubtfully. She wondered if she should order him to do it. She did not want to. Whip people because they were afraid? And what would the crowd do to them if he did?

But what would the French do to them if they could not get away? They would be robbed! Or worse!

And they might turn out all the trunks. She remembered the pleading letters on the table of the green judge – shoes, hats, neckties – all stolen. They stole everything.

They would find the package. They would open it.

She thrust her head and shoulders out of the carriage window. 'Ehrlich . . .' she began.

'Friends!' cried a voice in the crowd. 'Hear me. If the French enter the city, we must all keep calm . . .'

It was a stout, sober-suited man who was standing on a water butt to make himself heard. Perhaps he was a guild-master. He must have been running, for he was red in the face and sweating on that winter day. The crowd turned their faces to him.

'They've abandoned us!' yelled someone. 'They've handed us over – like goods!'

'As God wills,' said the man. 'Remember that our duty is to God, our Elector, and to our families. We can serve none of them if we lose our reason . . .'

'Sir!' cried Maria. 'Please – could you make them move?'

The man looked her way, and frowned.

'Sir,' begged Maria. 'For pity's sake, we shall be trapped here!'

'Trapped right enough,' said someone.

'Come now,' said the man, still frowning. 'Where is our courtesy, in Mainz? Move away from the horses, there, I beg you, friends. Let them pass.'

'Why them and not us?'

'Let them pass, friend, and then come reason with me,' said the man. 'Thank you, there. Now, friends, we do not know what lies ahead for us . . .'

The horses were moving. Thank God, they were moving! And they kept moving. She heard Ehrlich calling for room, again and again. She heard the whip crack threateningly. Then the coach stopped, and her heart stopped with it. But it started again. A few minutes later it stopped once more. They had reached the bridge.

There was a great throng of wagons and carts at the bridge already, crowded around and waiting to cross. Many people seemed to have snatched up whatever belongings they could lift and climbed into their vehicles in whatever clothes they had on. Maria saw more than one fugitive still in their nightshirts, with blankets thrown around them. Ehrlich roared and roared for room, forcing their way to the bridge with all the habits of privilege. People yelled at them, and cursed, and Maria, ashamed and fearful, shrank back inside. She heard the whip again, and a horse whinny, and more cursing. Then they were moving once more, and the window showed her the grey Rhine flowing steadily north, deaf to the human terrors on its banks.

No one checked papers at the far end of the bridge. A few Rhinelander soldiers stood about, looking helpless as the ragged column of townsfolk debouched into the fortifications and out onto the east bank. An infantry battalion – part of the Imperial garrison – was drawn up by the roadside there. Officers were moving down the ranks, inspecting packs and boots and the contents of wagons. The men looked idly at the people who poured past them, with faces that said it was no concern of theirs.

Maria sat back once more, with a horrid, guilty, empty sense of relief inside her.

'Anna,' she murmured. 'I'm sorry. I was unkind to you in the inn. It was very wrong of me.'

'Oh,' said Anna dismissively. 'You said nothing that I do not know well enough. Look, I have saved some of the bread for you. Will you have it now?'

It had been something to do with the Treaty. Clauses had been signed in secret between the Austrian representatives and the French General Bonaparte, handing over Mainz, the city of the first-ranking Elector of the Empire. The innkeeper in Frankfurt, an Imperial city, declared that this must certainly have been done without the knowledge of the Emperor himself. And anyway, when the news reached the Congress at Rastatt, the ambassadors of the princes would surely protest at once.

'No doubt,' said Maria. 'I am sure they will protest most vigorously. In the meanwhile, I wonder what else has been given away.'

'Oh do not fret, my darling,' said Anna. 'Remember, it is just two days now, and we shall be home.'

'Yes,' said Maria dully. 'I hope so.'

They slept late after the demands of the day before, and gathered themselves at about mid-morning for the journey up the north bank of the Vater. Another weary, jolting coach journey, thought Maria, with nothing to do but watch the landscape pass. She had had enough of the steep hills and woods and of the sound of the coach-wheels grinding over stones and into mud. She very much wanted to be home. She wanted to see Father again, and embrace him, and read to him. And once she had done that, she thought she might live her life between Erzberg and Adelsheim, and never travel again. Oh, that it would soon be over!

They changed horses at Hanau, paid a toll and ate a meal; then they pressed on into the grey afternoon. Steep, wood-covered slopes rose to their left. To their right the Vater rolled brownly on down towards Frankfurt and the Rhine, and on the far bank were more woods and hills, and the occasional hamlet, clustered at the waterside. There was little traffic on the river. The road was bad, much damaged by winter rain. The going was slow.

After another hour or so they halted to rest the horses. Maria, Anna and their two maids climbed out. They were in another little village: a collection of huts clustered around a small church, wedged between the forested slopes and the river. It was good to be able to walk and stand in the air after all that long swaying inside the coach. Two ragged, dirty children ran up and started to beg. She ignored them.

'Are we in Erzberg yet?' she asked Ehrlich.

'Still in Hanau, my Lady. But we should see the border-stone very soon.'

'Good.' She walked a little by herself while Ehrlich began to unhitch the team and the maids shooed the urchins away. The road they had travelled swept back along the wooded banks, curving to the left with the line of the river. They had passed no one on it for the last hour.

But there were people on it now.

In the grey light she had to screw her eyes up to be sure. But yes, there was movement on the road, perhaps half a mile away. Horses and their riders, she thought. There were maybe a dozen of them. There were no carts. They must be revenue officers, or soldiers.

A dozen of them. Maria did not think that the tiny county of Hanau could have even that many horsemen altogether. Who could they be, then? The colours of their uniforms were lost under the muddy greys and browns of their greatcoats.

Her mind leapt to the picket on the road outside Mainz.

'Ehrlich!' she called.

'My Lady?'

'How far is it to the border?'

'Not far, my Lady.'

'There are soldiers on the road behind us. I want to cross the border immediately.'

Mother Mary! And he already had one of the beasts out of its traces!

'Hitch it up again, and hurry,' she said.

He stared for a moment over his shoulder at the road. Then he

346

muttered something, and went to back the horse into its place once more.

'Into the coach!' Maria snapped at her maids.

'Who do you think they are?' asked Anna.

'I do not know who they are,' said Maria. 'And really I do not think we should wait to find out.'

They bundled into the coach. In a moment they heard Ehrlich climbing back into his place. The whip cracked. They were moving.

Maria looked at the faces of the other women. They were drawn, tight-lipped. The two maids were holding hands. They were afraid. Maria knew she was afraid too. She had been afraid before all of them. It was carrying that packet from the Rhineland. It meant she could never leave fear behind her – not in Mainz, not in Frankfurt, not here. And she would flee from the sight of strange horsemen, rather than wait to discover if they were indeed the portly customs-men of Hanau that all reason said they should be.

They were rattling up an easy slope above the river. How far was it to the border? They should have asked in the village. Maybe the horsemen would stop at the village. Maybe they would not come on. If only they could pass the frontier stone, they should be safe. How far was it?

The carriage paused at the top of the rise. Through her window Maria could see the river foaming gently at the foot of a great bluff. The road did not go that way. It must circle the bluff inland. Where were they? Why had they stopped? Ehrlich must be looking back down to the village, to see if they were followed.

Ehrlich cried out, and the whip cracked. The coach lurched forward, level for a space and then downhill. The women were thrown against one another. The window showed the forest beginning to rush backwards. Ehrlich cried again, and the horses broke into a canter. They were going at speed – at speed on this bad, stony slope. What if they were overset? The faces of the maids opposite Maria were white, and one of them was moaning. On, on they clattered and lurched down the slope. The wheels hit something with a bang that lifted Maria for a moment from her seat. Someone shrieked. They were all clinging to each other, because there was nothing else to cling on to. The ground levelled, but still Ehrlich was whipping and calling to the horses, and they trundled and swayed fast, fast along the forest road. Where was the border stone? Where in heaven was the border? Surely the horsemen would not follow them over it? Trampling on tiny Hanau's ground was one thing. Crossing unbidden into Erzberg was another. Erzberg had dragoons, patrolling. This road of all roads would be watched, surely. Oh, please Heaven . . .

Now she heard the hooves – the heavy, multiple drumming of hooves close behind them. Men were calling. She could not hear the words. Something cracked loudly. Mother of God – was it a gunshot? But Ehrlich was still in his seat, still whipping and calling to the horses, and the carriage bounced and swayed as if it were a dice-box in a giant's fist.

Where was the stone? Had they missed it? Surely they were past it by now!

A great, brown shape appeared outside Maria's window. It was a horse, cantering hard along the verge of the road. The rider had his reins in one hand and a pistol in the other. She saw him actually duck under the branches of a tree that would have swept him from his saddle. For a moment the horse hung level with them, and then it seemed to leap ahead as the horseman saw his

348

opening and set the beast at it. Even in that moment Maria was awed by the power and daring of it. She heard the man calling to Ehrlich, '*Arrêtez! Arrêtez ou je tire!*' And the coach slowed.

One of the maids was sobbing. Ehrlich was still calling to the horses, but his voice had changed. The relentless clatter of the wheels eased. They were down to a walk. Other horsemen were crowding up around them. For a moment it was a relief, a relief to have surrendered, and to be spared that headlong drive. Then the coach stopped. The door opened. A face swathed in moustaches and long bristles, topped by a battered tricorn hat, peered in.

'Out, everyone,' the man said in French. 'Onto the road.'

Slowly, stiffly they climbed out. The soldiers had brought the coach to a halt in a little forest clearing, so small that the coach and the horse-party crowded it. They gestured to the women to stand a little apart. Maria saw them take the pistols from Ehrlich and the other groom, and the purse from Ehrlich's belt. They made the grooms sit down. Then one of them walked behind Ehrlich and kicked him in the kidneys, viciously, so that he rolled over and lay groaning. The soldiers laughed, and spoke to one another.

They were French. She heard their voices, and saw the blue uniforms peeping from under coats and cloaks. She saw them lifting trunks and bundles down from the roof of the coach. Knives gleamed and straps were cut. The lids were forced open.

They were French. What were they doing here?

'Maria, dear,' whispered Anna. 'Stand behind me.'

One of the soldiers had looked her way and grinned. She shrank back. She could not help it. What would they do? Beside her one of the maids had begun to moan again. The stupid, animal sound sawed at her nerves. She wanted to shriek at the girl.

'Keep behind me, dear,' said Anna stiffly.

Anna had put herself between the rest of them and the soldiers. Her head was up. Her right hand, low by the skirts of her dress, was curled into an angled fist, as if she was holding an imaginary stick or riding-crop. Maria stared at it. She saw, in that moment, how very white the fingers were at the knuckles.

Oh Father, she thought. If you could see me now ... Oh Father, I don't think I'm going to see you again.

They had opened her trunk. They were spilling her clothes and petticoats – things so familiar that they were a part of her – out onto the muddy road. One of them picked up a petticoat and held it against himself, did a few dance steps and laughed. Another lifted out a black dress and was about to do the same, when the package fell from its folds. He stooped and picked it up. He broke the seals and ripped it open. For a moment his body concealed it from Maria. Then he grinned, and held it out for his comrades to see.

It was a painting, of the tortured face of Christ. Someone laughed.

And someone bellowed with fury.

Crack-crack-crack and smoke in the air! The clearing was suddenly full of riders, horses turning. Men roared in rage and in hatred. The Frenchman before Maria was trying to mount, one hand still clutching the painting. Maria saw a white-uniformed horseman appear beyond him, point a short carbine at him as he rose into the saddle, and fire from a range of two feet. The man fell, heavily into the mud. The riderless horse bolted. Other horses were turning in the clearing. Swords flashed and there were more cries. Horses, some of them with riders, were galloping along the road. More horsemen followed, many in white uniforms, pounding after them with wild shouts and laughter.

The sounds of pursuit diminished. Wisps of smoke drifted in the clearing and stung the eyes. A half-dozen mounted men, wearing the white uniforms and black boiled-leather helmets of the Erzberg dragoons, idled around the coach. One paused over the fallen Frenchman, who was moving feebly on the ground.

'Ho, you naughty boy,' the dragoon said. 'You're not dead yet!' He lifted his carbine, sighted it down on the fallen man, and fired. There was a rush of smoke, and the Frenchman lay utterly still.

'Are you all right, madame?' asked a sergeant, touching his helmet to Anna.

'I believe so, thank you,' said Anna faintly.

'Ehrlich is hurt,' Maria added. Her throat was sore. She must have been screaming. She hobbled over to the fallen soldier, and, closing her eyes, fumbled for the painting that lay on the ground beside him. Then she looked at it, at the oiled, dying face; in the clearing with the dead man at her feet.

'I don't understand,' she said hoarsely.

XXVI
The Reading Glass

Wéry sat at his desk in the barracks with his head in his hands. It was night. Before him, in the yellow light of a candle, lay a copy of the hurriedly-written report from the commanding officer of the dragoon squadron. He had read it three times. He knew every word that was in it. Now he was no longer reading but staring at the page.

Once, in a skirmish, he had seen a soldier's hat knocked from the man's head by a bullet. The man had simply stood, in line with his fellows, looking stupidly at it where it lay on the ground. Then, all of a sudden, he had sat down. He had remained there, with his limbs shaking, until an officer had come walking along the line to put the hat back on the man's head and tell him to stand up again.

Wéry knew how that soldier had felt. He felt the same now . . . *By good fortune they were not inconvenienced, and only a coachman suffered injuries . . .*

The dragoons had had a good day. A half-troop of French cavalry routed, prisoners taken, and ladies – one of them god-daughter of the Prince – rescued from distress. The squadron leader must hope for promotion for this. Certainly he wrote to make the most of his foresight in arranging patrols up to the border markers. But he was also careful to emphasize that the clash had taken place within the borders of Erzberg. He said so more than once, leading Wéry to suspect that he was in fact not quite sure on the point, and feared that it might lead to trouble.

Never, by God, never! thought Wéry. And if his word counted for anything, the dragoon would have his promotion and more. If anything had happened to her . . . (*By good fortune they were not inconvenienced* – what delicacy of phrase!) If anything had happened to her, he thought, he might have blown his brains out. Dear God – what had he been doing to involve them? What had he been doing?

How could he face her – even supposing she was willing to see him again?

But, he reminded himself, he had had nothing to do with her going. He would have begged her not to go, if he had known. And – and the danger she had fallen into had not been his making. Freelance banditry by the French was a common hazard of the roads these days, although it was unusual so far south.

Or could he be sure even of that? A half-troop, with no wagons, or at least none mentioned in the report. That was a scouting mission, not a foraging party. Probably it had been part of a larger force that had divided itself to cover a wider area. Heaven knew what they had been looking for. But yes, couriers to Erzberg could be a possibility. They knew Erzberg was hostile. And they knew too (because Lanard would have told them) that in Erzberg there was the man Wéry. They would have guessed what he did, and why.

And that was the truth. Whether he had asked her to go or not, whether they had been looking for her or not, he had made her a part of what he did. Against all the iron and powder of France, against that blind and savage will – how could he hope

353

that she would not suffer, as Kranz had suffered, and some day he too must suffer, for what he was choosing to do? He could picture himself sitting here in this same room, with a report from the same man in front of him, except that this time the dragoons had arrived a half-hour too late to prevent rape or murder.

Yes, in the small hours he might indeed have turned to his pistol.

He sat and looked at the page. A bell in the city tolled eleven o'clock. He was still there when it tolled the quarter hour. A carriage rattled in the street and distant voices spoke in the barrack square. He knew that he should go to bed. Late nights and early mornings left him dazed and foggy, and he was due to see Bergesrode at dawn again the next day with the report that he had written about the Illuminati meeting in the Adelsheim house. But he did not think he could sleep.

Steps sounded on the steep wooden stair – more than one set of feet. He wondered wearily who it was. The sounds stopped at his door. There was a knock.

'Yes!' he groaned.

The orderly sergeant looked in. His face was wooden.

'Person to see you, sir,' he said, and withdrew.

It was her.

He jumped to his feet with an exclamation. His chair tumbled and clattered on the floor.

'I am sorry to disturb you,' she said.

In his astonishment he had to fight for words. 'Are – are you alone?'

'My maid is on the stair.'

She was tired – as tired as he was. It told in her voice.

'I – regret I have nowhere for you to sit,' said Wéry. 'Please,

354

er . . . please take my chair.' He turned and fumbled for it. In his confusion, and the dim light, he felt very clumsy. 'Please sit,' he begged, and then recollecting himself, 'When did you arrive?'

'Thank you,' she said. 'We reached the house this afternoon. My mother supposes me to be resting, and has gone to Lady Jenz's. I must be back before she returns.'

'Indeed you should be resting,' exclaimed Wéry. 'I have read . . . such terrible things.'

'Thank you again,' she said. 'Indeed I have been much distressed. Yet I know it was nothing to what you and my brother and so many others must have seen. I have come with a message.'

A message?

Wéry almost sat down. Just in time he remembered that his chair was gone from behind him, and that she was sitting on it. He settled awkwardly on the edge of his desk. It put him above her, and also rather close.

'I fear it is not what you were hoping for,' she said, looking up into his face. 'It is from Ludwig Jürich. He says you must expect no more help from his house.'

He drew breath. 'I – see. Did he say anything more?'

'He knew I had come to see if I could bring you what you wanted. But he – he fears for his house, and the people in it. He says he is under suspicion.'

'I see,' said Wéry, digesting this.

She seemed to have been expecting some rebuke, or at least disappointment, for she said, 'I almost decided to stay, nonetheless. But I was given something and I assumed it was what you wanted. He said it was for you.'

'He?'

'One of the servants. It must have come from Maximilian

Jürich, but I did not know that.' She took from a bag a tattered sheet of parchment and spread it on the desk for him. The haunted face of Christ rolled its eyes at the low ceiling.

'I see he has sent you one of these already,' she sighed, indicating the picture on the wall behind Wéry. 'He is mad, of course. I did not realize that he knew you.'

Wéry stared at the painting. For a long moment he could not speak. Then he said: 'He is not mad. Well, I do not think he is.'

'He paints this face, again and again. Nothing else.'

'Yes, it weighs on him. This face . . . There was a man, you see. One of his own men, when he was with the republican militia during the siege of Mainz. Maximilian had him arrested, and shot by firing squad. I do not even know why – perhaps he thought the man would betray us to the French. I saw the body afterwards, when I was waiting to cross the river. It was lying against the palace wall with the lice crawling out of its clothes . . .'

He touched the painting with the tip of his finger.

'This is the face of that man.'

It lay on the desk, rolling its dying eyes in the gloom. It was real. It had come at last.

'It is what I needed,' he said hoarsely. 'I am most truly grateful.'

She frowned at it. Plainly she could not see how it could be so important. She said, 'Well, I am glad, then,' in a voice that had no gladness in it.

'You should rest,' said Wéry.

'I cannot rest without forgetting,' she said. 'And I do not think I can forget.'

She rose to her feet. He copied her.

'Lady Maria,' he said formally. 'I have said I am grateful. I cannot truly express how grateful I am. But I beg you to believe

356

me that had I guessed what you would do or the risk you would run, I should not have suffered you to do it. Indeed I have slept poorly for many nights, thinking of you. And I wish . . .'

Something in his tone had caught her attention. She looked at him.

'I wish to say . . .' he stammered. 'How much – how much I admire you. I have feelings for you that I find it difficult to express. It is surprising but . . . I have to tell you this. I do not know that I can ask you . . . I mean, you are . . .'

He flushed. There were no words that could tell her what she was in his thoughts.

'You must not say such things,' she said.

'I must not. And yet also I must.'

She gave a weary gesture with her hand, and he fell silent.

'I must go. Sir, you have helped us, but it will do no good to talk any more.'

'Yes,' he sighed and looked at the floor.

'All that I ask is that as little should be said of our journey as possible. My mother is already angry with both Anna and myself. The more she hears gossip of it, the worse it will be.'

He cleared his throat, fighting for composure. 'I shall do whatever I can. I will . . . May I see you to your carriage?'

'I think . . . Thank you, but it is better not.'

It was a quarter to midnight. Wéry lifted his head from his hands and groaned.

Work, he thought. Work was the remedy.

He lit another candle, and placed both candles close to the paper on the desk. He rose, took the other picture from the wall and set it on the desk beside the new one. Then he drew from a

357

drawer a curved reading-glass. He looked at the two pictures, side by side. The anguished faces of the man on the cross writhed before him. With a dull heart he placed the reading-glass on the new picture and bent over it. The face of the dead Christ swelled from the canvas, blotting out the memory of the face that had left the room.

He had to look beyond the suffering. That was the secret. As if he were a general or a prince, he had to look past it. He had to look at the detail of the background beyond.

It had changed. Where the old picture had shown a general receiving his orders, there was now only empty middle distance. The town, with the camp around it, was still there – painted rather larger than it had been in the previous picture. And the river was still busy with boats crossing. Probably there was some significance in the detail here, but he could not see it at once.

To the left of the face there were also changes. The picture of the Roman soldier stepping across the river had been replaced with a group of figures. The Roman was still there. He had his sword drawn and raised to strike. Moving the glass directly over him and peering closely, Wéry could see the letters at his belt: **A d A** – *the Armée d'Allemagne.*

Kneeling before the Roman, with his head bowed for the blow, was a man in a bishop's robes and cap. On the robes of the bishop were a pattern of lions, like the lions on the arms of the Prince-Bishop of Erzberg.

A number of other figures stood by, watching impassively. One wore an Emperor's crown. Another had an Elector's cap and the blue and white diamonds of Bavaria, Erzberg's largest German neighbour. And among them was a figure with two faces, holding an hourglass: the Roman god Janus.

Janus: January. *The Army of Germany will strike at the Bishop in January*.

January was already on them. But the left side, Maximilian had said, would be for the interpretation. The facts would be on the right. And Wéry could find nothing there that was new.

He swept the reading glass over the right hand side of the picture again. Hills, trees, bushes, and the town in the distance with the camp around it and the river beyond. All was as before. He placed the glass over the camp and peered down at the enlarged, distorted image. He counted the tents. Seven, as before. And horses and cannons . . .

Wait! The cannons!

There were four shown, lined in a row before the tents. In the previous picture there had only been three. He re-centred the glass on the fourth and peered closely.

It was shown larger than the others. A tiny figure of a man had been painted in by one wheel to make that clear. This was not a field gun. This was a siege weapon.

So that was it. Fact: *The Army at Wetzlar is being reinforced with siege guns*. Interpretation: *They are preparing to strike at the Bishop in January*.

This, these two sentences, was the message. This was what he had bought, at the price of Balcke-Horneswerden's honour, and his own.

This was what Maximilian and Hartmann — yes, and the unwilling Ludwig, and his wife, and Maria too — had risked so much to bring to him.

Now he must decide whether he believed it.

He sat back and rubbed his aching eyes.

There were so many drawbacks to this form of communication.

Details might be missed, or misinterpreted. A page full of writing would have told him more. But even writing could only get him so far. He could not question the written page, demand more details, or check his understanding of the meaning. And a page of writing, even in cipher, would have betrayed itself to the enemy if ever it fell into their hands – as this one nearly had. This was a far better disguise. *They will see only the head*, Maximilian had promised him. And indeed they would. It was Maximilian's device, and Maximilian's way. The dead man from the streets of Mainz. The man whose face Maximilian carried in his head every moment of his day, whom he had had shot by his own men, and whose innocence, by this means, he proclaimed to all the world. No, he was not mad. Not quite.

The Army of Wetzlar has been reinforced with siege guns. It was exactly the sort of thing that Hartmann, travelling up and down the Rhine, would be able to find out. Getting guns that size across the Rhine could not be done easily. Covered barges, gathered at night, loading . . . No. Even then there would be too much movement, business, noise. The crews and barges must come from somewhere. Man them with soldiers, and still the soldiers would talk. Take it as fact.

The interpretation was another matter. Wéry remembered bitterly how he, how everyone in Erzberg – had mistaken the news of the return of Hoche to Germany. So there were siege guns at Wetzlar. Why should they be intended for Erzberg?

Well, who else might they be intended for? Frankfurt was garrisoned by the Emperor. They would not strike at Frankfurt so soon after the peace. Indeed, if they had wanted Frankfurt they would have made the Emperor abandon it to them, just as he had abandoned Mainz.

If they meant to march north, or east, into the lands dominated by Prussia, they would have to reinforce Wetzlar with more than just a siege train.

But Erzberg, now. The walls were breached. But they would know from Lanard that the breaches were small and could be repaired. Erzberg, with its motley army, its control of the Vater crossings, and its position in the heart of Germany. They had what they needed, if it came to that. Had they a motive, now that d'Erles had fled? But only they would know what motive would be sufficient.

And there was corroboration of a sort, if they were patrolling down to the Erzberg borders. That was the sort of action that discouraged spying and patrolling in the other direction. Certainly it would be harder for him to confirm the presence of siege guns at Wetzlar if the roads were alive with French patrols. It might mean more lives lost – more of his own people. And yet he must try, and they must try. The double faces of Christ groaned soundlessly on the desk before him.

Outside a bell tolled the quarter hour. Midnight had come and gone and he had not been aware. And now he had a report to write, which must be ready before his meeting with Bergesrode tomorrow morning. He must write it carefully. He pushed the two paintings aside, found pen and paper, and set them before him. But before he began he remembered something else.

Taking a small lever from a draw, he bent down over a floor-board before the hearth. The nails that held it were loose. It came up easily. Beneath it, wrapped in canvas, were concealed the reports and papers he considered most valuable, or most dangerous. On the top of the pile was his own report to Bergesrode, strung together from his recollections of Uhnen's drunken ramble, and from meetings with officers of the police. It was short, because he had had so little to put in it. And it began baldly: 'On the night of 13 October notable members of the Canon Rother-Konisrat's party attended a gathering at the house of the Knight von Adelsheim . . .'

He removed it, wrapped the others back into their sack, and replaced the board. Then he made up the fire in the little hearth.

With shaking fingers, he fed his report to the flames.

XXVII
The Testimony of Papers

It was barely dawn when Wéry let himself into the Prince's antechamber, and found that Bergesrode's chair was empty.

Fernhausen looked up from his desk. He had a candle before him, which cast shadows across his face.

'Where is he?' asked Wéry. Never before had Bergesrode missed one of their early morning meetings.

Fernhausen shrugged. 'Off somewhere,' he said. 'Yesterday was chaos, and we are still picking ourselves up this morning. You'll have to deal with me.'

'What's happening?'

'Oh, it's everything really. Mainly the wretched ball for Candlemas. These things always take more effort than an imperial crisis. But Steinau has presented his report on Hersheim, and of course it's heavy against Balcke-Horneswerden, and last night we had half the Chapter in here one after another trying to find out what His Highness is going to do about it.'

'What is he going to do about it?' asked Wéry.

'How should I know? He just smiles and nods and hears each one out, and then it's on to the next one. And then right in the middle of it comes the news of d'Erles's assassination.'

'Assassination! I hadn't heard.'

'My dear fellow,' said Fernhausen smiling up at the ceiling. 'How should you? But no, it is true. Although . . .' he pulled a face. 'When I say "assassinated", that makes it sound deliberate. Apparently he was on his way to Rome, to seek asylum there. Of course he had to pass through French-held Italy. The French have been setting up this Cisalpine Republic of theirs, and there was a lot of excitement about it. A mob saw this aristocrat's coach, pulled him out of it, and, well, it ended with him *à la lanterne*.'

'I'm sorry. I had thought better of him after he appeared at the Chapter.'

Fernhausen rolled his eyes. 'You don't imagine that was his own idea, do you?'

'He was put up to that?'

'Of course. Although perhaps,' he glanced momentarily at Wéry, 'perhaps we shouldn't go too far into that. His Highness was not pleased. And now he thinks we all betrayed him, and betrayed poor dear d'Erles too. Of course he goes on smiling and nodding, but no one's getting anything they want out of him. And so we are all having to jump a bit.'

'Did you put d'Erles up to it?'

'Not me. Not Bergesrode either, if you want to know. He was all for fighting to the last man.'

'So was I.'

'Oh, I know. Fortunately there were wiser heads around. What can I do for you?'

Wéry rallied his scattered thoughts.

'Has he seen the report from the frontier dragoons yet?'

'No. I have it here. I'll put it in to him as soon as I . . .'

'No need. Here's the full story, in half the space.' Wéry handed over the pages he had written at midnight. Fernhausen lifted an eyebrow in surprise. But he took it, moved his candle over and began to frown at the page. Wéry sat back, aching with tiredness, and watched the light growing at the window.

So! Once again he found that he was far behind events. He had come up here expecting his most important interview with Bergesrode for weeks – intense on the report from the Rhine, difficult on the Illuminati – and had found instead that he and his concerns were almost the last things on anyone's minds. Really, he thought wearily, he should get his office moved up here to the palace – into this very room, perhaps. That way he would not miss two-thirds of everything that went on.

And d'Erles was dead. That wasted life, the waster of so much and so many others, was gone. And the man's one act of redeeming gallantry had been the gallantry of a dupe. Somehow, someone had manoeuvred him into offering to leave the city. And so he was dead.

Weariness and depression felt very much the same, thought Wéry.

'Yes,' said Fernhausen, after a little. 'Yes, he must see this.' He turned the page, reading with uncharacteristic attention. He came to the point where Wéry had told the story of the capture of the coach in four clipped sentences. Fernhausen read them, and finished. He frowned again, tapping the page.

'You don't mention . . .'

'No.'

Wéry had not said who had ridden in the coach. She had asked that he should not.

It was one of those rare moments when Fernhausen looked him in the eyes.

'Shouldn't you?'

'It is better not.'

'But she's his god–daughter.'

'All the more reason.'

Still Fernhausen was looking at him. But now he was unsure of himself. Wéry kept his expression firm, marshalled his arguments (security, scandal, the reputation of the Prince himself . . .). He waited.

'Very well,' said Fernhausen at last. He placed the report with a small pile of others. 'As you say, it takes half the space.'

'May I have the dragoon's report?'

Fernhausen hesitated. Then he said, 'I suppose so.'

He passed it over. Wéry took it and pocketed it. So much for the dragoon's hopes of promotion, after all. He was sorry about that. But she wished to keep her name from public notice, and he was going to track down every copy of that damned report if he possibly could.

'He values you because you are dedicated, you know,' said Fernhausen a little sulkily. 'He likes people he thinks are incorruptible. It's why he's put up with my priestly colleague for so long. If he thinks a fellow has loyalties elsewhere, he starts to worry.'

'I understand what you are saying,' said Wéry.

In the heavy silence, he rose to his feet. 'I had better let you get on with the truly important matters – like the Candlemas Ball,' he said.

Fernhausen smiled. 'For once,' he said, 'that is not my concern. His Highness has asked Bergesrode to manage it.'

'Unusual.' Such things almost always fell to the more junior aide.

Fernhausen's grin broadened. 'I think Bergesrode was indeed a little surprised.'

Maria was in her room, reading her dead brother's letters.

She had kept them for so long, tied in bundles with ribbon. She had not touched them until now, because the thought of them had always been so painful that she had shied away. She had needed a reason, more than mere remembrance, to make her pick them from her trunk, untie them, and begin to leaf through the pages, covered in that achingly familiar hand. This morning, at last, she had one. Her reason was Michel Wéry.

Of course it had been impossible. Of course she could not have stayed, and listened to what he had been trying to say to her. She had done what she must, and had done it quickly, so that neither of them should suffer more than they had to.

And yet – now that she had done it indeed, and left him there – why should she not look back after all and wonder?

Who was he really? Red-faced and stammering last night, he had barely been able to speak for himself. But he did not deserve to be dismissed. He had seen and done so many things. Was his birth his fault? Someone should speak for him, since he must now be silent. She knew of only one person who could.

Michel has returned from another of his forays, chattered Alba, half-way down the page she held. *He seems surprised and a little disappointed to be still living, but I am glad to see him. Of course he is angry because the army has done nothing but sit and feed itself while he was away. He expects too much of everyone, and of himself most of all . . .*

The weak winter sunlight strayed across the room. Her bed

was unmade and her fire unlit. She had sent her maid away so that she might be undisturbed. When the girl returned at the appointed time, she sent her away again. She read for hours. And, as the time passed, her pace of reading slowed. She no longer skipped half-seeing through the pages for Alba's words about his friend – who was mentioned in perhaps one letter in three, and sometimes only fleetingly. She began to read, at last, for Alba himself as well, as she had long wished to, and yet had never felt she could.

All those half-familiar, half-forgotten phrases that he had written to her were there before her eyes again. They were bringing her closer to him, closer than she had felt for a year. They spoke to her in his voice, a little distantly, as if they came from another room, but nonetheless clear, and nonetheless Alba. She could smile at them again – at his stories of the ridiculous and farcical happenings in camp, at the practical jokes that he and young Friedrich Rieseck-Tauen had played on other officers, and at his triumph on the occasions when he had managed to entice even the earnest and dour Michel Wéry to join in.

As she read, she began to feel grateful. She was grateful for the titbits about Wéry, but also she was grateful to Wéry himself, because she saw that it was because of him that she had come to remind herself of Alba in life. Because of him, she could see now that the memory of Alba was something she should also feel grateful for. Strange friends! She could almost picture the two of them together, walking towards her across a sunlit lawn, one short and laughing, the other tall and abrupt. And though neither of them would speak of themselves, each might speak to her of the other.

My dearest and most delightful Maria . . .

. . . to Darmstadt with Michel to visit Friedrich in the
hospital. Friedrich is worse, I fear. He did not rest himself
when his malady first appeared . . . Afterwards Michel took
me to the hospital for the ranks. I own that I was horrified.
The poor wretches lie in terrible conditions. There are not
enough beds or even rooms, so some must lie in the
corridors . . .

'Lady Maria . . .'

. . . I thought that Michel would be angry too, but he said that
he had seen so much worse. It is a wonder to me that a man
who can be so compassionate may also be so hard in his
thoughts . . .

'Lady Maria!' It was Pirenne again, the French maid. She
bobbed in the doorway.

'I have not finished, Pirenne,' Maria said. 'Did I not say you
should come back in another hour?'

(Another hour? What time was it?)

'Yes, Lady Maria. But the Knight wishes to see you in the
drawing room – he said *now*, if you please.'

Father? And *Now*. What was the matter?

Puzzled, Maria followed Pirenne down the stairs. A footman
was waiting for her at the door. She was ushered in, as if she were
a guest.

He was sitting on the settee on the far side of the room,
decked out in his great wig and frock coat as if for a formal
occasion. He looked up as she came in.

He saw her, and frowned. Still frowning gloomily, he looked at a point on the floor before him.

'Father?' said Maria. 'Is something wrong?'

'Displeased,' said Father, without lifting his eyes. 'Displeased.'

'Your father is displeased with you, Maria,' said Mother.

She was standing motionless by the fireplace, with eyes that seemed very bright and hard.

Franz was also there, lounging against the wall, looking at his feet. He wore a hangdog expression, as if he knew that someone was guilty of something and feared that he might be guilty too.

Like Father, he was carefully arrayed. It must have taken his valet an hour to tie that cravat.

'Your father is displeased with you, Maria,' said Lady Adelsheim. 'As too am I. I wonder if you can imagine how very, very disappointed we are.'

Maria could feel herself colouring. 'May I . . . know why?' she managed to ask.

'I cannot believe that you do not already know why.'

When Maria did not answer, she went on.

'I had thought it was plain to you that your father and I consented to your going to Mainz because we were growing concerned about your conduct, which, as I told you myself, was less than it should have been from the sister of our dear Albrecht. I had been concerned in particular to hear that your name was becoming linked in gossip with that of a certain foreign officer, of whose bearing and conduct you well know my opinions.

'Yet directly – *directly* – upon your return, when you had led me to believe I might leave you safely at this house, I find that you took yourself to visit this man in his barracks, at an hour and in a manner that you know could not possibly have been countenanced if we had been aware of it. Do you have an explanation for your father, Maria?'

'I . . . Is it my father who so accuses me?' she said, and met her mother's eyes.

Mother waited an instant, looking coolly into Maria's stare. Then, deliberately, she said, 'August?'

Maria swung appealing eyes on her father. But he did not look up.

'Displeased,' he growled.

'Your father is ashamed of what you have done,' said Lady Adelsheim. 'And you have as yet offered no explanation for your conduct – to him, or to me.'

Maria looked at the figure of her father, slump-shouldered and sorrowful. She willed him to look at her, to see that it was her, Maria, who loved him and stood there. But he would not.

She must have been at him all morning, Maria thought. She had been coaching him and instructing him against his daughter, while the servants dressed him like a doll! She had been trying to poison him against her!

It would not work! She would not allow it!

'Mother,' she said, as evenly as she could. 'I remembered that an acquaintance of this officer had given me a memento for him – a picture. I had agreed to deliver it . . .'

'Indeed? But such a thing could have been sent. There was no excuse for you to see the man yourself.'

'As I say, I remembered it late in the evening, and was angry with myself. I did not recollect the hour, it is true. But I was accompanied, and I did not remain above fifteen minutes.'

'So I have learned from the coachman and the maid.

Nevertheless it was very wrong of you, as you know. And do not proffer us your "fifteen minutes" as if it might excuse what you have done. It would have been too much, as well you know, even if the man you called upon were honest. But I have spoken to you of this one already. He is the basest and most treacherous man in all the city. One minute in his company is too much. There will be no more.'

Maria felt herself losing control. 'Indeed, Mother,' she said with a lift of her chin, 'I think you are unjust!'

'That is *quite* what I imagined you would think. I am told you have spent this morning reading letters from your brother. You should be ashamed to have touched them, and yet I feel sure you are not. I can only conclude that you are utterly blind to the fact that you have disgraced his memory by your association with that man. Blind, Maria! *I* knew that man was vile the first moment I saw him. Now Major Lanard has confirmed it to me.'

Lanard? Lanard?

What had he to do with all this? And what could he have said?

'Mother,' she said. 'Lanard and Wéry are enemies after all.'

'Once again you are mistaken. You have no wit in these matters. Lanard was quite reluctant to oblige me, I assure you. But I remarked some words that passed between them when they happened to be in my coach together – and I sought an explanation. Now he has sent me this.'

She held up what seemed to be a printed pamphlet, folded to comprise several pages.

'When your father has dismissed you, you will go to your room and read it. If you want to know who is responsible for Albrecht's death – who is truly responsible – this will give you the answers. I wish you then to reflect on what you have done to your brother's memory. His letters will be removed from your room until I judge your conduct to be more becoming for his sake. And you will no longer wear mourning, Maria, for it is plain that you no longer honour him as you should.'

She looked at Pirenne. Obediently, the maid crossed the room and took the paper from her hands. Lady Adelsheim turned her shoulder. Speaking now to the air, she said, 'I can do no more for you but write to my cousin Rother and arrange your marriage as soon as possible. August?'

Father gathered himself and frowned into the space before him.

'Go,' he said.

There was nothing Maria could say. In the icy air she accepted the paper from Pirenne. She looked her mother in the eyes. She looked at Franz, who hung his head. She looked at her father, and then she left them there.

Her feet carried her heavily up the stairs. She was dazed and miserable. She might have been ready for a confrontation with her mother. She had almost expected it. But Mother had known that. That was why she had brought in Father – so that Maria could not reject her without rejecting Father as well.

And as Maria climbed, she began to understand that her mother had taken revenge on her in the most wounding way possible. For Father would not forget, now, that Maria was in disgrace. She would be reading to him, or talking to him or sitting with him, and she would see that hurt and puzzled look cross his face as he remembered, once again, that Maria had done something that was not to be forgiven. He would not remember what it was, or when it had happened. But he would remember that it had. Maybe he would remember for the rest of his life.

Mother had stolen him from her.

No, it was not the late hour. It was not even Wéry. It was because Mother had sensed that one day, one day soon, Maria would defy her. That was what had made her do this, using Father, and Albrecht. And Albrecht, Albrecht, Albrecht – she was stealing Albrecht's memory too, taking his letters, denying him to Maria. She was making him into something he hadn't been.

She was stealing both of them!

When she reached her room, Pirenne was making the bed. Maria did not speak to her. She could not. She was shaking. Her fingers gripped the paper in her hand and made it crinkle. She looked down at it. She did not want to read it. She did not want to do anything that her mother directed. She wanted to burn it without looking at it and then to tell Mother what she had done.

The top sheet was headed, in French: *BRABANT HAILS THE CHAMPIONS OF LIBERTY*.

The lower line of the title ran: *A copy of a speech given by Delegate Wéry of the Revolutionary Club of Brussels to members of the Jacobin Club in Paris on 11th Nivoise, in Year One of the Revolution.*
She read.

Free citizens of France, I, a delegate of Brabant, salute you! We are your brothers in the struggle for liberty. Like you we have sought to throw aside the yoke and rid ourselves of the ancient abuses of those who would be our overlords. In this we have been inspired by your example, and we are inspired once again as we take up arms to return to our homeland.

Citizens of France! You are like a light that pours out far beyond your borders, into every cranny of oppression and

374

obscurantism. Nowhere is there a country that has not heard of your doings. Nowhere is there a people that does not yearn to be free like you . . .

Maria sat down, scarcely aware of what she was doing. She remembered prints of the revolutionaries making speeches, in those early days when all the news had seemed to be of excitement and hope. She could imagine him, speaking in those crowded rooms with the eyes of Paris on him. But to see his words! What dreams he must have had – and the chance to realize them!

. . . there is no space left between the rightful demands of the people for liberty, and the bayonets of the princes who oppose it. The choice for you, citizens of France . . .

She turned the page.

In the margin in a hand that she knew as well as her own, her mother had written one word: WARMONGER.

. . . is of action, to sustain the lights of liberty that glow beyond your borders, or, if you believe the princes will be content to leave you undisturbed, of inaction, to see our lights extinguished and only yours left alone. Which will you choose?

WARMONGER, barked the word at the side of the page, written so deep that the pen had dug a black rent in the surface of the paper.

Citizens of France, I say only this. That my countrymen know your honour, your spirit, your fraternity. You are our hope. And that if you choose action, yes, a thousand, perhaps many thousands may die. But you will work such a great good in the name of liberty beyond your borders that it will never be forgotten, but continue, like a river of light down the years and the generations to come.

Citizens of France, in the name of Brabant, and of all who love liberty beyond your borders, I thank you.

At the bottom of the page, Mother had written her own verdict.

Such words have brought more deaths than those of Nero against the Christians.

Maria put the pamphlet down slowly and stared into space. She barely saw Pirenne drop her final curtsey and make to leave the room. She barely heard the soft knock at the door, Pirenne opening, the low murmur of servants' voices.

Pirenne returned into her line of vision. Expressionless, the maid went to Maria's dressing table, gathered up the pile of Albrecht's letters and left the room.

Still Maria stared at nothing. And she thought that all the world was mad.

If men were not mad from within, like Father, like Franz, then the world crowded on them and drove them into madness of another sort, like Maximilian Jürich – and like Michel Wéry. And Alba had died because of it.

In her mind she saw again the black guilt for his death broken out and out and passed to thousands and thousands of his murderers, whose fingers took it in little black crumbs and put it to their lips, and their lips swallowed it, and it was gone. And one of them was Michel Wéry.

In a moment she would burn this pamphlet on the low fire in the grate: a small, useless act of defiance against her mother. But her heart was already ash.

PART V:
THE DOORS OF
HEAVEN

January—March 1798

XXVIII
Candlemas Ball

In mid-January the world learned the Emperor's price for Mainz. French troops withdrew suddenly from Venice. Imperial forces moved in to occupy the ancient city and its territories. The Doge was not restored. After eight hundred years of independent history Venice was absorbed into the territories of the Empire. The Venetian republicans, who had overthrown their oligarchic rulers with French help, were abandoned to the mob and to the mercy of the Austrians.

Wéry paced to and fro in his room, raging. *Why couldn't they have learned from what happened to us? Had they really believed that they would not be betrayed?* There was just one thing to be sure of in the huge, callous calculations of powers. Whatever they said about liberty, honour, or generosity, they would act in fear and selfishness. It had happened in the Lowlands, Italy, Mainz and Switzerland. Could not the republicans of Venice have seen it coming to them?

Perhaps they had. Perhaps they had suspected that they too would be doomed. But they had been trapped, powerless; their only choice had been to flee or wait helplessly for the end.

In his fury he wept, and bit his hand.

A week later French troops moved into Holland to support a republican coup. And on the Rhine, twenty leagues upstream from Mainz, shots were fired and men killed when the French forces seized a fortress on the west bank opposite Mannheim from the German militia that held it.

Two days later they invaded the canton of Vaud, after uprisings there.

But in Erzberg, January passed with no sign of an attack, except for the constant reports of French cavalry trespassing freely in neighbouring Hanau and Isenberg, and all the way up to the border. Wéry cursed, and racked his brains for new ways to find out what was happening at Wetzlar.

'Here,' said Bergesrode, in one hurried dawn meeting. 'You had better look at these.'

'These' were a sheaf of papers from the city police. The first was a report to the effect that Doctor Sorge had been in the city and had been followed. There was a list of houses at which he had been received. Wéry scanned down the names. Adelsheim was among them.

'These are not republicans,' he said shortly. 'These are damned fools.'

'Is that not always the case? Look at the rest.'

They were copies of letters, all written in the same hand and signed 'Nestor'. They were addressed to colleagues called 'Memnon' and 'Diogenes', and described the writer's doings in a number of cities, all with Greek names such as 'Sybaris' and 'Syracuse'. Most of them commented unfavourably on the rulership of these cities and in particular on the church – yes, clearly, and despite the classical names, the modern Catholic Church was meant. One letter contained a report of a continuing attempt to recruit someone by the codename 'Atlas'. Wéry looked up.

'What are they?' he asked.

'Discarded drafts taken from Sorge's office. It's the Illuminati, of course. The Bavarians found letters just like these when they broke Weishaupt's ring.'

'Has he been arrested?'

'Not yet, but he will be. That's not your concern. What I want to know is when I'm finally going to receive your report on all this.'

'These far overtake what I had.'

'I thought you would say that. Which leads me to wonder what it was you did have – if anything. The important question is whether there's a French hand in it. Don't forget you yourself told us the Illuminati had a highly-placed agent.'

'Maybe. But we are jumping at shadows.'

Bergesrode slammed his hand down flat upon his desk.

'And what if there's something *in* the shadows? You don't know until you've looked. So look hard. You've three days – until the Candlemas Ball!'

Three days? He would hardly be able to achieve much in that time. Bergesrode was demanding the impossible – again. Wéry smiled grimly, and looked at the papers once more.

' "Sybaris" is Erzberg, is it?'

'That's what the city police say. But pay no attention to that. You work it out for yourself, and see if you come to the same conclusions. And make sure you bring them to me personally and to *no one* else.'

'If you say so,' said Wéry, conscious of Fernhausen at the further desk, who was studiously not paying attention to their talk.

'Now, another thing.' Bergesrode picked up what appeared to be another list of names. A look of exasperation crossed his face. 'You have not replied to your invitation to the Ball. I know you have been keeping to barracks, but this one you will accept . . .'

'It is shameful of him,' said Lady Adelsheim. 'It is quite shameful.'

'Yes, Mother,' said Maria.

The two women sat opposite one another in the drawing room of the Adelsheim house in the Saint Emil Quarter, waiting for Franz, whose cravat had failed Lady Adelsheim's inspection, to reappear. Then the three of them would take the coach for the short journey up to the Celesterburg to attend the Ball. The women's hair was piled high in styles that had taken hours to prepare, set with jewels and covered in powder. Powder was thick upon their skin and their great silk ball dresses swathed out over their seats. There would be no new styles tonight – no feathers in the hair, no drapes gathered like Roman pillars in high waists beneath the breasts. Tonight the old order, braced with hoop and decked with ribbon, would sweep across the dance floor, perhaps for the very last time.

'He should have decided before this! It has been almost a month since the War Commission made its judgement. Did he imagine we would forget?'

'Surely he cannot have done, Mother,' said Maria automatically.

'Oh, you say so. But I know him. He is a fox, this Prince. He will hide wherever there is a bolt hole. But tonight we shall dig him out. Tonight we shall. And then we shall have justice on that man Balcke-Horneswerden at last.'

'Yes, Mother.'

In the past few weeks Maria had said as little as possible to her mother, and had agreed with her whenever she could. It did the least to provoke her and kept the conversations short. She would not risk another confrontation. It was better to sit with her eyes down, and loathe her, and pray quietly for the day that she would die.

'That man should be executed for what he did to Albrecht,' sighed Lady Adelsheim. 'But I suppose it will just be disgrace.'

'Yes, Mother.'

That particular act of submission cost her nothing. Albrecht was lost and Mother was a monster. But Maria could at least agree that the murderous Balcke-Horneswerden should be punished. He was a part of the world that had done all these things to her. And the thought of him, still unjudged so long after Albrecht had died, made losing her brother (the one sane and good man who had ever lived) even harder to bear.

Now it was her turn to sigh. She was going to a ball – one of the great balls of the year and her first since she had put off mourning – and she could go with no sense of joy in her heart.

He was dressing in his office in the barracks and they were calling him from below.

'Wéry! Hey, Wéry! Are you not ready yet? We're waiting!'

'A moment,' he bellowed in reply. He looked down at his boots. The shine on the left still plainly did not match that on the right.

'Once more,' he muttered to the valet. 'And quickly!'

The man knelt before him for the fourth time, and busied himself with his cloth.

Wéry was late. He knew that. The other hussar officers were impatient. But he could not attend the Ball with his boots in this state. He wanted to curse the soldier at his feet and tell him to hurry. But he knew it was his fault and his alone that he had run out of time. He had spent most of the afternoon over with the city officer of police, comparing notes on Sorge's list and trying to identify who really lay behind the Greek and Roman names the man had used.

'The report's got to go up,' the city officer had kept saying. 'The palace wants it before tonight!'

'Then we'll have to do our best in the time we have,' he had snapped. 'See here, if "Nestor" stands for Sorge himself, then "Telemachus" will be a younger man he has entertained – the younger Löhm possibly. Very good. Now what's this? You think "Cassandra" is the Lady Adelsheim? What evidence have you for that?'

'Who else could it be, sir?'

'If we're not sure, we don't say it.' And he had scored it out.

He had done it quickly, and never let the man go back to it. And he had stayed and stayed, to keep his eye on the report until the moment it was sealed and sent hotfoot up to the palace, to make sure that the name was not reinserted.

And so he was here struggling with his boots while his fellow officers hailed him from downstairs.

'Hey! Wéry!'

'Just finishing!' he answered. He looked down to check progress. 'It will have to do,' he said.

He remembered to add 'thank you' as he hurried out of the door.

A crowd of officers were waiting in the common room. The senior squadron leader leapt to his feet as he came into the room.

'Right,' he said, without looking at Wéry. 'Let's go.'

The officers began to troop out. Uhnen appeared at his elbow.

'Where's the colonel?' asked Wéry.

'He's been up there half the day,' said Uhnen. There was

something cold about his tone. Perhaps it was just that he had not liked to be kept waiting. 'Some conference or other – no one knows what. But he sent word that he wanted a full turnout from his officers. And that we were to make sure you came too.'

'Why?'

'No doubt we'll be told. Come on now. You're riding in my carriage.'

The barrack square was dark, and crowded with horses and carriages waiting to take the hussars up to the Celesterburg. They found Uhnen's and climbed in.

'Thank you,' said Wéry as they closed the door. 'I'm grateful.'

'There's no need,' said Uhnen. 'I wanted to talk to you.'

Still his voice was cold – cold and distant. Wéry eased himself back in his seat and felt the leather-covered boards press against his spine. He had barely exchanged a word with Uhnen since his confinement to the barracks had begun.

Von Uhnen waited until the coach had begun to move, following the others in a long line of carriages and gigs and barouches that snaked out of the barrack gate and down the narrow streets towards the bridges. Then he said, 'You remember some time ago you asked some of your fellow officers to choose someone from among them?'

'Yes.'

'I spoke with them. It will be me.'

The carriage rocked and clattered on its way through the darkness. From the carriage immediately ahead came the sound of excited laughter. They passed a street lamp. The momentary glow through the coach window showed Uhnen's face, yellow and blank-eyed as he looked at Wéry. Then gloom took the inside of the coach again.

'I am sorry to hear that,' said Wéry slowly.

'Oh, I wanted to do it,' said Uhnen. 'I thought you were a good fellow. I did not believe it when they first told me about you. Then I found out that you've also allowed your name to be linked with that of a young woman whom you should never have approached or laid eyes on. That's when I realized I was wrong.'

Wéry opened his mouth to protest. Then he shut it again.

They'll close ranks around you, unless you give them a reason not to. Von Uhnen had a reason now.

'And what do the other hussars think?'

'It's none of their business. And I wouldn't try to hide behind them.'

'I was not. But I was the aggrieved party. If there is a challenge, it should come from me.'

'I thought you might say that. Possibly you have forgotten what was said to you in the coffee-house. If you like, I will remind you.'

Wéry drew breath.

'No need. If you insist, I . . . I will think about it.'

Von Uhnen said nothing, and in the darkness between the street-lamps Wéry could not see his face. But the outline of his head and shoulders was rigid, and the air was iced with his contempt.

'I said I would think about it!' snapped Wéry.

'I heard what you said.'

The rest of the journey was completed in silence.

The Countess was receiving the guests. She was a huge, white-skinned figure in a dress of shining blue silk, and her white hair was piled massively upon her crown. Maria swept low in her curtsey. She rose and smiled as she did so.

'How wonderful you look!' cried the Countess, taking her by the hand. 'It is good to see you in your finery at last. Now my dear, surely you will dance tonight? Will you try the Lightstep for me? I remember you dance so well.'

'I shall be delighted, Countess, if it pleases Mother.'

'Pish!' cried Lady Adelsheim. 'One must be wary not of what one dances but whom once dances with, in my opinion. Countess, is His Highness not to join us?'

'Oh, there is some tiresome matter that he feels he must deal with. But I count on him appearing before midnight and have told him so.'

'Then we may be assured of it.'

In a flicker of the Countess's eye Maria read that her mother was presuming too far. Fortunately, Franz provided a diversion. He kicked his feet sullenly and said, 'Mother, can we not go in now?'

'Ah, and you would part me at once from my dear child,' said the Countess, still holding Maria by the arm. 'Come, my dear. You will dance with us. Of course you will.'

'Of course, Countess.'

The fat, white-gloved hand stroked her wrist for a moment. 'There is so much love in me,' she sighed. 'I cannot keep it for just one. I must share it with all our children.'

'Countess,' said Mother, with one more curtsey.

'Of course you must,' said the Countess, and with a broader smile dismissed them into the room.

'Maria, you should not support her so,' hissed Lady Adelsheim as they made their way in among the guests.

'Mother,' said Maria wearily. 'She treats all the young women like that. You know she does.'

389

'Indeed!' huffed her mother.

With that moment, and to her surprise, Maria began to enjoy herself. Faces turned towards her and cried out in welcome. Karl von Uhnen, in his green-and-white hussar uniform, came to beg a dance off her. Katherina Ölich and Elisabeth Machting-Altstein-Borckstein sortied from the crowd and surrounded her with exclamations, telling her that it had been *far* too long since she had last been out, asking about fashions in the Rhineland and insisting that she must have been in hiding for a month waiting for her dresses to be delivered.

'Why no,' said Maria. 'I did not order a single one. But to tell you the truth, my journey was such a trial to me that I have not wished to stir abroad until now.'

'Oh, but how *selfish* of you to deprive us of your company!'

'Now, Maria, tell us. Will you dance the Lightstep? And will you be in our set?'

'Yes, and yes!'

'Oh – and who will you dance it for? Say it isn't for Karl von Uhnen. I shall be so jealous if it is!'

Maria hesitated. 'As to that,' she said. 'I do not know.'

Standing alone in the gallery, looking down on the crowd, she saw the long figure of Michel Wéry. She thought his eyes met hers, and she looked hurriedly away. In the last few weeks she had begun letters to him. *Sir, I have had occasion to read a speech that you gave to a certain assembly in France, and it has concerned me deeply. I wish to know* . . . She had torn that one up, and begun again. *Sir, I have had occasion to read a speech that you gave to a certain assembly in France, and it has concerned me deeply. I wish you to know* . . . She had destroyed that one too, burning both it and its predecessor in her grate and stirring the ashes until they were truly gone.

She did not know what it was she wished him to know. And as for what she wished to know – that he repented of his words, that he saw all the cruelty and foolishness of them, that he understood how the war he had called for had caused so much suffering, and the death of her brother and his friend the last and greatest of all its blows – she had no way of asking such questions.

She could not address him at all – not on the page, not in word, not in so much as a look – without risking gossip and further confrontations at home.

'You had better decide quickly then,' said Elisabeth. 'They are about to begin.'

'Ah, ladies!'

It was the First Minister, Gianovi, performing an elaborate bow over his buckled shoe. The girls bobbed obediently. 'Sir,' they said.

'Permit me to avail myself of your beauty for a few moments,' said Gianovi. 'It would be charming for me, for once, to have my own choice of company, rather than that of every lady or gentleman who imagines that His Highness will do as they wish me to tell him to do.'

'Why, sir,' said Elisabeth, giving him her hand. 'If you wish to escape such attentions, you must go to him and persuade him to come out himself.'

Gianovi bowed once more. 'Again you overestimate my influence, my Lady. Although I am sure he will appear as soon as he may.'

'And what is it that is keeping him?'

'Ah, various things. Internal, external, a matter of justice and another of order. They all seem to gather into one at the moment.'

'Sir,' said Elisabeth. 'You are fascinating, although I think you do not mean to be. What matters are these?'

'Well, if you want to know the truth of it . . .' said Gianovi and knitted his brows.

'Yes, sir? Yes?'

'Well, I believe your best course would be to go and ask him yourself.'

'What!'

'Oh no, Lady Elisabeth. You should not be offended. I meant only that tonight you have a better chance of obtaining what you seek from him than I. No, do not laugh. I am absolutely earnest . . .'

'You are a tease, sir. I declare it!'

'. . . But it is the simplest matter for you. You see the doorway at the end of the gallery? You go down there, three, four doors to the room where you will find his secretaries. Knock at the inner door and inform His Highness that his presence is, most definitely is, required in the ballroom. What effect it will have, I do not know. But one may only hope.'

Maria smiled. She knew quite well that her mother would number Gianovi among those that one should not be seen with. And yet his company was more enlivening than that of anyone of whom her mother might have approved. (Was it not *always* so?) Now this bright-eyed, bird-like Italian had Katherina Ölich giggling so hard that she was in danger of weeping tears down her powdered cheeks.

At the same time Maria wondered at what he had said to them. He had a reputation for deviousness. Gianovi must know quite well what was delaying the Prince. He had rather skilfully diverted Elisabeth from probing too closely about it.

'I suppose it is army matters,' Maria said. 'His Highness is forever interested in the army, is he not?'

Gianovi shot her a look and his eyes were blank. 'Lady Maria, as to that you must ask a soldier – if you will not ask His Highness himself.'

Again, this proposal that one or all of them should accost the Prince. But surely he was joking?

'Oh!' cried Elisabeth in a different voice. 'Where are they all – the soldiers?'

Maria looked around. It was true. A few minutes ago there had been scores of uniforms mingling in the crowd. Now she could see a bare half-dozen. Two or three of them were moving swiftly along the gallery, as if hurrying somewhere. Wéry was still in his place. But she looked for Karl von Uhnen, and Katherina's brother Franz Eugen, and others that she knew. They had all slipped out of sight. The only officers she could see were the very youngest, cornets and ensigns, standing out like a handful of saplings in a copse that had been cleared of mature wood.

'I wonder if something is happening,' murmured Elisabeth.

At that moment a liveried footman banged three times on the floor with a great rod and, as the babble subsided, announced the Lightstep. The crowd began to part to clear spaces for the dancers. Maria looked and looked for the soldiers, hoping that she was mistaken.

She saw one. A huge, white-uniformed figure emerged from the corridor at the end of the gallery that Gianovi had been indicating. He glanced down at the throng, and instead of descending, began to make his way along the gallery, with the uneven, stumping gait of a man with a false leg. As he passed a footman he said something and laughed.

Katherina's hand was on Maria's arm. 'We must take our places,' she was saying.

But Maria was transfixed. A sudden misgiving had seized her. There was something wrong – something very wrong about the large man who had looked down on them all from the gallery.

'Sir,' she said to Gianovi. 'Tell me, I beg you. That man up there. It is not . . . ?'

Gianovi looked up and smiled tightly. 'It is indeed. That is your Count Balcke-Horneswerden.'

As Maria stared, wordless, at her brother's murderer, he added. 'I believe I did say that certain matters of justice and order have come together this evening. The reason Count Balcke is in good humour is that he has been informed that the charges against him will be dismissed. And they will be, shortly after ten o'clock tonight.'

Her friends were gone, hurrying away towards the dance floor. The candles were being lit there. Still she stared up at the man who made his painful, cheerful way along the gallery.

'It – is most unjust,' she whispered.

'If you are to make your plea,' murmured Gianovi. 'It must be now – before ten o'clock.'

She heard him distantly, as if his voice had come from far away. She nodded.

'First I must dance,' she said.

'Officer's conference, sir,' said a young hussar, hurrying past. 'Now. Down the east corridor, third door on the left. There will be orders.'

'I've heard,' said Wéry.

He did not move from the gallery rail. Orders – whatever they were, however urgent – could wait. He wanted to watch the Lightstep. With all this wretched, useless skulking in the barracks, he had not had the chance to see it for months.

He had arrived at the ball with a great sense of detachment, and had gone at once to find a place where he would not be bothered by anyone. His mind was full of his talk with Uhnen. He knew he was going to have to issue a challenge. He was going to have to fight. And he did not want to.

It was his own fault. His own damned fault. If he could only have kept his temper in the coffee house! But no. His fault went further back than that. He should never have allowed himself to be tempted into his bargain with Maria von Adelsheim. He should never have looked at her. Weakness, always weakness! And everything he had been doing was a shambles because of it.

No, that was not true either. The latest report had been a good one – the best he had ever done – even if the prediction of action in January had been astray. It had been a real blow, at last, against the enemy he had to fight. But the cost, to himself and to her . . . Too much? If in the end he lost his life?

He would not try to kill Uhnen. He would shoot wide, if it came to that. It would give Uhnen every chance of killing him, if he wished. And he did. *I wanted to do it.* It was not just loyalty to the army, or outrage at the betrayal of Balcke. Von Uhnen was jealous – jealous of the man whose name had been coupled in gossip with Maria von Adelsheim. In every way, she was becoming his downfall.

And still he waited. After all, it might be the only time he would see her dance.

She was there, taking her place in the middle set with her candle in her hand. Because she had arrived after most of the others, she would be one of those to begin on the outside. It would be some minutes before her turn. He would wait at least until she had changed in and out again. The music was beginning. From up here he would see it all very clearly.

'This is a fine time to be dreaming about women,' said a voice at his elbow.

It was Balcke-Horneswerden himself. He had been stumping at his best pace along the gallery towards the east corridor and had checked at the sight of the officer at the rail.

Wéry drew himself up, conscious of the first swaying movements of the dance below him. 'Sir,' he said.

'I've called a conference, Wéry,' he said. 'I expect *all* officers of Captain rank and above to attend. You especially. Come on.'

Reluctantly Wéry forced himself away from the rail. 'What's happening, sir?'

'I'll tell you if you come with me and speak to no one until we've got the door closed behind us. It's martial law, starting at ten o'clock.'

'Martial law!'

The Count grinned bitterly.

'And a heavy fist. I tell you, some of those fine folk down below will find they don't need their carriages tonight. Come on, now. There's a new post for you – promotion again. And a transfer. You'll have no time for daydreams after this.'

Dazed, Wéry followed him down the soft-carpeted corridors of the palace.

XXIX
The Painted Room

The charges dismissed!
  Dismissed!

She danced in a dream, barely seeing the circling women around her. Her feet moved in time, her hands took the light and guarded it with care. Her eyes lifted images from the room and brought them to a mind distracted. She saw her mother making her way brusquely through the crowd. She saw Canon Rother and Baron Löhm conferring among a group of their hangers-on. They had heard the news. They must have been planning to confront the Prince as soon as he appeared, anticipating victory. Now they would be debating whether to press their attack or to withdraw at once. But they had not listened to Gianovi. Before ten o'clock, he had said. And she – she, Maria Adelsheim, must go to him. Against these old practitioners of intrigue the Prince would be armoured. He would be expecting them. He would not be expecting her.

She danced, with her face pale, and the ghost of her brother at her shoulder.

She would go. She knew it with certainty. The clock at the end of the ball room showed twenty minutes past nine. It moved slowly. It barely seemed to move at all. The dance went on and on, in and out and round and round. She knew every figure.

Everyone around her was smiling. What was there to smile about? No one should be smiling at a time like this.

Now they were in the final pattern. She parted with one candle, placed both hands on the other, and followed the line – two-three and one-two-three and a final one-two-three and *up* to make the crown of lights above the group. The music ended. The crowd applauded. Maria brought her candle down, and looked at it. Then she blew it out.

'Oh, Maria!' cried someone. 'Why did you do that? Didn't you want him after all?'

'He's dead,' she said absently, and gave her candle to the footman. Then she slipped away into the crowd.

They knew. They all knew something was happening. She passed someone who was talking hurriedly and low about something the soldiers were doing. Another man was saying to his wife that they should go home, and his wife was protesting that it was impossible to leave before His Highness appeared. She threaded her way onwards. Her feet carried her up the red-carpeted stairs to the gallery. Wéry, she saw, had gone from his place. She was glad, because she did not want to talk to him now. The door to the west corridor was open and shadowed like a cave. There was a footman standing by it.

'Are you lost, my Lady?' he asked. 'May I help?'

'No,' she said, and walked past him with her head high.

Down the long corridor she went, moving in a rustle of silks that grew louder and louder as the babble of the ballroom was left behind. The air was cooler here, away from the lights and the press of bodies. She felt it on her skin. Her breath was coming in quick gasps. She tried to steady herself. It was important, very important, that she did not think too much about what she was doing.

It was the fourth door, Gianovi had said. The door was tall and dark and, unlike the others in that corridor, it was slightly ajar. There was a light burning inside. There were secretaries in there. How was she to pass the secretaries? She raised her fist to knock, then withdrew it. A distant memory dropped into her mind, of old Tieschen at Adelsheim, begging to explain that it had not been his fault that Wéry had tricked him.

Instead of knocking, she pushed the door violently open and leaned on the doorpost, breathing hard as though she had been running.

'Help!' she gasped.

There was only one secretary in the room. It was Adhelmar Fernhausen-Loos, whom she knew slightly. That was good.

He was staring at her, pen in hand.

'The First Minister!' she exclaimed. 'I think he's having a fit!'

'What!'

'He's in the ballroom! He's saying the most dreadful things!'

'What's he saying?'

She waved her arms helplessly. 'About the Prince. About the army! I thought he was only angry to begin with, but he's sick! You must come quickly.' She spoke urgently and low as if to conspire. And she spoke with all the force of her will, knowing that if she believed it enough Gianovi would be there, reeling and spouting the Prince's darkest secrets among the horrified crowds on the floor of the ballroom.

Fernhausen snatched a watch from his desktop and peered at it. '*Damn!*' He leapt to his feet. 'Who is down there?'

'No one!' she hissed helplessly. 'They've all gone somewhere!'

'The old ...! He's doing it deliberately! There'll be the devil to pay for this!' He hurried round the desk and out into the corridor. He looked left and right. There was no one there.

'Come on!' she exclaimed, picking up her skirts and beginning to stride down the corridor. He caught her sense of panic, went with her, and in a few paces was ahead. She started to run. He ran, too.

She let him get a little further ahead, then turned back as silently as she could and slipped through into the empty antechamber. In a moment, just a few moments, he would realize what had happened. She crossed the antechamber quickly. The door to the inner chamber was shut. She turned the handle without knocking and went straight in.

For the first time in her life she stood in the office of the Prince-Bishop. She had an immediate sense of space – great space, in dark blues and golds, stretching away far beyond the walls and up above the high ceiling. Vast, winged figures hung there, shadowy in the dim light. There were curling drapes and naked torsos. Saints in gleaming haloes pointed upwards, up to the very crown of the ceiling where, in a dull sunburst, a figure sat among battlements upon a high throne. And many eyes were on her, from above, from all around. They brought a verse from the Scriptures leaping to her mind. *So great a cloud of witnesses surrounds us* . . . Was this what the writer had meant?

Out in the corridor a man was running. Fernhausen had realized he had been tricked. She dragged her thoughts from the paintings and looked at the man at the desk. He had risen from his seat. He was watching her with a bemused expression.

'An unexpected assassin,' he said mildly. 'Or am I mistaken?'

She had never seen him like this. He was not wearing his wig. His hair was short, black and grey, and his head was very round. His cheeks and eye bags were heavy semi-circles of flesh, and there was stubble on his chin. If ever he had been planning to attend the ball that night, he must have changed his mind. He wore no powder, no doublet, no finery. His shirt was rumpled. His skin had a yellow hue in the light of the lamp on his desk. He looked very tired.

One hand was out of sight, in a drawer of his desk.

'I am no assassin, Godfather,' she said evenly. 'And I beg your pardon for my intrusion. I have come to ask for justice in the name of your godson, my brother.'

Steps sounded in the antechamber. Fernhausen appeared at the door, angry and flustered. She ignored him.

Very slowly the Prince-Bishop of Erzberg closed his drawer and resumed his seat.

'It is Maria, isn't it? And your brother was Albrecht von Adelsheim. He was a very fine young man. What justice may I do him?'

'That you act on the charges laid against his commanding officer by the Inquisitor of Erzberg.'

'Yes, I see. Of course it is very important to you that the officer in question should be punished. And that is why you have chosen this moment to come rushing up to see me?'

'I had heard, sir, that the charges against Count Balcke-Horneswerden are to be dismissed.'

He nodded wearily. 'That is true.'

'May I ask why, Godfather?' She could not keep her voice from shaking.

'Ah. That is the question that at the moment I do not feel I can . . .'

'Your Highness!' broke in Fernhausen.

The Prince glanced at him, sourly.

'I beg your pardon, Highness,' said Fernhausen, looking pale. 'I – I had not intended that you should be interrupted so. But I believe you would think it wrong of me if I did not now inform you that the courier whom the dragoons rescued in the incident was none other than Lady Maria von Adelsheim.'

The Prince's eyes swung back upon Maria.

'Truthfully? I had no notion. Not the slightest. Well . . .' he paused and looked down at his papers, as if debating something with himself. 'You place me yet deeper in debt to your house. Very well. Perhaps in that case it is right that I . . .'

Instead of finishing his sentence, he picked a broad, buff-coloured sheet from his desk and peered at it in the light of the candle.

'*This unprovoked and murderous excursion . . .*' he read. 'Mark how they will not admit they were on our territory . . . *demonstrates beyond all doubt that you persist in your hostile and malicious intent towards the Republic of France, despite all our patience and forbearance. Under these circumstances, the Republic has no option but to insist upon the following conditions for a lasting peace. That you shall . . .* Well, I do not think I need go into their terms in detail. It is signed by their General Augereau, and was delivered this morning. You will see that, notwithstanding what has gone before, it is difficult to part at this moment with the most senior and experienced officer left to Erzberg.'

'I – hardly understand you, Godfather. Are you saying something has happened because of me?'

He frowned, thoughtfully. 'I did not mean so. I think it is no more about you than it was ever about my unfortunate godson d'Erles. No, I suppose it is, and always has been, largely because of me. They know well that I hold their revolution to be among

402

the worst things men have invented and that, peace or war, I feel it my duty to oppose them as I may. So now they mean to be rid of me.'

'And what will you do?'

'I must surrender the city. Or I must strengthen myself in every way I can, and appeal for help to the Emperor. What would you have me do?'

It sounded – surely it could not be, but it sounded as though he truly wanted her advice. She hesitated. Huge things, finely poised, seemed to be revolving around her. She could put out her hand and change them, if she chose. But to what? To what? The eyes of the painted witnesses were on her, like a pressure in her skull.

'It would be easier,' he said, 'if we knew the consequences of our choices before we made them. We cannot. But you at least have been in the Rhineland. Tell me. Should I surrender the city?'

Memories tumbled in her mind, hopeless and incoherent. The Liberty Tree. The litter of pigs in hiding. The face of Madame Kaus. The face of Emilia, as the soldiers roared at her man in his study.

'Sir,' she said, agonized. 'I – I do not believe I can advise you.'

He sighed. 'I am sure that is a wise answer. It is not your choice, and I do wrong to lay it on you. In any case . . .' he glanced to a long-case clock, decorated with angels, which stood in the shadows by the door. The hands stood very close to ten o'clock.

'Now, I have been frank with you,' he said. 'I hope you will be frank with me. Who was it you were talking to, before you came up here?'

She hesitated. But indeed he had been frank, even if he had given her nothing she wanted.

'My choice to come to you was my own,' she said. 'And if I have done wrong, may it be upon me. But the man I was speaking with was your First Minister.'

'My Italian fox. I suppose he meant to remind me of the costs of the choice I have made, just as he did with poor d'Erles. And now . . .' His voice trailed off, and he turned his eyes to the clock once more.

He had misjudged it. The pendulum ticked and ticked reproachfully. They waited, listening to each second as it slipped like a last chance beyond their reach. Then the mechanism whirred and the light, bright chimes sang in the shadows of Heaven.

'I think you should go back to your mother,' the Prince said. 'Tell her, if she will listen, that I too grieve for Albrecht. But whatever you say, see that she goes home. Evidence of a conspiracy has been laid before me, and I must pursue it. I fear some of my guests will be inconvenienced tonight. However, so long as she comports herself properly, she will not be one of them. She will not be impeded. Somebody among my servants seems to have protected her. I am glad, for otherwise I should have had to do so myself.'

There seemed to be nothing more that could be said. She dropped into a slow curtsey, and left the painted room. Fernhausen pulled the door shut behind her.

'I am sorry,' she said to him. 'It was wrong of me.'

'It doesn't matter,' he said curtly.

But he still came to the door of the outer chamber to watch her make the long walk down the corridor to the gallery.

There were armed guards at the end of the corridor now, where the servant had stood earlier. And down in the shocked and murmuring ballroom, the first arrests were beginning.

XXX
A Turning in the Road

For the next ten days the Adelsheims kept to their house in the Saint Emil quarter. There was no guard at their door (as there were outside the houses of Jenz and Löhm, further down the same street), but Lady Adelsheim resolutely acted as if she too were under arrest. She kept to her study, morning and afternoon, writing letters of petition to the Prince and the Countess on behalf of her neighbours, on behalf of her cousin Canon Rother, imprisoned in the citadel, and even for Doctor Sorge, who had been caught by the frontier dragoons on the road to Nuremberg. She also wrote more widely, to influential acquaintances in the city and in neighbouring states, telling them that the supposed threat to the city had been fabricated to allow the Prince to rule like a dictator, and urging her readers to offer him no comfort. Maria knew what the letters contained, because her mother read them to her before sending them. She had never done such a thing before.

'But what if the French truly are preparing to take the city?' Maria ventured.

'Pish! It is lies. He lies about us and he lies about the French too. It is all to win himself more power. He gulls the Ingolstadt set with stories of invasion, so that they do not protest as he builds up his strength. But soon he will move against them also. He is devious. Do you know whom he has made jailor to my cousin? That man Wéry – now *Colonel* Wéry indeed! Commander of the citadel! And Gianovi is Governor of the city, I hear. Fanatics and foreigners, you see. He can find so few honest Erzbergers to back him.'

'Even so, is it wise? What if the Prince came to hear of what you say?'

'I am not so stupid, child,' said Lady Adelsheim. 'Our own people will carry these and will see that they arrive safely.'

Maria was in agony. However loyal the messenger, there were risks to any message – as she knew well. And there was also the danger that the next Ingolstadt canon that she addressed might simply hand her letters over to the palace. Moreover, she remembered her talk with the Prince in the Painted Room. She remembered, very clearly, the hunted look in the man's eyes as he had lifted the buff sheet of paper from Wetzlar. She did not think he had been lying about the French. And if they came . . .

But if she were to say that, then in the eyes of her mother she would have joined the Prince's party. It would mean another quarrel. Perhaps, after all that had passed between them about Albrecht, it would be the final one. And she knew this was why Lady Adelsheim was subjecting her to these letters: it was to test her loyalty, and to force her to choose her mother's side. For it was not possible to listen to the things her mother had written and yet remain neutral. If she did not oppose, she must acquiesce. She did not want to do either. She wished only that none of this was happening, and that she and her father and Anna at least were all safely away at Adelsheim.

At nights she woke up in fear. And then she thought that her mother was afraid too. But what mother feared was not punishment or siege but the loss of control. The world would no longer obey her, and she knew it. Under her wilful and confident manner, she was becoming less certain. Perhaps that was another reason why she called in Maria to hear what she had written and confirm her in what she had to say.

Damn her! *Damn her!*

But nothing seemed to come of the letters. Soldiers tramped the streets, with their long muskets sloped at their shoulders. They never stopped at the Adelsheims' doors. Maria watched them pass, wondering where they had come from. Most of them would indeed be honest Erzbergers, whatever Mother said. And soon they might have to level those muskets, and fire on thousands and thousands of oncoming Frenchmen. And their bodies would be exposed to French fire. And what would become of them?

'Well,' said Lady Adelsheim, putting down a letter at breakfast. 'He will take us. But what a fool he is!'

Franz, Anna and Maria looked up. Father went on burrowing over his food as if nothing had been said.

'A fool, Mother?' said Maria warily.

'See for yourself, if you wish.'

It was from Effenpanz, the butterfly-collecting Count with whom they had stayed in Bohemia when Erzberg had last been threatened by French armies. The Count wrote, in his own cramped hand, in reply to a letter Lady Adelsheim must have sent him very soon after martial law had been declared.

Of course, it said, he would shelter his dear, brave cousins. How much he admired them! What a noble thing it was to stand firm in the face of threats from these terrible revolutionaries! He only wished that the Emperor, so ill-advised by the spineless men around him, would gather such courage as was shown by the city of Erzberg. Surely with the example of Erzberg to inspire them, the soldiers of the Empire would be irresistible. He himself was now spending many hours a day in preparing his militia. But his home would for ever be open to those who could make such a courageous choice . . .

Anna was looking at her inquiringly. But instead of handing it on, Maria lifted it to her eyes again. The thought of that distant, peaceful Count leaving his butterflies to see his peasants in boots and straps and muskets was very strange. He had no doubt where the right lay. So little doubt, it seemed, that he could hardly have read Lady Adelsheim's letter closely.

She wondered if he remembered to wear his wig on his parades.

'I think we shall accept his invitation all the same,' said her mother dryly. 'I no longer wish to weary myself with this town.'

Maria put the letter down slowly.

'Why, Mother?'

'Why?' repeated Lady Adelsheim sharply. 'I have said why.'

'Mother, if you weary of the city, perhaps you should go to Adelsheim. I see no cause to go to Bohemia, unless we truly fear invasion.'

'Maria, you are impertinent. To go to Effenpanz is merely prudent. I will not debate it.'

He mother's tone was final, of course. It always was, especially when there was something that might indeed be debated. Maria felt her skin tremble slightly as she drew breath.

'I do not wish to go,' she said.

For a long moment Mother looked at her. They all looked at her – Anna, Franz, Johann the footman, poised at Mother's shoulder. Only Father muttered and chomped on over his food.

'What concern is it of yours?' said Lady Adelsheim. Her face was very white.

Maria did not know. She had not thought. She had not prepared for this moment. Yesterday, if she had been offered the chance of leaving the town, she might have cried for joy. But . . .

'I believe Effenpanz misapprehends us,' she said.

'Why should that sway me in the slightest?'

'If we were indeed as he sees us, we would not flee to him at all. We would remain here.' *We would face the siege*, she might have said. But Mother had not yet admitted that there would be a siege – although it was plain now that she believed it.

'There is no purpose in remaining here.'

'I am sure that there is as much and more as there has been over the past fortnight.'

'Enough! Maria, this is scandalous! I cannot support this! You will go to your room and remain there, at once. And there you will make yourself ready to leave.'

'But I believe that Father would also wish to stay!' cried Maria.

Father made no sign.

'Maria! You may *not* presume to speak for your father. You are at times a great disappointment to him and to me. No, it is impossible. He will accompany me. Nor, much though I might wish to abandon you, can I spare Anna to remain with you. Now go to your room *at once*!'

Seething, Maria trod the stairs. She was furious with her mother, and with herself. How stupid – how *stupid* – to speak out before she had thought what she would say. It had been stupid, too, to invoke Father. Mother could not allow herself to lose control of him. Of course not. Without him, what was she – except for an over-educated woman with a sharp tongue? So Father must go. So must Anna. They all must. Mother would drag them all along with her, accessories to her existence. And Maria would never be free of her, until at last Lady Adelsheim stirred herself to bring about her daughter's marriage.

There is no purpose to us remaining here. Was there not, now that all her petitions had failed? But a terrible hour was coming for the city. Everyone knew it. Even in Bohemia they knew it. Would they flee now? Like lice that could not longer live on the body that had fed them because it had become a corpse?

Mother was a louse. She was a louse, heavy with the blood she had sucked, heavy with the things she had stolen! She had stolen Father. She had stolen Albrecht. She had even stolen Michel Wéry – or the man Maria had imagined him to be.

He would stay – the flawed, twisted, brave man. He would face the spirits of war that he had once summoned in Paris. From the window of her room she could look south along the crags above the river and up to the walls and angled bastion of the fortifications around the Celesterburg. There, in the breach made last autumn, a crowd of tiny figures were labouring, digging out the rubble that had fallen into the ditch and dragging it, in barrows towed by long ropes, up to the line of the wall again. Things that looked like hurdles had been placed along the gap in the wall. Slowly, painfully, the earth was being piled around them to fill the defences in.

'I cannot help it,' she said, to the man she imagined was looking down upon her. 'I cannot help it. I am her prisoner.'

'This will be your room from now on, your Excellency,' said Wéry, lifting the lantern. 'Your servant will sleep here. There is a sleeping chamber for you beyond that door. I regret that it is not as convenient as the gatehouse, but it will be more sheltered from cannon fire. You have my word that we will do everything in our power to make you comfortable.'

Canon Rother-Konisrat peered around the slit-windowed, narrow room in the south-east bastion.

'Your powers appear to be limited, Commander,' he sighed. 'Although I do not blame you.'

'There will be a guard at your door, to whom you may pass requests at any time. Nothing in reason will be refused you. You will continue to have the opportunity to walk the walls for half an hour in the morning and again in the afternoon.'

'And what hour is it now?'

'It is just past ten of the clock.'

'I did not hear the bells.'

'The cathedral bells are being taken down, sir, to be placed in hiding in case the city falls.'

'I see.'

Wéry watched him moving around the narrow room like a man in a dream. The Canon paused by the plain wooden chair and ran his fingers over the back of it as if to assure himself that it really was there.

'Did I see my colleague Steinau being brought in under guard last night?' he asked suddenly.

'You did, sir.'

'So our Prince has now turned on the Ingolstadt set too. I warned Steinau that he would. And what of our friend Bergesrode?'

'He has been dismissed from his post, sir, for association with the Ingolstadt clergy.'

'Arrested?'

'I believe not, sir.'

'The man shows some gratitude, in the end,' muttered the Canon. 'Yet I cannot see how he strengthens himself by making enemies of two-thirds of the Chapter. We have no sympathy with the Republic. We have only a certain lack of sympathy with those who wish to gather all power into their own hands. Was it thus in Paris, Commander?'

'I beg your pardon, sir?'

'That the rulers, having seized power against one faction, then persuade themselves they must remove *all* other actors from the scene, in order that their power should be secure?'

Wéry swallowed uncomfortably. 'Sometimes, sir, yes it was.'

Canon Rother smiled thinly at the chair back. 'You see,' he said. 'Well, it seems I now have no part but to wait upon events. Many more worthy than I have been persecuted for their faith. I shall make their example my own. Is there such a thing as a Bible in your citadel, Commander?'

A Bible? Wéry had no idea. After ten days in this neglected fortress he was still reckoning the ratios of powder and shot to cannon on his walls.

His mind was so full of many things now that siege loomed: duties and manpower and stratagems and supplies; a hundred little blows that could be struck, a thousand preparations to be made. His thoughts consumed him all the time: at table, in the middle of conversations, striding from place to place, and waking in the night from dreams of the days to come. And deep beneath the turbulence of his brain was the voice of the demon within him, bellowing, *At last! The fight! At last!*

'Sir,' he said. 'Your books will be brought across from the gatehouse as soon as possible and I am sure . . .'

'Perhaps you would grant me the loan of one for the morning. There will be one at least in the chapel.'

'Yes, sir,' said Wéry.

He was turning to go when the Canon, now peering through the narrow slit of the window, spoke again. 'And how does our Prince think he is going to deliver himself from this situation?'

'I believe he has a plan, sir.'

'I hope it is something other than to stand and be crushed.'

Maria walled herself in silence on the morning of their departure. It was the only protest she could make.

She sat by herself with a stole around her, eyes on nothing, waiting to be called. And when the time came to leave she climbed tight-lipped into the second coach and took her place by one window. Everyone knew she had been put in the second coach because she was in disgrace. Franz was to travel with her, but that was only because Lady Adelsheim could not endure the way he would fidget on a journey.

'I do not want to talk,' she said bluntly.

'I know that,' said Franz, and gawked out of the other window at the leading coach, which carried Father, Mother and Anna, and also Icht, so that Lady Adelsheim would have someone to converse with during the day.

At length the grooms stirred the horses, and the coaches lumbered into motion. Maria stared hard at the house front as it rolled past, as if she could hook herself to it with her eyes, Dietrich, Johann, Pirenne and the other servants drawn up at the door. She wondered if she would ever see them again. She wondered, too, what instructions Lady Adelsheim had given to them should the French come. Very likely she had told them to count the spoons!

They crossed the bridges, climbed to the Church of Saint Simeon, and passed on down the broad Bamberg Way towards the eastern gate of the city. There they were halted and soldiers asked to see their papers. Maria prayed that they would be turned back. Her hopes grew when she heard her mother beginning to protest to the officer from the window of the leading coach.

'I beg your pardon, my Lady,' came the officer's voice. 'It's the siege, you see.'

'There is no siege,' said Lady Adelsheim. 'And, Captain, I am not used to being treated this way.'

'I beg your pardon, my Lady, but we have our orders.'

'Do not speak to me of your orders. I see no sense in them. I see no sense in what you are doing on these walls, sir. Your duty is folly, Captain, and I think your uniform a butcher's apron.'

'Damn her,' muttered Maria aloud. 'I am going to scream.'

Franz gave her a startled look. Then he went back to leaning out of the window.

The grooms must have found the papers, for the voices sank to murmurs. Maria sat, fists clenched, waiting for more expostulations from her mother. There were none. Perhaps Anna had managed to soothe her. Perhaps she was simply preparing her next salvo.

The next salvo did not come. There were friendly calls ahead, and suddenly the sound of the leading coach beginning to move. The next moment their own followed it. They passed out of the city. Goodbye, thought Maria, looking at the faces of the soldiers and the last few people at the roadside.

Goodbye. We are abandoning you. I cannot ask you to forgive us.

The faces were gone. No one called after them.

'How far is it now?' asked Franz sullenly.

She was silent for a moment longer. And then she realized that with Franz there was no point.

'It will be most of the day,' she said. 'You must be patient. We are going to spend the night at Adelsheim. If we stop before that, it will only be for horses.' She supposed that there were still horses to be found on the roads that ran to war.

Franz's face brightened. 'Can I go riding when we get there?'

'It will be dark.'

The roads were busy. They passed cart after cart heading for the city. Some were in trains with what must have been supplies for the garrison. Others carried families with their belongings: people who had heard that invaders were coming and feared to wait in their villages to find if it were true. They also passed small columns of soldiers on the march – poorly uniformed peasants, for the most part, led by some landlord or landlord's bailiff on his horse to assist in the defence.

Goodbye, thought Maria bitterly. I would be with you. I would carry a pack and a musket gladly. I have seen a man die, and I am not afraid of it. But I am luggage, no more.

An hour and a half from Erzberg the coaches stopped at an unmarked turning in the road. Craning through her window, Maria saw that another file of soldiers was approaching down one of the roads. The way was narrow. The coaches had checked at the junction to allow the men to pass.

On they came. She could hear the patient squelch, squelch, squelch of their feet as they legged another mile away. She heard the horse blow and the rhythm of the noises change as they sidled past the coaches. She heard calls exchanged between the grooms and the horseman – friendly, surprised calls, as if the men had recognized one another. She leaned from her window again. It was a very small file – twenty men at most, and one on horse. The horseman was guiding his mount past at that instant.

And she did know him. It was Windhofer, the bailiff from Adelsheim.

They were from Adelsheim! From their own estate, going up to the war.

She pulled herself hurriedly back from the window, thinking, Please! Mother Mary, please! Don't let her realize! Don't let her see!

'Stop!' said Mother's voice. 'You there, stop, all of you!'

The door of the leading coach swung open. Lady Adelsheim stood on the step, steadying herself with a hand on the door. The horseman checked his mount and looked back at her.

'My Lady!' he exclaimed.

'Down you come, my man. Come and speak with me.'

He dismounted obediently.

'Where are you going?'

'To the city, my Lady. Lord Harzen, he says all militias in our district to go up to the city.'

'You are not Harzen's people but mine.'

'No, my Lady, but Harzen always . . .'

'If Harzen has orders from the Prince, he can furnish him with his own men. But it is wrong of him, and wrong of you to go without my let—'

Franz suddenly exclaimed, 'That's my horse.'

Maria looked at it. And yes, it was Dominus, the horse that had

417

been Albrecht's: a great, brown, handsome animal, waiting patiently there in the road.

Windhofer had taken Albrecht's horse! That was impertinent of him. But perhaps there had not been much choice. And perhaps Albrecht would have given it to him freely, if he had known where Windhofer was planning to go.

Yes, he would have done. Albrecht – the real Albrecht – had been like that.

Franz had climbed out to pet the animal. But Dominus lifted his head away from Franz's hand, as if there was no time for that now, and other things that an honest horse should be thinking about.

'It is a shameful thing – shameful – that he is calling you to do. I will have no part in it. I will not sully myself with support for what this Prince does . . .'

Maria's fists were clenched. She could not shut her mother's voice out. She looked at the horse, Albrecht's horse, still facing back the way they had come, waiting to continue his journey. The memory of her brother sat in that long, gentle face.

Where are you going, Dominus? she thought suddenly, remembering the apostle Peter on the road outside Rome. *Domine, quo vadis?*

Venio Romam, the Lord had replied. *Iterum crucifigi.*

To be crucified again.

'My Lady, I have been sent papers . . .'

'He's taken my horse, Mother,' said Franz. 'This is my horse, from the stables there.'

'Begging your pardon, my Lady, but there were not many suitable . . .'

'It is an outrageous liberty,' said Mother. 'I will not

418

countenance it. Now, you will turn these men around and we will proceed to Adelsheim together. And when we are there . . .'

'They are not your people!' Maria cried aloud.

She jerked herself out of the coach and stood swaying on the step. All the faces were turned to her. Mother, on the step of the other coach. The factor, the men, even Franz looking up from where he stood at the horse's head.

'They are not your people!' she screamed. 'They are Father's! Have you asked *him*?'

She swayed, and nearly lost her balance. To steady herself she put out her hand and touched the horse's saddle. It shifted. The stirrup was near her foot.

'Maria!'

It began as an effort to save herself from falling. Her toe found the stirrup, her hands the saddle. And then it was just natural, one move following another with the inevitability of a dance, that she should swing herself up onto the horse's back.

At once she found that her dress was wrong and the saddle was wrong too. She swayed. Her hand reached instinctively for the rein. Everyone was staring at her. No one, not even she, knew what was going to happen. (And whatever happened she must not fall!) She controlled the beast beneath her.

'Let go!' she cried to Franz.

Gawping, he obeyed.

'Maria — get down at once!'

'I will not get down,' she said over her shoulder. She had her voice under control now. 'I will not get down for you.'

She steadied the horse, swayed — it was impossible to ride side-saddle in a seat like this! — and spoke over her shoulder again. 'I am going back,' she said.

'You will not!' exclaimed Lady Adelsheim's voice.

Maria laughed, and set the horse at a walk along the road.

'Stop her!' commanded her mother from behind her. 'Stop her! Catch that horse!' Lady Adelsheim repeated.

Maria looked back. The men were still standing there, astounded. Now three or four of them were moving towards her. She kicked the horse, and it lumbered into a short trot that nearly threw her from the saddle. There was nothing for it but to bring her leg, dresses and all, over the beast's neck and sit astride with all her skirts rucking up and her shins and ankles in view to every man's eyes.

'Maria, it's my horse!' called Franz plaintively. But he had stopped coming after her, knowing it was hopeless. Some of the militia, weapons discarded, were still chasing her. She could not stay.

'Catch me if you can,' she called cheerfully to the men.

Then a last look, back at the coaches. Mother still on the step, watching her go. Anna, dismounted on the far side. Franz. Father was the only one she could not see. Only the hulk of the coach, like a sturdy old gentleman oblivious to all around him, faced on down the road to Bohemia.

'Goodbye,' she whispered.

And then she rode, hard, until the last of the militiamen gave up their vain pursuit.

Never in her life, never in her dreams, had she been so alone. There was no one to help her but Dominus (a good, responsive animal). There was no one to point the way – she must find it for herself, making her own choices when her memory of the morning's journey failed. There was no one to house her, dress her, feed her. She had no money, unless by the mercy of some saint, Windhofer had been carrying his wallet in his saddlebags. She should stop and search them. There might be many useful things. But she did not want to stop. If she stopped she would have to think. She would have to think about what she had done, and about what could possibly happen now.

They might be pursuing her. They could have turned the carriages around and be hurrying after her. They would not move very much slower than she. So of course she could not stop. Because she was never, never going back. She saw again her mother's face, looking at her from the coach step.

'Never,' she said aloud.

She would starve or drown herself first, she thought.

She was going to the city. That was what she was doing. She was going back to be one of the people there. Perhaps people under siege all cared for one another in a way that they did not when at peace. She did not know. Whether or not they did, the city was the only place to go.

Saints grant that the enemy had not already arrived!

The long miles passed. She grew saddle-sore because she was not used to this way of riding.

She saw people in fields and on wagons. They stared at her. They stared at the long white gleam of her stockings exposed by her rucked-up travelling gown. She looked firmly ahead. Let them think as they wished. This was war, was it not? And they did not know who she was. They could not possibly know, because she no longer knew herself.

But when she saw a file of militia ahead of her, struggling under load towards the city, she turned off the road and made a wide circle across country. She did not want to be stopped and have questions asked of her. And she was not sure she would be safe with soldiers, even those of her own side. So it was that when she finally approached the city, it was from the north-east and not the north, and it was to the Saxon Gate that she came.

There was a crowd there, and many soldiers drawn up in ranks, wearing their packs and grey overcoats. On the opposite side of the road was a full squadron of hussars, facing north. The horses tossed their heads. Stirrups and steel gleamed in the sun. Officers were moving to and fro, checking boots, straps and horseshoes. The men were preparing to march. The crowd around them were families and townspeople, come to wave them good-bye. Where could they be going? Heads turned to stare at her as she came up, and went on staring. She felt awkward; obvious and at the same time indecent on her perch with her legs showing at her horse's flanks. Stiffly, she dismounted.

There was no one to hold Dominus for her. She would have to hold him herself, or let him go.

'Stay,' she murmured to him and made her way into the crowd. She moved slowly, for she realized now that she was very sore indeed.

The people had come out to see the soldiers. They were calling to them, some weeping, some laughing. She saw ragged children run up and hug a man in the back rank by the leg. He fluffed their heads, and told them to leave him, but they went on hugging his leg and calling up to him until a sergeant yelled at the man and the children ran away.

An officer was standing near her. She knew him. It was Karl von Uhnen. He had not looked her way.

Her first instinct was to shrink back a little. She could not have said why, but she did not want him to see her. He was too much part of her old life. He would only be shocked by what she had done. Besides, he must be busy. He must be about to depart with them. He could hardly help her find her way in the city.

But who else would there be? Here at least was someone she knew. There was no need to tell him yet what she had done.

Still uncertain what she would say, she began to approach him. He had not noticed her yet. When she touched his arm he would fairly jump out of his skin . . .

Another green-and-white uniform shouldered its way through the crowd and stood in front of Karl. It was Michel Wéry. Maria stopped.

Slowly, Karl lifted his hand in a salute.

'Sir,' she heard him say.

'No need for that,' said Wéry. 'I came to say two things.'

'What would they be?' said Karl. Maria did not think his voice sounded friendly.

'First, good luck.'

'Thank you.'

'Second. If, when this is over, you and the others come to me, I will say whatever you need me to say.'

'I see.'

'I think it will satisfy you. And if it does not, I will meet you when and where you want.'

'I see.'

Wéry seemed to be waiting for more than that. He was looking at Karl with his head cocked on one side. 'Well?' he prompted.

'I'll think about it.'

A loud bellow from the ranks cut short whatever Wéry had been about to say. Karl von Uhnen saluted him once more, and

423

strode to where a man was holding his horse at the head of his squadron. Wéry watched him go. His back was towards her. She stole up to him and touched him on the arm.

He did jump. It was very satisfying. And as he stared down at her she felt her own face break into a mirthful grin.

'I thought you had left!' he stammered.

'I came back,' she said.

She had so many things to say to him. *I have displeased my mother. You would oblige me if you did not ask me about it.* And: *Can you tell me how I may help?* And: *I must speak with you about things you said in Paris.* And: *Can you have someone look after my horse?* She did not say any of them. For the moment she wanted only to look at him and know that she had arrived.

With a long clattering of hooves the hussars wheeled onto the road. People were cheering now, waving hats, and weeping. She saw Karl von Uhnen at the head of his squadron. She saw him look down and see her, standing at Wéry's side. She waved and smiled. His face was wooden. Then he was carried away down the road to war.

There was a lump in her throat. A flood of wordless feelings engulfed her as the people called and the dust rose. She turned to the man beside her.

'I came back to help,' she said. 'Can you tell me how?'

'You can keep me sane,' he said.

'Now, the Dürwalds,' called the colonel of the infantry. 'Let's nip those buggers' arses.'

'Ho! Hurrah!' bellowed the ranks, and the lead company surged onto the road in the wake of the hussars.

'Surely he should not say things like that!' exclaimed Maria.

Wéry looked at her helplessly.

A voice in the second company had started to sing. Others joined it, first here and there among the regiment, and then all along the ranks as the song swung into the chorus.

> *. . . And we've fucked our mothers and we've fucked our hogs*
> *And we fucked the Frenchies and we fucked their frogs.*
> *We're the damned, damned, dogs of the Dürwald,*
> *Rolling in Blinki's train.*

'Oh – but we should have our own *Marseillaise!*' she protested, putting her hands to her ears. And then she smiled. These were soldiers, and their feet would soon be sore. And this was the world she had entered, where all ties were broken and women rode bare-legged, where the world might end tomorrow, and until it did the soldiers would always sing like this.

'Who – or what – is Blinki?' she asked.

Wéry took a moment to answer. 'Old Blinkers,' he said at last. 'Balcke-Horneswerden.'

He was still staring at her, as if he could not believe that she was there. And on the road the soldiers swung by, singing as they passed, as if their leader's honour had never been tarnished, as if it had not gone downstream in a coffin almost a year ago.

XXXI
Confession

There was no *time*, thought Wéry.

She was here, and the fight was here, both at once. Either would have taken every moment, every power and ingenuity he had – were it not for the other.

They walked back through the city together, leading their horses because she was not dressed for riding (and how had she and her mount come here, then?), and his mind was all confusion. The engineers wanted more labour for the breaches. The Knight von Uhnen, whose militias would provide the manpower, was expecting to be consulted about it. According to his own plan he should already have switched effort from the walls to building barricades and strongpoints inside the town. He still had not spoken to the artillery officers about bringing guns down from the walls to the concealed battery at the Church of St Barbara. And the plan for the Mercers' Guildhall would not work. He had woken in the night knowing that. But if they abandoned it . . .

At last, the war-demons yammered in his brain. *At last!*

But now there was a new voice among them, strident, shouting against them, *She's here! Look, she's here, beside you!*

And she had said that she did not wish to stay in the Adelsheim house in the Saint Emil quarter. And that was as important as anything else.

'There is the Celesterburg,' he said, hardly daring to hope. 'Many of the rooms are empty now. And it is within the citadel, which will be the safest place.'

'Is His Highness not in residence?'

'He has accompanied the cathedral treasures to safety. He will not return before the siege is lifted.'

'Oh.'

'Of course you will need a maid to escort you,' he said hurriedly. 'I will see that one is found from the palace staff – unless you wish to send for one from the Adelsheim house?'

'No,' she said, firmly shaking her head. 'No, they must not know that I am here. And yes, if a maid could be provided from the palace, that would be most acceptable.'

'And perhaps,' he heard himself say. 'Perhaps you will dine with me this evening?' (You, the child of an Imperial Knight, dine with someone like me? A thing not to be thought of – until now).

'I should be delighted,' she said. 'But as I have said to you, what I most earnestly desire is to know how I may give something to the defence. And this you have not told me.'

Heavens! Did she want to pile rubble in the breaches? Or tear rags in the hospitals? (Hospitals! There were still too few. But if they were no longer going to make the Mercer's Hall a strong point, perhaps . . . He must think about that.)

She was waiting for him to answer.

'You should talk to people,' he said.

'Talk?'

'It will help them. Waiting is always the worst thing.'

When she came that evening, accompanied by a maid from the palace, he thought she was the loveliest thing he had ever seen.

427

He did not notice that she was still wearing her travelling dress until she apologized for it. Over supper, by the light of two candles, her face was beautiful, and his heart was moving heavily within him. He allowed himself more wine than he would drink in two evenings alone.

And they talked; first (conscious of themselves, and of the corporal who served them and the maid in the room) of commonplace things: of the Celesterburg, now booming in its emptiness, with only Gianovi left to occupy even one wing of it; of the officers left to help prepare the defence of the city (and he explained why in such a situation an engineer or an artilleryman was worth any ten infantry officers, however well born they might be); of words, and wordplay; of what she had read, and he had not.

But as he sat and looked at her in the candle flame, he was more and more aware of things he wanted to talk of – private thoughts and fears that it would be a relief to say, and that wanted to be said. And bit by bit he found himself yielding to them, and was glad. He thought that the same was true for her, too. He listened soberly to her account of her return to the capital. He guessed at things she had left unsaid, about what had passed between her and her mother. He guessed, too, that she did not wish him to ask after them. So he did not.

She put her glass down and her hands to her head.

'I have killed the woman I was,' she said.

'How?'

'By my conduct.'

She was thinking that she would be disowned, and perhaps disgraced. She would be left penniless and with no future. And yes, perhaps – even probably – she would be.

'Do you regret your conduct?' he asked.

'No.'

He waited.

'What do you think?' she asked, dropping her hands to look at him.

'I think that in a very few days it will not matter.'

'Because of the siege?'

He nodded. 'We know a force has left Wetzlar and is on its way. They will have reached Hanau by now. From there, they may take one of two routes. If they come direct, we will see them tomorrow. If, however, they follow the north bank of the Vater, it will take them longer, and they will find Balcke-Horneswerden and the army blocking their way at the Pullen stream . . .' He broke off, seeing her face harden at the name of her enemy.

But all she said was, 'Why would they not come the straight way?'

'Because then they must approach from the west, and both the citadel and the river will stand between them and the town. The citadel is strong – the wall is breached on this east side, yes, but it is not difficult to block and is well sheltered. If they come along the north bank of the river, however, the city is open to attack. We are trying to fill in the city breach but even so it is vulnerable. That is why we have sent almost all our regular units to block the road at the Pullen crossings. Those men you saw leaving the north gate were the last of them. No doubt they will be pushed back onto the city. But we gain time. The longer we resist, the more chance the Emperor will intervene.'

'And if he does not?'

'We shall make them pay as high a price as we can – in the field, on the walls, and in the city itself.'

In this light, her eyes were dark. He watched her thinking about his words.

'Michel – why has His Highness left the city?'

She had called him 'Michel', like a friend or a cousin or . . . or someone very close. His blood was tingling – was that just the wine? He must stay in control. He must not do or say anything foolish. It might simply have been a slip. Or she might think better of it.

'He did not want to go,' he said. 'But in the end Gianovi persuaded him. The enemy want both him and the city. We cannot move the city. But we can keep him out of their reach. As long as he is not caught, the fight may go on.'

As he spoke, a thought stole like a shadow from the back of his brain. She had said she had killed herself. Coming here, she might have killed herself indeed. She had come to a city where the plan of defence was to continue the fight within the walls, no matter what the cost.

It was *his* plan. If she died, it would be he that had killed her. And her face, now solemn and thoughtful, would be twisted in shock and pain. If he lived he would carry it in his head forever, as Maximilian Jürich carried his tortured face of Christ.

Hey, Michel – have you ever looked at somebody?

He was seized with a feeling that he had found something glorious: that his hand had closed on it, unexpectedly, as he had fumbled for something else in a dark place. And he was weighing it, looking at it, and knowing that he should – he should – put it back. It did not belong to him.

Her life did not belong to him. He should send her away. He

should put her, willing or not, into a guarded coach out of the city. And he knew that he would not. He wanted her to stay with him. He wanted her to stay, in the knowledge of what was coming.

'They must be fought, everywhere and with everything there is,' he said. 'I have always thought so.'

'Not always. You were one of them once. You made speeches in Paris.'

Dear God! She knew *that*!

'Yes.'

She was looking at him.

'. . . Yes,' he said. 'I – I made speeches in Paris. I wanted the French to come and help our revolution in Brabant and the Netherlands . . .

'Of course it was not the only reason France went to war. It was not even the main one. Nevertheless, I urged them, and to war they went. Then . . .' he sighed. '. . . The war brought fear to Paris, and fear corrupted the revolution. And my country became spoils of war. I think . . .'

He covered his face with his hands. Then he laid them on the table before him. The white marks of his scars seemed to float from his skin in the gloom.

'I think . . .' he said at last, 'it is because I know what I said then, that I will now do anything in my power to drive this revolution back where it came from, and to kill it if I can.'

He had never linked the two thoughts before.

'What can I say?' he said helplessly. 'A monster was made, and I had thought it would be a god.'

A god. The god of Christians was the dead and innocent

431

Christ. The face of Maria was before him, and it was all that he could see. Her eyes were on the table.

'We thought that, too,' she said. 'Albrecht and I.' Then she said, 'So this is why the Prince made you Commander of the citadel.'

'Yes.'

'Because you hate them so much. Because you will fight, when no one else would.'

'Maybe, yes.'

If he had been speaking to anyone else, he would not have said 'maybe'.

In the muzziness of wine, he thought: I should have known you before this. If I had known you before this, I would not be as I am. I would not be ready to throw cities on the fire. I would believe that people were to be loved and cherished, not buried with markers to say what they died for.

'But he put Gianovi over you, and Gianovi does not think as you do.'

'I have orders concerning Gianovi.'

(Oh, why had he said that? It sounded so childish, as though he was determined not to be diminished in her eyes.)

'Orders?'

He had said it because it weighed on him. Something in him begged to confess to this too, just as it begged to speak about the Inquisitor and the Prince's other political enemies who were now penned in the cells and strong rooms of the citadel. But it was weakness, foolishness. He could hardly talk about his orders in front of the maid and the corporal. And even if they were alone, how could she help? All the tawdry, repulsive choices that went with this post – that always went with *any* post where he must command other people beside himself – there was nothing she could say that would help him with those. If the time came, the orders would still have to be carried out.

It seemed to him that he had shown her the casket of his soul. She had looked into it, and found that it was empty. No words of his could fill that emptiness. A word of hers, now, could destroy him.

'It doesn't matter,' he muttered. And he waited, afraid.

She put a hand up to touch her eyes.

'I am tired,' she said.

It was with a strange sense of relief that he rose to begin saying goodnight.

The maid led, with a lamp in her hand. Maria followed her across the walled space between the commander's house and the palace. They made their way around to the towered gateway where the porter opened the gate for them, and then across the inner courtyard. The palace was dark, and quiet. Only in one row of windows on the first floor were there lights burning. That must be Gianovi, and perhaps his clerks, kept up late by the government of the city. Maria wondered if Gianovi even knew there was another inhabitant in the palace. There was no reason, surely, why he should. But she was anxious that he should not know and so she drew her shawl around her head and hurried across to the grand steps, forcing the maid to keep up with her. The doors were open. In the ill-lit hall the footmen nodded blearily in their chairs. Maria and her maid mounted the grand stair, and another flight of stairs, passed down a dark corridor and found the door to the room that had been made ready for her. There she could thank the maid, bid her good-night, and be alone at last.

Someone had put out a night dress for her. Other dresses were laid ready for the morning. Whose had they been? They were all far too fine and formal, she thought. She would have to speak to someone about that. In the meantime, the sheets had been warmed and the pillow was soft, and she could lie down.

She could lie down, but she could not sleep.

I have killed the woman I was. Was that true? She had abandoned all the supports and protections that had surrounded her every day of her life. She lay in a city whose enemies were coming closer. Her life might indeed be very close to its end, but she did not fear that. What she feared was losing whatever moments of her life were left in wasteful idleness, as all the rest of her life had been lost. And yet – what had held her back?

She was free, to do as she chose. In a few days it would not matter. Why had she not dismissed the maid, walked around to his side of the table and let him see with her eyes that the corporal must go too? Oh . . .

Thump, thump went her heart in the darkness of her sheets. Who cared what was thought or said? In just a few days . . .

But why him? Why him? Simply because he was the first man here she had spoken to? No! She would do as she chose, but she would not choose to be a harlot. They had parted properly. However wild her thoughts now she would act properly again when they next met.

She had determined to be herself. Should she therefore throw herself away at once, just to prove that it was true? This was madness. These were just night-thoughts, loose from the restraints of reason. She was longing to be in love. Yes, she was. And so she must take care. Not for the sake of society, or the fear of gossip. For her own sake, she must.

He did not regard himself. It seemed to her that so many people regarded themselves – Mother most of all. He did not. He had his own belief. It was a terrible one, but it was not of himself. She remembered Hofmeister's words over wine in the Rhineland – '*Ay, there's a man I envy!*' She did not envy him. His beliefs meant pain to him, and pain to those around him. Like the words of Nero, or Pilate, they brought death upon the innocent. She could not share them.

And yet if she did not, why was she here?

She turned over again, and put her arms around herself to embrace her own body.

I shall invite him, she thought. Tomorrow, he will dine with me.

Even Pilate had had a woman who loved him.

XXXII
The Last Dance

She had come to the city full of vague notions about helping in its defence. Now she rose the next morning with one clear plan in her head – that Michel Wéry should dine with her that evening. She spoke with the maid who came to dress her. A senior footman came to hear what My Lady wanted, and she instructed him as if she were in her own home. Then, commandeering a maid for escort, she set out to find the citadel Commander. She had decided that it would be better to give her invitation in person. He must be beset by so many duties. It would be too easy for him to decline a note that had been put into his hand.

At the Commander's house they told her that he had gone out before dawn. They believed there had been a conference in the Prince's antechamber. She remembered the antechamber, and went there boldly. It was empty. But a militia officer in the corridor told her that the Commander had gone to the west wall of the citadel. She smiled ruefully at her maid, and they went out to the wall together. It was a vast, long sweep of masonry, with many soldiers on it looking out to the west. She searched among them for one man only.

She found him on the gun-platform of the north-west bastion, among a group of his officers. He was looking through a small telescope at something on the hill opposite. Some of the others had telescopes too. She hesitated. She did not want to give her invitation before so many witnesses. He might be embarrassed. But if she waited a little way away from them, he would see her and maybe make his way across to her.

Beside the group of officers were half a dozen soldiers gathered around one of the long cannons. Their leader was looking now to the officers, now to the hillside opposite. She stepped up to the next embrasure and looked out, too.

At first she saw nothing to be interested in. The side of the Kummelberg was as it always was. There was the farm and the road. The hillside was mainly pasture but the crest was crowned with a stand of trees. That was all.

Then movement caught her eye, and she saw the horsemen.

They were moving in a little group, some way down the pasture from the hill line. There were – she could not count them but she thought there were more than twenty. More than twenty men, on horses, to the west of the city. The riders' coats seemed to be blue and white.

The enemy!

There they were, in full view, moving gently down the hillside towards the city. Maria stared at them. In the bright air she could see the detail of their hats and boots and the lift of a horse's head as a rider controlled its reins. Already they were a little below the level of the bastion on which she stood. The space between her and them must be less than a thousand paces. Her heart had begun to tap against her ribs.

They were such a short distance away! She felt she could have launched herself from the walls and flown down to them. Certainly she could have walked down to the lower gate and on down the hillside to meet with them in the valley bottom in a matter of minutes. And if she did? The air between her and them was as thin as the verge of death. What was it, really, that moved on the far side of it? What demon cloaked those men that seemed to be only men and yet would kill her if she stepped down to join them? Soon – today, or in a few days – she would know, because soon she would meet them indeed. She dreaded knowing it. But she longed to know it too. And for the moment, in the bright sun with the tense and excited men around her, she felt as strong and cheerful as she had ever been in her life.

The gun captain was gesturing to the crew. Inch by inch, on the gun trail and the wheels, they were levering it around so that the barrel followed the progress of the doll-like horsemen on the far slope. The captain stepped forward to do something at the breech of the gun. The barrel dropped an inch or two. Now the man was looking across at the officers again. Michel lowered the glass from his eye.

'Try it,' he said to the gun captain.

The captain squinted along the line of the barrel. He seemed to be waiting for something. On the far slope the horsemen were still moving.

'Stand clear,' said the gun captain and stepped aside. He jerked on a string. There was a spout of white smoke at the breech.

FAGH! barked the gun, bounding back with appalling weight and speed. A cloud of white smoke flew over the battlements and into Maria's eyes. She knew the smell of it at once. A clearing on the road. A wounded man. *Naughty boy, you're not dead yet!* And her ears rang and stung with the violence that had been done to them.

This is it! she thought wildly. I am in a battle!

438

The smoke thinned. Michel and the other officers had their glasses to their eyes again.

'Short,' said one.

'Short, and to the left.'

'There they go.'

Her ears were still ringing. The voices of the men sounded light and dead to her. She wondered if her hearing had been damaged. There was a tear in her eye from the smoke. She put up a hand to wipe it away.

On the far hillside the horsemen had changed direction. They were moving steadily back up the hill in the direction from which they had come. They showed no sign of hurry or panic. Had none of them been killed? She almost felt disappointed. She had not seen where the shot had fallen.

'Sketching party,' said one of the officers. 'Taking a look at us, that's all.'

'If they come that close again, you may fire on them,' said Michel. 'Otherwise, save your powder. We don't want to let them know how far or hard we can hit, yet.' He bent to listen to a portly, grey-haired officer who had come panting up to the group. His eyes met Maria's. For a moment her heart leapt. Then she realized that the officer must be speaking about her.

'Lady Maria.'

'Yes, Commander?'

He made his way over, and bowed over her hand. Plainly he wanted to be formal in front of all these officers.

'I am informed that a coach has come up from the city,' he said. 'There is a woman in it who is asking for you.'

A coach. A woman. It would be Mother, come to storm at her and insist that she be carried away. Her heart deadened within her.

Why could they not leave her alone?

'Where is she?'

'In the palace courtyard.' He looked at her, and his eyes were concerned. 'If we may be of any assistance to you . . .'

'You are busy already, Commander,' she said.

They were standing a little apart from the others. The men were watching them, but there would be no better chance than this. Now, surely, was the moment to thank him for his hospitality the night before, and to offer her invitation. She looked at his face, and thought the words she had prepared to say to him. But she did not say them. It seemed too great a step then. The enemy was below the western walls. And another enemy was waiting in the courtyard of the palace. She must face that first. Gently, almost reverently, she restored her words to the closet of her heart.

'I only ask that your messenger may return with me,' she said. 'To see that I am taken nowhere by force.'

'You will stay, or go, as you please and for no other reason,' he said.

Her ears were still ringing as she left the gun platform.

It was an Adelsheim coach, with Ehrlich in the driver's seat. And a woman was pacing slowly beside it, with little short steps as if she was waiting for someone who was making her late for church. She looked up as Maria and her maid followed her officer escort into the courtyard.

'Anna!' cried Maria.

She ran. She flew across the courtyard and embraced her governess in a whirl of dresses.

'Oh my dear,' said Anna. 'I am so glad you are *safe*.'

440

'But how did you come here? How long have you been in the city?'

'I came back yesterday, my dear. I went straight to the house, because I thought you would be there. Since then we have been searching the city for news of you.'

'We?'

'Ehrlich and Dietrich and I. Your mother and father and Franz are all in Adelsheim.'

'In Adelsheim!' repeated Maria, relieved.

'Yes, my dear. They are waiting for us there.'

So mother had sent Anna back to bring her. How very like her.

'Anna, I do not wish to go.'

'Oh but, my dear – you *must*. Your mother . . .'

How like Mother, thought Maria, to send poor Anna on an errand like this, assuming that the errand would succeed simply because she willed it. If she had come herself there would have been a battle indeed. Perhaps her mother had foreseen even that, and had sent Anna simply because she was unwilling herself to enter a confrontation she might not win. And of course she must guess, without ever voicing it to herself, that it would hurt Maria far more to reject Anna than it would to reject herself.

'I know you were angry with her, my dear. But really you must not let that overwhelm your reason. Surely you see what danger you are in if you stay here? Surely you do.'

Danger – the siege?

'This man,' said Anna, moving closer to her and lowering her voice so that the bystanders could not hear. 'This man – what is he? No doubt he is very clever. But he has no birth, no means – your family could never permit a match. Surely you see that? If

441

you stay it can only be ruin on your name. You have such prospects, and you will throw them all away.'

'Oh!' said Maria. She put her hand to her mouth as if to stifle a laugh. 'Why is it,' she asked gaily, 'that all the world imagines I am in love with Michel Wéry?'

Anna eyed her doubtfully. 'Are you not? But you have come here! You have passed a night in the citadel already. Really, you should not be surprised if people begin to think things. And what they think matters, my dear. It does.'

'Why should I listen to gossip? This is simply idle tongues, Anna. It always has been.'

'My darling – it does not need to be true. It only needs to be widely supposed. Even if your mother chooses to believe you, the world will not. You will not be received. No proper house will look at you for a marriage. You must see that surely!'

See it? Of course she did. She had ridden up to the gate of the city, unescorted and with her legs showing. She had thrown herself into the company of a foreign officer, who was more a mercenary than a gentleman in the eyes of the world. *I have killed the person I was*. She had.

'It is madness!' exclaimed her governess.

'It is war, Anna. And what you call "the world" has fled away.'

'Oh, but the war will not last forever. Next year, things will be as they were . . .'

Maria laughed. How ridiculous, to think that!

'Dear Anna. We have already seen their scouting parties. We have fired on them. Soon they will be swarming over the west bank. You must leave. Now, or at the latest tomorrow morning. After that they may have crossed the river, and it will hardly be safe.'

'But I am not leaving without you, my dear.'

'Anna – I am staying here.'

They stood facing each other under the bright sky of the courtyard. After a moment Maria added, 'I feel it is my duty to stay. And I will not go back to my mother.'

Anna sighed. 'Then I suppose I must stay with you.'

'Oh no! Anna dear, it will not be safe!'

'It will be as safe for me as for you,' said Anna dryly. 'Perhaps even more so, since I am old and unattractive.'

'Oh, Anna, dear Anna, no!' cried Maria. She took her governess's hands and caressed them. At all costs, she was determined to prevent this. She did not want Anna in danger. And she did not want Anna at her shoulder now, in this world of glory and freedom that she had barely begun to explore.

'You must go to my father and mother,' she said. 'They will need you. I have caused them great grief. And . . .' she hesitated.

She hesitated, because the thought that had suddenly presented itself to her was enormous. The consequences would go on, and on, far beyond the horizon of her understanding. In a flash she saw that. And also she saw how very little, indeed, was required from her. People were already thinking it and saying it. It was almost as good as done already.

'Anna,' she whispered. 'You must tell them it is too late.'

'What . . .'

'The thing you feared, about that man. It is true.'

A sudden blankness, as if of pain, had entered Anna's eyes.

'Oh, my dear . . .'

It is true, thought Maria firmly. It is true, for the moment, for this hour, because I will it to have been true. *Mother, see how I use your weapons against you!*

'It has already happened, Anna. And I have never been happier.'

'I so wished I had been in time,' groaned Anna.

'Anna! You must not blame yourself! Blame me, if you must. Blame him, although truly he has done no more than I desired. Blame my mother, who has driven me to put myself beyond her recall. You are guiltless. You are the most wonderful creature that ever lived . . .' (Oh, she could believe that, and say it, and say it all the more fervently because it was true, even buried in the middle of her lies!) '. . . and Anna, I tell you this, because I believe you will understand it – although I cannot hope that Mother will, and I know she will say such things to Father and to Franz that they will surely disapprove. But I truly believe that if Albrecht were still with us, he would counsel me to stay. You must see that, Anna. For you truly loved him, too.'

'Yes, my dear,' said Anna, in a horrible, tired voice. 'And now I have lost both of you.'

'No, Anna. You have not lost me. You can only lose me if you will it, for I do not renounce you! And I do not believe you will it. Wherever you are, and wherever I am, I shall think fondly of you as long as I live. Oh, Anna,' (for now she was borne along by the flood of her own drama, saying all the things she felt and that normally she might have hesitated to give voice to). 'I would keep you here with me, for just one night. You will dine with me in the palace, for I have rooms here. And I shall have a room made ready for you too. Say that you will, for me?'

'My dear – I cannot meet him. You understand that.'

'You will not, I promise. You and I will dine alone. Say you will, please, Anna. For I do not know when I shall see you again.'

'Of course,' said the older woman. There was a hoarseness in her voice and a shimmer in her eye. 'My dear, of course.'

* * *

So her plan to invite Michel Wéry to dinner was discarded, at least for one night. And instead she played hostess to Anna, who came sober-faced to her rooms in the palace at seven in the evening. With her came servants from the house in the Saint Emil quarter, carrying a trunk of Maria's things, and Pirenne, her own French maid, to look after her. Maria hugged them all, and thanked them, and the servants blessed her gruffly and went back down to the coach with instructions to return for Anna in the morning. Then she led Anna into the room opposite, where footmen of the palace waited with the furniture cleared and a table laid, and they sat together at the meal that Maria had intended to share with another.

Maria was gay. Some of her gaiety was natural, out of the lingering abandon that came from declaring herself to be a fallen woman. But some of it was an act because that was how she supposed a fallen woman might be expected to behave. She realized that if Pirenne stayed she would not be able to keep up her pretence for long. But that did not matter. All that mattered was that Anna should believe, for the next few hours, that there was nothing left to save or to chaperon in the woman who had once been her charge. Out of respect for Anna's feelings she did not mention her supposed lover once. But absorbed as she was with matters of the siege, she could not help speaking of things that she could only have learned from him.

'There is just one company of regulars left in the town,' she said. 'That is the depot company of the Erzberg battalion, here in the citadel. The walls are held by a mix of the country militias and the volunteers supplied from the guilds.'

'Really?' said Anna politely.

445

'The countrymen are the more reliable soldiers, I am told,' said Maria. 'That is because they do not think as quickly as the townsmen. And also the townsmen have not been friendly towards the army this last year. But the townsmen will be fighting for their homes and their churches, so we warrant that they will show spirit enough.'

'I am sure, my dear.'

'But it was so wrong of Mother,' she exclaimed, 'to turn those men around when in truth they need everyone that they can have here!'

Anna pursed her lips and looked down. Instantly Maria felt a pang of guilt.

'Oh, I am sorry, Anna,' she said. 'Let us not speak of it. Only I had – I felt suddenly and very strongly what Albrecht would have thought if he had been with us and where he would have wanted them to go.'

'He was a dear boy.'

'Oh, always. Do you remember him in the fig tree, refusing to come down?'

'Of course,' said Anna, smiling sadly. 'I am surprised that you do, however. You cannot have been five years old.'

'Oh, I was so frightened for him! But he was not.'

'Such a time he gave me, that day . . .'

And they laughed, and they wept together. And then they remembered other things, terrible and dramatic as they had seemed at the time, now bathed golden in the afterglows of childhood: all their little rebellions, torn clothes, scraped knees, a broken door, a horse ride and a fall in a pool. And they smiled at each one, and sometimes they laughed too.

'Now,' said Maria, putting down her glass. 'I want to dance. Will you dance with me, Anna?'

'If you wish. Although you might want an accompanist more.' She looked around, puzzled, as though she felt that every room in the Celesterburg should have its harpsichord in the corner.

'No, you will dance with me. We will do the Lightstep and I will hum the music for us. Look, here are candles. Do you know the Lightstep, Anna?'

'I have watched you often enough.'

They had the footmen clear and move the table to give them room, and the rug beneath it to give them something hard to dance on. Then they dismissed them. Maria took the candles and stood to one side, motioning Anna to take position in the middle of the floor.

'Now,' she said, and she began to hum. Silently, Anna went through the opening movements. Maria watched. You did not often see Anna dance, unless she was showing you how something should be done. She had a slow, stately style, so Maria naturally found herself humming and tonguing the music rather slower than it was normally played. But Anna knew exactly what she was doing as she swept through one figure after another to the end of her sequence. She came to a stand before Maria, and the candles changed hands.

'Now,' said Maria again, and flung herself into the dance. She had speeded up her music without thinking about it, and she followed it, imagining the throng of other dancers, the smiles, the great orchestra humming in her head and her heart as her feet flew and her body floated on the moment.

'Did you know it was a charm?' she gasped, as she changed places with Anna again.

'A charm?' Anna was turning dutifully in the middle of the room without the benefit even of Maria's humming.

'It's for a man,' Maria said, knowing it might be tactless and yet wanting to say it anyway. 'To bring him home, and keep him safe.'

'My dear, I am dancing for *you*.'

'Dance then,' laughed Maria. 'And I'll dance with you.'

And now, together, a candle each, and one-two-three and one-two-three and turn and back-two-three and humming the music to its climax and up!

She held her candle above her head for a long second. Then she brought it down to the level of her eyes. She was breathing hard, as if she and Anna had indeed danced the full dance and at the speed set by the Prince's Orchestra playing in high season.

It had not been tonight, she thought, as she looked the candle in the eye. This was a debt I owed to Anna. But it will be soon. Tomorrow night. I have already committed myself.

She put the candle gently back on the table and left it trembling in the draughty palace air.

'We must go to bed now, Anna,' she said. 'You will need to start early.'

XXXIII
Third Night

The next morning she sent to the citadel headquarters for an escort, and to the palace stables for Dominus to be made ready with a side-saddle. She would accompany Anna to the east gate, to be sure she was away safely. But she did not want to ride in Anna's coach, just in case there was a last, loving attempt at kidnap by the Adelsheim party. Anna smiled wanly when she emerged to see Maria waiting by her horse's head.

'I will be like your cousin Ludwig,' Maria said. 'I will open the doors for you.'

'Dear man,' sighed Anna. 'I hope all is well with him.'

'I am sure it must be,' said Maria firmly. 'He is very wise, I think.'

Their escort arrived, already mounted. He was the same portly, grey-haired officer who had accompanied her from the west wall the day before. His name was Bottrop, and he told Maria that he had orders to be available to her whenever she required it. He led them importantly out of the citadel and down into the city.

The Bamberg Way was heavy with wagons, loaded with goods and with those well-to-do families who could afford to flee the city. Maria looked from face to face as she managed her horse along beside the window of Anna's carriage. She saw their empty,

449

anxious eyes fixed on the distant gate, begging for a chance to get through it before the trap closed. She remembered the crowded streets of Mainz, the day the French had come. *Friends, whatever happens will be as God wills.*

There was no shouting, though. There was no panic yet. Maria, indeed, felt very calm. She was not struggling to escape. She was going to stay, and be unashamed.

The wagons ahead of them moved on. The coach followed. The gate was near. A sergeant came to check papers that Bottrop handed down to him. Anna leaned through the window.

'My dear . . .'

Maria checked her horse, smiling pleasantly. She was armoured against any last appeal. Perhaps Anna saw that. Her face was lined and heavy with emotion.

'Saints be with you,' she said. 'Write to me as soon as you can.'

'I will. I will write to you at Effenpanz. Oh, Anna . . .'

She wanted to embrace her. But that was impossible from the side-saddle. And Anna had turned away inside the coach. Maria thought she had begun to cry. Suddenly she wanted to cry, too.

'Go on, Ehrlich,' she called throatily to the driver. 'Don't stop before Adelsheim.'

'Yes, my Lady.'

'And don't let anyone come back. After today, the roads may not be safe.'

He nodded, but did not answer. Perhaps even Ehrlich was having trouble with his voice now. He shook the reins and grunted to the horses. The coach rolled forward, out under the gate, bearing in it, weeping, the dearest woman in all Maria's life. She watched it dwindle down the roadway. She felt sorry, and guilty. But she could not, even at that last moment, have climbed into the coach and let it carry her away.

'No sir, not you. I'm sorry. You'll have to turn around.'

It was the gate sergeant, standing by a cart in which sat a heavy-set man in a good buff coat, a woman and two boys.

'I shall do no such thing!' cried the man. 'I have business in Bamberg, and I must go there at once.'

'To be sure you have, and your lady and boys too, no doubt. But reasons of state, sir. You can't go.'

'Reasons of state? You want to press my boy, I daresay. Sergeant, he is just twelve. Damn me if I'll let you take him!'

'I'm thirteen, Father!'

'Hey!' called a voice from the next wagon down the line. 'What's the hold-up there?'

'It isn't the boy, sir, as I'm sure you know. It's you. Your papers say you're a doctor. Doctors, carpenters, bricklayers and blacksmiths — they're all needed in the city. None of them's to leave without a special pass. And you haven't got one, sir.'

'Special pass? What nonsense is this? Who's giving out these special passes that I've not heard of until now?'

'I guess it must be the Commander of the citadel, sir.'

'I see.'

The doctor in the wagon seemed to think for a moment. Then, leaning forward, and with less bluster, he said, 'And what do you suppose one of these special passes might cost, hey, sergeant?'

'Couldn't say, sir.'

'Thirty gulden?'

The sergeant hesitated. Then he, too, dropped his voice. 'A bit more than that, sir, I guess.'

Because of the gap between them, and the background hubbub, they could not sink to whispers. Their words carried to Maria clearly.

'Well, sergeant. I just don't have time to go to the citadel and get a pass. But I can see you're a sensible man, and helpful too, I dare say?'

'That depends, sir.'

'Oh, I wouldn't ask you to go out of your duty, sergeant. But maybe you can save us both a bit of time. If I give you the money, perhaps you could let me through now and see that the pass is obtained in due course? Then it will be just as if I had it all along, won't it?'

The sergeant hesitated. 'As to that, sir . . .'

'Sir!' broke in Maria.

The two men looked up and saw her. Both men straightened at once.

She had spoken in a kind of agony, knowing that a bribe was being offered and that if it were accepted the city's defences – Michel's defences – would be weaker. But as she reined her horse closer she was conscious that they were all looking at her: the sergeant, the doctor, the mother with her arms around the boy. Just another family, desperate to escape the city.

'Sir,' she said, addressing the doctor. 'I should tell you that I have just come from the citadel. I fear that what the sergeant says is true. You will need to apply for your pass in person. I am quite sure of it.'

And now Bottrop, her escort, had ridden over to see what the fuss was about. In his cocked hat and white uniform he glowered at the conspirators, an emphatic symbol of authority.

The sergeant cleared his throat.

'You'll have to apply in person, sir,' he said to the doctor.

The doctor scowled at Maria, and at Bottrop beyond her. 'But . . .' he began. Then he stopped.

His wife pawed anxiously at his arm as if to urge him to keep trying.

'No, my dear,' said the man irritably. 'It is no good. Plainly it is an offence to care too much for our children now. We will go back to the house.'

'Perhaps, sir,' said Maria desperately, 'perhaps it will be possible for you to find someone else to escort your family?'

He only glared at her.

There was an awful time, of cursing and pulling at the horses, before the cart was able to turn in the gateway. The doctor fussed and swore and told the soldiers to expect no mercy if their bodies landed on his table in a day or two. The sergeant was abrupt and officious, as if no one should ever think that they might approach *him* with a bribe. The woman sat beside her husband, with her arms around her youngest child. Her head was down and her eyes dull. Only when the men had at last managed to face the cart around to head off down a side street, did she look up.

She looked straight at Maria as the cart trundled away.

How could you? her eyes said. *How could you?*

Grimly now, Maria demanded that someone watch her horse. The men saluted as if she was an officer indeed. She and Bottrop climbed the steps to the great bastion north of the gate, but when she finally reached the wall the Adelsheim coach was no more than one of a number of distant dots upon the road. She turned away with a heavy heart and wondered how many people she had made miserable that morning.

But it is war, she told herself. People must go where they must go and do what they must do. If they do not, there will be far greater misery.

There were a score of men on the bastion, in various militia uniforms. Most of them were doing nothing except sitting and looking glum. She remembered what Michel had said about talking to people who had nothing to do but wait, so she went across to them and spoke with them, just as if they had been a party of peasants resting from some labour in the woods or fields at Adelsheim.

In fact, they came from an estate not far from Adelsheim. None of them had actually seen her home or knew any of the Adelsheim folk. But their voices recalled for her the accents of that country and she was glad to stay and talk with them. There was no officer present, but one of them was an old soldier who clearly had some rank with his fellows. He took Bottrop and Maria to the north side of the bastion.

'This is where they'll come at us, see,' he said.

Below them was the Craftmarket, a long, narrow space inside the wall, which was usually filled with the stalls of tinkers and woodcarvers and bustling with townspeople. It was bustling now, but with altogether different activities. This was where they had blown the breach in the city's defences while she was away in the Rhineland. A long, low dyke of earth and rubble had been piled up on the line of the old wall. The top of it was being closed with a fence of timbers, with more earth piled on both sides of it. Some of the rubble in the ditch had been cleared away, but it was still possible for determined men to scramble in and out down there. Men were doing so now – working parties, with buckets and barrows, still toiling away to make the moat a fraction deeper in whatever time was left.

The makeshift earth wall looked very low and thin. The massive bastions to north and south of it cradled it between them like the big brothers of a delicate child.

'Will it be strong enough?' she asked.

'No telling, my Lady,' said the man. 'As long as the guns up here are still going, there's a chance. But we don't plan on it. When we get the signal, we fall back and fight them from in the town. Those streets, there and there, they're to be barricaded. Our post is the church there – can't remember what it's called . . .'

'The Holy Child.'

'That's the one. And then if that goes, we fall back again. There's a guildhall we're supposed to hold. But by then it'll all be a mess, so I don't reckon to see it. Those tailor-boys won't back us up anyway, that's my thought . . .'

Bottrop was glaring at him, red-faced. In a moment he would call the man to order.

'Thing is . . .' the man went on, not the least overawed to be speaking to an officer and an aristocratic lady, '. . . they should have started on those barricades by now. Should blow this row of houses here down, too. Then we'd have a clear shot at them as they came over the top. But if they don't start soon there'll be nothing to hold them when we fall back . . .'

'Hey, Peter,' said one of the recruits. 'Hear that?'

'Don't you interrupt a lady,' snarled the old fellow. He turned back to Maria. Then his expression changed.

It was a curious noise, like distant wind, coming from the north. It was so soft that it might only have been a heaviness in the air. It did not sound like thunder.

'Peter, what's that?' said the recruit again.

They all strained to listen. For a moment they heard nothing.

455

Then the sound came again, borne to them down the Vater river.

'I reckon,' said the old fellow.

They all watched him as he stood, stooped in the act of listening, frowning at a space in the air before his nose.

'Is it guns?' asked Maria.

'I reckon it may be,' the man said.

'Ours and theirs together, it'll be,' he added. 'Up where the army is, on this side of the river.'

There was a sudden excitement on the platform. Two or three of the militia ran for their muskets.

'Now where would you be going?' jeered the old soldier.

They stopped, sheepishly.

'You won't see nothing for hours yet. Not this side of sundown anyway. Bide where you are and don't go frightening me with those pop-guns of yours. Half of you can't hold them straight anyway. This afternoon, if His Lordship leaves us alone, we'll have them out and go through the drill again . . .'

Down in the streets Maria found she could not hear the noise any more. She wondered if the firing had stopped. Nobody about her seemed to have noticed it. Some of the shopkeepers and stall keepers were still trying to do their business. There was a crowd around a miller's wagon, and another at the baker's. Other people were hanging around, singly or in small groups, when they should have been working. Carts passed, bearing people and their goods out of the city. She wondered what the doctor she had seen was doing now. Perhaps they had simply tried their luck at a different gate, and had managed to get through. She hoped so. She, who had felt ashamed to leave the city, now felt ashamed to have prevented a family from leaving it.

At the west end of the Old Bridge men were knocking loop-holes in the walls of a merchant's house. Two girls were watching them – the merchant's daughters perhaps. The younger, who could not have been more than five, was delighted and clapped her hands and laughed as the iron point of a pick broke through from inside, tumbling fragments of stone and plaster into the street. She ran and jumped up and tried to see in through the new little window that the men had made in her home. But her sister, who must have been a couple of years older, watched in silence. Her eyes were solemn, and she held her thumb to her lip, as if she had been about to start sucking it and had remembered only just in time that she was a big girl now. There was something wrong, her stance said, something awful, about what the men were doing. She knew that, even though everyone had told her that everything would be all right, and her little sister ran about chuckling as the holes were torn in their home. Maria looked away.

How could you? said the hooves of Dominus, clipping and scraping on the cobbles.

She reached the citadel, and gave her horse over to the foot-men at the palace door. They had a message for her. It was an invitation to dine in the palace that night. It was signed 'Gianovi'.

The neat square of paper trembled in her fingers.

Gianovi! How had he known she was here?

'I had intended an engagement for myself,' she said aloud.

'We were to say, my Lady, that he especially hopes that you will come. He has also invited the citadel Commander.'

'I see.'

This was maddening! She had been promising herself . . . And now, with the firing to the north, there might be no more chances. Why had she delayed?

Maddening! She could almost picture Gianovi, as he handed his invitation to some clerk, saying, *She may be a little reluctant. If so, please tell her that I have also invited the citadel Commander.*

The vile, manipulating man! She could believe every bad word that her mother had said about him, and double. What right had he to presume so?

But she could not dine alone with Michel now. He would be with the Governor. So she would dine there too. Perhaps it would at least be possible to leave together, to have the maid drop back, to put her arm in his . . .

Perhaps.

Disconsolate, she ordered pen and paper and went to her room to write her acceptance. Then she penned a note to Michel, to let him know that men were expecting barricades to be put up inside the breach, but that this did not appear to have happened yet. At the foot of the note she allowed herself to add that she hoped to see him that evening. After that she went up onto the north east bastion of the citadel to see if she could still hear the noise of firing. She was not the only one. A number of officers, soldiers, and a couple of maids from the palace, were up there too, straining their ears to the wind. And yes, it was there: that dull, irregular noise, flowing down the chill north wind.

Like a headache, it pursued her for most of the day.

Gianovi received her in the Blue Chamber: a long, high-ceilinged room in the south-east corner of the palace. The great windows, unshuttered, were dark with night. The chandeliers were not lit. A few candles gleamed here and there, and a fire fluttered busily in a hearth. The light glinted on the polished dining table and on the three settings of silver and glasses laid at the end nearest the hearth. Footmen stood like statues in the shadows.

'I fear my other guest may be delayed,' said Gianovi. 'But I believe you are already acquainted.'

'We are, sir.'

'He must be very busy,' Gianovi said. 'Still, we shall hope. Perhaps you would care to sit?'

There was nowhere to sit but at the table. She took the chair at the head. Wine was poured for her. She sipped it, and looked carefully at the little man who seated himself to her left.

He was unchanged. There were none of the marks of short sleep and frantic activity that she had seen on the faces of Michel and his officers. This was a man who was accustomed to workloads far beyond ordinary experience and who bore them lightly. He had not bothered with powder. His skin was pale, even in the lamplight. The lines around the eyes and little muscles of his face were clear, but they had always been there. His eyes moved quickly, or did not move at all.

'Have you any news from the fighting, sir?' she asked. It did not seem the time to bother with the ordinary nothingnesses of conversation.

'We know that a strong column of the enemy has made its way along the north bank of the river. Presumably what we heard was their attack on our positions. How it has gone, I do not know. We can only wait, and depend upon our dear Count Balcke to deliver us.'

Balcke. She had forgotten that it was he who was commanding the army.

'I am sure, sir, that we are depending upon all of them.'

'Oh, quite. Now, may I entreat you to try some of these dainties while we wait? The palace master is so obliging to me when I ask for his favours, and really it must be difficult now for his people to come by such caviar . . .'

It seemed to Maria that they were not waiting at all. They were seated, they were eating, the wine was poured. He was not expecting Michel to join them. Had he invited him at all? Yes, almost certainly he had. But he might well have known that Michel would find it difficult to come now. She should have known that too.

She clung to the feeling that if she had invited Michel herself then he would have come, even if the enemy were already in the breaches. But that was useless. She would have to deal with her host alone. And she had already realized, even if she had not known it before, that he was the very cleverest man that she had ever met.

Gianovi had no time for politenesses either. He talked about politics – grand politics and the manoeuvres of princes. He did not do it to impress or even to instruct. He spoke simply, as if he were an observer describing things that passed his window.

'In a few years, I think, we shall look back and tell ourselves what fools we were, because we did not see what was happening. And yet it is very difficult to see, because so many things might be happening that it is hard to tell which will and which will not.'

'Are you speaking of the siege, sir, or of the Revolution?'

'Both and neither. This siege, immediate though it may be to us, is but a very small part of the whole. As for the Revolution . . .' He frowned. 'Its exponents did not take very long to learn the limits on idealism. It has lost its way, and must find a new direction. But what – or perhaps who – that direction may be is beyond guessing. These days there is much talk of Buonaparte . . .' (he gave the name its Italian pronunciation)

'. . . However, until last summer, the same things were said of Hoche. I will not predict.

'What I will predict, however, is that the Empire, a thousand years old though it may be, must also change. Indeed that when we look back we may realize that it has already changed, without our realizing it.'

Maria scrabbled among the memories of conversations she had overheard in her mother's salons. 'You are talking of secularization, sir? The end of the prince-bishops?'

'That has long been mooted. Also, I fear, the end of the independence of Imperial Knights. And at the same time, one imagines, the growth of the greater secular princes – Bavaria, Saxony, Wurttemberg and the rest. Perhaps they will even come to rival Prussia and the Emperor.'

'But the Emperor will not permit such a thing. It would not be to his advantage!'

'So we have told ourselves. I often think we fail to understand that there is a difference between a thing that will not happen, and a thing that has simply not happened yet. Yes, there has been an alliance of convenience – I put it no more strongly than this – between the Emperor and the prince-bishops. But now we have seen Mainz abandoned in exchange for Venice. At the same time we have seen the Rhineland abandoned too. That means losses for those princes with lands on the left bank. How are they to be compensated? The secularization of the bishoprics – ours included – suggests itself. A nice problem for our delegates convened at Rastatt. Meanwhile, as we chatter, the French continue to make facts on the ground.'

'So . . . you do not believe the Emperor will help us?'

'I have never believed it, and I have told His Highness so.

Oh, the Emperor will go to war again. He cannot co-exist with this new France. But when he does, it will not be because a few thousand Germans cry out to him. It will be because he has English gold. He does not have it yet.'

'A sorry thing, that Germany's pain should mean nothing to the King of the Germans.'

'But what is Germany? When I hear the word *Germany* I find that it means only what the speaker wishes it to mean. No, pardon me. I do not mean to patronize. I am an Italian, and we are in no better case. But the present truth is that any German who thinks himself (or herself) a German has little to be proud of. Too many princes treat their subjects scandalously. I believe the only reason Germany has not itself fallen into revolution is that in Germany there is no Paris.'

Maria frowned. 'Do you include your own prince in that, sir?'

'Not especially. If I set aside this present situation (which has indeed come upon us largely out of his conviction) I find that he has meant well by his subjects. If I have a regret, it is that his attention has so often been taken by others. I am First Minister, indeed. And yet I have had to contend with many ministries other than my own: especially those I may call the Ministries of Family and of Favour, which demand so much of a prince's resources. Also important is the Ministry of the Night: the confessor, even the merest bedchamber servant, have opinions that they may whisper in a prince's ear when wiser heads are not present to urge caution; and of course the mistress, who owns a part of the man's very soul.'

Maria looked at him sharply. She was sure that the word *mistress* had had more than one target. He smiled thinly.

'What, after all,' he said, 'should one think of a state in which

Family and Favour all avert their eyes from the sight of an ordained bishop practising incest?'

'Indeed, sir,' said Maria sternly. 'In my family I believe we are careful with our words. But if you would tell me that we and others like us have been an inconvenience to you, I should say for our part we have sometimes had occasion to regret policies that have been advised by His Highness's servants.'

His eyes flicked quickly, and his small, tight smile was like a stiletto.

'No doubt. We have hardly been kind to one another. And yet I suppose that you are aware that you and your family have cause to be indebted to His Highness's servants – particularly to his foreign servants, whom I suspect to be the butt of much that you have heard?'

'I do not know that I am. But no doubt you will make me aware.'

His shrug said that, if anything, he was a little surprised by her answer. 'Since you ask. The prime excuse for the arrest of Canon Rother-Konisrat and others of his party – I do not include here the Ingolstadt set, whose purge I feel was long overdue and undertaken only for the wrong reason – the prime excuse, as I say, was that they had entered a conspiracy with the Illuminati. The mentor of this conspiracy was a Doctor Sorge. So much was reported and acted on. What was also known, but not reported or acted upon, was the name of the house in which the first meetings were held.'

The look in his eyes told her that he meant *Adelsheim*.

Maria met his look levelly. She had sensed that an assault was coming. Now it seemed to have risen from nowhere to be inside her defences.

'You are saying that you suppressed this report, sir?'

'I? No. I should not even have been aware of it. But I had an interest, and the man responsible for suppressing it had seen fit to requisition a clerk from my offices as a part-time assistant – which, after a suitable show of reluctance, I had allowed. I simply reconciled it with my conscience to pay the clerk a second salary. It is not a course I am generally in agreement with, but on this occasion I felt it justified. From then on I knew everything the clerk knew of his master's work. Which was rather a lot. The master in question has many qualities, but in some ways his mind is insufficiently – ah – devious for the world he inhabits.'

His mind *is*. A foreigner, still serving the Prince . . .

'You are speaking of . . . ?'

Gianovi inclined his head to the empty chair on Maria's right.

'As I say, the report was never forwarded, and later it was destroyed. You are saying to me that he never mentioned it to you?'

'On my word, sir,' she said, with a tremor in her voice. 'Never.'

'I had wondered if it could possibly have lain behind the unusual dealings that appear to have occurred between you and him. He did not seem to me to be obviously capable of black-mail, and yet . . .'

'No sir, he is not!'

He smiled again at her firmness.

'And, sir,' she added. 'I may say that I do not believe any such report could have had merit. My mother's opinions of His Highness's policies were well known. So too was her curiosity of mind, her interest in government and personal improvement, and her willingness to explore what dogma and fiat forbade. If this is enough to spin a story of conspiracy, then I must doubt very much the case against the unfortunates who have been charged with it.'

'Oh, I agree with you. I fear it has ever been so with the Illuminati. It was the fault of the founder, Weishaupt, who had dreams far beyond his capacity to realize them. Unfortunately for his order, the Bavarian authorities took him seriously, and so have other authorities ever since. Sorge may dream the same dreams as Weishaupt, and with the same self-admiration, but with even less mental or practical capacity. In my opinion Baron Knigge was the best of them. Alas, he is dead now.'

'You seem to know them very well, sir.'

'I did say I had an interest. The report that our friend destroyed referred also to an Illuminatus high in the ranks of the Prince's government. That Illuminatus is of course myself.'

For a moment she could not speak. He smiled again.

'I make no excuses. In Italy I was a freemason, but I became dissatisfied with my colleagues and sought something better. The Illuminati, too, promised to work for the good of man. I was eager to learn their mysteries. Therefore Sorge knew of me and later, in his efforts to revive a failing order, sought to claim me. I burned every letter I received from him. Nevertheless, I still believe that the virtues to which the Illuminati dedicated themselves are good ones to live by, and I flatter myself that I do.'

He paused for her to comment. She said nothing. To speak now would be to scuttle like a mouse when the cat plays with it.

Why is he telling me this?

'I tell you this so that you understand that I wish to deal fairly with you. Above all I wish you to understand that I am not attempting to compel you.'

'Compel me? To do what?'

'Not yet. I think we are not yet ready. But let me move closer to the matter. I have been watching our friend Wéry for some time. It was a curious decision of his to destroy that report. I wanted to know why. Despite what you say, it was a powerful weapon – and a coup for him if he had delivered it. It may not have been destroyed as a result of some bargain with you. But I feel sure that it was because of you that it was destroyed. This, as I say, interested me. Until that happened I had come to fear that he was incorruptible.'

She drew breath sharply. But she did not rise, or demand to be allowed to leave. Instead she put to one side her wineglass and signed to a footman for water. She could feel the drink humming in her temples, but she did not think it was too much. Her mind was poised like a fencer's. Now she knew who she was fighting for.

'A strange thing to fear, sir,' she said. 'It is more usual to honour such a quality in a man. And indeed I may tell you he is worthy of honour in this, for I have myself seen him take great offence at the offer of a bribe.'

Let us be honest devils with one another.

The devil opposite her smiled again, and his eyes did not waver.

'But the incorruptible quality is also to be feared. A thing which is more than human is for that very reason not human. I fear that Wéry is driven chiefly by hatred of the men who betrayed his own revolution. And also by an idea of – ah – heroism, that I think very dangerous. I find that the longer I live, the less I am in love with death. But with these young men it is different. Consider Hoche. Consider Buonaparte, with his flag at Arcole. They stride the dark fields with their young eyes and fierce looks, and men flock to their banners. I see it in Wéry too – although to his credit I believe that he lacks some of the self-belief of these men we would make into idols. Nevertheless I think it has a place in his soul.'

'That is the second time you have talked of *souls* tonight, sir.'

Her interruption checked him.

'You also said a mistress had a part of a man's soul,' she said deliberately. 'I understand that it is widely supposed that I am the mistress of Colonel Wéry. I am not. Since we are being frank with one another, I will confess to you that – that I have had some thoughts on the matter. Nevertheless, I am not. And even if I were, I would beg that you address him yourself, if there is something that you would endeavour to persuade him of!'

'Ah. Yes. You detect my intention. Although, please be assured, I think of you only as someone to whom he might listen. If he had been able to come tonight, perhaps we could have considered the matter together. But I confess I had also thought that if he did not come you and I might usefully say these things to one another. As for approaching him myself, I am a little nervous. I know – again, I am not supposed to know, but I do – that he has orders to place me under arrest if he suspects that I incline towards surrender.'

'And you wish me to persuade him for you.'

'I wish you to consider the people who will suffer if he does not.'

Now their eyes locked, like swords at the hilt.

'Sir, you know that I know something of the loss war brings. My thoughts are indeed with the people who defend this city, and I returned here to be with them. But I have not heard that they wish to submit themselves to occupation. And I believe

467

that His Highness could have chosen few men better to lead the defence than Colonel Wéry.'

'Yes. Yes, I believe that you believe what you say. And of course you defend him. But dare I suggest to you that you also profit from this war? That you may have reasons – which with your waking mind you have not considered – for wishing that it should take its course?'

Her mouth shut like a trap.

'How else,' he insisted, 'if there were no war, could you come to be in the citadel that he commands, and with no restraint but your own will?'

'You are unkind, sir.'

My Lady, I am desperate, said the voice of Ludwig Jürich in her mind.

'I ask you only to consider it,' said the man who sat at her left. She drew a long breath.

'I would honour this more,' she said slowly, 'if it came from one whom I thought of with honour.'

Now it was his turn to gather breath and shift in his seat, because he knew she had rejected him.

'And you do not?' he murmured.

'It is not the first time, I think, that you would have used me as a tool. At the Candlemas Ball, as the Prince was about to defy the French, you sent me to speak to him of my brother.'

'My voice had been heard and disregarded. That of the peace party had not. I seized upon its most able member, and the only one I thought had a chance of counting with His Highness. I do not think this dishonourable.'

'Yet even this was not the first time, as His Highness told me. I think you must have done the same thing before. I think it was

468

you that sent the Comte d'Erles to plead before the Chapter in September.'

'Indeed. And do you know how I persuaded d'Erles – that famously selfish young man – that he must prevent his godfather from fighting for his sake? I outlined to him, in detail, the plan that our friend Wéry had composed for the defence of this city. The very plan that he is now about to put into action. Shall I tell you? He intends to fight . . .'

'Within the city. For every street and church and guildhall. Yes, sir, I know.'

There was a long silence, in which the only sound was the low hissing of the hearth. At last she said. 'You see, d'Erles has suffered for your persuasion. And we must still fight. Only now our honour is tarnished, and there is a hole in the wall.'

Gianovi sighed. 'Honour? We know the truth about ourselves. The truth is that we are mites, and history is far, far bigger than we.'

Even as he said it, the sound of a cannon shot rang out across the town. Maria started.

'That was from the east wall!' she gasped.

'Yes. They have found something to fire at, whatever it may be. I fear our time has run out.'

He looked gloomily at the remains of his meal, which had lain untouched on his plate for the last quarter-hour.

'Well. I can no longer be of use here. Matters must now reside in the hands of the Commander. I do not envy him his task.'

'You are resigning?'

'I am leaving. I believe I am the last shred of reason in this city. Now I must yield it to the romantics and return to my Prince. Perhaps I may still be of service at his side.'

'But – if the enemy are east of the city, the roads must be cut!'

The enemy! What had happened to the army?

'The roads, but not I think the river. They will have to work fast to have a boom across it before tomorrow. I have an oared barge ready at the quays and will be gone tonight. I wonder . . .'

He looked at her.

'Perhaps, since you say you have not taken the step that some might suppose . . . Perhaps you should come with me.'

'I . . . thank you, sir. But I had thought you intended me to stay – at least until I have been able to speak with Colonel Wéry?'

'Since you have made it plain that you do not wish to sway him from his course, I see no advantage in you staying, and every advantage, to you especially, if you leave at once.'

'May I ask if it is my reputation that concerns you, or my safety?'

'Both, of course. And my own reputation too. I would not be known as the man who abandoned you to the perils of a siege.'

'But my reputation is already lost, sir. And as to my safety – who is to say whether it is indeed more dangerous to stay than to go?'

She almost said *to go with you.*

'Come, it is not so bad. You have remained – what? Two nights in the city? It is awkward, I grant you, but I can vouch . . . no? You would not want me to do even that? I see. Then is it useless also for me to beg you to consider your own safety. I am sure you realize that if indeed things go as we expect, birth will be no barrier to the most cruel suffering. Come, my dear. This must be your very last chance. It would be a terrible tragedy if you were lost.'

'Sir, if you would have pity on a potential victim of the

470

siege, you will find as many in the streets as your barge will bear.'

'So. Again you refuse. Very well. Very well.'

He leaned back, joined his hands at the fingertips and looked at the ceiling.

'I consult my conscience,' he said.

'Your – conscience, sir?'

'I do have one. Does it surprise you? But I only consult it when it suits me to do so.'

Her eyes flew round the room. He had four – five footmen standing in the shadows. Her nearest help was Pirenne, waiting for her in another wing of the palace. And after that Michel and the men of his garrison – all fixed on the coming enemy. Blessed Saints! Did he mean to capture her and carry her back to her mother by force?

'Very well,' said Gianovi again. He sighed, and drew a letter from his breast pocket.

'I must, of course, respect your choice. Therefore, since I am sure you will be seeing him, I beg you to deliver this letter to Colonel Wéry for me. He knows what is in it. As the city is now under siege, he is to have responsibility for all the matters to do with the governing of the city that have hitherto fallen to me. If you would do this, it would ease me greatly, since at least I will not have to abandon one of my fellows to hunt for him while I make my escape down the river.'

She took the paper from the table and held it in her fingers.

'You may be sure I will deliver it,' she murmured.

'There is no need for you to take it to him now,' Gianovi said. 'He will be out somewhere, on the Saxon or Bamberg gates as likely as not. In any case he will not be expecting it before tomorrow. He can shift for himself until then.'

With a nod, he allowed her to rise, and he rose with her. They bowed and curtseyed to one another.

'This has been a most interesting evening,' he said.

In the courtyard she paused. The air was cold and the sky clear to the stars. She drew a long breath to drive the wine and the talk from her brain. The chill bit into her throat and blew out again in a cloud of frost. She stood and listened for a long while. There was no more sound of cannon, near or far. Abruptly she turned away from her quarters and made her way out to the stable block. The single duty groom gawped at her in the light of his lantern. It must have been nearly midnight.

'I wish you to saddle my horse again,' she said. 'And send someone for Lieutenant Bottrop. I am going down to the east wall.'

XXXIV
The East Wall

Wéry looked down from the bastion upon chaos. The road into the city was crowded with shapes and shadows. Carts inched forwards, blocked in the crowd. Voices called in the darkness, 'Get on! Get on!' Other voices wailed or cried out in pain. In the tiny pools of light by the Saxon Gate he could see that men were cramming themselves forward in an effort to push past a wagon that was at a standstill under the very arch. The wagon was not moving. The press of bodies around it was making it impossible. Voices, hoarse with yelling, bellowed for men to keep still or to move out of the way. No one heeded them.

'Ho there,' called Wéry down into the crowd. 'What unit is that? What unit?' But his voice lost itself in the struggling mass and he heard no answer.

Beside him the bastion commander, a short man in a huge cocked hat, was craning over the parapet.

'There's French among them!' he gasped. 'I'm sure of it!'

Panic was in his voice. It was panic that was breathed out by the crowd below them. Every man down there, at the end of their terrible march from the battlefield, was seized with the fear that in an instant they would be snuffed out. Their comrades around them, wounded, exhausted, were nothing but obstacles. They pressed unthinking for the last yards to the safety of the gate. The gates were jammed back by the crowd. There was no possibility of closing them until the blockage freed. If there were indeed a strong force of French mingled in the mass, the gate might be lost in minutes.

'We must fire, sir. We must disperse them.'

'Don't be a fool,' snapped Wéry. 'Do not fire. Do *not* fire.' He strode to the top of the inner steps and bellowed down again.

'Ho there! What unit?'

Some hero had got the wagon moving. It sidled forward a few yards into the city: a big rattling shadow among other shadows that eddied forward in a rush as the way was freed.

'What unit is that?'

A voice from the cart, strained and pained, answered, 'Second company, the Fapps.'

The Fapps battalion – or a fragment of it. What of the rest? What in God's name had happened up there on the banks of the Vater?

'Officer to the bastion to report, please.'

When nothing seemed to respond to his cry, he bellowed again, 'Up and report, damn you!' He could feel his own voice going hoarse with the strain of shouting. But something was happening down there now. They seemed to be lifting something – a man, in the cart. He heard a gasp of pain. Then another voice, faint in the tumult, said, 'No, no. He is wounded. Put him down.'

It was a woman's voice. He thought he knew it.

'*You* go,' he heard her say. 'Don't be afraid. I will come with you.'

'Commander!' called a voice from across the bastion.

'Wait!' he snapped.

People were climbing the steps to the bastion. Pale uniforms

474

glowed in the lamplight. Bottrop appeared, leading a young, bewildered soldier with his arm in a sling. Behind him, biting her lip as she picked her way up the last few steps, came Maria von Adelsheim. God's teeth, what was she doing *here*? At *this* hour?

Here where the enemy might appear without warning, and death might take any of them in a moment?

'Their officer is wounded,' she said. 'This man will tell you what has happened.'

The bastion commander appeared at his side again.

'Report,' he said importantly to the soldier. The man came dazedly to attention.

'Second company, the Fapps?' said Wéry.

'Yes, sir. Wounded detail.'

'What happened up there?'

'Don't know, sir. They caught us up on the march and said the position was overrun, and the enemy cavalry were after us . . .'

'Stop. Who caught you up?'

'The other fellows, sir. The Erzbergers. In a mob they were, no officers . . .'

'Stop again. You were sent back from the lines, as part of a wounded detail?'

'Yes, sir. After the first attack. Captain Herz and the badly wounded in the carts, the rest of us walking. And . . .'

'And then some men from the Erzberg battalion caught you up and told you they had been overrun and the enemy were in pursuit with cavalry?'

'Yes, sir.'

'When was that?'

'Around an hour ago, sir.'

'Did you see the enemy?'

'We heard horses, sir. But it was dark.'

Dark. It had been dark for hours, and these men had been marching, running, riding, dazed and wounded, all the way. What chance of a sensible report from any of them?

'Right. Well done. And you are safe. Now what we need you to do is get yourself to the hospital — what is it? Sabre-cut?'

'Don't know, sir. After we cleared them out of the position I found I couldn't use it. That's all.'

'Get yourself to a hospital. They'll see you right. The nearest one's at the Saint Cyprian church. Know it?'

'No, sir.'

Wéry turned to the bastion commander.

'Spare a man to take him there, would you?'

'Yes, sir.'

'And there are men of the Erzberg battalion in the crowd. Bring at least one of them to me.'

'Yes, sir.'

The woman was still standing there, watching them.

'You have blood on your dress,' he said.

'It was his — the officer's. I think his wound broke open as they tried to lift him down.'

'Please — you should not be here.'

It was agonizing to see her standing there, when shots might break out at any moment.

'I know. I have a message for you from the Governor.' She held out a paper. 'He has left the city. You are now to take over his responsibilities.'

He nodded dully. Gianovi was gone. Well, at least that simplified some things.

'What has happened?' she asked.

476

'I do not really know. The army was attacked in their positions. They must have held against the first assault, if they were able to organize a wagon train for their wounded. But there must have been a second attack, and at least one of the battalions has broken.'

At least one. And if the Erzberg battalion had gone, that would be a third of the position. What chance for the rest of them, after that had happened?

'We heard cannon fire in the citadel.'

'That was the Bamberg gate. They saw — or heard, rather — cavalry somewhere out in the fields. The cavalry rode off. We do not know where they have gone . . .'

'Commander!' said a voice behind him urgently.

'Yes, what is it?' he snarled.

It was another militia officer. One of the guildsmen, he thought.

'We think we have finished the barricades, Commander. What are your orders?'

Mercy of saints! We *think* we have finished the barricades . . . 'I will come and inspect. If they are satisfactory, the next thing . . . Have you prepared fire-buckets in your quarter?'

'Fire-buckets, Commander?'

Damn it — had these people never heard of incendiary shells?

'Earth, sand, water — whatever you can find. And twice as many as you think you will need. And we need earth and dung on the cobbles to damp shot as it falls. I will come . . .' He looked around.

He could not leave the bastion, not yet. The men were leaderless. He had sent their officer to find him someone to interrogate. At any moment they might take it into their heads to shut the gates on the fugitives or start firing at imaginary Frenchmen. And they were all looking at him – the gun crews with their implements in hand, faces blank in the darkness, all turned towards him. Tomorrow, or the day after, iron shot would be hurtling in to smash those men to pieces as they worked here. They were looking at him, waiting for him to speak.

The lamplight was on Maria's face. She was biting her lip, still. He saw her shiver. He saw her breath frosting on the air. She had come without a coat, or even a shawl.

He unbuttoned his own greatcoat and peeled it from his back. He handed it to her.

'You must wear this,' he said. 'If you are staying.'

To the guildsman he said, 'I will come as soon as I can.'

The late February dawn found them both still on the wall. The gates were closed now. Since the arrival of the train of wounded the inflow of fugitives had dropped away to single men or small groups, many arriving on horses that must have been stolen from wagons. There were more of the Fapps battalion, some Erzbergers, and a handful of the dragoons. All those they questioned confessed that their units had been broken. There was no word of the Dürwald battalion, or of the hussars, or any of the artillery. No one knew what had happened to Count Balcke. No officer above the rank of captain reached the city.

But the grey light showed them masses of cavalry, circling the city beyond gunshot of the walls. Wéry counted at least six squadrons of light horse, and three more that might have been dragoons, accompanied by a battery of horse guns. Their presence put all thought of a sortie beyond question. His nervous militias would never stand in square against such a force.

Balcke-Horneswerden, and the main body of the retreat (if there was one) would have to fend for themselves.

He found himself looking at Maria in the first light. Her hair was tousled and her eyes marked with lack of sleep. She looked like a walking tent with his greatcoat draped around her. The beauty had fallen from her – gone altogether, except, perhaps, for the line of her jaw as her chin lifted and she listened to what was said.

Hey, Michel – have you ever looked at somebody? Have you tried to see their past, their hopes, their fears, all written on their face?

That was the real person, he said to himself. Take away the grooming and the training, and now you see her as she really is. Her past he knew well, and her hopes for freedom. Her future, he dared not guess.

And supposing he could paint, as Maximilian painted, then this would be the face that would look out from his canvas. How might it change in death?

He could not bear to think of it.

But the idea was infectious. He found himself glancing again and again at her, to reassure himself that she was still alive. He cursed himself for his weakness and looked away. But immediately he had to look back again at her, to be sure that she was there.

He tried to replace her with someone else. He looked at the men around him and let his mind play its death-games with their faces instead. There was a round headed, crimson-cheeked militia officer, with a hairy wart growing by the side of his nose, and another on his chin. So what was his past? What were his hopes and fears? He was a country gentleman from Zerbach. His hopes: probably to go back to being a country gentleman as soon as possible and to have another try at persuading his obstinate peasants to raise that clover crop, which would make so much difference to their lives. His fears: smoke, and a line of charging Frenchmen, and his men melting away around him as he stood there. His future: short.

Or the sombre-looking Master in the Guild of Crossbowmen. Or the thin-faced official from the mayor's chambers, whom Wéry had imagined would desert his post at once, and somehow was still here. Somehow they were all here, every one of them wrenched from their lives into a world that was utterly changed. The same tired expressions were stamped on all of them. They had even begun to defend him, as he had seen Fernhausen and Bergesrode defend the Prince from petitioners.

But still the petitions came. Here before him were two more faces, two nuns from the Convent of Saint Cecilia, whose Mother Superior had sent to know in what way they could assist. (Dear God, what would happen to *them* when the French broke in?)

'Clear your largest rooms for a hospital,' he said. 'And make as many bandages . . .'

'Oh, but Commander! The Mother Superior says it is impossible to admit men to the convent buildings!'

'They will be wounded, and doctors and orderlies only. I am sure that if she understands the situation . . .'

'She will not agree to this, Commander.'

Dear God! thought Wéry again. He felt very tired.

'Say to her that I most earnestly request it . . .'

'No,' said another voice. 'Do not say that.'

Beyond the two nuns, a figure loomed out of the twilight – a familiar shape, in a black priest's robe. It looked just like

Bergesrode. But surely that was a trick of the light. That would be because the thought of Bergesrode had flitted across his mind only a few moments before . . .

It *was* Bergesrode. It was that face, that unforgettable face, with the dark brows slanting down and the dark patches below his eyes slanting up like the remains of an ashen cross. It was a man who only weeks ago had been one of the most powerful in Erzberg. He looked at the two nuns with eyes of stone.

'Say to the Mother Superior that when men are wounded we are not commanded to pass on the other side of the road. And also say to her that if she is too stupid to understand even that, I shall come and explain it to her myself.'

'Thank you,' sighed Wéry, as the two nuns fled.

'She is a fool, that one,' said Bergesrode.

'What are you doing here?'

'After I left my post, I returned to the cathedral. When the Chapter left the city, I volunteered to remain. So now I have charge of the cathedral, and of the cathedral troops. I came to tell you that we are at your disposal.'

'Thank you,' said Wéry again.

The 'cathedral troops' he supposed, would be the ragged band of beggars and clerks, clanking with pikes and relics, that the priests had been organizing over the last week. Of course they would expect to provide the defence of the cathedral. And he had already assigned it to . . .

He could not remember to whom he had assigned it. Here was one more matter to be resolved, among all the others.

Wéry and his party inspected the barricades inside the breach and ordered that one should be rebuilt a few yards back down the street so that the buildings on either side could enfilade it. They went to the cathedral and climbed the west tower to gain a view of the Kummelberg, where an enemy battalion had appeared and was beginning to dig trenches opposite the citadel. Then they returned to the east wall in time to see a column of infantry emerging from the woods to the north of the city.

'There, sir. They are ours!'

'So they are, by God!' said an aide. 'Hurrah!'

'Wait,' said Wéry.

He trained his field-glass on them. Distant figures danced in the circle of his vision. The uniforms were white, yes. But that meant nothing. Much of the French infantry still wore its old royalist whites because the Republic had had neither the time nor the money to replace them with the new patterns. And after the fugitives of the night and the arrival of enemy cavalry in the morning, it would be extraordinary for a formed body of Erzberg infantry to appear now.

Of course, extraordinary things did happen in war. But if these were Erzbergers, surely they should be making for the Saxon Gate, rather than circling the city?

'Should we not sortie, Commander?'

'No.'

He swung his glass a little to his right. A squadron of French cavalry had halted on the eaves of a wood, not far from the head of the advancing column. The men were dismounted. The horses were picketed. Soldiers did not do that in the presence of an advancing enemy.

'No,' he said again. 'Those men are French.'

He felt the mood of the group around him sink as under-standing set in.

'So,' he said, closing his field-glass. 'We must assume that

Balcke-Horneswerden has had to retreat in another direction. There is nothing we can do now but wait.'

'How long?' said Bergesrode.

'At least as long as it takes that column to march all the way round to opposite the Ansbach Gate and for their fellows to come up and circle the city. After that, it depends where their guns are. They will be slow to arrive because they are big beasts . . .'

'Commander!'

Again that urgent cry from beyond the ring of faces.

'What is it?' said one of the militia officers gruffly.

'A flag of truce, sir, at the Saxon gate. There is an officer of the enemy who wants to parley.'

'Truce, eh?' said someone.

'Do not put your hopes up,' said Wéry. 'They will speak only to scare us. But we will hear what they have to say. Have them blindfolded and brought up to the palace. I will meet them there . . .' He looked around at the faces. '. . . With the quarter commanders. The rest of you should find yourselves breakfast and some rest. You will need it before long.'

'There will be a special mass for our deliverance,' said Bergesrode, as the group broke up. 'Six o'clock, at the cathedral.'

'Very good.'

Maria stood beside him. He looked at her, and all their faces were gathered into one in hers.

She asked, 'What may I do?'

He allowed his eyes to linger on her for a moment, to remind himself that they were both still living – that all of them were, for now.

'Breakfast, and rest,' he repeated. 'It is an order.'

★ ★ ★

483

The effect of placing a white hood over a man's head was to make him seem headless, like a blood-drained corpse from the guillotine.

So Wéry, dazed from lack of sleep, mused as he watched the blindfolded French officers led on horseback across the courtyard of the Celesterburg. There were just two of them. Their hands were tied behind their backs to prevent them from removing their hoods without warning. The militiamen guided their horses gently up to the palace steps.

'Very well,' said Wéry. 'Let them see.'

One hood was pulled roughly back, revealing a solemn face with black brows and a grey moustache surrounded by tightly-curling grey hair. The Frenchman looked impassively away as the militiamen reached to cut his bonds. Then they lifted the other hood.

It was Lanard.

Colonel Lanard, it seemed, to judge by his insignia. And he was in a foul temper. 'Ah. Good day to you, Wéry,' he said. 'I find the hospitality of Erzberg is not what it was at my last visit. But perhaps that is because the Brabançons are now in charge.'

'Perhaps,' said Wéry. 'Perhaps it is also because at your last visit you were a welcome guest.'

'Not welcome to everyone, even then,' he said. 'But it was my duty, as it is now.'

He climbed stiffly down from the horse.

'My aide, Capitaine Rouche,' he said, indicating the grim-faced, grey-haired officer beside him.

'I regret that we have made you uncomfortable,' said Wéry. 'Of course you will appreciate the necessity.'

'Frankly, Commander – and may I congratulate you upon

your promotion, albeit disposed at the whim of some aristo-crat – I find it hard to appreciate the necessity of any of this most considerable folly. I had thought you a man of better sense. Nevertheless, I have prevailed upon my General to permit me to see if there is any possibility of avoiding a disaster. And therefore I am here.'

'How thoughtful of you,' said Wéry coldly.

'Oh, but I like you, Commander. You remind me of my former General. An angry man, but a good one. So I am going to do my best to save you. Also I understand that at least one person from a household I remember fondly is in your fortress, and I would very much wish that she were not inconvenienced in the coming days.'

He stopped. The amused smile that Wéry remembered played for a moment across his face. Wéry realized that his eyes must have flicked across the courtyard to the windows of the apart-ments where Maria would be sleeping.

'How did we know?' said Lanard. 'Oh, there are always comings and goings, even in sieges, are there not? You know that even better than I. And we were not so very surprised to hear that Gianovi has slipped away, leaving you to hold the bag. Such a clever man.'

'We will go up to the conference chamber,' said Wéry.

'To the Prince's room, I hope,' said Lanard lightly. 'After all, it seems you have the run of all the palace. Surely there is no better place to find agreement than surrounded by the representation of Heaven.'

'If you wish to see the Prince's chamber, you will have to go back out and force your way in.'

'Ah, but that might damage it!'

'If you value it so much you should leave the city undisturbed.'

'So sad, that to enter paradise one must destroy it.'

In tight-lipped silence they entered the palace. They climbed the marble stairs, their boots and the boots of their aides clattering in a long harsh trail behind them. The paintings and statues seemed to look away as they passed, as if the soldiers were an unwelcome truth that the palace figures still hoped they need not acknowledge. On the carpets of the first-floor corridors the sound of their tread deadened to a low thunder that rolled down the dimly-lit passages and rumoured the end of the Prince's world. The door to the antechamber was open. Inside, the two desks of the secretaries had been pushed to the wall and a long conference table had been set up. More of the officers commanding the defence of the town were gathered there, staring out of the windows or pacing up and down. They came to attention as Wéry entered.

'You may sit,' he said to the Frenchmen, indicating seats in the centre of one side of the table. He himself made his way around to sit opposite them. The other officers arranged themselves on either side of him, a long row of eighteen white uniforms facing the two foreigners.

Capitaine Rouche took some paper, a pen and an ink-bottle from a satchel that he carried, and set them out before him. Lanard leaned forward and looked directly into Wéry's eyes.

'I am authorized by General Augereau of the Army of the French Republic to speak for him to those in command of the defences of this city.'

General Augereau. So it was that man, of all of them, who was to be the opponent in his last fight. He remembered dimly that Lanard had once called Augereau an 'ape'.

'Let us hear what General Augereau has to say.'

'I shall begin by outlining the situation as General Augereau sees it. In brief, the Army of Erzberg has ceased to exist. All three of your field battalions have been broken, and one of them has been completely destroyed. Your Count Balcke is dead. We found his body after the last square of the Dürwald battalion was over-run. We have taken six guns, which we believe to be the sum total of your field artillery. If you will appoint officers for the purpose, they may accompany me back to our lines under flag of truce to interview some captured infantry and artillery officers of yours, who will confirm what I have told you.'

'I see,' said Wéry, conscious of the rustle that was spreading down his side of the table at the Frenchman's words. He fumbled for something to say. 'You have not yet mentioned the hussars.'

Lanard shrugged. 'Hussars will be hussars. They made their ride to glory. I regret to inform you that we have yet to find a single hussar officer among the living.'

'I see.'

'To prevent any further recurrences, General Augereau requires that all remaining forces of the Prince-Bishopric be disarmed and disbanded. All incumbent officers and officials of the Prince-Bishop's administration are required to surrender themselves for parole. In addition, and to provide for the security of the city of Erzberg, my general proposes to leave a garrison of his own troops in the city. I am authorized to discuss with you the terms under which this garrison is to be installed and maintained.'

Wéry knew that he had expected nothing else. He fought to control his anger, and to let his voice roll coolly out to the ears of his subordinates, like an officer rallying a wavering line.

'I see. But I am not authorized to discuss these things. If you wish the town to be surrendered, you must address yourself to His Highness.'

'His *Highness*, we believe, is as far away as Bamberg, and may very well be farther still – on his way to Bohemia or Bavaria, perhaps. We shall certainly endeavour to discover his whereabouts but we most certainly shall not wait until we have done so before finishing matters here. Therefore we address ourselves to what remains of the armed force of Erzberg, and most specifically to those who have the responsibility of command of that force.'

'Very well. You may tell your general that we will not surrender the town.'

Lanard gave a little gasp of exasperation. 'This answer will achieve nothing but further loss of life, chiefly among the soldiers you are responsible for, and the citizens it is your duty to protect. Erzberg is not a proper fortress. You have no outworks, few trained gunners, and the single ring of your walls is breached. No doubt you have done your best to repair the damage. Even so, your defences are hardly adequate. I should also inform you that we are equipped with heavy guns.'

'We know this.'

Lanard lifted an eyebrow. 'Then I hardly see what you will gain from prolonging the conflict.'

'In the first place, Colonel, I remind you that this city is not yours or your general's, but that of the Prince. Every man of my garrison and every citizen in the town knows that, and will uphold it. In the second, we are subjects not only of the Prince, but of the Emperor, who may yet interest himself in this case. And thirdly, the responsibility for every shot you fire over our wall, every house demolished, every man, woman or child whom you cause to suffer, will be seen by all of Christendom to rest with you.'

Lanard gave an impatient gesture. 'But this is to clothe yourself in chains! The Prince has fled. And will Paris tremble at what the Emperor thinks? Eventually, I suppose, we may hear from the Emperor his thoughts upon the matter – and upon our operations in Switzerland and Rome at the same time, no doubt. It will change nothing. Such . . . obeisance to powers past ill becomes you. You of all people, Commander. This is your choice, and I put it to you again. Either commit your people to suffer and die, or let them be free of the yokes you have named. Which is the choice of the sane man?'

'Free, you say!' cried Wéry. 'Free like Liège, Brussels, Mainz? The only freedom they know is that they are free to weep!'

'Damnation, Wéry!' exclaimed Lanard. 'If I return with these answers to my general, the end is certain! He is not a forgiving man. And our soldiers, when they have climbed your fence – they will not simply be petulant. There will be no stopping once we are in. You know what that will mean.'

'So do you. And may you live long with it.' And he looked at the officer before him, in the uniform of the Republic. And his mind bellowed, *It will be your doing! Your doing, not mine!*

'So,' said Lanard. 'I had hoped that in this parley at least I might have better luck than in my last. But it seems to be forever my fate to negotiate with bone-headed fanatics.'

'You have taught us to be fanatics, sir. This, too, I lay at your door.'

'Enough. For our part, it remains only to bring up the guns and take position. Until then, you have yet some time to reconsider. I bid you do so – and to consult before you do.'

'But as I have said, Colonel, there is no one with whom we may consult. Therefore you should not look for our answer to change.'

'Bof!' said Lanard wearily. 'Then consult the devil at your elbow, my friend.'

He rose from his place, and the grim-faced Capitaine Rouche rose with him. As the aide stowed his things in his satchel again, Wéry saw that not a mark had been made on the paper in all the conversation. Not one word of his had been recorded for Paris.

The militiamen at the door escorted the Frenchmen out of the room. Their footsteps thudded dully down the corridor and clattered distantly on the gallery steps. The silence after their departure seemed as thick as the air before a storm. The officers were waiting for him.

They were waiting for him, with pale cheeks and shaken eyes. Faces, faces . . . the gentleman from Zerbach; the official from the mayor's chambers. *How many of us will live through this?* they were thinking. *Half? Less than half?*

And seated at the very end of the table, the gaunt Knight von Uhnen himself.

Their eyes met. The old aristocrat was as grey as weathered stone. His nose was sharp, and his mouth a little line. His gaze was absent, as if his thoughts were all turned inwards upon some hidden pain.

Hussars will be hussars, Lanard had said. I regret to tell you . . .

Another face to remember: the Knight von Uhnen, who had just learned that his son was dead.

He is dead, your son, thought Wéry. Following a plan that I helped to devise. And if he had not died, then I would have met him with pistols anyway. He would have killed me, or perhaps I him. And why? For a woman. For a crazy notion of honour that should have died long ago.

How can I tell you that I am sorry?

He drew breath, and found that he was trembling.

'I prefer it when they are firing cannon at us,' he said aloud. 'At least we know they mean it, then.'

No one laughed. He must take command again. Now, if never before, he must *not* fail.

'Knight von Uhnen. I should be grateful if you would follow our French guests and avail yourself of their offer to interview those of our officers they may be holding. The more we can learn about what happened out there, the better.'

The Knight glared at him. He seemed slow to understand what had been said.

'Why should it be me?' he asked, in a voice as hoarse as a crow's.

'Because you will know them, sir,' said Wéry. He kept his tone short. This was no time for empty condolences. The Knight would not welcome them either. 'The rest of you gentlemen, please rejoin your units. I will begin an inspection at nine o'clock, beginning with the Mercers' Bastion.'

But of course they did not all leave at once. Many of them had matters for him to resolve – disputes with other units, and excuses for what he would find when he came around. One by one he dealt with them and the group around him diminished. At last there was only one man, standing on the opposite side of the table. It was Bergesrode, frowning at him from under those dark, crossing brows.

Yet one more face. One more past: the man who had held power in this very room, who had fallen and whose seat was now occupied by Wéry himself. His hopes: to be a martyr for his faith. And his future: his wish granted.

'Yes?' said Wéry.

'There is a matter we must discuss.'

'Sit, then.'

Slowly Bergesrode drew up a chair on the opposite side of the table, in the room where he had once had his power. His face showed no emotion. Wéry watched him, and wondered what was coming.

'The Knight von Uhnen,' said Bergesrode. 'He is not to be trusted.'

'Why do you say that?'

'He resents your position. He believes he should command the defence.'

Wéry shrugged. This was hardly a surprise. Von Uhnen was one of the few remaining Imperial Knights in the city. It must have irked to find that his Prince had put him under the command of a foreign-born upstart.

'He plans to arrest you, and take your place,' said Bergesrode.

'What is your evidence for that?'

'I cannot tell you.'

'I have to trust what you say. I have to act on it.'

'I know.' Bergesrode looked down at his hands. 'But . . . It is difficult.'

Wéry raised his eyebrows and waited. (How like Bergesrode he had become!)

'Again, no one has taken the Prince's gold for this,' said Bergesrode grimly.

'Nevertheless.'

'Can you not take my word?'

'In the Terror, a word was enough,' said Wéry dryly. 'But I believe our standards should be a little higher.'

'You are asking me to violate a sacrament.'

'It was a Confession?'

Of course it would be. Half the city would be confessing themselves now.

Bergesrode hesitated for a second more. Then he nodded, abruptly. 'One of Uhnen's men came to the cathedral yesterday evening. We hear many things in the booths. Little shocks us. Even so, the priest who received him was troubled and came to me.'

'And you in turn have come to me.' Wéry thought for a moment. 'Why?'

'I believe it is God's will that the city should be defended. Von Uhnen is not the man to do that. I think you are.'

'I see,' Wéry said, and sighed. 'Thank you.'

There was something awful about Bergesrode's faith in him. Twice, at least, he had betrayed the secretary's confidence – over the Frenchman's passport, and the meeting of the Illuminati. And none of the services he had provided to Bergesrode had been enough to prevent the man's fall from office. Yet here he was, now the subordinate, uncomplaining of his demotion, dedicated only to his cause. And he was ready to break even the sacred rules of his church, to insist that Wéry was the one to defend the city. Why?

Because of the seed of hate in his heart. Because he knew it in Wéry, too.

Wéry felt very tired.

He should call Uhnen in, harangue him, turn him around. Perhaps he could even appoint the gaunt old aristocrat as his second-in-command. The defence was weak enough already. A struggle at the top would shake the men badly. But . . .

But he could not see himself succeeding. He could not imagine that anything he said would persuade that arrogant old noble. Not now. All he would achieve would be to put the plotters on their guard.

The man had just lost his son. And that must count for nothing. It would only make him the more unpredictable.

The safe thing to do – the only thing to do – was to strike first. What mattered was that Uhnen's subordinates should still take orders afterwards. So the blow should not be struck in front of them. Once it was done . . .

Bergesrode was waiting for him.

'Your cathedral troops,' Wéry said. 'Are they loyal?'

'Yes.'

'Could you arrange an arrest?'

Again Bergesrode looked at his thumbs.

'If I must,' he said.

'When he returns from the French lines. He will come to the Saxon gate. Do not wait until he has rejoined his troops inside the city. Take him to . . .' He hesitated.

It would be a risk to hold Uhnen in the citadel. Some of the garrison might be sympathizers.

'Is the cathedral secure?'

'It could be made so – if necessary.'

'To the cathedral, then. And see that you hold him there.'

To fight them you must be like them, he thought, as he watched Bergesrode's retreating back. The Prince had said it, and denied it. Then he had gone on to arrest and imprison his political opponents one after another.

And he, too, had denied it. And now he, too, was striking out like a tyrant: striking at an innocent man before he could become guilty.

'Commander!' called a voice from the door.

'Wait,' he said.

He put his hands over his face.

He had become the very thing that he most hated.

XXXV
The Grate

In her rooms in the Celesterburg Maria lay between waking and sleep. Her body was weary but her mind could not rest. She dreamed that she was wandering through the palace around her, and that it became her home at Adelsheim, which she had never left after all. The place was full of people, many people, and the fighting had begun. Before her stood the doctor's wife, with her arms about her son. *Naughty boy, you're not dead yet*, said a soldier and fired his gun. And the boy was dead after all, and the woman stood with her arms around him and looked at her, and her eyes said *How could you?*

In her dream she escaped through a door into the study of the green judge. The room was empty. She looked and looked for the thing she was trying to remember. It was not there. But she knew that if she waited for it, it would be brought to her. And yes, here was the servant standing there at the door. (Only it was not the servant. It was Ludwig Jürich, with his green coat and his patient eyes.)

This is for your friend, he said. *He must have it as quickly as possible.*

She recoiled at the memory of the tormented head. But the thing in his hand was not a painting. It was a book. And his finger marked a page that she remembered. 'When he was set down upon the judgement seat, his wife sent unto him, saying Have thou nothing to do with that innocent man . . .'

She woke, sour and confused. She tried to think where she might go and what she might do, but could not. The only thing that seemed to offer her any purpose was to find Michel and stay with him, as she had stayed all the night before. She remembered that Father Bergesrode from the cathedral had said that there would be a mass at six o'clock. He might be there. Indeed he certainly should be, since the purpose of the mass was to allow the garrison and the city to pray for deliverance. He should be there for everyone to see.

Strange that a young foreigner, of no great birth, should be their Hector now! Strange, too, that she should hardly think it strange. The time brought these things, just as it brought wild, bare-legged rides to the city without thought for censure. The city looked instinctively for a leader, and one had been appointed for them. But was he ready? How would he carry himself?

She must find him.

There was no clock in her room. To judge by the fading light she still had time, but not very much. She roused up Pirenne, who was dozing by the fire, and made her help her get ready. She sent for Bottrop, but after waiting for him for ten minutes she lost patience, and the two women set out on foot for the cathedral together. By now it was nearly dark. There were no lights on the looping road that led down from the Celesterburg gate to the river.

It was as they were crossing the Old Bridge that she heard the cannon from the east wall. The sound, coming from the far side of the low rise on which the cathedral and much of the city stood, was a dull *thump*, like someone dropping a sack of corn onto hard ground. After a few seconds it was repeated. And then it was repeated again. Something was happening out in the dark beyond the wall. She quickened her pace, as if the cannon shots only made it more urgent that they should be at the cathedral on time.

In fact they were early. And yet already there were a number of people there, gathered in little groups in the aisles for the comfort of one another's company. As she stood by the door many more were coming in, rich and artisan and poor, all with the same pale faces and worried eyes. Again and again she heard the question asked: was it the enemy, firing into the city? Or was it only our side, so far? Voices, some anxious, others self-important, declared this or that about what was happening and what was going to happen. But she did not understand how any-one could be sure. There were very few uniforms in the crowd. She looked and looked for Michel. She stood by the great doors and searched every new knot of entrants with her eyes as they came in. But he did not appear. Perhaps . . . perhaps he was on the wall instead. Perhaps he thought it was more important to be there rather than here. She did not know. But the townspeople would miss him. She was missing him too.

Thump, went the guns on the wall. *Thump-thump*.

The choir was filing in, in silence. The people were drifting forward up the nave. Still she hung by the door, waiting for each late entrant, to see if he might come after all. He did not.

When the first Kyrie Eleisons began, she crossed herself in the direction of the distant altar, muttered to Pirenne and left.

It was night outside now. She turned at once for the eastern exit from the cathedral square. She heard Pirenne exclaim and sensed her footsteps falter as the maid realized where they were going, but she pressed on, down the broad Bamberg road towards the east gate.

Something flashed, like weak lightning, and the dark shapes of the roofs and the buildings showed black for an instant before retreating into shadow. The thump! followed a second later and much louder than before. And then there was quiet, and nothing but the darkness and the sound of their feet hurrying as they made their way down the hill. She could hear nothing else – no voices, no screams, no crashing among the buildings. The eastern side of the city seemed quiet and dark, indifferent to the cannonade and to the two women who scuttled through its streets like mice.

Thump-Thump!

It was much louder now, and sharper. It was coming from a little to the left of the Bamberg gate – from the bastion just south of the breach. That was where they would come, the old soldier had said. Were they coming already? But there were no sounds other than the irregular beat of the cannon on the wall. The sweet smell of smoke eddied in the night air.

'Lady Maria . . .!' exclaimed Pirenne. She was afraid.

'Come on!' Maria muttered.

They scurried into the deep shadows behind the Bamberg Gate. There were people here, muttering, handling weapons. White uniforms drifted ghost-like in the darkness. Within the bastion a cannon barked its coughing roar, and now she heard the rattle and squeak of the wheels as it hurled its huge weight backwards with the force of the shot. She could see the light of the lanterns in the casement, filtering out through the bastion door.

And now her heart almost failed her, as she stood with her

foot on the open stair that led up to the platform. What was she doing here – here of all places, in this hell of noise and smoke? Her limbs congealed with the thought of the open space above her, and the men and the guns and the enemy in the night.

But surely he would be up there – surely he would! And if she did not move in a moment, she might never move at all.

'Come on!' she exclaimed to Pirenne, to herself. And her feet forced her upwards.

He was not there. Her eyes hunted among the crowd of men at the wall, but she did not find him. The men were aiming their muskets outwards and peering at the darkness. Someone called and pointed. Out there below the walls, perhaps three hundred yards off, a lantern had showed fleetingly. The men in the gun-casement below her must have seen it too, for again a cannon bellowed and the air was full of smoke.

'Quiet! quiet!' called a voice among the men.

Silence flowed in behind the gun-shot. But it was a silence that prickled with little noises. From somewhere away before her came the low *chink, chink* of picks and spades in earth. It seemed to be coming from more than one place. And it seemed to be horribly close. Even at so innocent a sound, Maria could not help shuddering.

'Listen!' said one of the men.

That was not digging. That was a softer noise, and much closer. In the blackness out beyond the ramparts, someone had stumbled.

The men were pointing their weapons.

'Shoot! Shoot!' cried the officer suddenly. The muskets flashed and spat. Maria fled down the steps into the dark behind the wall.

Pirenne had disappeared. She had not come up the steps. Now

the shadows behind the bastion door were empty of her. Maria cast left and right, and saw no sign of her. Deep in the casement a gun bellowed, and she ran.

She ran north from the Bamberg Way, up the long Craftmarket, which curved along the inside of the wall. The thought in her head was of reaching the bastion on the north side of the breach, because if he was not at this one then surely he must be there.

Or perhaps he was here, at the breach itself, where the line of the wall above her broke down into a low dyke of rubble? The Craftmarket seemed to be full of lanterns and white uniforms. The heads of men looking out over the makeshift palisade showed clearly against the sky. Calls and orders filled the air. Men hurried along the inside of the fence, stumbling in the darkness on the uneven ground. A long, thin man in a greatcoat was up there, turning now and then to shout more orders at the men on the wall and in the street. Maria came up to him.

'Please . . .' she said, and her voice was a whimper.

His head was only a black shape as he turned to look down at her. But he must have been able to see enough in the light of the lanterns to know who she was.

'Is he coming?' he asked her.

It was the question she had been going to ask him.

'I don't know where he is!' she pleaded. 'Have you seen him?'

'No, I damned well haven't!' he snapped.

'Captain!' called a voice along the wall. Again, muskets were being pointed outwards. The long man craned to look.

'Please . . .' said Maria again.

At that moment the muskets went off *crack-crack-crack!* on the palisade to her left and were answered by more shots from outside. Something went *spat!* against the wall of the building ten yards behind her and dropped lightly to the street.

'Get out of my way,' the man screamed at her. '*Get the hell out of my way!*'

So many times that night she asked for news of him, from uniformed men hurrying or loitering about their duties on the wall. On the north-eastern bastion a militia officer whom she knew slightly said that the Commander had been there perhaps an hour before, but he did not know where he was now. He had gone back into the town perhaps. She went in the direction that he pointed, almost feeling her way in the dark streets, and found more soldiers crouching in the doorway of the Ironworkers' Guildhall. They had not seen the Commander but they pointed her on to other places where he might be. And so it went on. Some of the men were tense and excited, some angry, some pretended to be bored. But each time she heard that hesitation in their voices as they answered her. *Where is he? Yes, where is he?* The Prince was gone, and the Governor was gone, and now where was the Commander? But he was there, somewhere. He must be. Lost in the night of the besieged city, they would point off hopefully in the direction that they supposed their orders were coming from.

And then, well after midnight, there was the sentry, standing by a lamp-lit arch in the Saint Lucia street, who looked at her with sleepy eyes.

'The Commander?' He jerked his thumb over his shoulder. 'He's inside.'

This man, too, must have known who she was, because he let her pass without a word. She walked down a short gate-tunnel, and found herself in a courtyard so filled with wagons and indistinct piles of supplies that for a moment she did not know where she was. Then she realized that she was standing in the barrack square of the hussars. She could still hear the sullen thump of the guns, but all around her the building was dark and quiet. The wagons were lined up wheel to wheel and teetering with high loads, which smelled like baulks of freshly-cut timber under canvas, but might have been something else altogether. There was no one else there.

But there was a single light, high in the building on her left hand. He had had his old office there. She had come here before, and had climbed up there to give him the painting. It seemed very long ago.

She felt her way among the wagons and found the door to the building. It was open. The stair inside was utterly dark, but she groped her way up it, counting the flights one, two, three, until she was greeted on a narrow landing by a thin line of lamplight coming from under a closed door. She stole up to it and knocked softly. When there was no reply, she went in.

He was there, kneeling by the grate in which a small fire was going. He had placed his lamp upon the bare floor by the hearth. Scattered in front of him were a range of papers. It looked as though he had taken them out from hiding, because a floorboard was up, showing the black and filthy space beneath.

He looked up at her in surprise. He must have been so preoccupied that he had heard neither her footstep nor her knock. There was a dazed look in his eyes. She remembered that he had not slept the night before and probably not during the day either.

'What is it?' he asked, as if he thought she must have some message for him.

'I heard you were here,' she said. 'So I came.'

'I see.'

He looked back at the papers in front of him, picked one up, looked at it, and lit it carefully in the grate.

'Thank you,' he added.

With a whispering noise the paper withered into brittle black talons of ash. He picked up another and looked at it.

He had moved his chair and desk to one side to give himself more room. She set the chair to face the hearth and settled in it.

'They are fighting, on the walls,' she said. And as she spoke a cannon thumped distantly in agreement.

'I know.'

'The enemy are coming up close. They are using muskets.'

'Yes,' he said. He put another paper on the fire. 'They do not want us to sortie against them while they are digging their works. So they are patrolling up to the walls. Also they are trying to assess the depth of the ditch before the breach.'

'I understand,' she said. It was a relief to be told that the enemy were not attacking in earnest – at least, not yet.

He sighed, and looked at the papers on the floor before him.

'My clerk has gone,' he said, as if to explain himself. 'There is no one else whom I can allow to do this. And after tonight there will be no more time.'

She supposed that the papers must be important. But she could not imagine that their importance mattered now. There must be a hundred other things the Commander should be doing. With the guns firing from the walls, he had shut himself away to do this. And even the guns were not that important, she thought, compared with what would be happening soon. He was already exhausted. He should sleep. But perhaps he could not.

'You should stay in the citadel from now on,' he said.

'I know, but . . .'

'It is the safest place,' he said.

And where will you be? she thought. In the smoke, and looking for the door of death? But she did not say it. And he did not press her. Like a drunk to his bottle, he was drawn back to his papers again. Through the window came the sounds of three or four cannon firing altogether. He did not look up.

They have all gone, she thought suddenly. All the clever people who brought him here. And now they have left him. They had left him with the city, its people, its defenders – and the enemy outside, creeping closer in the darkness.

'. . . But may I sit with you, for a while?' she asked.

'Yes. Please do.'

He took a roll of paper and uncurled it so that he could feed one corner of it into the grate. It was one of the paintings of the face of Christ, and it burned with a flare and a faint hiss. Another head of Christ was still in its place above the mantelpiece. It hung in a pool of light thrown upwards by the lamp on the floor.

The madman's painting looked more life-like than ever. There, on the wall, was a picture of living pain. A head lolling in the brown hues of the brush; a mouth opened with a silent howl, as if the man was undergoing his agony even as she watched.

And perhaps He was. Perhaps He was even now writhing and groaning with all the thousand inexcusable follies being committed that night. The irregular thump of the guns was the sound of nails being driven into his hands.

There had been women who had watched Him die like this, just as she was watching Him now. There had been Mary his mother. And there had been Mary of Magdalene, a younger woman, fallen in the eyes of her people, who had come to watch her hope extinguished on the cross. And now there was Maria von Adelsheim, also young, also fallen, looking up at the head. At the man on the cross, and the man on the hearth.

'Before this,' the man said suddenly, 'there was nothing but the war. Now there is the war, and there is also you.'

He stated it as if it were a choice, and one that he regretted.

'The war made it possible for me to come,' she said.

Then she wished that she had said *for me to come to you*.

He nodded. And he did not ask her what she meant.

'To enter paradise, we must destroy it,' he said.

The war had made it possible for her to come. It had brought them together. And now, or very soon, it would tear them apart. And it would tear all Erzberg apart too. How many Michels and Marias were there in the city, talking or thinking these things with one another? But they had been given no choice. He had chosen, and so had she. Why should they pity themselves? She remembered the face of the dead Frenchman, the eyes of the doctor's wife: *How could you?* The man in agony on the wall had sacrificed only himself. But the man at the grate must condemn them all. No, he was not Christ, and she must not think it. It was blasphemous and stupid. And she was not Mary Magdalene.

But there had been another woman in the story, a woman who had sent to her husband as he sat in judgement.

The man at the grate glanced at one more paper. His eyes followed a line, and then a few more. Then he shrugged and fed it carefully into the fire. It was an act curiously like washing his hands.

She drew breath and checked herself. She felt her hands grip upon her knees.

'Michel.'

He paused at the sound of his name.

'There are . . . innocent people in the city,' she said. 'Even now.'

For a moment he was still, staring at the air in front of him. Then he said, 'I know.'

Suddenly, angrily, he snatched a paper from the floor and scrunched it into a ball, which he jammed into the low flames. For a moment it sulked there, still obstinately paper in the glowing mass. Then with a bright flare of flame, it changed into an instant of glory. But already Michel was gathering up the other papers, balling them with savage movements of his fists, and adding them to the fire. One by one they went and the flutter of the flames grew into a brief roar. Maria rose from her place, took the face of Christ from the wall and offered it to him. That went, too, frame and all. On his hands and knees he watched it until the light wood caught and the face began to blacken with oil-smoke. Then he rose to his feet.

For an instant they looked at each other, either side of the hearth. Then – and she never remembered who moved first – they stepped towards one another, and his arms were around her neck, and hers were around his chest. And his ribs were strong as oak beneath his tunic, and she put her head to his breast and heard the tap, tap of his heart against her ear.

'Oh,' she whispered. And she could not say *my darling*, or *sweetheart*, or *my dear*, because she had never used those words before. She said, 'Whatever you do. Whatever you do. I will be as close as I can. I promise.'

'Yes,' he said, and bowed his head so that his cheek rested on her hair.

'There may be a chance,' he said. 'There may yet be.'

'Hush,' she answered. 'You should sleep. You should sleep if you possibly can.'

But still she clung to him, and the thumping of her heart and of his seemed far louder to her than the distant cannon from the wall.

XXXVI
Before the Doors

From the Bamberg Gate Wéry looked out into the dawn. The night had been paling steadily for the last hour. Now the lines of the world could be seen again, colourless under the sky.

Some three hundred paces away across the field a long earth-work had been thrown up. Over the rim of the brown wall poked a line of gun-muzzles. He swung his field glass along the row, noting the size of the bore and the carriages – big pieces, all of them. He counted twelve. A similar work had been built to his left, opposite the north-east bastion. And there again there were heavy cannon, although from this angle he could not count them easily. Say, twelve again. Further to left and right more batteries had been constructed – field guns this time, he thought: six- and eight-pounders, ready to pepper the defences and bombard the town. But it was opposite the breach, his weakest point, that the enemy had deployed their greatest strength.

He brought his telescope back to focus on the siege guns. There was something almost peaceful about that cold row of heavy muzzles: those little black 'o's that cooed silently as he swept his glass along them. *Death*, they said. *Death. There is nothing to do any more.*

Here, then, was the reality of the message from Maximilian Jürich, which he had fed onto the fire last night. The Army of

Germany had been reinforced with siege guns. Here they were. The message had not stopped them from coming. Nothing he or anyone else could have done would have stopped them. And nothing the city gunners had done last night had prevented them from taking position.

'That's where we were firing, over there,' said an officer. 'By the farm. You can see the ground's torn up with shot.'

'That's where the lights were,' someone answered him. 'We saw them.'

'Decoys, then. We've wasted a night's worth of powder, that's all.'

Only grumbles answered this.

'They've trenched the road, look.'

Wéry looked, and raised his glass again. Yes, there were low earthworks opposite the gate, further off, but still within mid-range for the city guns. There was a battery of field guns there, and infantry. Further away still, a mass of cavalry – a regiment at least – was circling into position beside the road.

'They fear a sortie,' said a voice near him. That was the country gentleman from Zerbach.

'They don't fear it,' said another, gloomily. 'They just want to be ready for it if it comes.'

'Where's old Uhnen, anyway? Shouldn't he be here?'

'Ssh! Haven't you heard?'

The voices dropped to whispers. Wéry ignored them. Softly, he closed his telescope.

The contempt of it was staggering. He remembered, years ago, watching from a church tower in Mainz as the Prussians had begun to dig their siege lines. They had started well out of cannon shot from the walls, with long circling earthworks to protect their positions. They had pushed the garrison back in from the outer villages and works. And day after day they had dug their way forward, in zigzag trenches, to a line two to three hundred yards short of the main defences. They had sited their batteries on the heights and had begun the bombardment in earnest. And then they had dug forward again, aiming to build new battery sites within fifty paces of the walls, from which their guns could pound the defences at close range until they crumbled.

This enemy was bothering with none of that. Augereau knew the town was held not by twenty thousand regulars but by only a few thousand ill-trained militia. He had thrown his main batteries well forward, shrugging his shoulders at the risk of cannon shot from the walls. A single low bank of earth trailed backwards from each enemy position, presumably covering a shallow trench in which people and supplies could be brought forward in some shelter. As for preparations against a sortie . . .

'Guns ready, sir,' came the call from the bastion door, behind and below.

'Tell them to wait,' he murmured.

He measured the distances with his eye. The batteries were closer to the gate than to their reinforcements, certainly. A running man could be on them in minutes. But the field battery and the infantry dug in opposite the gate would have to be attacked as well. And that farm was a strong point. He would have to get a sizeable force out onto the road and formed up before the wall. If those cavalry closed in quickly . . .

How many would he lose if it went wrong? Practically the whole force. Four or five hundred. It would rip the guts out of the defence. And even if he overran the guns what could he do but spike them and blow up whatever powder they had brought forward? He would win a day, or two days at best, before the enemy made good what he had done.

This was the truth. You could dream of heroic deeds, imagine cunning attacks and ambushes, and win the war you constructed in your mind, with brilliance and with glory. But under the grey, real skies there was no answer to overwhelming force. As well shout at the wind.

'Commander?'

He should fire on the batteries. No doubt there would be other targets during the day, as the enemy extended his works and brought supplies forward. But they would be pounding his guns. He must pound theirs – until they saw storming parties massing in forward positions. *They won't do that in daylight. It will be tonight, or dawn tomorrow . . .*

As he hesitated, a puff of smoke flew from the muzzle of the left-hand gun in the battery before him. A moment later, and almost together, came the crump of the shot and a small fountain of rubble rising lazily on the slope below the breach, a little to his left.

'Short,' said someone.

'Yes,' he said, and did not add *but it's heavier than anything we've got.*

'Ready?' he called over his shoulder, and then remembered that they had already told him they were.

'On the batteries, Commander?'

'Yes, I think . . . No, wait.'

There was movement down at the enemy battery. Men were clambering up onto the earthwork, lifting something pale, waving it . . .

'Flag of truce, sir.'

There it was, a great, dirty, grey rag, dancing in the field of his glass. His arms seemed to be trembling with tiredness. He could not steady his telescope. He lowered it, and squinted with his naked eye at the pale fleck in the distance.

Well, well. So there was indeed a chance after all. A chance to do something.

Now he must decide whether he would do it.

'Very good,' he said. 'Find something white to wave back.'

'Horsemen on the road, sir. Two of them.'

Did they know his mind so well already? They had not even waited for his signal.

'Very good,' he said again. 'Blindfold them and bring them up to the citadel. And pass the word to quarter commanders. There will be a conference at nine o'clock.'

'Nine o'clock, Commander?' That was still two hours away.

'It will do our unwelcome guests no harm to kick their heels for a while,' he said briskly. 'In the meantime, keep a sharp eye on those batteries. If they start building up their earthworks, give them a warning shot. And if they keep at it you hit them with everything we have.'

And he made his way off the platform, and slowly down the bastion steps, picking his way stiffly like an old, old man.

'Bah,' said Colonel Lanard, as his blindfold was removed in the courtyard of the Celesterburg. 'These hoods! When you are my prisoner, Wéry, I shall make you stand and wear one from dawn to noon. Perhaps then you will be more gentle.'

Beyond him, his stony-faced, grey-haired captain dismounted, exactly as he had done the day before.

'Forgive me,' said Wéry dryly. 'But your general continues to threaten the town, and I see no reason to relax my guard.'

'Do you not? Well, we shall see. May we go in?'

'I regret that it may be a little while yet before I am able to assemble my quarter commanders.'

'It is fortuitous. My orders are to speak with you alone in the first instance.'

Alone. Sometimes this Frenchman seemed to read his mind.

'Of course we can move to a full session after this,' said Lanard. 'But alone, to begin with. I must insist.'

'And if I refuse?'

'My orders are to return at once to our lines.'

'I see.' Wéry feigned a further hesitation. Then he shrugged. 'It will change nothing. But if you are willing to repeat yourself in front of my officers, I am amenable to it.'

'Bravo.'

They made their way up to the Prince's corridor and along to the antechamber once more. A few of the quarter commanders were already waiting outside the door. Their eyes were sullen, and bewildered. Why this delay? they asked. Why not just get on with it? None of them relished the thought of another fruitless parley, any more than a condemned man could wish to hear his death sentence read a second time.

All the same, he resented the way they looked at him. And that made it easier to brush them aside.

'I must beg your patience, gentlemen. The conference will not be held until nine. There is time for you to breakfast if you have not already done so.'

They left the officers and the stiff-faced French captain to stare at one another in the corridor and closed the door behind them.

The antechamber was quiet, and in its emptiness it seemed very long. The full grey light of winter poured in from the windows. They sat. The scrape of their chairs was loud in the room.

'Well?' began Wéry.

Lanard was looking at the door of the inner chamber. There was something longing in his expression that was almost comical. But the door was shut fast in their faces, and he must have known better than to court another rebuff. He turned back to the table, rubbed his eyes and yawned hugely.

'Pardon me,' he said affably, when he had finished.

'I fear you have not slept well, Colonel,' said Wéry woodenly.

'And no doubt you are beautifully rested,' said Lanard. 'But I have spent many hours with my general overnight. He is not at all pleased with you, I fear. Nevertheless, there came a time towards morning when he was more ready to hear what I had to say.'

'And?'

'Well, you have observed our preparations for yourself . . .'

Wéry leaned back in his chair and lifted his eyes to the ceiling. It seemed a long way above his head. Chains of tiny gilt scroll-work adorned the edges of the ceiling and curled around the hooks that held the chandeliers. Some hand had done that, labouring with great care for many days. In all the times he had visited this room he had never seen it before.

'. . . To tell the truth, I think my general has not yet made up his mind how to proceed. He may choose to dig his way in from our current position. Or he may choose simply to lean against your fence and see if it falls over. Much may depend on how your gunners do. So far we would judge that they are willing, but perhaps not so very accurate. Even when we give them some-thing to aim at . . .'

'I am not disposed to listen to threats this morning,' Wéry murmured.

'Of course you are not. But I am not threatening you. I merely review facts of which we are both aware.'

'Very well. Proceed if you must.'

'Well, then. Perhaps tomorrow, perhaps in a week's time, we shall have topped your barricade. So. We understand you mean to fight through the town. We judge that you are capable of it. You see how your reputation has spread, Wéry. And I dare say that your people will continue to fight until you yourself are knocked over. After which it will indeed be all over. But consider. Your men are farmers, burghers, housewives with rolling pins, perhaps. Very soon we will know the ground as well as you. You must lose four or five for every one you kill of ours . . .'

'Less, perhaps.'

'I do not think so. But what I am sent to say to you is that you have a responsibility . . .'

The light creak of a door opening interrupted him. He looked over his shoulder. Wéry sat up. It was not the door to the passage outside. It was one of the big leaves that opened onto the Prince's chamber.

'I beg your pardon, gentlemen,' said Maria von Adelsheim. 'But I wish to join you.'

'Ah,' said Lanard, evidently perplexed.

Wéry looked at her. His first feeling was a simple leap of joy that she was there. But immediately it mixed with other things. *I wish to join you.* That was a command, not a request. This was an Imperial Knight, he thought. She must be almost the very last one at liberty in Erzberg. What was he to say? *I am afraid it is impossible*. It was impossible to say that to her. But if she stayed . . .

At the sight of her he felt, strengthening within him, his resolve to do what he was planning to do. She was herself: one of the few good things that had happened to him since he had left Brabant all those years ago. Yet she was not only herself. In her eyes and face and thoughts he could see all the people of the city of Erzberg, huddled under their roofs, waiting for the fire.

'I do not know that my orders . . .' said Lanard. He stopped, and looked at Wéry.

'What were you doing in there?' Wéry asked.

'Waiting,' she said. 'I had heard there would be a conference, so I came down. I would like to sit with you. I shall say nothing, I promise.'

'Of course,' he said.

Lanard shrugged. Then, elaborately, he rose to his feet, until Maria had made her way around to take the chair beside Wéry. Wéry supposed that he should have risen too. Really, he was too tired to remember everything. But he was acutely conscious of the rustle of borrowed silk as she took her place near, so near beside him.

And then, under the table, he felt her hand take his own.

Lanard sat, colouring slightly, and cleared his throat. He focused his eyes on Wéry.

'We were speaking of the likely course of events once we force our way into the town. And we need not quibble over figures. You know very well what sort of price the city will have to pay. Do you dispute it?'

'No.'

'Good. But the price need not be so dear. In the satchel of

517

Capitaine Rouche I have the terms I spoke of yesterday. I can set them before you. In essence they are that a garrison shall be installed and that the government of the town shall pass to a council of senior inhabitants, who will conduct their administration in consultation with the garrison commander. Of course there will also need to be contributions made to the maintenance of the Army of Germany. Of course this is not what the townspeople would necessarily wish. Yet offered the choice between this and a massacre, I imagine that they would choose it?'

He was searching Wéry's face as he spoke. Wéry gave no sign. The Frenchman's voice seemed to be coming from increasingly far away. The only real thing in the world was the touch of the woman's hand, lying in his own under the table.

'Bof!' exclaimed Lanard, after waiting for a reply. 'Maybe there are indeed fanatics in the town, Commander! Yet it is not a town of fanatics. And the point is, that *they* do not have this choice. Fate has given the choice to you, to make for them . . .'

Wéry sighed. The arguments of yesterday – whose was the choice, whose the responsibility for the coming deaths – lumbered into his mind. But he must not allow himself to be distracted. And he must not – *must* not – fall into another rage. Not now.

'. . . The men of the garrison will be disarmed and may return home. The officers will be required to give their parole, but they too will be released once that is done. A few will be held, of whom you, I fear, will be one. But you need not be anxious. We plan a gentle captivity for you. It would even be possible – I am authorized to say this – for you to be accompanied while you are our guest by any who are dear to you.'

A sudden, involuntary pressure from the hand within his own! He thought, too that she caught her breath softly. But her grip relaxed at once. After a moment, he felt her other hand come across to cover his.

Whatever you do, he remembered her saying. *Whatever*. Oh God, and he had clung to her as she said it! He almost wished, now, that she would speak. But he knew that she would not. She had promised that she would not, just as she had promised last night that she would be close to him, whatever he did. All that she had to say, she had now said. *Whatever you do.*

And also: *There are still innocent people in the city.*

Lanard's eyes were on them. After a moment he added carefully, 'Habits of thought change slowly, even in the territories administered by the French Republic. But I should have said that with us, a union between a former aristocrat and someone of a different station is now rather less unthinkable than perhaps it is here. Especially if both are strangers and guests of the state.'

And now he was silent. He was waiting for his reply. Wéry stirred.

'You have finished your blandishments, Colonel?'

Lanard frowned. 'I have finished, yes – for the time being.'

'And you suppose I will submit to them?'

'That,' said Lanard, 'is up to you and you only.'

'Then permit me to say that you should not have uttered those last remarks. Until you did, I had intended to surrender the town.'

Lanard looked up sharply. The hand on his did not stir. *Whatever you do*, said the touch of her skin upon his own.

'Commander . . .' Lanard began.

'I may yet surrender the town,' said Wéry slowly, fighting the anger that had risen in his throat. 'But I have two conditions.'

'Let me hear them.'

'First, that you put your bribes back in your pocket. I will go to Paris in chains if need be. But my second condition is that once in Paris I shall be permitted to address the houses of the Legislature. There are words I must unsay. And then I will have more to say to them yet. After that you may do with me as you will.'

Silence, and the low murmur of men in the passageway beyond the door.

'Ah,' said Lanard softly. 'Ah, I see.'

And he leaned back and looked at the ceiling. 'You will choose death in a prison, or perhaps on the guillotine. And you will go to it with your words ringing in the ears of Paris. I see.'

'I have words that I must unsay,' Wéry repeated.

He glanced at the woman at his side. His look would have said to her: *I am sorry. I could wish* . . . But she had closed her eyes. Her mouth was shut, firmly, as if she were in pain but would not speak.

'I think that I must refuse,' said Lanard at last.

'Then . . .' said Wéry.

'No. Before you pass the word to your batteries, Commander, you must allow me to explain. I understand what you would do. You wish to spare those you are responsible for. This is the action of a sane man. But you would also remain true to your cause. This is the action of one who would be thought of with honour. Alas, it is mere pride and delusion. There is no possibility that what you ask will be permitted.

'If I return to my general with your request, he will either lose his temper and begin the assault at once, or he will indeed agree your terms and send you in chains to Paris, knowing, as I know and as you should know, that the Legislature, the Directory or whoever you will, will not in fact hear you when you come. At best some clerk may be told to take your statement and some one or two persons may read it out of curiosity. That is all that will happen to the words of Wéry.'

Wéry drew a long breath. Beside him, the eyes of Maria were still closed.

'I do not ask much in exchange for a city,' he said. 'It is strange that we should break down over a few words.'

'You are mistaken. You ask more than I can offer. Even great men, in their hearts, would rather let a thousand die in a distant land than spend twenty minutes hearing that they are wrong. My masters for the present are not great but little. Eh, Wéry. I have in my pockets proposals for a pension for you, if you surrender the city. I should not advise you to take it, mind you, because the Republic has some difficulty paying its pensions at present. If we come to that, you should insist on a grant of land – perhaps even the return of your old estate in Brabant. Also I have some idea to what level it may be possible to reduce the demands my general wishes to impose upon the city. All this we can talk about . . .

'But *first* you must choose. If you insist on remaining pure, then between us we will kill the city. If you wish to save the city, you must consent to humble yourself – perhaps even to be a little bit corrupt. You should not fear this. To be corrupt is, after all, merely to be human, as I have said to you before.'

So they would give him nothing. All the things he felt, all the things he would say – they would not hear them. And if he surrendered now, no one would remember what he had stood for. A night's futile cannonading – it would not be worth a single line in Augereau's despatches to Paris. His words would have to be written in blood, or they would not be read at all. They must be written in the blood of the innocent.

Maria had opened her eyes. He looked into them, and she looked back.

In her face he found at last the strength to let go.

'Very well,' he said, and bowed his head. 'We will spare the city.'

'Colonel, I am delighted,' said the Frenchman.

Wéry frowned at the table. It was over. He had decided. He felt . . . No, to his surprise he did not feel uncomfortable with his decision. And suddenly there were so many things to think about. The terms . . .

He gripped her hand, hard, and felt her fingers answer his.

'It will be necessary to know what size your garrison would be,' he said.

'That will be for us to say. You may be assured it will not be bigger than we need. We do not have so many soldiers that we can leave a full brigade in idleness.'

'The levy,' he asked. 'How much?'

'The paper says four million livres. I suspect we shall not settle for less than three and a half millions. But how much is collected – it is always another matter, and one neither you nor I can control.'

'You mentioned requisitions.'

'The usual things. A thousand head of cattle. Five hundred horses. Five hundred mules or donkeys. Five hundred wagons. Leather, cloth, iron, copper. The church and cathedral bells must be surrendered to be melted down . . .'

'They have gone.'

'I thought they would have done. Ah, nails, straps, buckles – Rouche has the list. I cannot remember it all.'

'I shall need to confer with my officers.'

'I am sure they will do as you suggest. Particularly if you suggest to them that it is not worth losing their lives after all.'

Bergesrode would resist, Wéry thought. Bergesrode would resist to the last man, if he could. He and his fanatics would barricade themselves into the cathedral. He would have to be forestalled . . .

Maria, and Brabant. *I am corrupt.*

Corrupt. But – after all – what of it? Even sanity had its price.

'Another matter,' he said. 'I am charged with the custody of certain people in the citadel. What of them?'

'It depends who they are. These are political enemies of your Prince?'

'Yes. One of them is the Canon Steinau-Zoll, who took your testimony last season. There is also the Canon Rother-Konisrat, the Baron von und zu Löhm . . .'

Lanard shrugged. 'Of course we would examine the list. But I could not predict what we would do. If you wish your prisoners to be released, Colonel, you must do it yourself. And before we enter the town.'

'Very well . . .' Wéry leaned forward. His eyes were on the polish of the table, and his heart in the touch of the woman's hands. He heard himself say, 'Then I would ask you to wait in another part of the palace while I assemble my commanders.'

And while he arranged for the arrest of Bergesrode. There must be one last act of tyranny. He would have to be quick.

'Of course. But, Colonel . . .'

Wéry looked up.

'I wish that you would smile a little, when you have saved your soul.'

Maybe he did smile a little, then. And her hands pressed warmly upon his.

'That is better,' said Lanard. His eyes slid sideways to the door of the inner room. 'And perhaps – before your conference begins – perhaps we may all be admitted to Paradise, now?'

THE END

Acknowledgements

This is a work of fiction. The city and state of Erzberg that I have described never existed, and most of the events I have related did not occur. Nevertheless I have tried to make the historical context of my story as accurate as possible. I am deeply indebted to those scholars on whose work I have relied to help me understand aspects of this complex and crucial period: TCW Blanning (*The French Revolution in Germany* and *Reform and Revolution in Mainz*), Peter H Wilson (*From Reich to Revolution*), GP Gooch (*Germany in the French Revolution*), William D Godsey (*Nobles and Nation in Central Europe*), Philip Haythornthwaite (*Uniforms of the French Revolutionary Wars*) and many others, including compilers of websites and editors of letters, dictionaries and chronologies. I owe particular thanks to Dr William O'Reilly of Trinity Hall, Cambridge for reviewing the manuscript and for the many helpful suggestions he has made.

And like so many authors I owe thanks too to all those friends and colleagues who have read the book for me, and whose comments and encouragement have helped me so much as the story evolved: Pippa, Kim, Bruce, Amanda, Julia, Ginger, Peter, Peter, David, Linda, Ben, Dorie, Paul, Oliver, Jane, Anne-Françoise, Alex and . . . you all know who you are. Thank you so much.

The Kingdom of Ashes

Robert Edric

'An impressive tale of love and death in wartime . . . much contemporary fiction seems inconsequential and fleeting by comparison'
GUARDIAN

GERMANY, SPRING 1946. The Nuremberg Trials are underway. Three hundred miles north, in the Rehstadt Institute, a British 'Assessment and Evaluation' centre, Alex Foster interrogates a succession of lesser war criminals, exploring their pasts and their crimes, and deciding their futures in the soon-to-be-reborn Germany.

But Rehstadt, a town largely untouched by the war, is a place of old hostilities and burnished hatreds; a place still not entirely at peace; a place where the certainties of the past are still weighed favourably against the deprivations of the present and the vague, uncertain promises of the future.

As spring progresses, and as events in the wider world quicken to their own closely observed conclusion, Alex Foster finds himself at the centre of a conflict involving British, American and German interests; and for the first time in his career he also finds himself compromised – forced into subterfuge and deceit as he struggles to weigh personal convictions and loyalties against the greater political and military good . . .

'Edric's work constitutes one of the most astonishing bodies of work to have appeared from a single author for a generation'
DAILY TELEGRAPH

'Has a seriousness and a psychological edge that nine out of ten novelists would give their eye teeth to possess'
SUNDAY TIMES

9780552774178

The Given Day

Dennis Lehane

DANNY COUGHLIN IS Boston Police Department royalty and the son of one of the city's most beloved and powerful police captains. His beat is the predominately Italian neighbourhoods of the North End where political dissent is in the air – fresh and intoxicating. On the hunt for hard-line radicals as a favour to his father, Danny is drawn into the ideological fray and finds his loyalties compromised as the police department itself becomes swept up in potentially violent labour strife.

Luther Lawrence is on the run. A suspect in a nightclub shooting in Oklahoma, he flees to Boston, leaving his wife behind. He lands a job in the Coughlin household and meets Danny and the family's Irish maid, Nora, who once had a powerful bond. As the mystery of their relationship unravels, Luther finds himself befriending them both even as the turmoil in his own life threatens to overwhelm him. Desperate to return to his wife and child, he must confront the past that has followed him and settle scores with enemies old and new.

As Danny, Luther and those around them face increasingly turbulent times, they are forced to ride a rising storm of hardship, deprivation and hope that will change them forever.

Set at the end of the Great War, *The Given Day* is meticulously researched and expertly plotted, it will transport you to an unforgettable time and place.

'Lehane combines 20th-century American history, a gripping story, and the plot of a multi-faceted thriller'
PUBLISHERS WEEKLY

9780385615341

Now available from Doubleday

Mutiny on the Bounty

John Boyne

---

23 December 1787, Portsmouth.

A 14-YEAR-OLD BOY, John Jacob Turnstile, has got into trouble with the police on one too many occasions and is on his way to prison when an offer is put to him – a ship has been refitted over the last few months and is about to set sail with an important mission. The boy who was expected to serve as the captain's personal valet has been injured and a replacement must be found immediately. The deal is struck and he finds himself onboard, meeting the captain, just as the ship sets sail.

The ship is HMS *Bounty*, the captain is William Bligh, and their destination is Tahiti.

Mutiny on the Bounty is the first novel to explore all the events relating to the *Bounty*'s voyage, from their long journey across the ocean to their adventures on the island of Tahiti and the subsequent forty-eight day expedition towards Timor. A vivid recreation of the famous mutiny, the story is packed with humour, violence and historical detail, while presenting a very different portrait of Captain Bligh and Mr Christian than has ever been shown before.

9780385611664

Now available from Doubleday